Flight of the Blackbird

A NOVEL

Faye McDonald Smith

SCRIBNER

SCRIBNER
1230 Avenue of the Americas
New York, NY 10020

This book is a work of fiction. Names, characters, places, and incidents either are products of the author's imagination or are used fictitiously. Any resemblance to actual events or locales or persons, living or dead, is entirely coincidental.

SCRIBNER *and design are trademarks of Simon & Schuster Inc.*

Designed by Jenny Dossin
Set in Adobe Caslon

Manufactured in the United States of America

ISBN 0-684-82971-1

I believe in thank-yous. And so, with deep appreciation, I want to acknowledge those who in different ways helped bring this book to life:

my father, W. J. McDonald, who many years ago thought of the title *Flight of the Blackbird*, which became the seed of an idea that grew into this novel;

my "first draft" circle of readers, composed of relatives and friends who gave invaluable feedback and support: my mother, Lil T. McDonald; my sister, Yuletta M. Mitchell; and Gloria T. Lockett, Daphne Henderson, and Gail Syphax;

Lauren Sanders-Jones, for her superbly critical and detailed eye;

Paula Paul, who provided early encouragement and advice through the Writer's Digest Novel Writing Workshop

my wonderful agent Victoria Sanders, for seeing the potential and sharing the vision;

Leigh Haber, a dream of an editor, who truly believes in writer's autonomy;

and Janis Coombs Reid, a dear friend and fellow writer, who offered immeasurable assistance, and more than anyone, traveled with me along the way.

To them, and to all of you who take the time to read this book, thank you.

Flight of the Blackbird

Mel Burke felt a queasiness in her stomach as she sat at her desk. The birthday cake from lunch suddenly made her insides churn. Chocolate was her favorite, but it wasn't always kind to her digestive tract. She had overindulged, she knew. It didn't take much to get her system off balance. And now, this cryptic message from her boss: "Please see me when you return."

A note from Larson Cook was unusual; he rarely sent handwritten messages. He relished his role as a head honcho at the Atlanta Chamber of Commerce and preferred his secretary to handle the more banal communications. But equally odd was the "please," which didn't sound at all like Larson, who was normally abrupt and eschewed such niceties.

As she rounded the corner of her desk to head out the door, Mel sniffed the yellow roses that her husband Builder had sent by courier this morning. Today was her thirty-seventh birthday, and Builder had made hard-to-get dinner reservations at Nikolai's Roof, an elite Russian restaurant that was often booked weeks in advance. Mel had the sinking feeling that Larson wanted her to work late on a new corporate relocation project. *Not tonight,* she said to herself, and walked briskly down the hall.

"I've been summoned from on high," she said breezily, flashing the note in front of Larson's secretary.

"Go on in," the secretary directed, waving her into the inner sanctum. "And happy birthday."

Everyone at the office knew. As with most employee birthdays, they had celebrated in the morning over coffee and a huge specialty doughnut with candles lining the rim. Mel had received her share of teasing—that the doughnut was barely large enough to hold all those candles, that she was fast approaching the fourth decade and had good reason to be depressed—and on and on. There were a lot of fun people on the staff, and she enjoyed working here. But this overtime madness could get out of hand. Determined to be firm about not working late tonight, she took a deep breath, tapped on the large oak door, and poked her head inside.

"You made it back," came a heavy voice.

Larson Cook unfolded his bulky frame from a massive chair and greeted Mel with a sober smile. "Been out celebrating?"

His tone was light, but his face looked pinched. He moved toward one of two Queen Anne chairs in the middle of the room; Mel slid into the other one. They sat face-to-face, chatting about the quick passage of time and the mixed blessings of birthdays. Then, there was an awkward pause. Larson repeatedly clicked his pen as Mel waited expectantly.

"Look," he said finally. "There's no easy way to say this, especially today. It's terrible timing. But you know what the situation's been for some time, and—well . . ." He inhaled deeply. "Jesus, Mel—I've got to let you go."

Mel leaned forward in disbelief. "What?"

Had she heard him right? Was this a joke? Larson stood and walked to the window, giving her time to absorb the shock. Or was it that he couldn't bear to see her face? She vaguely heard him talk about downsizing, the sluggish economy, how difficult it was for the board to make the decision. But all she could think of was the seven years she had worked at the Chamber, worked hard to prove she was indispensable. All those nights of overtime, the long trips away from home, the extra effort she had put in. And this was the payback? She felt cheated and betrayed.

". . . especially coming on your birthday, like this," Larson droned on. "But I wanted you to know as soon as possible and not hear it from anyone but me. You know how valuable I think you are. I couldn't have pulled off half the things in this place without you."

It was true. For the past several years, Mel had made Larson look good. He'd gotten the praise and high profile awards but was wise enough to give her due credit. Despite his puffed-up ego, he'd looked out for her, fighting for promotions and a higher salary. It was in his best interest to have Mel around, and he knew it. Mel was one of two marketing reps at the Chamber and the only black female in management. She wondered for a moment if Jason Hall, her marketing colleague, had also gotten the boot. He was a hotshot graduate of Wharton, had family ties to a board member, and, most importantly, she knew, was white.

As if reading her mind, Larson assured her that race had nothing to do with the decision. She was not the only victim. "I'm going to have this same talk with Jason," he said. "The whole goddamn department's gettin' creamed."

Mel realized then that Larson's own job might be in jeopardy. He suddenly looked tired and much older.

"Listen," he said, trying to sound optimistic, "I want you to know up front that as soon as this budget thing is resolved, you'll be the first one I'll call, begging you to come back."

Mel rose slowly, her stomach tightening as she prepared to leave. In a daze, she heard herself say weakly, "You always did have a knack for surprises. But this one you could have kept to yourself." Her lame attempt at humor sounded flat and pathetic, even to her own ears.

Larson put his arm around her shoulder and walked her to the door. "Look," he said with sympathy, "go home. Get some rest. We've got a couple weeks before this takes effect. Let's talk again Monday."

Outside, the bright sunshine stung her eyes and seemed to mock her growing depression. Minutes earlier, Mel had grabbed her purse and fled the office, anxious to be home. It was only 2:30, but traffic moved slowly. A four-car pileup and a mammoth tow truck blocked her escape. Why now? she thought. Why today? She felt unusually hot. Her head pounded, sweat soaked her silk blouse, and her stomach erupted. She jerked her car over to the far right lane, nearly swiping the fender of the red Volkswagen in front. She swung open the door, not a second too soon. The rich food from lunch, laced with Larson's bad news, violently gushed onto the pavement. Again and again, the nausea rose in wave after wave, leaving her shredded and empty.

The mess below confirmed how much she had lost control. Somehow, she managed to make it home, and crawl into bed.

Mel awoke to the slam of the basement door, a telltale sign that Builder was home. He usually came in the house through the lower level, stopping at the makeshift "mud room" to wash off the day's paint and dirt. If his work clothes were especially soiled, he would remove them downstairs, and drop them in a dirty clothes basket reserved exclusively for them. "Those bad boys need their own washing machine," Mel often teased him, and was horrified when, as a prank, Builder once washed his sweaty work pants with her best lingerie.

As she walked into the bathroom, she heard him puttering around downstairs longer than usual and concluded he must be ironing a shirt for tonight. When he worked at VRT years ago, she'd taken his shirts to the cleaners; however, once he started his contracting business, he rarely wore a starched shirt, and when he did, he always pressed it himself. But if he was ironing one now, he wouldn't need it.

There was no way they would be going out to dinner tonight. Not after today's events. The idea of food sickened her. Mel splashed some cold water on her face and patted her pale cheeks. A bath and nap had helped, but she still felt drained from the earlier ordeal.

"There she is—the birthday girl!" Builder appeared at the doorway, stripped to his underwear and T-shirt. He handed Mel a few cards that had come in the mail, and deposited a robust kiss on her lips. "More to come later," he said slyly, tweaking his eyebrows. "Give me a minute to clean up, and I'll be ready to rock and roll."

"Wait a second," Mel began slowly, her tongue still heavy from sleep. But Builder was already shooing her out of the bathroom, humming his way into the shower.

When he emerged a few minutes later, Mel was curled up on the bed, her bathrobe still on, her unmade face transparent.

"What's the matter?" he asked, concerned. He sat next to her on the bed, his chest glistening with drops of water.

"Today was not my day." She laid aside her magazine and peered straight into his eyes. "You're looking at a soon-to-be ex-employee of the Atlanta Chamber of Commerce."

He stared at her blankly.

"I've been put out to pasture," she told him. "Laid to rest. Kaput."

He frowned at the announcement. "What are you saying? You've been fired?"

"Well, I wouldn't put it exactly in those terms," Mel said, a bit defensively. "But, yes, the end result is the same."

"What happened? What'd you do?"

"Me?" She was irritated by the question. "I didn't do anything. It's budget cuts, the economy—take your pick. It's not *my* fault."

She eased back against the pillow, her head starting to pound again. She watched Builder pace the floor, retying the sarong around his waist, visibly disturbed by the implication of her news.

"Damn," he said. "Of all times."

Mel felt anger swell up inside. How dare Builder blame *her*, as if *she* had done something wrong! Why should she apologize to him for losing her job? Where was the loving support, the gentle hand-holding, the comforting hug? She had expected him to say something like, "Don't worry, baby, that's par for the course." In fact, he was the one who frequently warned her that she had too much faith in the corporate system—that she was naive and overly trusting; that playing by the rules was no guarantee of success. Losing her job seemed to fit the scenario he had painted all along—that the corporate arena was politically fickle, and black folks, in particular, paid an unduly heavy price. Where was all that rationale now?

"When's your last day?" he asked, from the other side of the room.

"In a couple of weeks." She heard the living room clock chime faintly. One, two, three—on up to six times. What a difference a few hours makes, she thought. "Look," she said hopefully, "I should be able to find something pretty soon." But she could tell Builder hadn't heard her. He was lost in his own thoughts.

"A heck of a time for this to happen," he mumbled. He plopped down in the La-Z-Boy, splaying his fingers on the arm rest. His eyes gazed abstractedly, seeking to escape the problem at hand. "It's not good out there," he said, as if speaking to someone else. He shook his head sadly.

"I know it's not good," Mel said, shifting in the bed. She was tired of his self-pitying attitude and accusatory tone. "How do you think *I* feel?" she asked. "You're sitting there feeling sorry for yourself. What about me? I'm the one who'll be out of work. How about a little sympathy for *me?*"

Her headache returned full force, and she massaged her temples to relieve the stress. She stared at Builder, who, sullen and quiet, had sunk into the chair, his playful mood long gone. He stared back, almost gazing beyond her, and then, as if suddenly aware of her presence, sat up straighter to deliver the obligatory reassurance that should come from the male head of household.

"We'll work this out," he said. "It'll be tough for a while, but we'll be all right."

"I think you're taking it worse than I am," Mel said, softening. She knew things were not that great with his business lately. She had picked up snatches of conversation, here and there, and he had a bad habit of talking out loud to himself in the shower. Over the months, she had heard him moan about bills piling up. He certainly didn't need any more financial pressure right now, but Mel was confident that she would find a job soon.

"Between my references from Larson and the contacts I've made through the Chamber, I should be back in circulation soon." She offered this tidbit to console both of them. She was tired from the day's disappointments, tired from Larson, tired from Builder, tired from her body's vengeance. She wanted to sleep it all away.

For a few minutes, neither of them spoke. Then Builder started stirring. "We need to get dressed for dinner," he said, glancing at his watch.

"This is the only birthday you'll have this year, so we'd better salvage it somehow." He released a forced chuckle. "I could use some vodka right about now."

Mel cringed. "Oh, Nikolai's is definitely out. My stomach's been acting up all day. And I have a headache that won't quit."

"Guess we'll have to take a rain check then," Builder said. But he looked relieved. Mel could see him mentally tallying up the money he had just saved. "I think there's some spaghetti downstairs," he said, "so I'll grab that and bring you something light. Tea and crackers, okay? Maybe some soup?" He didn't wait for a response. "Why don't you lie down and get some rest?"

She did as she was told, lying against the fat pillows, watching him as he dropped his sarong in favor of a pair of running shorts from the armoire.

"Don't worry about the job. That's life. We've got to roll with the punches."

He was trying, he really was. But Mel got the impression that his comments were prerequisite words of confidence, spoken out of half-hearted conviction. As he leaned over to pull an afghan around her shoulders, she could see that he was troubled. Builder could charm and joke and tease, but the truth always shone in his eyes. Some of the light behind them had disappeared.

Mel crammed a barbecue-stained napkin into her pants pocket as she balanced an overloaded tray en route to the kitchen. So far so good. The day was going perfectly. Almost too perfectly. Not that she was superstitious about such things, but she sometimes got a little anxious when all the pieces seemed to fall into place—as though Lady Luck might suddenly change her mind and withdraw her shield of grace.

Relax, she told herself. Enjoy it.

Indeed, this was the first time since her "bad news" announcement last month that Builder seemed like his old self—laughing, cracking jokes, displaying his talents as chef de barbecue. He *could* handle a grill like no one she knew. His lemon-topped chicken and shrimp kebabs closely rivaled the peppered Italian sausage and sirloin, Mel's once-a-year concession to buying red meat. She had gone to the DeKalb Farmers Market yesterday and brought home enough food to pack both refrigerators.

She was glad she had pushed Builder into having the get-together after all. It was Memorial Day weekend, and for the last several years they had invited a huge crowd over to kick off the summer. Most of their entertaining was low key and small scale—having a couple of folks over for dinner, or bemoaning the latest political snafus over pizza and beer—but this was their annual big bash to welcome the summer, and, rain or shine, people knew that the Burkes were having a party. However, Builder had been so withdrawn lately that Mel had wondered if they should forgo the tradition this year. He had proposed as much last week.

"Let's do something later in the summer," he had said, "when things ease up a bit."

"Yeah, right," Mel had said knowingly. "Things never ease up for you. Why do I always have to drag you, kicking and screaming, to take a day off, and then you end up having more fun than anybody? Besides," she added, "people have already started calling to say they're coming."

He had murmured how "the Fourth of July would be better," but offered no further resistance.

She knew what was bothering him, of course. Losing her job at the Chamber had not been easy for him to accept. Builder had been particularly concerned about the loss of life insurance and health benefits. Since he was self-employed, the family had been covered through Mel's job. But with that gone, the burden of providing insurance coverage added to a growing pile of unexpected expenses that now fell solely upon his shoulders.

Mel couldn't really explain it to Builder, but at first, there was something strangely exhilarating about this professional uncertainty. In a way, she saw it as a blessing in disguise—a new opportunity, an uncharted adventure. Part of her felt like she did when she was fresh out of college, not knowing what the future would hold, but expecting only the best. However, it was now six weeks since she had left the Chamber, and she was still without a job. Worse, she had not received any nibbles from her many inquiries, and her optimism had begun to wane. She had decided that both she and Builder needed this party to help lift them out of the doldrums.

"Mel, need help with those drinks?" Amidst the ribbon of outside laughter and the husky voice of Vea Williams singing "You've Got the Magic," Builder's question still carried through the open door.

"No," Mel shouted. "I got it."

She rinsed a sprig of mint she had brought in earlier from the backyard, stirred it into the lemonade, and placed the pitcher on the tray between the ice bucket and a six-pack of Michelob. As she turned to go, Sasha bounced into the room.

"Mom, which one should I take? The red or the blue?"

Mel looked at her lanky thirteen-year-old daughter, sized up her choices in a flash, and said firmly, "Definitely the blue." In one hand, Sasha held last year's bathing suit, a cute aqua one-piece with a pink flower running down the middle. In the other hand was the "hot one"—a red popcorn bikini with fake rhinestones. Mel had watched Sasha try it on the other night—and she noted that the bottom was cut way too high over Sasha's rear end, and the top fit much too snugly against her budding chest. Mel would never have bought anything like that. It was a present from Maxx, Mel's younger brother, who liked to bestow gifts upon his only niece. Problem was, his selections were almost always too expensive or just plain inappropriate.

"But, Mom," Sasha protested, "this one's really more *me*, you know?" She bobbed the flashy bikini out front. "Please?"

"I told you that suit's too grown-up for you," Mel said, readying for yet another sparring round. She silently cursed Maxx for contributing the ammo for this latest dispute.

She was surprised that Sasha even asked her opinion, knowing how she felt about the suit. Then, she realized that Sasha knew her habits only too well. Regardless of how busy she might be with her guests, Mel would want to check Sasha's overnight bag to make sure she had all the essentials—toothbrush, comb, etcetera—and in her inspection, Mel would surely spot the offending swimsuit.

"I don't see why I can't wear it," Sasha persisted.

"Because it's a bikini, and it's too mature for you," said Mel, trying to hold on to her patience. Sasha had a way of taking her to the edge.

"It's not a bi-KEE-ni," mocked Sasha. "It's just two pieces. All the girls wear them. What's the big deal? You let me wear one when I was five years old! *Five*, Mom. Remember that picture in my room from Myrtle Beach?"

"That was different," Mel snapped. "And I'm not going to argue about it. I can use your help getting these drinks outside."

She could manage the drinks herself, but she was trying to change the subject. She and Sasha were both going through a period of adjustment. At times, Sasha was the affectionate, innocent daughter, seeking to please her mother. And then, sometimes in the very next hour, she'd transform into the typical teen—rebellious, argumentative, moody—displaying all the negatives of adolescent growth. "Whatever happened to my sweet baby girl?" Mel would often say to Sasha in the midst of a disagreement.

Now, she noticed Sasha's slow pout beginning to take shape—the lower lip protruding slightly; arms folded about the chest as her hands clutched both swimsuits, an evil eye fixed on Mel.

"That's *definitely* not going to help," Mel said firmly. She was tempted to reach out and tickle Sasha under the chin, a gesture that usually broke the tension and elicited a laugh from them both. But something about Sasha's stance indicated she would not be moved.

"So what did you decide?" Sasha's friend Ashley entered the kitchen with two plates of pizza crumbs and peach pits. The girls had been upstairs—trying on clothes, combing each other's hair, and, no doubt, talking about boys. That was the crux of the problem, Mel knew. Sasha was going to spend the night with Ashley, who was having a few friends over for a pool party tomorrow. If it were just Sasha and Ashley and other girls, that would be okay. But Mel knew that boys would be there too, and Ashley, who was a year older than Sasha, had already gone on a couple of double dates with fourteen- and fifteen-year-olds. Mel didn't want Sasha parading around this older crowd in her too-tight bikini.

"Mom wants me to wear this ol' blue one," Sasha said stonily to Ashley. She released her body from its fighting pose and stood shoulder to shoulder with her ally, who quickly came to her defense.

The girls presented numerous arguments, attempting to persuade Mel to change her mind. She had to admit she enjoyed having the power to say yea or nay, and she liked having the girls present their case in her kitchen courtroom. It'll help them develop good debating skills, she reasoned But she also knew this issue wasn't worth pursuing. Besides, she didn't want anything to spoil this day, so she decided not to prolong the impasse. She was about to give in when Builder barged through the kitchen door.

"The natives are getting thirsty," he said, grabbing his throat by both hands in mock desperation. "What's the holdup?"

Sasha wasted no time in staking her claim. "Daddy, I want to wear this bathing suit that Uncle Maxx gave me." She dangled the tiny suit in front of Builder and shoved the blue one to Ashley.

"Well, okay, baby, if you say so." Builder winked at Ashley and gave Sasha a bear hug. "What does your mom think?"

All six eyes turned to Mel expectantly. She shrugged her shoulders in concession. The girls jumped up and down, letting out squeals of joy. This victory needed to be celebrated.

Men are so blind, Mel thought, shaking her head. She busied herself with the things on her tray, and caught Sasha's triumphant glance before she sped out of the room. "Remember, it's just one night," Mel called after her. "Don't overpack."

"And come on outside," Builder added. "People have been asking about you."

He rummaged through the refrigerator, looking for more of the barbecue sauce that had been ready since last week. Mel was glad to see him looking so spiffy. He was still wearing his long white apron, spotted with smeared barbecue sauce, and a chef's hat that fit jauntily over his thick crop of hair.

"You two at it again?" he asked, opening a beer.

Mel gave an exasperated sigh. "She's growing up too fast."

"Ah. The universal complaint of all parents." He took a tray from the bottom of a cabinet and started stacking more drinks on top. "We should probably take another cooler out there," he said. "It would simplify things."

"We only have one cooler," Mel reminded him. She watched him deftly arrange the beverages in symmetrical order, a carryover, perhaps, from his skill of arranging houses. He was probably great with blocks as a child. He hummed happily.

"To what do we owe this wonderful mood?" Mel asked in proper English.

He feigned surprise. "Why, what do you mean? I'm always in a wonderful mood." He pulled her closer to him, his fingers cold from the refrigerated cans. "I've got a beautiful wife, a lovely daughter, and . . ." He twirled her around the kitchen in a sprightly two-step, singing, *We're in the money, we're in the money. . . . Dah dah—dah dah dah dah—dah dah dah dah dah dah.*"

"What's this all about?" Mel asked, laughing.

"Oh, let's just say that bank loan should be coming through any day now."

"Really?"

"Yep. Just got an inside tip."

"That's great! Tell me about it."

She didn't know much about his business. Not that she didn't want to, it was just that—well, it was *his* business, and he seemed to prefer it that way. Besides, she had been so involved with her own job and dealing with Sasha, that she never had a great desire to pry into his business affairs. They would talk generally, in that she knew he was working on this project or that, and he shared stories about demanding customers who wanted overnight miracles. But they rarely talked finances. Of course, she knew there were bank loans—even Atlanta's premier developers had bank loans—but she and Builder had never discussed specifics.

Even now, in this jovial mood, Builder acted as though he had said too much. He ended the dance, signaling a halt to further discussion. "Let's just say the loan will be right on time," he said, picking up his tray. "Can you handle the other one?"

"Sure, but . . ." Before she could say anything else, he was out the door. She heard him cheerily greet someone on the steps, and she turned to see an unfamiliar woman with tight black denim shorts, tinted red hair, and sprawling boobs spilling out of a yellow halter.

"Hi," the woman said brightly. "I was looking for the rest room."

Mel didn't usually make quick judgments, but all her instincts told her this person was a lightweight. Whatever happened to introducing yourself to your host? she wondered. She envisioned that if this woman were white, she'd fit the stereotype of the dizzy bimbo. Beautiful but dumb.

Mel extended her hand. "I'm Mel Burke—and—"

"Oh, *you're* Mel," the woman exclaimed. She shook Mel's hand heartily. "It's a wonderful party. My name's Nikki."

"Nice to meet you," Mel said. "There's a rest room downstairs, but since you're here . . ." She deliberately let her voice trail off as she pointed around the corner.

"Thanks," Nikki said, walking toward the hallway. "Oh, I love these older homes. The ceilings are so *tall*."

Mel didn't like having strange folks roaming through her house; that was the only thing she didn't enjoy about having a large party. Sometimes, a friend or two would bring along out-of-town visitors or other people that she didn't know. And she suspected that a few folks heard or saw the gathering and simply dropped in, testing their hospitality. She and Builder tried to contain everyone to the lower level, but inevitably a few stragglers would wander through. It was harmless, she supposed, but it made her a little uncomfortable. People were so weird these days, you could never be too careful.

She picked up her tray, once more, and headed outside to be with her guests.

It was the ideal day for an outdoor gathering—sunny and warm, but not yet the hot, sticky Georgia weather that would come later in the summer. The Burkes' backyard was full of people—over a hundred friends, neighbors, acquaintances, and friends of friends. It was a yard made for entertainment. The wooded one-and-a-half-acre space allowed ample elbow room for the athletic antics now occurring at the two badminton nets and in the volleyball game. The more sedentary types were playing bid whist, bridge, or pinochle at one of three rented card tables, and an assortment of colorful blankets dotted the right side of the lawn, designated for eating only. Two men leaned intently over a chess board, oblivious to a soaring Frisbee that whirled above their heads. A young couple nestled cozily in a hammock nailed to two of the towering oaks that formed a gauntlet of greenery along the property line.

Mel and Builder loved this yard. It was the icing on the cake that made them decide to buy the house more than a decade ago. It was unusual to find a house with such a spacious yard in an in-town neighborhood. They still talked about adding a pool and a tennis court "at some point in the future," but on the other hand neither of them was eager to see the lovely green space give way to concrete. The yard was a testament to the names of the streets in the neighborhood—Rolling Brook, Cedar Paradise, Spreading Oak. Over the years, Builder had put in a lot of time out here. While projects inside the house often went wanting, he managed to find time to work "out back"—landscaping, pruning, planting. Some type of flower was always in bloom, and today the yard was awash with purple gladiolus and brilliant pinks.

Mel caught a whiff of honeysuckle in the air as she slid her tray onto the table on the outdoor deck. Celeste and Ron Hamilton sat under the umbrella, nibbling on crackers and smoked oysters. Builder was tending the barbecue.

"Mel, I've been trying to get this stubborn man of yours to join us on the cruise we're taking next month," Celeste said. "Some people dropped out at the last minute, and it's not too late for you to sign on. We'll be doing some island hopping—St. Martin, St. Kitts, Martinique. It'll be fabulous."

"Sounds like it," Mel said enviously. "But I think we'll have to pass."

"Aw, come on," chimed in Ron. "All work and no play—you guys better enjoy the good life before it passes you by."

"I thought that was what we're doing," Mel replied good-naturedly. She knew that Builder was taking in every word, even though he appeared to be concentrating on the task at hand. He put more charcoal on the grill.

Ron reached over for a glass of lemonade and looked directly into

Mel's eyes. "You've got to use your powers of persuasion, sweetheart, and get this husband of yours off his duff."

"Well, actually, I'm going to have to get off mine. You know, I'm a lady of leisure these days."

"Yeah, I was surprised about that." Ron took a quick sip. "With the Olympics coming and more foreign-based businesses setting up shop here, you'd think the international division, of all departments, would be a safe bet."

"We've—uh—they've had some cash flow problems for some time," Mel explained. "I guess I can take comfort in the fact that I'm not the only one who was let go. You know the old saying—misery loves company."

"All the more reason why you should come with us," insisted Celeste. "The islands—ahh—I can't think of a better place to be miserable."

Builder flipped over a rib in an exaggerated way and placed the large barbecue fork on the table. "Well, we're going to Jekyll soon and that's going to have to be it for a while."

"*Jekyll?!*" Celeste spoke with disdain, almost spitting out the word. "You can go there *anytime.*" One by one, she ticked off reasons on her fingers why the cruise was a better choice. "Mel's not working right now. You're your own boss. You don't have to answer to anybody. And besides, you need a real vacation."

"Yeah, and how about some real cash to go with it?" Builder said sarcastically.

Mel thought she'd better speak up fast. "The way I see it, we don't have to go on a cruise to have a *real* vacation." She winked flirtatiously at Builder.

"All riiiight!" Ron said energetically. "Now *that's* the kind of talk I like in a woman." He playfully nudged Builder on the arm.

Celeste dismissed the idea with a fling of her hand. "Well, give me a ship anytime." She crossed her long legs and looked critically at her well-manicured nails. "I still have so much to do to get ready. Not to mention Ashley's stuff."

"Oh," Mel said. "Ashley's going?"

"Yes. We thought we'd make it a family affair." Celeste paused for a moment to select a celery stick. "Say, even if you two don't go, why don't you send Sasha? Ashley would love it."

"Hmmm," Mel mused. "How much would something like that cost?" As soon as she said it, she wished she hadn't. Builder gave her a look of betrayal, as though to say "How dare you ask any question related to money?"

"A couple of grand," Celeste replied lightly, "which is not that much when you consider that your food and entertainment are included." She held up her arms to embrace their outdoor surroundings. "You can handle it. Builder's a successful entrepreneur—land baron and all."

"Yeah, right," he replied huffily.

"But, hey, man, let me tell you," Ron inserted, "it's not the trip that does you in, it's the wardrobe. You should see what Celeste already bought for herself. Not to mention Ashley. That's the hurtin' part."

"Oh, you'll survive," Celeste said, munching on her celery. She fixed her gaze on Mel, and asked, conspiratorially, "So, are you going to let Sasha come?"

"We'll see," Mel said. She caught Builder's look of surprise, but he said nothing. Of course, she realized they'd have to watch their budget for the next few months, and sending Sasha on a cruise was not the least bit feasible, but Celeste and Ron didn't need to know that.

The basis of the friendship between the two couples was their daughters. Sasha and Ashley were inseparable. They had taken ballet lessons together since they were four and five respectively, and both attended the same northside school, Trent Academy. In the early years, the Burkes and Hamiltons took turns driving the girls to school, as well as to swimming practice, dance lessons, and scouting activities. Even after Ron and Celeste moved from southwest Atlanta to a high-priced house in an exclusive Buckhead subdivision, the girls continued their close friendship.

Ironically, Mel liked Ashley, the daughter, much more than she did Celeste, her own peer. She thought Celeste was too status conscious, and she frequently felt uncomfortable around her. A high-level manager at a Fortune 500 corporation, Celeste had worked her way into the executive ranks after graduating from a prestigious Midwestern business school. For years, she had made a hefty salary, yet she constantly complained: The money was never enough; the perks, including first-class international travel, never quite matched the "bennies" of her white colleagues. "But, Celeste," Builder once told her, "you've got to understand. To them, you'll always be a nigger." She would bristle at any suggestion that she got where she was, even in part, because of the sacrifices other blacks had made. With Ron working as a vice president at Landmark Universal, Celeste enjoyed their status as a successful, prosperous couple, embraced by Atlanta's black elite. She relished telling Mel about the many invitations she and Ron received, and how they attended this or that social event on behalf of their respective companies. In her own right, Mel received a lot of the same invites through her job at the Chamber, and in truth, she suspected that was largely why Celeste considered her a desirable person to know. Of course, now that her job at the Chamber was history . . .

Light, staccato beeps from a car horn heralded an approaching vehicle. A pearl white Lamborghini cruised lazily up the driveway to the foot of the yard. It purred to a stop, soaking in the rays of the sun like a translucent polished jewel. The car made such an impressive sight that all heads turned, freeze-framing any previous activity in honor of this newest entrant.

"Who is *that?*" Celeste asked, peering over the wooden rail.

"It can only be Maxx," Builder answered with pride. "He's really done it this time."

Ron whistled appreciatively. "A Lamborghini! Oh, man!"

Mel stood next to Celeste, and watched below as people crowded around the car. Majestically, the driver's door swung skyward to a chorus of oohs and aahhs. Removing his black leather racing gloves, Maxx emerged with a gleaming grin and a thumbs-up sign.

The girls burst out of the kitchen door, almost knocking over a chair in their glee.

"Uncle Maxx! Uncle Maxx!" shrieked Sasha. She raced down the steps, with Ashley close at her heels.

"Calm down before you break your neck," Mel called after them. She shook her head in amazement. A few moments ago Sasha was a near-woman, arguing over a bikini. Now, she was acting like a six-year-old. But Maxx had that effect on people. Wherever he went, excitement followed.

"Hey, Builder, did you know there's only about three of these cars in the whole state?" Ron said eagerly. "They cost well over two hundred thousand. I'm going to go check it out."

"I'm right behind you," Builder said. He piled up a plateful of smoked chicken and hurried down the steps after Ron.

"My, my, my." Celeste surveyed the scene below. "Maxx certainly has a way of becoming the life of the party."

"Yeah," Mel smirked. "And he's eating it up. I'm surprised he's not passing out autographs."

Celeste laughed. "He's sure cute enough. I for one wouldn't mind having a successful young lawyer in my pocket. I'll bet he's raking it in."

If only you knew how, Mel thought. She moved toward the untended grill, although there was no more meat on it and therefore no need to look after it. But she didn't feel like hearing talk about Maxx—Maxx and his women. Maxx and his cars. Maxx and his money. She was tired of people being taken in by him. They were so gullible to his good looks and smooth talk. They had no idea what the real deal was.

"I'm going down, too," Celeste said. "Want me to take some of these drinks?"

"Thanks."

Mel was grateful for the time alone. She needed a few minutes to collect herself before mingling with the crowd. The last thing she wanted was to get an attitude over Maxx's latest venture and show her obvious displeasure over his car. People aren't dumb, she thought. Everybody else is smiling and having a good time, and if I go down there with a glum face, they'll wonder what's my problem. Like Builder, she was never good at hiding her emotions.

"Hey, Mel, come on down." It was Maxx, waving from below.

She returned his greeting with a tepid smile and nod. The hood to the car was raised, and Builder, Ron, and several others were inspecting the electronic innards. Sasha and Ashley lounged on the buff-colored front seats.

In the last couple of years, Maxx had showcased a string of expensive autos. There was the black Porsche Carrera, the red Austin-Martin, and the '63 Corvette convertible that he had restored to mint condition. Each car was more flamboyant than the previous, and each represented a part of Maxx's lifestyle that Mel abhorred. "If anything, you need to keep a low profile," she once told him. "Use your head. How many black men run around in cars like that?"

"What I do is strictly legitimate," he had replied, using a phrase he had repeated many times before in their arguments about his work. But this time, she thought, he'd gone too far. The Lamborghini was a dead giveaway. He might as well be wearing a sign—Maxximilian Lincoln: drug dealer. Those are often the people who buy that kind of car. Who else could afford them? And a black man driving it too? Maxx was asking for trouble. The fact that he was an attorney for drug dealers and not a dealer himself would make little difference to the police. He'd probably be pulled over more often than he'd have the car on the road.

Mel walked over to the CD player to change the disk. She saw someone move out of the corner of her eye. At first, she couldn't make out who it was. Another first-timer, she thought, and looked away. But something about the man's walk pulled back her gaze. It wasn't quite right, that walk, more like a sway—slow, but determined, steadily moving up the driveway. Mel reached for her glasses in her pocket, and then remembered she had left them inside. She was extremely near-sighted, "myopic in more ways than one," Builder would sometimes say, and now she squinted against the sun, her left hand over her eyes, trying to get a closer look.

She noticed that the man wore a long-sleeved shirt and overalls, strange for such a warm day. There was something vaguely familiar about him, but he was still too far away for Mel to bring him into focus. A roar of laughter rippled from the crowd, and Mel glanced over in time to see the red-haired "bimbo" being hoisted onto the hood of Maxx's car.

She turned back to the blurry figure and then realized with a start what the problem was. The man was drunk! That explained the odd walk. Probably some passerby who'd heard the music and was looking for free booze.

Mel started to call out to Builder, but as she opened her mouth, a harsh voice stopped her short.

"Hey, Builder! Builder Burke! Where are ya?"

The voice was loud and mean, cutting through the merry crowd, whose attention turned to the stumbling figure in the driveway. Mel now recognized the man. It was Lenny. She couldn't recall his last name, but he was one of Builder's workers, a painter, and had even done a few rooms for them at the house just last winter. But the voice and unsteady walk seemed so unlike the usually soft-spoken and reserved Lenny she remembered. That's the liquor talking, she thought, recalling a saying from her childhood that she had often heard older folks use.

"Builder!" Lenny shouted again. "Where ya at? I want my money."

He lunged further into the driveway, tripped over an empty card table, and staggered in the direction of the crowd. Mel saw Builder emerge from the group surrounding Maxx's car. She could tell he was angry at this rude intrusion, but for the sake of appearances, wanted to keep Lenny at bay.

"Hey, man," he said, steadily walking toward him. "What are you doing here?" His back was stiff as he headed toward his uninvited guest. "If you've got a problem, we need to talk at the office."

"Nah, nah, nah," slurred Lenny, waving his hand in protest. "I want my money, and I want it now. No more puttin' off like last time. You owe me eight hundred bucks from the Luckett job, and I ain't leavin' till I git it."

At the word "git," Lenny stomped his feet, defiantly holding his ground. Mel watched Builder move closer, trying to get Lenny to lower his voice. He mumbled something, which only made Lenny more agitated.

"Nah, I don't want nuttin' to eat," Lenny sputtered. "I want my money. You ain't puttin' me off no mo.'"

The argument was getting out of hand. Get him out of here, Mel wanted to cry out. Shut him up! It was embarrassing to watch the scene unfold below—Lenny disrupting her party, disturbing her guests. How dare he come into her yard and in one swoop dispel the festive mood with his drunken demands.

Maxx made his way to Builder's side, as if uniting against a common enemy. She heard Builder repeat again to Lenny that they needed to talk inside, but nothing he or Maxx was saying would calm him down.

"You never finished payin' me from the last job," Lenny accused, "and I ain't lettin' you git away with that again. I want my eight hundred dollars for Luckett, and the forty-five dollars and fifty cent for the paint on the Jefferson place."

"Now you listen to me," Builder ordered, losing all patience and control. "Get out of my face, now. You hear? I told you I'd take care of this later."

As Builder reached for Lenny's arm to hurry him away, Lenny reared back. Seemingly from nowhere, he pulled out a shiny silver pistol and waved it erratically in the air.

"Look, he's got a gun!" someone shouted. People scrambled for cover, ducking behind Maxx's car, behind tables and chairs—behind anything they could find.

In a panic, Mel searched the crowd for Sasha, knowing that the girls were just a few feet from danger.

Builder, held back by Maxx, tried harder to reason. "Lenny," he said evenly, "drop the gun. Drop it before there's real trouble." He inched closer to Lenny, who brandished the weapon again, creating another surge of fear among the crowd.

"Don't nobody touch me," Lenny warned. "Stay 'way from me."

Mel could see that the gun was wobbly in his hand, and Lenny was trying hard to maintain his balance.

"I mean it," he threatened. "I'll use this."

Mel leaned over the rail and found herself pleading directly to Lenny.

"Lenny, *please*," she appealed loudly, amidst the hush below. "Put it away. Put the gun away. There are children here."

Something in her voice must have jolted Lenny back into reality. He looked around, newly aware of the terror he had created. He stared up at Mel as in a stupor, and suddenly, his ugly facade collapsed.

"Oh, Miz Burke," he said, sobered by her alarm. "I . . . I didn't mean no harm. I wouldn't hurt no children—or—or no one." His right hand went limp, and the gun fell to his side. Maxx quickly retrieved it while Builder and Ron strong-armed Lenny out of the yard. There was a collective sigh of relief as people picked themselves up, some laughing nervously, others huddling for comfort. Mel hurried down the steps to Sasha, who rushed into her arms.

"Oh, Mom! I was so scared!"

"I know, honey," Mel said, shaken. "So was I."

Maxx walked over with the gun still in his hand.

"You okay?" he asked solemnly.

Mel nodded, as she gently patted Sasha on the head.

"I'll get rid of this," he whispered.

Celeste, with Ashley in tow, approached with a worried frown on her face. "What was *that* all about?" she asked.

Mel shook her head and breathed deeply. "I'm just glad it's over."

Frank Kirby, an attorney known for his quick wit, dramatically put his arm around Mel's shoulder. "Darlin', I've got to hand it to you. Now I know what Builder means when he says, 'When Mel talks, people listen.' I'm glad you found your voice today." He laughed heartily, and a few in the crowd, relief on their faces, joined in. Frank continued with other comments, designed to break the tension. "You folks not only fix the best barbecue around, you provide real entertainment too. You should have charged admission."

Mel tried to muster a smile, but could not yet let go of the fear that had gripped her just moments before. She could understand that Lenny was upset about not being paid. But to come to her house with a gun! Someone could have been shot, could have been killed! And all because Builder hadn't taken care of business.

Mel limply wiped a stubborn grease stain clinging to the underlip of a glass bowl. The sink was stacked with dishes that needed hands-on attention, but she had no energy for tackling the dirty task. She decided to let the dishes soak. The warm water from the faucet felt good running over her hands. If only she could as easily wash away the last few hours. From the kitchen window, she watched the sun melt behind a red maple in her backyard. Mesmerized, she held on to the moment, grateful for the distraction.

It was barely eight o'clock and already all the guests were gone. In the past, this was about the time that things really got jumping, when the die-hard party folks would start to dance and get loose, staying until well past midnight. But Lenny had successfully broken up the party. After the threat of danger had been eliminated, people had quickly drifted away, making polite but speedy exits. Not that she could blame them. They weren't used to seeing a gun brandished about. Neither was she. This kind of thing wasn't supposed to happen here. Her home wasn't some ghetto pit where people resolved disputes by shooting it out. This was insane. She was angry at Lenny for causing such a ruckus and spoiling the day. But she was even angrier at Builder. She couldn't understand why he was so disorganized in handling his business matters. If he had just paid Lenny on time, none of this would have happened. She knew he had a tendency to put things off, but this was becoming a disturbing habit.

Just recently, the administrator at Sasha's school had called about overdue tuition. That was one of the expenses that Builder was responsible for, and when Mel reminded him about it, he said he would take care of it immediately. But several days later, another call came from the school about nonpayment. Embarrassed, Mel went to pay the tuition in person. Builder's negligence was becoming more public and unforgivable.

The telephone stirred her from her thoughts. She picked up the receiver, her hands still dripping.

"Hello?"

"Mel! What's this I hear?" The voice on the other end gushed with excitement. "You had a shoot-out over there in the backyard?"

Mel moaned. "No. No, it was nothing like that."

It was the third call so far, and she expected there would be more. People who had heard about the commotion but who hadn't been present were calling for the inside scoop. It sure didn't take long for tongues to start wagging. She wouldn't be surprised if by now, the story was that the SWAT team had been called in.

"One of Builder's workers came here drunk and out of control," she explained. "But everything's okay." She wondered if the caller detected the shakiness in her voice. She talked for another moment and then searched for a way out. "Gotta run. Sasha's calling me."

A lie. Sasha had gone to spend the night with Ashley, as planned, but it was the best way Mel could think of to abruptly end the conversation. She left the phone off the hook for a temporary respite, and walked onto the deck to clean off the table. Under the darkening night sky, she caught a glimpse of Maxx's white chariot. She was surprised that Maxx was here; she had seen him leave earlier with the red-headed bimbo—what was her name—Nikki? Evidently, he had come back. But for what?

She reached up to close the table umbrella when she saw Maxx and Builder huddled below. They didn't notice her, so intent were they in their conversation. She couldn't hear what they were saying, but she clearly saw Maxx hand Builder some money, which he folded and placed in his back pocket.

Mel was furious. She flung a stack of CDs across the table and stomped into the kitchen, slamming the door behind her. How could Builder do it? He knew how Maxx made his living, but more importantly, he knew how she felt about Maxx's ties to corruption. Her head was spinning. Was the whole incident with Lenny simply an oversight? Or was Builder really that hard up for money?

She heard Maxx's car start, and quick footsteps rattle the wooden deck stairs. Builder had barely entered the kitchen when Mel immediately pounced on him.

"Did you just accept money from Maxx?" she asked accusingly. She stood in the middle of the floor, hands on hips.

Builder frowned at the question and retrieved a beer from the refrigerator. "This is between me and Maxx," he said tightly. "Just 'cause you have problems with him, doesn't mean I do." He popped the top off the beer and walked out of the kitchen.

But Mel wasn't going to let him off that easily. "Wait a minute," she called after him. She followed him downstairs into his office, all her stored-up anger about to explode: Lenny; the botched party; the money from Maxx. "You owe me an explanation," she said, standing in the doorway. Her voice sounded both wounded and accusatory. "Someone could have been killed out there today. Do you realize that?"

Builder shifted some papers on his desk to make space amidst the clutter for his beer can. "I'm sorry that happened. Lenny was drunk. He had no business coming here like that."

"Well, why haven't you paid him? He said this wasn't the first time, either."

Builder plopped in his chair, exhausted, and anxious for her to leave him alone. "Look, the man was drunk. You heard him rant and rave. But what he didn't say was all the times I've given him advances on jobs before he even *looked* at a paint brush. This one time, when I'm a couple days late, he acts like I'm jerkin' him around. That's a bunch of bull."

"But you do owe him eight hundred dollars, right?"

"So to speak. But if you add it all up, he probably owes me. He's lucky I didn't have his ass locked up. Like I told him, if he comes by the office tomorrow, he'll get his money."

"So that's why you borrowed money from Maxx? To pay Lenny?"

"Look, didn't I tell you? This is between Maxx and me. Don't push it." His eyes turned cold and steely. He didn't like to be challenged, especially on what he considered private business.

But for Mel, the matter was no longer private, if indeed it ever was. If Maxx was involved, it was her concern too. She paced back and forth at the doorway and spotted a paperweight from their trip a few years ago to Disney World. She felt like flinging it across the room at Builder, anything to shake him up about Maxx.

"How can you take money from him?" she lashed out. "You *know* where it comes from. It's drug money, and when you take it, you're just as guilty as he is."

"It's a matter of perspective," Builder said hotly.

This was a point of contention between them—what Maxx did for a living. Mel remembered how proud she had been that sunny spring day when Maxx graduated from Harvard Law. Here was her baby brother, a handsome, bright African-American man who was well-armed to make a difference, to right some wrongs. She'd had such dreams for him, such hopes! She had envisioned he would become a defender of the poor and disadvantaged, and would use his sharp legal mind on behalf of the people who needed him most. But from the beginning, he chose a different path. For a while, he worked at Klein, Kingsdale & Hudson, one of Atlanta's high-powered corporate law firms, where he quickly gained a reputation as a tough negotiator. He was one of the few knighted blacks deemed eligible to ride the fast track of rapid promotions and premium deals. Later, when he made the move to open his own practice, he had no problem attracting business. But many of his clients, at least in Mel's view, had questionable backgrounds. The one time she'd gone to his office she'd seen a string of suspicious men in the waiting room—mostly young Latinos wearing $900 suits and pointed Italian shoes. Maxx himself was now looking like some of his clients. He had taken to wearing his hair brushed back, in a wavy style, and his clothes, while always well-tailored, had become sleeker, more high fashion. He spent about half his time in Miami, which to Mel was another sign that he had sold out to nefarious interests. "Why don't you just go ahead and move to Colombia," she had blurted once during an argument. He justified his work by stating that everyone deserves a defense, that he was providing a needed service, in the American way, and that his clients were simply legitimate business people. It infuriated Mel to hear him talk like that. Even worse, she received no backup from Builder, who admired Maxx for using the system to get what he wanted.

"I've got some calls to make," Builder said now. "I'll be down here for a while."

He was dismissing her, but she didn't budge. She wasn't ready to drop the matter. She wanted to tell Builder again how wrong it was to take money from Maxx. And she wanted to talk more about her feelings, about how scared she had been when Lenny had the gun. They hadn't really talked about the incident, the absurdity of it all, that paralyzing moment of terror.

Perhaps had she mentioned her fears, the conversation would have ended differently, on a better note. Perhaps they would have embraced, offering each other the support they both needed. But instead of talking about her fears, she brought up another aspect—one that Builder didn't need to hear at that moment.

"Do you realize how embarrassed I was out there today?"

"It wasn't exactly a picnic for me, either," he said. "Don't blame me because Lenny was drunk."

"I'm not blaming you for that. But I do blame you for not taking care of your business affairs, especially when it starts affecting all of us."

"What do you mean?" he asked incredulously. "*I'm* the only one who's taking care of any business around here, since *I'm* the only one working!"

It was a low blow, and Mel reeled back as though she had been struck. How unfair of him. Her losing her job had nothing to do with his not paying Lenny. *That's* what had started everything.

For a second, Builder looked as though he wanted to take back the words. Then, the moment passed. He got up and rummaged through a file drawer. "I have work to do," he said curtly.

"Yeah," Mel retorted. "In more ways than one." She marched out of his office and up the stairs.

His voice, still hostile, trailed after her. "Put the phone back on the hook."

She strode into the kitchen and jerked the receiver that had been lying on its side. She heard impatient clicking on the other end; Builder trying to get through. She wanted to scream at him, curse at him, to strike back in some way. But her mother's good breeding held her in check.

The best she could do was to bang the phone back into its cradle, slamming it loudly against Builder's ear.

From his hillside stance at the edge of the green, Builder watched closely as men in sand-colored uniforms queued up next to the prison bus below. A foreman walked back and forth along the line, spewing tobacco and instructions, while another prison official stood a few yards away, erect rifle in hand. Gardening tools were passed around—a hoe, a scythe, a few rakes. Builder surmised that these must be trusty inmates to have access to such potential weapons.

He noticed that the prisoners were black; the guards white. He shook his head, remembering the words of his father, who had often said, "If you grow up without getting into trouble with the law, I'll have done my job." Steadily, the wave of uniforms moved toward the underbrush that choked a row of trees and the prisoners began their day-long task of weeding under the hot Georgia sun.

Builder plucked the number 3 iron from his leather golf bag, patting his forehead with a damp handkerchief. He had been out since early this morning to make a seven o'clock tee-off and had left Mel snoozing contentedly in their rented condo. He took a deep breath before setting up for his next shot. Knees bent, he readied the club for the swing, tightening his grip for the downward stroke. The club whipped through the air, sailing the ball onto the fairway.

"Shit!" The lone word broke the silence around him. He had sliced the ball, creating an errant curve that would require a couple of extra strokes on this seventeenth hole.

He was a fair golfer, an every-other-weekend hacker who could be much better if he devoted more time to the game. Actually, he preferred high-energy sports, like running and biking. But what he liked about golf was mornings like this, when he could get out early, walk the course, smell the fresh cut grass, and reflect. During the past year there had been few opportunities for that. The stress of his business, the long hours, the never-ending financial jockeying to pay this creditor versus that—it had all taken a toll. And Mel's losing her job certainly hadn't helped.

He lifted his bag onto his shoulder to begin the decline from the hill.

He caught another glance at the prisoners below, who were bending over, whacking at the kudzu and overgrown brush. He wondered what they were in for, what were their crimes. Armed robbery, aggravated assault, petty theft? Guilty or not, they certainly had no influence in high places. He thought of all the financial swindlers and crooked politicians, the master manipulators of the system, who make a living from ripping people off, yet remain insulated and revered in their air-conditioned offices. *They're* the ones who should be paying a price, he thought. *They* should be out here in prison garb, sweating in the heat. But no, they enjoy the protection of other corrupt colleagues, making and breaking the rules in their own self-interest.

Builder sighed heavily as he lumbered down the hill. He could feel a lousy mood coming on, as though the further he descended, the more the reality of his own problems sank in. He had done pretty well these last three days, in starting to feel more upbeat. Mel had insisted that they come to Jekyll Island as planned. It was at Jekyll that they had spent their honeymoon nearly fourteen years ago, and since then they had made an annual trip here. Mel liked to come in mid-June and then go somewhere new around the end of August. But this year there would be no second vacation. They were doing well just to come here for a few days. In fact, after the incident with Lenny two weeks ago, Builder had told Mel that it would be impossible for him to get time away from work. But she had persuaded him to come, saying that, more than ever, they needed some time together, just the two of them.

As it turned out, Sasha had gone with the Hamiltons on the cruise. Mel had argued that Sasha would benefit from the cultural exposure. "It'll be one of those wonderful experiences she'll remember for a lifetime," she had said. But Builder knew that part of it was Mel's own ego and her competitive drive to prove to Celeste that she too could provide the best for her daughter.

For his part, Builder wanted Sasha to go, but was concerned about the money for her share of the expenses. He had felt so bad about what happened at the party that he thought Sasha's trip could be a way of making up for it. He didn't need any more ill feelings running through his house. Mel was already upset with him, and it wasn't fair that Sasha should have to pay the price for his financial problems. So he gave in. He had scrounged up a couple hundred dollars, but they'd gotten most of the money from Sasha's savings account. "That's what it's there for," Mel had reasoned.

It seemed that lately everything focused on money: Mel's losing her job; the unexpected cash for Sasha's trip; even this lightweight jaunt to Jekyll. His problems were exacerbated, he knew, because Mel had no idea about the fragility of their finances. He had decided some time ago that since he had gotten into this mess himself, he would get himself out of it. And he was determined that he would turn things around. What he needed was more time, that's all, just a little more time. But ever since Lenny had acted the fool at the party, it had become harder and harder to keep things from Mel. In the last couple of weeks, she had asked all kinds of questions. He usually gave vague responses or tried to ease into another subject. But if things kept up at this rate, it wouldn't be long before she found out the truth—that they were in serious financial trouble.

More than anything, it was important to Builder to be a good provider. He had little patience for men who shirked their responsibilities, didn't support their children, or deserted their families when the going got rough. It was an early message he learned from his dad, who had said frequently, "You gotta take care of your own, son. Ain't nobody else gonna butter your bread."

He had grown up in Dublin, Georgia, one of those "everybody knows everybody" small towns where the standard joke is, if you're driving by, "don't blink or you'll miss it." The black people of Dublin stuck together, had to because of discrimination. But Builder's father had had his own modus operandi, and his independent spunk often made things difficult for his black neighbors. He was always in the forefront of a demonstration, speaking out against some injustice, and making the more timid in the community very uncomfortable. People admired yet resented him at the same time.

Nathaniel Burke, Sr. (people called him Nathan), was a carpenter of high regard. He had started his business in 1942 when he bought a used pickup truck for $250 from old Mr. Bottoms, the lone black funeral director. For years, Nathan drove that truck throughout the small towns and dusty hills of middle Georgia, getting work here and there, wherever it could be gotten. He built wall-to-wall bookcases, bedroom furniture, kitchen cabinets. Sometimes he'd have what he called "special deliveries," like the delicate doll house he once fashioned for the mayor's granddaughter.

When he was old enough, Builder worked with his father during the summers when school was out. At first he would hold nails or sand wood.

Later, he graduated to taking critical measurements, and setting up exact cuts on the lathe. He learned quickly and loved the feel of the wood in his hands as he shaped and sculpted it into a baby chair or a finished pedestal. In the sixth grade he made a miniature chest of drawers without nails, just wood and glue, which won first prize in the state's science fair, beating out more elaborate pieces by older contestants. It was around this time that Nathan, Sr., bestowed on his son the nickname "Builder," and it stuck. In fact, Builder preferred it to the more mundane "Junior." He had always regarded his full name, Nathaniel Alston Burke, Jr., as too pretentious, and he never liked the shortened moniker Nate. But "Builder" fit him just right. It sounded strong and steady, which is what he wanted to be. Like his father.

Sometimes, the father/son duo would drink Coca-Cola and make up their own silly lyrics as they headed down the back roads of a country town, looking for business. Builder especially liked Wednesdays, advertising day, when they'd pass out handmade leaflets extolling Nathan's woodworking talents. Nathan Burke was an astute businessman—"Can't get no work if folks don't know you," he'd say. Certainly, the people in Dublin and the surrounding towns knew him. He had his share of run-ins with white people and prided himself on standing up to "the crow."

"Daddy, who is this Mr. Jim Crow?" Builder had asked once when he was nine years old. "Am I ever gonna meet him?"

Nathan had laughed cynically. "Son, you already have. And he don't deserve to be called no mister."

Builder found out soon enough that Jim Crow resided in the homes of many of the white customers that his father worked for. He remembered the time they were making a huge unit for a family named Allen. They had been working for several hours when Mrs. Allen, her blond hair stretched into a tight bun, announced she had made lunch for them.

"Well, thank you, ma'am," said Nathan. "That's mighty generous of you."

Builder grinned at the prospect. Today, at least, he wouldn't have to eat another limp sandwich that had no doubt wilted in the truck under the sizzling sun. The mayonnaise was sure to be smelling to high heaven by now.

"Come this way," Mrs. Allen instructed brightly.

Nathan and Builder followed her through the cool, spacious house, walking through the dining room and on past the kitchen. Builder was surprised to see that, except for a flowery centerpiece, the kitchen table was empty—no sign of any food, anywhere.

"Just step right on through." Mrs. Allen was smiling, opening the door to the outside. "I've got everything set up for you." She pointed to a shabby lean-to, separated from the house by a good thirty yards.

Builder moved in the direction of her hand, but Nathan froze on the spot.

"Go right ahead," Mrs. Allen prodded, noting his hesitation.

Nathan reached for Builder's shoulder and sharply held him back. He spoke slowly, punctuating each word with intensity. "There ain't no way my boy and I gonna eat out there."

"Well, I . . . " began Mrs. Allen, startled at the rejection. "Why wouldn't you want to eat? Surely you're hungry?"

Nathan gave no response. Builder knew better than to utter a word.

Mrs. Allen struck an indignant pose. "I'll have you know I spent a lot of time making that lunch. You should at least have the decency to eat it."

Nathan looked at her stonily and put his hand around Builder's neck, guiding him forward. "We got food in the truck," he pronounced.

Builder remembered how disappointed he was that he wouldn't get to see the feast that awaited him. His nine-year-old imagination visualized something deliciously exotic in that run-down shed. But he knew this was one of those times when his father was taking a stand, and evidently whatever was inside the shed would remain a mystery.

They climbed into the steamy truck and silently ate soggy chicken and mayonnaise sandwiches. When finished, Nathan passed Builder a warm Coke and fixed his dark eyes on the innocent face looking up at him. "Remember, son: just 'cause people treat you like a dog, don't mean you gotta act like one."

His golf game over, Builder headed back to the clubhouse. He missed his father tremendously, even though it had been many years since the old man died of a coronary. He missed the jokes, the cut-to-the-bone bits of wisdom. Over the years, the two had become good friends; in fact, Builder realized nostalgically, his father had been his best friend. No one else had really understood him. Not even Mel.

That was part of their problem—a failure to communicate. Of course, he had to take some of the blame for that. When they first married, they had pledged never to go to bed angry at each other, or leave hurt feelings unresolved. Builder had to admit that for some time now he hadn't held up his end of the agreement. But then, things were a lot more complicated now than when they were newlyweds.

"Hey, mister, need any help?" A well-fed black kid sporting faded chinos and fat cheeks came huffing up beside Builder. "I need the tip," he said unabashedly, "*and* the exercise."

Builder smiled at the boy's honesty. "Sure, why not." He released his heavy load to the ground, grateful for the relief to his shoulder.

The hefty young caddie bent his back to take up the weight of the golf bag. "You carried this for the whole course?" he asked with amazement.

Builder laughed. "No, I'm not Superman. I did rent a handcart, but it dropped a wheel around the fifteenth green."

"Oh wow. Sorry about that, sir. Wish I had seen you earlier. I could have brought you another cart."

"No big deal."

"You coming back out tomorrow?"

"Yeah. Early. Gonna squeeze in a quick nine before I leave."

The kid gave the golf bag a friendly tap. "Well, you can leave your clubs with me at the clubhouse. No need to lug them back with you. I'll look after them. And since the cart broke down and you were inconvenienced and all, I'll be glad to clean your clubs. It's on the house."

Builder smiled. "That so?"

"Yes, sir. And I can wax the handles, too. I'll take care of everything."

As they walked toward the clubhouse, Builder wished that everything in his personal life could be taken care of so easily.

Last night after Mel had gone to sleep, he'd walked the beach till nearly 2:00 A.M., running through his mind all the bills that were due, trying to figure out how to pay them. There was no way he could talk to Mel about this; she didn't know the half of it. It was bad enough that she'd found out about the money he owed Lenny. That was small change compared to the other stuff.

The main problem now was covering outstanding business debt. The sluggish economy had mercilessly seared his contracting business. His credit with some of his suppliers was threatened, and he needed to bring several accounts current right away. And then there was the damn second mortgage on the house. He was already behind two payments, and by next week he would be three months late. He'd had to use that money to cover some pressing business bills. He knew it was risky to keep juggling things around, the old "borrow from Peter to pay Paul" tactic, or, more accurately in his case, holding off Peter and stalling Paul. Somehow he'd get the money to bring the second mortgage current immediately. There was no way he could risk jeopardizing the family residence. As it was, Mel had agreed to sign the loan papers last year only when he told her he could pay off the total loan within three months, after the Wilson job. It was a sweet deal—a $40,000 room addition, with plenty of profit built in. But it all fell through when Wilson was suddenly promoted to a position at his company's headquarters in Kansas City. Soon afterward, a contract for building a new office space went sour when the client up and reneged. Lousy luck. Both deals had been virtual shoo-ins. He had had two signed contracts in hand and was just days away from starting—when the bottom fell out. It was as though once he finally got behind the 8 ball, it just kept rolling over him, dragging him down.

Not only did he have the additional expense of a second mortgage payment, but business bills were mounting again, and there were no major contracts in the pipeline. It was critical that the loan with Sunbelt Bank be approved, and he was awaiting word on that any day. "It's got to come through," he said aloud.

He had been in regular contact with Curtis Moore, a loan officer at Sunbelt's Cobb County branch. A former classmate, Curtis had come to the Memorial Day party and had told Builder that his chances were greater for getting the loan okayed at the Cobb branch, rather than the West End. "I'll be looking out for you, bro," Curtis had said. "I know it's tough out there."

Builder had received a few business loans before, but they were always small amounts—$5,000, $10,000—and everything had to be collateralized to the hilt. He knew of white contractors who landed a $50,000 line of credit over the phone, no papers to sign, nothing to put up. They were amazed that he was able even to handle the business that he did, virtually out of pocket. But now he needed a major infusion of capital—fast.

In recent months, Maxx had helped keep the business afloat by lending him several thousand dollars. Plus the $800 to pay Lenny. But Builder didn't want to borrow any more from his brother-in-law. The business needed to stand on its own feet, and he didn't want to become dependent on Maxx. The good thing was, Maxx never pressured him about repayment and was genuinely interested in giving support. He'd say things like, "Don't worry about it, I know you'll get to me when you can," and "We're family and have to look out for each other."

Builder thought of how Mel would hit the roof if she knew about the numerous transactions between him and Maxx. She could be so pigheaded and unreasonable. Maxx wasn't perfect, true, but he was an all-right guy, and he certainly had a head for business. A few years ago he had asked Builder to join him as an investor in a new medical supply firm. It seemed like a good idea and since his own company was doing well at the time, Builder could have put in his share without too much strain. He hadn't talked to Mel about it because he knew she would object to any idea, no matter how noble, involving Maxx and his money. He hadn't felt like having a guilt trip laid on him, so out of deference to Mel's feelings about Maxx, he'd declined the investment opportunity. A bad move. Almost immediately, the medical company turned incredible profits, attracting a lot of attention from corporate suitors with deep pockets. Maxx and the initial investors gleefully sold to the highest bidder and made a phenomenal return on their money. Builder considered how he might not be in such a financial bind if he had gone ahead and done what he had wanted, rather than hold back because of Mel. That's partly why he no longer told her details about his business. He was convinced that the less she knew, the better.

"Did you have a—good time—out there, today—sir?"

The boy carrying the golf bag was trying to make conversation, but he was having difficulty with his load. His face had turned red and sweaty, and he breathed mightily under the weight.

"Look, let me take that," Builder said with sympathy. "If you're not used to carrying clubs around, they can be pretty heavy."

"Oh, no, sir, I can manage," came the quick reply. "We're almost there."

As they mounted the steps to the clubhouse, Builder hoisted the bag on the bottom to provide an extra boost. Poor kid. He was probably here on the orders of determined parents who had demanded that he get a summer job and whip himself into shape. But at least he was trying. Not long ago, black youngsters wouldn't even be hired in a place like this.

Inside, Builder flipped through the bills in his wallet, looking for a tip. He had tens, twenties, nothing smaller. Somehow it seemed disrespectful to get change, so he gave his expectant caddie a fresh Andrew J.

"Gee, thanks a lot, sir! Your clubs will be all ready for you in the morning."

Mel would not believe it, he thought. She called him such a tightwad. He surprised himself too. Tipping a kid ten dollars just to carry a golf bag—for a few yards? Money came too hard for that. Of course, he rationalized, the tip was really to cover the "complimentary" cleaning. Somehow the boy reminded him of his own struggles, trying like heck to succeed, trying hard to please. Builder admired his enterprising spirit. Tenacity should be rewarded.

He could certainly testify on behalf of hanging in there. Not only in terms of fighting for the business, but also in relationship to Mel. Theirs had not been a storybook marriage; fidelity wasn't his strong suit during those early years. He loved Mel, but there was a coolness, an aloofness, that seemed to keep her from totally connecting with him. Maybe it had something to do with her New England upbringing, or the fact that she was so devastated when her father died that she feared getting close to any man who might ultimately leave her. Builder couldn't figure it out; he just knew that there was some indefinable void between them. At times he felt it more strongly than others. It was during one of these particularly vulnerable times that he met Nina.

It was right before he started his business and was still working at VRT Corporation. Things had deteriorated on the job because he was in the midst of a lawsuit against the company, and his bosses were making his life hell. He charged that he had been passed up for promotions and raises, even though he was one of the top-selling account executives in the region. He was getting flak from all sides—the corporate brass who punished him with penny-ass assignments that he could do with his eyes closed, and black folks in the company, who gave him the cold shoulder, believing that his legal action threatened their good standing, such as it was. He felt isolated and alone, and things at home were getting shaky. Mel had just landed her job at the Chamber, and was putting in substantial overtime, anxious to make a good impression. Mrs. Hawkins down the street was always available to take care of Sasha, who was five. Builder had a lot of idle time on his hands and, he realized later, a heap of insecurities.

During this period of discontent, he became involved with Nina, the new accountant who worked in the office building next door. At first, it was nothing serious; certainly nothing to risk his marriage for. But he liked being with her, and she became more than an attractive diversion. Their long lunches progressed to early dinners, then culminated in a weekly rendezvous at her downtown apartment. Nina was good for his ego, which had been battered and bruised on the job, and left unattended by Mel.

But despite the gaps in his marriage, he knew he couldn't sustain two relationships. And even though living with Mel was not totally satisfying, he believed strongly in keeping the family together. He also knew, intuitively, that Nina was not the answer; that no woman could give him what he was looking for because part of the problem was of his own making—uncertainties about himself.

The same week that he broke off the affair with Nina, an old boyfriend of Mel's emerged from the past. Evan Purcell came to Atlanta to speak at an architectural convention, and Mel invited him over for drinks. Actually, Evan was more than just an old flame; Mel had been engaged to him when they were both college students. "I was too young when I married *you*," she once told Builder, "so you know I wasn't ready for Evan."

He wasn't ready for Evan either. The man oozed self-confidence. A well-connected architect in Chicago, he worked on projects that Builder could only dream about. Mel had been eager to hear every detail of Evan's life since their college days, and Evan happily filled in the blanks. He had rattled on about the numerous skyscrapers he was working on, and passed out pictures of his attractive family (a wife and two sons) and of the sprawling suburban home that he had designed for them—a 7,000-square-foot monstrosity that, to Builder, had no character. But it was big and modern and new, and made his house seem almost shabby in comparison.

"You all must get lost in there," Mel had teased. "Ever play hide and seek?" She had laughed coyly, tapping Evan's knee. Builder checked her out more closely. She had kept on her suit from work, but had pulled her long hair into a jaunty ponytail and replaced gold stud earrings with jeweled hoops. She must have applied some industrial strength lipstick because even after two glasses of wine, her mouth remained a luscious, smooth red.

"Chicago's been good to me," Evan said, tucking his photos into his wallet. "But I'd never have guessed you'd become a genuine Southern belle. You must really like it down here."

"Oh, I've adapted," Mel replied. She leaned toward Evan, who was seated next to her on the couch. "Builder just gave me no choice, ya know?" She spoke with an exaggerated drawl. "It was either Atlanta or some teeny-weeny town way down in south Georgia. So we decided to stay here. 'Cause there's South and then, honey chile, there's— Soouuuth—know what I mean?" Her voice dripped sugary sweet in an affected Southern accent.

Even Builder chuckled. Sometimes Mel's put-on accent could get tiresome, but he had to admit she did a great imitation of some of the Southern—or, as she would say, *Suthun*—women he'd heard all his life.

The conversation turned to Builder's job at VRT. He mentioned only the bare essentials. He wasn't about to tell Evan that he had a lawsuit pending, was charging racial discrimination, and considered persona non grata by top management. He was surprised and angry when Mel brought it up.

"Builder was the top selling marketing exec in the Southeast last year," she said proudly. "But some folks were threatened by that, and he hasn't gotten the bonuses that were promised. So he filed a lawsuit."

"Hmm," Evan said. "That's going to make it hard to get promotions in the future."

"Tell me about it," Builder replied huffily. "If they were passing me over before, then you know what my chances are now. I have no illusions about that. These folks'll stomp on their grandmamas for a buck. Either you're in, or you're out. It's as simple as that."

"Yeah."

Evan's response was lukewarm, but Builder understood why. After all, Evan was one of the "in" crowd—for the moment—and most likely didn't appreciate being reminded that he too could fall out of favor. But Builder saw an opening here. Perhaps Evan Purcell, renowned black architect, needed a jolt of reality about life on the other side.

"Black men in corporations catch it both ways, man, you know that," Builder said. "You've got to be twice as good to get in, but then, you're not supposed to be *too* good. You see, if you're too aggressive, or sign up too many new customers too quickly, then you'll show up the white guys, and that's just not allowed." He leaned toward Evan, his eyes narrowing. "And when you propose some idea that's shot down as unworkable, don't be surprised when six months later it reemerges in some proposal that a fairheaded white boy put together. Then, of course, it becomes the greatest idea since chopped liver. And the white guy?—why, he's brilliant, outstanding, getting all kinds of accolades. But when *you* proposed the same thing, the line was"—and here Builder put on his own affected white voice—"'Oh, absolutely not. There's no way we can do this. It's too radical.'"

Mel shot him a warning look with a distinct message: "Back off, don't spoil the evening."

"Maybe things are better in Chicago," Builder continued, ignoring Mel's glare. "But I tell you, man, down here, these crackers don't cut any slack. They'll let a few of us slip through, but only a few. The rest of us keep knocking on the door like crazy, yelling, 'Let me in, let me in.' But, hey, ain't nobody home."

He didn't want to show his frustration this way, especially not to an old lover of Mel's. He wanted to come off as strong and secure; he wanted Evan to see that Mel had made a good choice in him, a better choice. But whenever the subject of blacks in corporations came up, and this whole racist thing, it was hard for him to simply say that everything was cool. It was too close for him to pretend otherwise. But he also knew he was coming across as embittered and cynical; another black man who wasn't making it and who therefore blamed the system.

"Isn't there anybody at the company you can talk to about this?" Evan asked. "You know, a mentor? Or a grievance committee?"

Builder looked at him in disbelief. Had the guy not heard anything? A lawsuit had been filed. Obviously for it to reach that point, the problem couldn't be resolved internally. For all his outward savvy, Evan was almost dangerously naive, and Builder felt like telling him so. Restraining himself, he simply said, "The guy who hired me was pretty decent and might have been in my corner, but he was shipped off to New York last year. That was part of the problem. A new v.p. came in and wanted to bring in his own crew."

"Tough break."

"Well, in the long run, it could work out for the best. It's making me reconsider my time frame, speed things up."

"What do you mean?"

"Corporate life's not for me," Builder said. "I've always known that. I just wanted to gain some experience and put some money away. For the business."

"Builder's going to start his own company in a year or two," inserted Mel.

"Really? What area?"

"Contracting," Builder said. "Mostly home renovation, at least to start." He held up his hands. "This was my first project. Right here."

"Nice," Evan remarked, taking a renewed look around the room.

"You should have seen it when we moved in," Mel said. "It was a VA repo. Really rough. None of the major systems worked; we had no running water except the downstairs bath. What a nightmare."

"You did a great job here," Evan complimented Builder. "Have you thought about the commercial area? Any interest there?"

"Sure, depending on how things go. Nothing at all on the scale you're involved in, but I might move into light commercial projects—doctor's offices, professional buildings, things like that."

"Well, good luck. But if for some reason, it doesn't pan out, get in touch with me." Evan flipped out a business card from his shirt pocket. "Maybe you can fit into one of my projects. That is, if you don't mind dealing with the Hawk."

Builder surveyed the gold embossed card as the conversation turned to

Chicago's brutal winters. Evan meant well, he supposed, but the offer to help seemed condescending, as though he really meant to say, "Okay, Southern boy, if you can't cut it down here, let me show you how it's done—big time—up north." It wasn't so much what he said, concluded Builder, but the way he said it. The arrogant son of a bitch. The prospect of working for Mel's ex-fiancé was almost as bad as putting up with the bull at VRT.

It was on that night, seven years ago, that Builder decided to make his move. No more talking about it, no more dreaming. He would take the plunge and start his own business. Ironically, he had Evan Purcell to thank. Evan, with his pompous ass, had pushed him over the edge, aroused his ire enough to make the leap. And VRT? That was over—no more long-winded meetings to attend, no more asinine reports to write, no more petty office back-stabbing. From now on, he'd be his own boss. He had to admit that his excuse about saving money was only partially true. Deep down, something else had been holding him back: fear of failure. In a way he had been hiding behind his job, afraid to let go. He had been suckered into thinking that he needed a certain amount of corporate experience before setting up his own shop. But that was a cop-out. Hell, he was as prepared as he'd ever be. He could hear his father say, "What are you waiting for, son? Get to it." Yes, he would rise or fall on his own merits, like his dad. Screw Evan. Screw VRT. He'd show them all, damn it.

Walking toward the condo, Builder chuckled to himself, recalling how naive he was back then. He had no idea he'd have so much difficulty acquiring working capital and getting customers to pay. Not to mention dealing with the vagaries of the economy. But even now, with all the problems he faced, he had no regrets. The business was worth fighting for, and he'd get out of this financial bind. Somehow. Besides, what else would he do? Apply for a nine-to-five at some corporation? Hah. What a joke. What company would hire a forty-two-year-old black man? Most were trying to get rid of the ones they had. No, he'd just have to ride this wave out—and he *would* ride it out. The key was getting the loan from the bank. Curtis had virtually assured him that it would come through. And then, he could really take care of business: catch up on bills, bring the second mortgage current, square up with Maxx. Yeah, it would all work out. You gotta have faith.

As he neared the condo, Builder decided to check out the beach before going back to the room. He removed his shoes and socks and sank his feet into the smooth, loose sand. Rows of sunbathers paid homage to their celestial golden god. It amused him to see the zeal in which white people worked on getting a tan. Spending hours on one side, then, flipping over, like pancakes, to even out the color. Ridiculous, he thought. They try to get darker, yet don't want to be around us. He moved slowly along the edge of the water, watching the waves come in and enjoying the gentle ripples against his legs.

"You came out in the wrong outfit, didn't you?"

He turned to see a blond woman on a blanket, rubbing lotion on her legs. Now, she *did* need color. Her pale, pale skin looked ghostly white compared to the bronzed bodies nearby. But her smile was warm and friendly, displaying porcelain-like teeth.

"Just taking a quick walk," Builder said. He moved a few steps toward her, stopping at her feet. "I'm coming out later to do it right."

She squinted up at him. "I love this place, don't you?"

"Anywhere there's a beach."

"You been here long?"

"Three days. Going home tomorrow. To Atlanta."

"Oh. Well, we just got here. We're from Greensboro."

"Greensboro? Nice city. I went to school there—at A&T."

"Mommy! Mommy! Look at what I found!" A little boy came running up, holding a yellow pail. A man, stepping quickly, followed close behind, his jelly roll of a stomach bouncing with his every step. The boy poured out his treasures on the blanket: baby sharks' teeth, black and tiny, and an assortment of shells.

"Wow, that's quite a collection," Builder said.

"I found this one way deep in the sand," said the child, pointing to a twisted mollusk.

The man scurried up to them, giving Builder an evil eye.

"How's it going?" Builder asked.

"Fine," came the terse reply.

Builder could tell what the man was thinking—that he was trying to rap to his wife. Give me a break, he thought. For a second he debated having some fun with it. He could act as though he and the woman had been heavy into some deep conversation. But then, he decided not to. This dodo might end up beating his wife, or even tackling *him!* He was a big guy, at least 260 pounds, and was evidently the type who'd get bent out of shape over nothing. Right now, he was hovering over his wife, hands on his hips, as though shielding her from some ominous threat.

The woman stood up, tugging on the bottom of her suit to assure ample coverage. "We were just talking about how lovely it is here," she explained.

"That so?" The man remained unsmiling, and was now glaring at his wife too.

Builder felt sorry for the woman. She was just trying to be nice and make conversation. But obviously this idiot she married was insanely jealous. He probably didn't let her out of his sight for two minutes.

"Well, you take care," Builder said, shifting his shoes into his free hand.

The woman nodded, almost apologetically. "You too," she said softly.

Builder looked down at the little boy. "I hope you find some more sharks' teeth. They're pretty valuable, you know."

He weaved through the outstretched bodies on the sand, eager to get to his room. The last thing he needed was an altercation with some redneck who thought he was trying to hit on his wife. He'd had it with white men and their insecurities.

"Mel," he called, entering the front room. "You up?"

As soon as he asked, he knew the answer. The patio door was open, causing the curtains to billow slightly from the ocean breeze. Magazines and papers flickered over a section of the coffee table, and the faint scent of nail polish punctuated the air. A half glass of water sat alone on the kitchen counter. Builder gulped it down.

"What do you mean, 'am I up?'" Mel glided down the steps, Loretta Young style, keeping her drying fingernails aloft. "I've been up for hours." She pranced across the room, hands to her side, and kissed Builder on the cheek. "Waiting for you."

"Yeah, right," he said, in an unbelieving tone. But he was delighted that she was in such good spirits. "Maybe I should go away and come back more often."

"Maybe you should," she teased.

This trip to Jekyll had been worth it. During their time here, they had rekindled their romance—taking midnight walks on the beach, making love twice a day. Things between them had gotten less tense. They had vowed not to talk about financial worries and to concentrate on enjoying each other. But Builder knew they couldn't forestall tomorrow indefinitely.

"How was golf?" she asked, blowing her nails. "Get a hole in one?"

"Hardly." He gently pulled her aside and turned on the faucet to fill his glass. "I'm ready for lunch. How 'bout you?"

"There's a clambake on the beach. At three o'clock."

"I can't wait that long."

"Well—" She massaged his shoulders from behind—"I can think of lots we can do to fill up the time."

He loved it when she talked this way—the teasing, the flirting jabs, he had missed that. This place did work magic. It brought back memories of their torrid honeymoon and newlywed passion, memories that needn't stay buried in the past.

"Oh, I almost forgot. You got a message from your daughter."

"Sasha?" he asked incredulously.

"The one and only." Gingerly, Mel took him by the wrist, careful not to bump her nails.

"Is she okay? Everything all right?"

"Of course," Mel said calmly. She led him to the sofa, reached for a sheet of paper from the coffee table, and bestowed it on him with a command. "Read."

"What's this?" Builder glanced at the top of the paper. HOLIDAY CRUISE LINE. It was a fax from Sasha, or more accurately, from Ron and Celeste, outlining some of the activities that the girls had enjoyed so far.

"This is really something," Builder said.

"They're having a ball. Really getting the royal treatment." Mel sat next to Builder and read the fax, again, with him. In addition to the regular activities on the ship, Sasha and Ashley were playing starring roles in a video that the cruise staff was making, and they reveled in their newfound celebrity status.

"How'd this get here?"

"Well, Sasha knows your fax number, so evidently they sent it to your office. I guess Fatima thought it'd be fun for us to receive it here, so she must have called the condo office for their fax." Mel pulled her legs up under her and leaned her knees into Builder's lap. "I must admit, when the guy brought it over this morning, I didn't know what to think. At first, I thought he had a telegram or something. With bad news."

"The wonders of technology. Even if you *wanted* to get away, you couldn't."

"Yes, dear, and you remember that," Mel said, tickling his chin. "We're going to always find you, no matter where you are."

"Hey, I'm not going anywhere." Then, with a serious look, he focused back at the fax still in his hand.

"I can't believe she's growing up so fast. Off on a cruise all by herself."

"She's not exactly by herself, Builder."

"Well, you know what I mean. Without us. Next thing you know, she'll be off to college and out on her own." He sighed heavily. "See, that's why I'm working so hard, putting in fifteen-hour days and bustin' my butt, to make sure she'll have what she needs when she gets out there. I'm sick of each generation of black folks starting from scratch, with nothing. It's not going to be that way for her."

"I know, I know," Mel said, in response to the familiar refrain. "Did you ever imagine you'd be so much in love with your daughter like this? She's got you wrapped, dear. Wrapped tight." Mel twirled her baby finger as she spoke. "And to think how disappointed you were when she came out a girl."

"Aw, come on. I wasn't disappointed."

"Yes, you were. Face it. You were steeped in male chauvinism, from head to toe."

She was right, of course. They had talked about this several times over the years, and Mel seemed to delight in bringing it up, as an "I told you so" reminder of his narrow-mindedness. He remembered how silly he had acted when Sasha was born. On the one hand, he had been exhilarated—he was a brand new father with an adorable baby girl. But there was a nagging letdown that the baby was not a son. Mel's pregnancy had been difficult, and the doctor had told them it was unlikely she could have more children. So he had pinned his hopes on a healthy baby boy, even though Mel had felt intuitively that it was a girl. The sonogram showed a normal baby, but Mel didn't want the sex of the baby revealed, preferring to maintain the suspense until the delivery.

When Mel was pregnant, Builder was still working at VRT, but even then knew he would eventually start his own business. He envisioned that in the years ahead, his son would work with him, side by side, just as he had with his own father. His father had done the best he could with what he had, and Builder wanted to carry on the legacy, take it to a higher level, leave his son something concrete to hold on to. But when Sasha was born, he felt an emptiness he couldn't explain. It was as though the cycle had been broken. His dream of a father/son legacy had collapsed; the Burke name would die with him.

In time, his feelings changed. Mel had shamed him into realizing that girls, too, could be groomed to become effective business managers. And he had come face to face with his crazy fixation about having a son. He realized that Sasha was a wonderful blessing, a miraculous, beautiful gift. He also realized how ludicrous it was to expect any child of his to take up his business automatically. Male or female, they should be allowed to have their own dreams, and deserved a chance to pursue them in their own way. It was unfair to pressure Sasha to come into the business, just for his ego. But he did want to build the business to a point where it would provide a healthy income and serve as security for her future.

"Yep, our baby girl is growing up," he said, letting the fax slip out of his hand.

"It's a natural process."

"I know. But it makes me realize how much I've got to get my act together. Time is moving on." He sat up straighter, with new determination. "Soon as I get back, I'm calling Curtis. Find out where things stand with the loan. Once that comes through, I can get back on track."

Mel planted a finger on his lips. "You promised. No talking about the business."

Builder looked into Mel's deep-set eyes, those bedroom eyes that had first snared him fourteen years ago when he had met her at a clubhouse dance at the apartment complex where he had just moved. Being an eligible young bachelor with an appreciation for the ladies, he predicted he would get his share of female attention, since functions of that type usually had a paucity of men. He was right. The place had been packed with attractive young women, several of whom had eagerly latched on to him the moment he arrived. But in the midst of so much bobbing beauty, and during a particularly thrilling bump-and-grind dance routine where his partner brushed up against him quite suggestively, it was Mel who caught his eye.

Slender and tall with kind of wild, bushy hair, she stood on the outskirts of the dance floor, nodding to the music, a slightly amused expression on her face as she watched the swaying bodies in motion before her. She conveyed a certain mysteriousness, a seductive distance, that Builder found oddly appealing. It was as though she was *in* the crowd, but not *of* it. He felt himself drawn to her with an almost hypnotic pull. A few minutes later, he worked his way across the room and looked into her bedroom eyes. After that, he had no chance.

Fresh out of graduate school, Mel had come to Atlanta for a job interview, and had opted to stay through the weekend with a girlfriend. Builder had crossed his fingers that the Atlanta job would come through, but when it didn't, and Mel accepted a less favorable position in Philadelphia, Builder immediately launched an intense, long-distance courtship, beginning a period that he would later say "helped guarantee the solvency of Delta Airlines."

Before meeting Mel, he had been in no rush to tie the knot, had been in no hurry whatsoever. But Mel changed all that. He didn't want to lose her, and he believed that if he didn't act quickly, he would. So, after just a few months of dating, he asked her to marry him. At first, she resisted, saying that at twenty-three, she was too young chronologically and not yet ready emotionally. But Builder's persistent profession of love, and Mel's growing love for him, persuaded Mel to pack up her newly laid life in Philadelphia, and start all over again in Atlanta—as the wife of Nathaniel Burke, Jr. The next year, Sasha was born.

Now, Builder moaned contentedly as Mel stretched her long brown legs around his, strategically placing her right knee against his groin. She moved her knee back and forth, years of lovemaking giving her the advantage of knowing just where to apply the pressure—a light touch here, a tad more there. The motion caused her shorts to inch up her thighs, exposing black lace panties underneath.

"Let me take a quick shower," he whispered. "I'm still hot and sweaty from the golf course."

"All the better," she whispered back, continuing her knee massage. "That's the way I like it."

Her arms were tight around his neck, and she was face to face with him, rocking back and forth with a steady rhythmic thrust.

"Oh, yes," Builder groaned again, feeling himself harden. It didn't take long with Mel. It never did. But he didn't want to come quite yet. Not this fast. As much as he wanted to, he didn't give in. Despite what Mel said, he could smell his own funk from the morning's outing. He wanted to be clean for her, just as she was now, for him. And he wanted to be inside her, to slowly ride the waves, to savor the rush, feel her cushiony softness against his burst of tide. With great resolve, he gently disengaged her limbs, and pushed down the bulge in his pants.

"Believe me, it'll be a quick shower. I don't want you changing your mind."

"Well," Mel said, pouting and folding her legs. "You realize you're taking a risk." She held out her hands, spread-eagle, into the air. "While you're in the shower, I just might put on another coat of polish. And then, when you get out, I won't be dry."

"Good!" Builder leaned down and kissed her powerfully on the mouth. He greedily grabbed her tongue while putting his hand inside her pants. "I don't like my women dry."

"Ahhhhh!" She grabbed a nearby pillow to hit him, but he was already at the staircase by the time it landed at his feet.

Happily, he took the steps, two at a time, peeling off his shirt in transit. As she had downstairs, Mel had let in the fresh air up here too. The bedroom windows were wide open, permitting a misty ocean breeze to encircle the room. He threw back the bedspread and the starched top sheet, in anticipation of the special treat that awaited him. Mel had brought candles and incense for their trip, and in the last couple of days, she had burned both during their long hours in bed. Now it was his turn to arrange the trappings.

He fished a fresh vanilla taper out of a bag, lit it, and twisted it into the ebony candleholder that Mel had packed with other goodies. He held an incense stick to the candle, letting the tip burn just enough to catch hold. He blew out the tiny flame and balanced the smoldering stalk astride a glass ashtray stamped Seven Seas, Jekyll Island. The smell of sandalwood engulfed him and he pushed his altar makings to the rear of the dresser, watching thin ripples of smoke cross the mirror. Great, he thought. The gentle breeze in the room would swirl the incense to just the right level, not too overwhelming. He pulled the curtain sheers together, dimming the bright sunlight.

From his designated drawer, he retrieved a red suede case, and placed it in the center of the puffed pillows on the bed. Mel would love the colorful seashell necklace inside. She liked bright, vivid jewelry that made a statement, not the dainty stuff that was so tiny you needed a microscope to find. This necklace had her name on it. He had found it in one of those expensive shops he had browsed in during their first day here. Now was the right time to give it to her.

The scene set, he stepped into the shower, humming. He had barely soaped up and rinsed, when he was out again. He peeked into the clear mirror which hadn't had a chance to steam. He rubbed his face—it wasn't too rough—and so chose to forgo a shave. He didn't want to keep Mel waiting. Naked and damp, he eagerly opened the door, in anticipation of the long afternoon with his wife.

The drive back was torturous. An hour before they left Jekyll, they went for one last walk on the beach, "to hold us till next year," Mel had said. When they returned to the condo to finish packing, the telephone was ringing. Builder dashed to pick it up, only to hear a click on the other end.

"Damn!" he said, to the monotonous dial tone. "I wonder if that was Curtis."

"Why would he call here?"

"I gave him the number, just in case. Told him to let me know the minute he heard something."

Mel made a clucking sound with her tongue and shook her head in disapproval. "How quickly we forget."

"I'm gonna see if he's home." He searched for the piece of paper he had scrawled the number on, finding it in the zippered section of his tote. Hurriedly, he dialed, letting the phone ring several times before finally hanging up.

"I'm sure it wasn't Curtis," Mel said, nonchalantly, putting ice cubes in the silver thermos Builder carried on job sites. "I'll bet it was the condo office making sure we're checking out today."

"Yeah. Maybe." Builder slumped into the chair, staring at a dark smudge on the wall where an unlucky fly had gotten splattered.

"Besides," Mel was saying, "if it *was* Curtis and he had good news, he'd leave a message at the condo office, wouldn't he? And if it's bad news, well . . ." She stopped in midsentence, her eyes meeting his. "I doubt that he'd call and spoil your vacation."

She had a point. Mel could be so damn rational at times. Even though he had insisted that Curtis call, had made him swear to it regardless of how things went, it made sense that if the loan didn't come through, Curtis might wait until he returned home to drop the bomb. Promise or not, Builder had to admit that's how he himself would handle it.

"We'll check for messages on the way out," Mel said brightly. "Come on, be optimistic."

She chided him about his gloomy mood during the waning hours of their time away. "Think about yesterday," she urged, "and these last few days together."

Indeed, how could he forget; it had all been so fantastic. But in preparing to go home, he felt this dogged downward pull, a heavy dragging sensation that he couldn't shake. They stopped by the office on the way out, but the only thing waiting was the bill. No word from Curtis.

Now, with each revolution of the wheel, as they inched closer and closer to Atlanta, he felt more and more boxed in. Sadly, he watched the face of the landscape change, as they left bucolic open spaces for the heady cramp of city life. He found it hard to push aside an impending feeling of doom. He wanted to reach deep down, scoop it up, and toss it aside. Toss it far, far aside. If only it were that simple.

An Exxon station beckoned on the right, and he eased off the highway onto the service road. Although it was only a five-hour drive, they had already stopped twice. Mel's Honda was nearly full of gas, and he didn't need to stop again, but he wanted to try Curtis one more time. The not knowing was killing him. He was sure the banking committee had made a decision, and he was obsessed about finding out, one way or another. Cruising to a stop, he parked the car behind the convenience store, several yards from the pumps.

"Whaaa?" Mel awoke groggily and looked around in a stupor. Straightening up, she slowly rubbed the back of her neck. "Where are we?"

"Outside Augusta. About eighty miles."

"Oh." She stretched and yawned in sync, her long nails grazing the roof of the car.

"I'm going to get some juice," he said. "Want anything?"

"No, I'm okay."

He entered the store and was immediately met by the strong aroma of coffee. It smelled so good that he started to get some, then changed his mind. He had already had three cups this morning, and Mel would get on his case about the caffeine. He picked up a couple bottles of apple juice, knowing Mel would want some of his, and he didn't feel like sharing. He placed the items on the counter and reached for straws, as the young, gum-chewing cashier gave him a nod.

"How ya doing?" the teen asked, smacking loudly.

"Good. You have a phone around here?"

"Out back. Use the one on the left. The other one'll just gobble up your money."

Builder thanked him for the warning, took his brown bag, and headed toward the phone. He noticed that Mel was out of the car, talking to a tall man and pointing to a map. He kept his eye on them as he dialed Curtis's number.

"Hello?"

He had half-expected to get another series of rings, and was surprised when a child answered the phone.

"Hello," he said quickly. "Is Curtis Moore there?"

No response.

"Is your dad home?"

There was a slight pause, and then, "He's not here right now."

"Do you know if he'll be back soon?"

"Maybe. I—I don't know."

"Okay," Builder said hesitantly. "Would you tell him that I called?" He spoke slowly, distinctly. "Builder Burke. Can you write that down?"

"What'd you say? I—I don't have a pencil."

Builder was exasperated. Why do parents let their children answer the phone if they're not old enough to take a message? From the background, he faintly heard a woman's voice asking who was calling.

"Listen," said Builder, hope renewed. "Can your mother come to the phone?"

The child spoke plainly. "She's on the toilet."

Builder chuckled in spite of himself. Out of the mouths of babes. "Never mind. I'll call later."

He returned to a bright-eyed and expectant Mel.

"I met the cutest couple with the most adorable baby girl. And they're going to Atlanta too."

"Oh, yeah?" he said, disinterested. He twisted the bottle cap and handed her a juice.

"They're coming from Valdosta," Mel continued. "His parents just retired and moved into a house in one of those new subdivisions on Cascade. Well, you know, that's five minutes from us. Anyway, they weren't sure exactly how to get there, so I told them we'd lead them in." She delivered this last bit of information casually, but gave him a careful look.

"You did what?" He had already started the car and was about to back up when she placed a hand on his arm.

"It's not at all out of our way."

"Mel, I'm sure these people have directions on how to get to where they're going." He couldn't believe that she had volunteered him to serve as guide. And on his time too. He was anxious to get back home. There was a lot to do, and he wanted no more delays.

"You know how it is when you're in a strange city," she was saying. "One wrong turn, and you can be lost for hours. Besides, they have the baby, and—"

"Okay, okay," he interrupted. "Let's get going."

"Well—they're not quite ready yet. She had to go inside, and he's still pumping gas."

"Oh, good grief." He followed Mel's gaze to the tall man he had seen talking to her moments ago. With his free arm, the man gave a broad wave. Builder grudgingly responded with a half-salute. "So now we're on *their* timetable," he said, irritated. He cut off the engine and slurped his juice.

"Just relax, we'll go in a minute. See, there she is."

A slim woman holding a yellow bundle came out of the store and strapped the baby into an infant car seat. Her husband hung up the pump and jogged over to Builder. He extended a hand through the open window.

"Hi. I'm Johnny Gray. We really appreciate you doing this."

He was young, in his early twenties, with the lean and hungry look of youth, eager to tackle the world. He had an engaging smile that was full of trust, and in an instant, Builder couldn't help but like him.

"No problem," he responded. "Glad to."

"I'll stay right behind you." Johnny tapped the window frame, as though sealing a contract, and sprinted to his bright blue Mazda.

Mel settled back with a satisfied look. "He's nice enough, isn't he?"

"Yeah, yeah, yeah."

Maybe it wouldn't be such an imposition after all. But the drive would definitely take longer. Normally Builder ran seventy-five or eighty miles per hour, keeping watch for the cops, especially near the ramps. But with these people following, he couldn't do that. He'd have to pace himself the rest of the way.

Their mini caravan left the gas station, and once on the highway, Builder set the cruise control to seventy-two. Mel read aloud the lead paragraphs of several stories from an outdated *Newsweek,* occasionally looking back to make sure their charge was close behind.

They were an hour from home when Builder heard the honking of distress. From his rearview mirror, he saw the Mazda roll to a stop, barely making it onto the shoulder.

"Uh, uh," he said to Mel. "They've got a problem."

"Oh, no."

Slowing down, he pulled off to the side and backed up several yards, to the front of the disabled Mazda. He and Mel jumped out simultaneously.

"What happened?" he asked. Johnny had opened the hood and was peering aimlessly inside.

"I don't know. All of a sudden it just stopped. The alternator light is on."

"Had any problems before this?" Builder asked, getting out a handkerchief.

"No, not a bit. It's been running great."

"Let me see. Maybe it's just a broken fan belt." He peered alongside the radiator and saw that the belt was intact.

"The belt's still on," said Builder. "It must be the alternator. You have jumper cables?"

"No. No, I don't."

He shouldn't have been, but Builder was surprised. These young guys of today just never seemed prepared. They didn't grow up working on junky old cars, never experimented with trying to make things fit, and were afraid to get their hands dirty. Everything was given to them, brand new.

"You should always carry jumper cables," he scolded. "That's basic. Like a flashlight or a jack."

Johnny nodded humbly. "You're right."

The baby started to cry. Johnny's wife and Mel walked alongside the car, alternately patting the baby's back and trying to console her.

"I'll get mine," said Builder. He grabbed a set of cables from the trunk of his car, then turned his car around to face the Mazda. He left the engine running. It was a long shot, but he thought he might be able to jump-start the battery so the car could make it to Atlanta. He connected the cables, feeling the vibration of the cars whizzing by. He didn't like being so close to the road—it was too dangerous. The last place he wanted to be was on some highway working on a car. But he did get a certain pleasure, a sense of pride, from knowing that he could potentially fix this problem. Mel and Johnny and his wife crowded around, surveying the operation. In a sense, their fate rested with him.

"Okay," he directed. "Start her up."

Johnny climbed behind the wheel. They held their breaths as he turned the ignition. The engine answered with an even purr.

"All right!" exclaimed Builder, pleased with his handiwork.

Johnny thanked Builder generously, voicing amazement at the feat. His wife, all smiles, had dropped her worried look. Mel clapped her hands and bowed from the waist in homage to Builder.

But the celebration was short-lived. Like a wretched animal in pain, the engine shut down, spewing a final scratchy wail.

"Well, that's that," said Builder, disappointed.

For a moment, no one spoke.

"See, Johnny, I told you we needed Triple A." Johnny's wife rolled her eyes in disgust.

Mel attempted to put an optimistic face on the setback. "I'm just glad we're with you. It'd be terrible if you were out here alone, all by yourself."

Builder proposed action. "Look, I'll drive up the road and ask around. There has to be a wrecker service nearby. Or a place we can get some help."

We? He surprised himself at his use of inclusive language. But clearly someone had to take charge. He couldn't leave them stranded. Their problem was now his problem. Mel and her soft heart! But he couldn't blame her. In an odd way, he felt responsible.

"Well, at least it's not pouring down rain," he heard Mel say, reaching for some solace. She offered to get everyone water and almost giddily stepped to the car for the thermos and cups. It was as if she considered this unexpected detour an extension of their vacation. She acted like a student on a field trip, primed for excitement, poised for adventure. But to Builder, this was a costly intrusion that was sucking up time and energy. Suddenly, he felt tired. He wanted this to be over.

"Be back in a flash," he said, trying to project some of Mel's light-heartedness.

The "flash" turned out to be nearly an hour, and even then, he returned empty-handed. Virtually everything was closed on a late Sunday afternoon. The two gas stations he went to were far from full-service stations. An attendant gave him the names of the nearest wrecker services, thirty miles away. When Builder called the first, the woman on the phone had drawled, "It won't take Button long to git there, but he ain't here ride now. He's out havin' suppa." Builder told her no, not to bother to page "Button." It amazed him, how, this close to Atlanta, the small-town mentality still prevailed. Mel would have another word for it—country. The other wrecker service he called had just sent their lone truck to pick up a car that was in an accident and estimated "maybe an hour, maybe two" before someone could get to them. Heck, they could be in Atlanta by then. That's when he decided, there was only one thing to do—take Johnny and his family with him.

It took a while to load up. Builder had to repack the trunk totally to accommodate Johnny's and Evelyn's (he found out her name) suitcases. Not to mention the baby's things: a carrier seat, a portable crib, and two jumbo bags of diapers, all of which had to share space with Builder's golf bag. Plus, there was an awkward-shaped chair, a gift for Johnny's parents, that ended up tied on top of the Honda.

Back on the highway, they told him about the people who had stopped to help while he was gone: an old black man with poor eyesight, who Mel said shouldn't have been driving at all, and a salesman from Tifton who had a car phone and seemed overly anxious to use it. "You just never know about people," Evelyn was saying, "or what their intentions are." Builder thought of their own situation. What if he and Mel were different kinds of folks? They could be whisking away this young family to some horrific fate. And no one would be the wiser. But at some point people had to trust each other. From his mirror, he could see that the baby was out of the car seat and in her mother's arms. The yellow fringe of the blanket covered the infant's bobbing head. Evelyn was breast feeding. She noticed him looking and drew the blanket closer. Quickly, he glanced away.

The sun was setting when he drove through the entrance of The Cascades. They looked for number 2315. Builder went around twice; the subdivision wasn't that large. But again, no 2315.

"I don't believe this," Johnny said.

"Are you sure it's the right place?" Mel asked, concerned.

"Of course," he said, emphatically. "They told me The Cascades off Cascade Road. It's a new house."

Johnny leaned forward to get a better view, his hands grasping the back of the front seat. Builder felt his warm breath from behind.

"This is ridiculous." Evelyn was nearing hysteria. "Why do we always have so much trouble?" She looked ready to pounce on Johnny, but the baby's car seat provided interference.

"Let's go by the office and call," Mel said calmly. She turned directly to Johnny. "You do have a number, right?"

"Yes," he said humbly.

Builder kept quiet. Deliberately. He had figured it out. He was going to deposit this cargo, somewhere, now. Enough was enough. They had been scammed. This innocent looking couple had planned the whole thing from the start, using the baby to play on their sympathy. And it had worked, yeah, it had worked. They were like so many people he had dealt with, customers and suppliers itching to cut a deal, plotting to get over.

He wondered what their next move was. They'd make the phone call, and, of course, there'd be no answer, so then they'd probably weasel Mel into putting them up for the night, maybe even at the house. They knew they'd have a better shot with her than with him. But it would have to come off as Mel's idea. They'd look pitiful and with the baby and all, Mel would naturally propose to help them out. No way. This was the end of the line. He'd take them to a hotel, and that'd be it. They'd have to screw somebody else.

That Johnny, with his damn grin and friendly facade, was a con man through and through. Builder hadn't given him enough credit; he had fallen for the nice guy routine. Yep, assumptions can get you in trouble.

And the whole deal with the alternator—that was pure luck, icing on the cake. They'd probably just planned to follow them to Atlanta to this nonexistent house. Then work their scheme from here. But driving together in the same car made things more legit. And now, of course, money would become an issue; perhaps they'll claim not to have any and give some kind of sob story: not being able to reach their in-laws, somehow stuck with a wrong address, and having no place to go. People like that lied so well, they often believed it themselves. They stalk their prey, and use any tactic to suit their goals. Short term, long haul, no telling what was up their sleeve. But why target him? They must think he and Mel were financially well-off. Ha! If only they knew. Johnny, my man, you're sniffing up the wrong tree. Like Dad used to say, "Ain't no sap in this bark."

"Builder, wait, let's ask this guy."

They had pulled up to the model office and tried the door. Locked. Builder was about to drive down the street, so they could use a phone, for appearance' sake. He knew that when they'd call, there'd be no answer. But that was all right, he was onto them now. And he'd play along to see how far they'd go. Soon, their butts would be on the street.

"Maybe this guy knows something," Mel was saying.

She called over a teenage boy, shadow boxing up the lane. "Excuse me. Can you help us? We're looking for . . . ?" She looked back at Johnny to fill in the blank.

"The Grays. Erta and Thomas Gray. It's a new house." He spoke loudly, close to Builder's ear.

The boy pondered, then shook his head. "I don't know any Grays, but most of the new houses are up there." He pointed a long arm to the top of the hill.

"But we've *been* there," said Evelyn, close to tears. "Two-three-one-five. We're looking for two-three-one-five!" Her shrill voice startled the baby, who woke up crying.

Builder was totally disgusted with the act. But he had to admit, she was good.

"Sorry, I can't help you," the teenager said, backing away. "I don't think the numbers go up that high."

A weird sound came from the back seat. At first, Builder thought Evelyn had hit Johnny. More dramatics, he supposed. But when she shrieked, "What is it?" he realized that Johnny had slapped his own forehead. Builder watched him pull out a crumpled envelope and hurriedly scan the insides.

"Gosh, I'm sorry. I was wrong." Victoriously, Johnny waved a piece of beige stationery, the missing critical evidence. "Says here it's *across* from The Cascades. This must be the address on Cascade Road, not inside the complex. No wonder we couldn't find it!"

Evelyn let out a long sigh of relief, followed by a nervous laugh. Then she hammered in on Johnny, saying he should have given her the directions in the first place.

"Well, I'm glad the mystery's solved," Mel said. She turned back to Builder. "Come on, honey, let's get going. It must be that other subdivision. You know, the one with the white gate?"

"Yeah," Builder said quietly. "Right."

Could he have been that wrong? Were they really okay after all, or was this another ploy? The explanation made sense, but still . . .

It wasn't until he pulled up to the house and Johnny's parents came out that he realized the truth: His imagination had gone haywire, at the speed of light. He felt foolish and guilty at the same time.

As atonement for his sin, Builder single-handedly unloaded the car. Johnny's parents made a fuss over everyone and insisted that Mel and Builder come in for a glass of lemonade.

In his good-bye, Johnny gave a firm and grateful handshake, making Builder feel bad all over again that he had suspected foul play. His misgivings dissolved, he felt strangely protective of this fervent young man.

"Don't forget which exit to get off to pick up your car," he said as he left.

"Don't worry," Evelyn inserted. "*I* wrote it down."

They were home in a flash. Finally. Mel had talked about the happy family reunion they'd helped bring about. Builder hadn't said a word about his suspicions, which seemed ludicrous now. Maybe later he'd tell her. Of course, she'd accuse him of being paranoid and not giving people the benefit of the doubt. She always said that. It's just that he'd been burned so many times before. You had to be suspicious to protect yourself. But maybe he did need to be more trusting. Needed more faith.

It felt good to be home, back in familiar surroundings. It must have rained a lot while they were gone, because the grass had sprouted an inch, and the marigolds stood taller than he remembered. Mel announced she was going next door to collect their newspapers and mail. Builder needed to clean out the car, but that could wait. First: Curtis.

A lightning bug beat him into the basement, and he left the door open to let out the dank air. He dialed Curtis's number, this time by heart. Busy. He turned on the answering machine, which flashed a red number 5. He fast-forwarded the tape. The first two messages were from customers; the third was a charity plea; the fourth was from Mel's friend Anne. And the fifth—Curtis Moore.

Quickly, Builder turned up the volume.

" . . . and you know the committee was supposed to meet on Wednesday, but one of the members got sick so they postponed it until Friday."

"Yeah, yeah, so what the heck happened?" Builder talked back, impatient.

There was a pause on the other end. Then, "Listen, man, I'm sorry, but the loan didn't come through. The numbers looked good to me, but the bank—"

"SHIT!" Builder's right fist slammed the desk top with vengeance. "Goddam those motherfuckers."

The voice on the machine droned on, explaining the bank's rationale. Builder heard none of it. Swearing, he paced the room, beating a trash can with his foot. He knocked books off an open shelf, threw blueprints on the floor. His neck veins pulsated fiercely from anger gone awry.

After a while, he fell, exhausted, into the chair. With hands pressed to the back of his head, he stared at the ceiling above. His fury spent, he lowered his chin and squeezed the bridge of his nose. A thinker's pose by proxy, the resemblance ended there.

Mel found him that way when she entered; Builder's head dropped in defeat.

CHAPTER 3

Shimmering lights amidst streams of red velvet clung to the inside columns of the shopping mall. Towering evergreens with chunks of gold created a startling overhead phalanx. And gilded foil at the entrance of each shop shouted a Yuletide greeting of cheer. But for Mel, the glorious decorations only added fodder to the frenzy around her.

"We were crazy to come today," she complained. "It's a zoo out here."

Her friend Val had talked her into attending a matinee movie at Phipps Plaza, and when they emerged from their quiet cocoon, they were assaulted by the midafternoon Christmas crowd.

"These people act like they're possessed, buying everything in sight," Val said. "You could sell them warmed-over spit, and they'd lap it up." She sucked her teeth in disgust, watching the bustle around her, as she picked her way through the morass. "This is insane."

Mel started to say "This was *your* idea," but thought better of it. Neither of them was in the best of humor, and at this point, Val might not take too kindly to criticism. Overweight, she was already huffing and blowing. They had ventured into a few stores, bemoaning the expensive prices ("larcenous," Val called them), and after several unsuccessful attempts to get a reduced price on a silk skirt that had a tiny run, and a sweater whose horizontal lines didn't meet exactly on the seam, even Val gave up the fight, which, for her, was quite a concession.

Mel considered Val the consummate shopper, partial to discount houses and designer outlets, the ideal settings for astute bargain hunters. It was amazing to Mel how Val managed to snare such incredible deals. The down jacket and matching hat that she wore now, Mel noted, were the spoils from an aggressive negotiation during their last shopping spree. Val had meticulously pointed out that the jacket was missing a button (even though there was an extra one sewn inside) and that the hat had a flaw (barely noticeable, in Mel's view). After some haggling, the clerk reluctantly reduced the price, all the while pointing out that the outfit was already on sale and was to be sold "as is"; but Val, not satisfied, insisted on seeing the manager, who, anxious to nix an attention-getting scene, agreed to drop the price further. Chalk up another win for Val Bellinger. Flaunting her flair for the dramatic, she was a one-woman show for consumer rights, using charm, tears, or loud protest, whatever the situation required.

They inched toward the main food court, but after finding standing room only, decided they should simply leave. Even the sofas and benches along the corridors overflowed with packaged people. All Mel wanted was to get outside so she could breathe. She felt a headache coming on.

"Oh, wait!" Val pulled her to the side, her eyes locked onto a flowered Oriental scarf in the window of a ritzy women's store. "Now *that's* gorgeous." She tilted her head to the side for a better view.

"I thought your energy level was low," Mel reminded her.

"It is, but I'm not dead yet!" She peered closer. "Wonder what they want for it."

"Whatever they're asking," Mel retorted. She meant to discourage Val from any more bargaining antics—not this day, not now. But she could tell by the set of her friend's jaw that this new challenge would not go untested.

"Come on, let's check it out."

"No, you go on," Mel begged off. "I'll wait here."

"Okay. This shouldn't take long." Armed with fresh determination, Val flung back her head and marched into battle.

Mel was glad for the respite. Adjacent to the store window was a narrow alcove, which accommodated her slim frame perfectly. She liked this vantage point. Protected from the crush of people, she had a front-row view that made her part of the crowd, but not in it.

"Mel? Well, I'll be."

Stopping in front of her was Jason Hall, who used to work in marketing at the Chamber and was laid off the same week she was. Mel had heard that he had immediately gotten another job with an electrical supply firm, owned by a distant relative. He was a tenacious go-getter, a steam roller who was not at all shy about tooting his own horn.

"It's—really—good—to see you." He emphatically stretched out the words, as he pumped Mel's hand.

"You're looking well and prosperous," Mel observed.

"Hey, 'tis the season, right? I can't complain." He edged as close as he could into Mel's cramped corner, trying to ward off the jostling around him. "This has turned out to be a heck of a good year."

"Really?" said Mel, raising her brows.

"Really. Larson actually ended up doing me a favor when he handed me that pink slip."

"Business must be booming in electronics."

"Oh, *that*," he said distastefully. "That was just a stopgap for a couple of months. No, I've been handling international marketing for Bascomb Global since September. Focusing on accounts in Latin America."

"My, I'm impressed. You really hit the jackpot. You like it a lot?"

"Love it. Been to Rio three times already. Let me tell you, that's the place to live."

As Jason rambled on about his new job, Mel thought how ironic it was that he had landed such a sweet deal, while she, despite having more experience, was still looking for something decent. Bascomb was one of the places she had applied to months ago, but was told the company promoted from within and was not in a hiring mode. She could hear Builder now, if he were here. "He's a fair-headed white boy," is how he would explain it. "You shouldn't be surprised."

"So what are *you* doing now?" Jason asked.

"Nothing nearly as exciting as you," Mel said through a forced smile. "I've been developing a few marketing proposals for a couple of firms, and doing some lightweight consulting here and there. But I'm still footloose and fancy free." She hesitated a moment, then took the plunge. "Got any leads?"

She had never liked Jason; he was a manipulator and schemer, and she felt uncomfortable asking him for information. Also, she was embarrassed to reveal her vulnerable position, with all her supposed qualifications and credentials, she should have found something after all these months. But clearly, Jason had an inside track. And it was silly not to network. She knew that most companies didn't hire via the personnel department; that was just a sanctioning procedure. She had been in the corporate arena long enough to know that the real hiring took place under wraps and off the record, that jobs were often issued as pay back for uncollected favors from deals past, awarded on a recommendation from a senior manager, or a nod from the CEO. She knew she was competing against people who had those kinds of connections, but the least she could do was make it known, whenever possible, that she was still available. She hated playing these games, but to do less would short-circuit her chances. Perhaps Jason could throw her a bone—which might even have some meat on it.

He creased his brow, considering her question. "I haven't heard of anything lately, but if I do, I'll let you know."

"I'd appreciate it."

They exchanged cards, but Mel suspected that hers would end up in the trash can in his expensively decorated office, if indeed it made it that far. So much for colleague loyalty.

Jason was leaving as Val reappeared, clutching a silver bag with green tissue paper peeking out. "Who was that?" she asked curiously.

"Someone I used to work with. Did you get the scarf?"

"No. They wanted three hundred dollars for that thing, can you believe it? But—I did get this." She pulled out a black suede belt with a turquoise stone. "It was on sale, marked down to eighty-five. I got it for forty."

Mel shook her head in admiration. Val could be brash and a bit much to take at times, but she knew how to get her way. That's one of the reasons Mel liked being around her—in the hope that some of Val's punch and gutsy style would rub off.

"Say, isn't that Miss Tooty Fruity? You know, what's-her-name."

Mel followed Val's gaze to the middle of the crowd where an attractive woman in vivid blue stood out among the throng; but even before she saw her, Mel knew to whom Val was referring.

"It's Celeste," she said, like a parent correcting a child, "and you very well know her name."

Mel caught her eye, but upon seeing her, Celeste quickly looked away; then, realizing she was caught, looked back again, breaking into a smile. She detoured from the main push of the crowd, heading in Mel's direction.

"You mean the mountain is coming to Mohammed?" remarked Val, in a cynical tone.

"Be nice," Mel directed. "In fact, why don't you try another store?"

But Val planted her feet firmly, positioning herself for the ready.

Mel realized now that it had been a while since Val and Celeste had locked horns. A bad cold had kept Val away from Mel's Memorial Day party, and had denied her the opportunity to spar with her favorite adversary.

The two women didn't like each other, but, for Mel's sake, operated within an atmosphere of tense tolerance. Whenever they met, usually at Mel's house, Mel often had to play referee, ushering Val to another part of the room, imploring her to be polite and not start anything. Val deplored Celeste's obvious obsession with money and social strata, and had once questioned how Mel could be friends with someone who was so passionately self-centered. "You have your faults too," Mel had teased, although she also found Celeste tiresomely suffocating on the issue of status—on who's in and who's out, on how much money X is making, the new Mercedes that Y bought, and all that "keeping up with the Joneses" that places so much value on the exterior. Whenever Mel feared she was getting too wrapped up in material things, she compared herself to Celeste, and knew, thankfully, that she had not gone that far.

In a way, both women served as Mel's barometers—the one with a shameless preoccupation for materialism, the other with an overblown self-confidence that, Mel suspected, covered up a deeper insecurity. In a way, Mel's friendship with both Celeste and Val said a lot about her life in other areas. A balancer of extremes, she considered herself the mediator, the buffer, the taker of the middle road.

Celeste walked up, burdened with several packages and a bulging dress bag hanging over her arm.

"Whew! Everybody and their mother is out today." Breathless, Celeste dropped her packages beside her, forming a small bunker that forced the flow of people to detour around them. "How've you been?" She brushed her cheek against Mel's and gave Val a curt nod, which would be the extent of her acknowledgment.

"And a Merry Christmas to you," Val said sarcastically.

"Looks like you're all set for the holidays," said Mel, hurrying past Val's remark. "Did you leave anything in the stores?"

"Oh, I barely made a dent. Just picked up a few last minute gifts. And getting ready for the Mayor's Masked Ball tomorrow. You're going, aren't you?"

"Uh, no," Mel replied dully. "Not this time."

She and Builder had attended the annual affair for the past several years, but this year they had not received an invitation—another sign, she concluded, that they were no longer part of the in crowd. Not that they ever had been. The best that could be said was that they had hovered along the edges, bordered on the periphery, and that had been mainly because of Mel's job at the Chamber. Once that was over, things rapidly went downhill. It took a while for her name to be scratched off the preferred mailing lists and deleted from the computer files, but gradually, over these last few months, it had happened. The social invitations that had previously flooded the house had trickled to an occasional announcement, and most of those were from nonprofit organizations whose affairs were open to the public. Mel and Builder had fallen from grace, their names dropped even from the C-level mailing lists among politically correct black Atlanta, not to mention the white social functions, which were in another league altogether. Mel had to admit, though, that even if she and Builder had been invited to the Masked Ball, they would not have gone. Forking out over two hundred dollars per ticket just wasn't practical. Every penny counted.

"Well, it's too bad you're not going," Celeste said, in a tone that failed to convey genuine sympathy. "I hear there'll be a special guest, probably someone like Whitney or Gladys."

Celeste liked to throw celebrities' names around, as though they were close personal friends. Val unleashed a bored, give-me-a-break sigh.

"So, did you get a dress for the occasion?" Mel asked politely.

"Yes." She proudly patted the plastic in her arms. "A really cute pink chiffon."

"*Pink?*" Val pounced. "At Christmas?" She made it sound like a cardinal sin.

Celeste curled her lips at Val. "It's very festive," she said haughtily. "And quite appropriate."

Mel had visions of the two of them brawling on the floor, pulling out each other's hair. It would be quite a dogfight, but she had no doubt who would win. She laid a hand on Val's arm, restraining her.

"Sasha's been wanting Ashley to spend the night," she said to Celeste. "I think she's asked her a few times, but it seems there's always a conflict. When do you think they can get together? They just see each other at school and that's it."

"I know." Celeste fluttered her eyebrows. "This school year's been so hectic. Ashley's new flute teacher wants her to practice hours on end, and then there's jazz class and the scholars' program—"

"Well, maybe during the holidays," Mel broke in. "When they have a break."

"Good idea," said Celeste. But she left it there, quickly changing the subject. "So what are you doing these days? Found a job yet?"

There it was. The inevitable question. The one that came up no matter where she happened to be. Anyone who knew she no longer worked at the Chamber would undoubtedly ask what she was doing. It was a natural question, she supposed, but she was tired of answering it. She felt like wearing a sign that said, "No, I don't have a job yet, but I've updated my résumé and made contacts and called people, and networked, and am doing everything I can to become employed again." Or, maybe she should simply wear a sign that admonished, in all caps, DON'T ASK!

But she had no sign, and Celeste was waiting for an answer. So she took a deep breath and went into her spiel, the same spiel she had just given Jason Hall, except with a bit more detail, because, after all, Celeste was a friend, despite her selfish ways.

"I'll keep an eye out," Celeste said, "and if I hear of anything, I'll let you know."

A strange gurgle came from Val, which both Mel and Celeste chose to ignore.

"Actually, I'm scheduled to see Ron tomorrow," Mel volunteered.

"You are?" Celeste drew back in surprise. "He didn't tell me."

"It took a while to get an appointment. He's a busy man."

"Tell me about it. Sometimes I've got to make an appointment myself."

Mel had talked to Ron back in the summer when he had told her that Landmark Universal was not hiring, and the fall would be a better time. She had tried to reach him several times at the office, but he was either out of town or in a meeting. Her calls were not returned. She thought about calling him at home, but decided against it. Builder had warned her that Ron was a "by-the-book" player, and would not favor any action that might in the least be deemed unprofessional. So she continued to call him at work, finally reaching him last week when his assistant was out, and he answered his phone directly. He'd seemed reluctant to set up an appointment and didn't sound too encouraging. But, heck, he was vice president of personnel. If he couldn't help, who could?

"I'm sure he'll do what he can," Celeste said, "though he keeps saying it's such a tough market nowadays. There're so many people looking."

"Yeah, right," ventured Val. "But then again, it depends on who's looking out for you."

Celeste gathered her packages. "I need to press on. You have a good holiday." Her "you" was clearly in the singular voice, accompanied by a wink at Mel. "Chin up." She disappeared into the thrust of the crowd that veered toward an exit.

"Chin up," mimicked Val. "God, she has some nerve. If her own grandmother was lying out on the street, bloodied, she'd step right over her."

"Oh, Val, she's not that bad."

"Ha. All the people she knows? I bet she hasn't said boo about you to any of them. See, that's the problem, we don't help each other."

Mel's shoulders ached and her head pounded. The movie earlier had been a welcomed distraction, but seeing Jason and Celeste reminded her of the stress and tension at home: the damn money thing that wouldn't go away. And all these people with their pasted-on smiles, seasonally adjusted, dissipated what little Christmas cheer she had. Tiredness came down on her full throttle. "Let's go," she said in a weary voice. "I don't want to see another soul."

Minutes later, at the north parking lot, Mel inhaled deeply, thankful for the crisp December air. She vaguely remembered that she had parked her car on the back row of vehicles facing the outer gate. Hours ago, she had complained about having to park so far away; now even that space was a hot commodity. Several cars were circling around like buzzards, looking for an opening anywhere. As she stepped off the curb, a long Lincoln immediately pulled up behind her. She extended her right arm out, indicating a distance to go, but the Lincoln trailed her all the way and, patience rewarded, captured the prize.

She wanted to go straight home and curl up in bed, at least for an hour or so. Going to sleep was her usual remedy for stress, and lately she had a lot of that. But sleeping would have to wait. She needed to stop by Builder's office to give Fatima her Christmas gift. For the last few days, Builder had left the house without it, even though she had placed it, clearly tagged, next to his keys. When he forgot again this morning, she decided to deliver it herself. That would at least be one less thing for him to do. She knew he was exhausted. For weeks he had been coming home late and leaving early, working feverishly. Mostly, they communicated by note and phone; rarely did she see him.

Mel slid into one of four empty parking spaces in front of Builder's office. She couldn't help but contrast the deserted area surrounding her husband's small southside business with the jostling mob she had just left. How they needed some of that activity here! She never did like this location. Builder's neighbors consisted of side-by-side boarded-up shops and a vacant gas station that loomed idly across the street. Years ago, she had argued that it was not a good investment. But Builder had seen potential here. The site included a large storage facility out back, where he could safely secure his dump truck, pickup, and lumber, as well as materials for current jobs. Beyond that, the main facility could house several offices. He planned to use one side for himself and rent out the other. Mel remembered how diligently he had fixed up the place, hoping to spark an economic brush fire that would spread throughout the block. But despite a trademark reconstruction that surpassed even his own expectations, Builder's singular flame failed to induce similar action by others. The street itself remained downright depressing, with an empty, eerie feel. At one point there was talk of city funds for revitalization, but that never materialized. Builder's renovated stucco, painted yellow with white trim, stood alone and defiant against the ubiquitous blight.

A loud buzzer answered her knock, and Mel walked into the small reception area. Fatima was on the phone, speaking in her lyrical Barbadian accent. She was more than a secretary; she was Builder's office manager and right arm, keeping subcontractors and supplies in line.

"Be with you in a minute, love," she said, cupping a hand over the receiver.

Mel noticed silver icicles hanging from the rubber plant in the corner and an artificial Christmas tree decked out in the center of an end table. Definitely Fatima's touches. She was surprised to see a few half-packed boxes stacked against a wall. Fatima was so meticulously organized, it was unusual to find even a stray paper clip. Perhaps she was setting up a new filing system.

"These people—they can be so rude." Off the phone, Fatima walked over and took Mel's hands into her own. "Oh, love, look at you! You are a sight for sore eyes, you know that? You shouldn't be such a stranger around here."

Mel smiled at Fatima's enthusiastic welcome. Count on her to be cheerful and upbeat.

"You just missed Builder. He was in here checking on an order."

"I didn't come to see Builder. I came to see you." From her deep coat pocket, Mel pulled out a box covered with leaping reindeer. "Merry Christmas."

"Ahhh! For me? Oh, love, you're simply too too wonderful."

"It's just a thought," said Mel, enjoying Fatima's delight. "I wanted to give it to you before you left." She knew that Fatima spent the Christmas holiday in Barbados with her parents, just as she had every year since working for Builder.

Suddenly, Fatima's mood turned sober, and her eyes teared. "Oh, my. I promised myself not to get all worked up again." She fingered the shiny ribbon on her present.

"What is it?" Mel asked gently. "Is something wrong back home?"

"No, no, nothing like that." She wiped her eyes and collected herself. "It's just that you and Builder have been like family to me. I'm going to miss you so much."

"Miss us?" Mel was confused. Why would Fatima miss them for just a couple of weeks? And what was all this about "family"? "I don't under-stand." She paused slightly. "You're going home for Christmas, right?"

Fatima nodded.

"—and then, you'll be back here the first of the year, like always." It was a statement, not a question.

"Oh no, love. I mean, I'll be back in Atlanta, but—I won't be working here."

"You won't? Why are you leaving us?"

Fatima gave her a startled look. "You don't know? He didn't tell you?"

"Tell me what?"

"I—I have no choice, love."

Mel's eyes widened. "But we can't lose you," she protested. "You're what keeps this place going."

Fatima walked over to a file cabinet in search of some papers. The sil-ver bracelets on her forearm jangled with each movement. "It'll be okay," she said softly. "Things have a way of working out."

Suddenly, for Mel, the lights came on. "He can't pay your salary, can he? Builder's letting you go. Is that it?"

Fatima stopped her busywork and turned to Mel. "Yes, love," she admitted.

"My God," said Mel, shaking her head.

Fatima shut the file drawer and headed back to her desk. Now that the news was out, a rush of words overcame her. "Friday's my last day. It hurts me that I have to leave like this. I've tried to hang on, but—"

"Oh, I understand," Mel said lamely. "I just wish I had known."

Not that she could have done anything. Things must really be bad if Builder had to let Fatima go. What else was going on? How much more did she not know? "When did all this start to happen?" asked Mel, think-ing back. "In the summer?"

"Oh, I've seen the signs coming for some time," Fatima replied. "First, there were these creditors calling, day in and day out, demanding money. They can be very nasty people, you know. I held them off as best I could." She sighed heavily. "Then, there were the bounced checks—"

"Bounced checks?" Mel had noticed several returned checks in the mail from Builder's personal account, and she had already talked to him until she was blue in the face about the money that was wasted with returned check charges. But here at the office too? "I thought *you* han-dled the books," said Mel. She tried to push back the accusatory tone creeping in her voice.

"I do. I—I did," Fatima said quickly. "But some days Builder just comes in and takes the checkbook with him. And then it's hard for me to keep a correct tally on the accounts."

"I know it is," Mel said, chastened by Fatima's sincerity. "I certainly don't blame you. It's just that I had no idea things had gotten so out of hand."

"It's that loan," Fatima said, frowning. "We would have been okay if only that loan had come through. But you know, love, so many people are hurting now. I keep telling Builder he'll be all right—if he can hold himself up until business turns around. It's only a matter of time, you know?"

"I hope you're right," Mel said quietly.

"He's a hard-working man. He's doing a lot of the work himself so he won't have to pay out to other people and can use that money to pay these bills off faster." Fatima lifted a fat manila folder on her desk. "I worry about him, though. He's working all the time to keep things going. But he's only one man, love. He can only do so much, you know?"

As she listened to Fatima, Mel started to feel that perhaps she hadn't been as attentive to Builder as she should have been, particularly during this period. He had been coming home tired and dirty from juggling two renovation projects. He was doing much of the work himself to cut down on subcontracting costs. Most times, he got in around midnight, after Mel had long gone to sleep. She would leave dinner for him on the stove, but it was usually still there in the morning. Too exhausted to eat, or appeasing his appetite by an overload of fast food throughout the day, he would gather just enough energy to take a shower before falling into bed. He had even allowed work to intrude on Sundays, which had always been exclusively reserved for family. Mel had objected, saying he needed to take better care of himself. He said it was only until things got back on track, and then he'd slow down. How many times had she heard that before! So she hadn't pushed the subject, knowing there was no sense arguing with him. But perhaps she should have been firmer, should have insisted he get more rest. When she did see him, she noticed that his hands were callused and rough, and he had long stopped any exercise routine, even an occasional bike ride with Sasha. Work had become all-consuming.

Fatima was right—Builder couldn't continue at this pace. And for what? The business was obviously in trouble, and her husband was sliding downhill with it.

Mel looked at her closet with disdain, not liking the options. She had two meetings today, an interview with Ron and a board meeting at

Humphrey Treatment Center, so she had no choice but to "dress up," meaning, hose, heels, and a suit. She pulled her terry cloth robe closer, not yet ready to relinquish it, savoring its toasty warmth. One benefit of being out of a job was being able to dress as she wanted. She practically lived in cottons, exchanging her cotton pajamas and robe for cotton pants and a top. Even her shoes were cotton, the wash-and-wear canvas type. *"The touch, the feel, of cotton,"* she sometimes sang, repeating the words to a favorite commercial. She loved to wear the soft, cuddly fabric. Well, not today. She'd wear a silk blouse, wool suit, and patent leather heels. She needed to look corporate.

She plugged in the curling iron and took stock of her hair. She had given it little attention during this period of unemployment, mostly pushing it back into a ponytail or hiding it under a headband, or scarf. She had convinced herself that this projected a youthful, carefree look, but the bottom line was she needed a trim and regular maintenance, and some highlighting to pep it up. It was naturally curly, too curly. But when it was long like this, it didn't hold much body, so she relied on the heat of the curling iron to transform it into a smoother, polished style.

Actually, she preferred the more natural, wild look. She had started wearing her hair like that about midway through her "tenure" at the Chamber, when things were riding high, her confidence was up, and she could get away with just about anything. There were a few raised eyebrows and titters, but Larson, her boss, had liked it, or at least, didn't disapprove, and that was all the incentive Mel needed. In most of the meetings for Chamber business, she was frequently the only black woman present. During the period before she wore her hair untamed, people would often question her ethnicity, asking if she was part Hispanic or Arab— anything but USA black. She knew part of it was racist—an unwillingness to believe that an African-American woman could put two sentences together without breaking syntax, or could design a proposal intelligent enough to lure multimillion dollar companies to Atlanta. She decided that since she couldn't do anything about her light brown complexion, at least her hair would set the record straight. Therefore, she shunned the predictably permed, pasted down hairstyle that was standard issue among black female managers in the corporate world. No, if she was going to be noticed, then she would express her racial identity in no uncertain terms. And hair was one way to do it. So she had worn it long and natural and free.

For a moment she thought about brushing back her bushy mane, plunking on a fancy headband, and calling it quits. But if Ron saw her like that, he'd probably really be put off. He was such a stickler for convention. She suspected that anybody he recommended for *anything* had to look superconservative, properly pressed with no rough edges.

She touched the top metal of the curling iron to see if it was warm enough. The ready light hadn't come on yet, but she needed to get started. Thankfully, her nails looked presentable. Last night, she had given herself a much-needed pedicure and manicure, while she waited for Builder. She had beeped him earlier to find out why he hadn't told her about Fatima. It had taken him nearly an hour to return her call, and when he finally did, she had almost forgotten why she had called.

"Why'd it take you so long to get back to me?" she had demanded. "This might have been an emergency. Sasha could be sick, or anything."

"Mel, please. It's hard for me to get to a phone sometimes. I just can't stop everything at the drop of a hat. What's up?"

"I saw Fatima today. I found out she's leaving. Why don't you tell me these things?"

"Look, I can't talk right now. Some guys are coming in to hang the Sheetrock, and I've got to get back. We'll talk about this later."

"When? You're never home. I hardly ever see you. You keep saying we're going to talk, but we never do."

"All right, all right—uh, I'll try to wrap things up early tonight."

"*How* early, Builder?" she had pressed.

"I don't know." He had sounded exasperated. "As soon as I can. Tell Sasha hi."

The late news had gone off, and she had put the final coat of polish on her nails, and still Builder hadn't come home. She dozed off briefly, then jumped with a start when she heard his truck pull in. She lifted her head toward the clock—1:42 A.M. She tried to keep her eyes open, but by the time he came upstairs, she was asleep. True to his usual pattern, he'd left this morning before she'd awakened.

She was angry with Builder, but she couldn't spend time thinking about that now. She needed to concentrate on this meeting with Ron, to have all her ducks in a row. Even though he was a friend, Ron had been evasive about discussing potential job opportunities at Landmark Universal. Not that she expected him to create something for her, but—good grief—as vice president of personnel, he had *some* clout. Why was he so afraid to use it? He was mysteriously tight-lipped about sharing just basic information, things she could find out from midlevel managers or from reading divisional newsletters. She didn't understand what Ron's problem was. But she intended to get some answers.

By 9:25 she was in the lobby, waiting for someone to accompany her to Ron's office. She couldn't believe the security: All visitors had to sign in, get a badge, and have a personal escort. In a few moments, a frail young woman with an expectant look surveyed the lobby, then walked over to Mel.

"Miss Burke?"

"Yes."

"I'm from Mr. Hamilton's office. I can take you up now."

The young woman signed a sheet at the receptionist's desk, and in response to a question from Mel, explained that not only visitors but employees had to have an identification badge at all times. There had been a recent break-in, where some hackers had stolen equipment and charged thousands of dollars of telephone calls on people's accounts, so security had been beefed up.

"I went out last week to get something from my car, and they wouldn't let me back in," she said. "Mr. Hamilton himself came down to vouch for me. I had left my ID in my coat pocket on my chair, and even though I walk by the receptionist desk every day, and they know me, Mr. Hamilton had to verify that I work here."

"My goodness," said Mel.

"It's silly, but that's the rule."

It was a lot more detail than she wanted, but Mel was grateful for the small talk. As they approached Ron's office, she realized she was nervous, as though this were her first job interview. It had been years since she had done this. Self-promotion was not her strong suit. She could sell the city of Atlanta to a roomful of business people considering relocation, but talking about her own assets was another matter. There was a thin line between sounding confident and sounding pompous.

When he saw her, Ron appeared more enthusiastic than when they had spoken a few days ago. He took her by the elbow and led her to a small conference table in the center of his spacious office, which was lined with floor-to-ceiling windows.

"This view is magnificent."

"It is, isn't it? I really enjoy it. Walk on over and take a closer look." He proudly pointed out different landmarks as though they were his own offspring. It was another ten minutes, after an update on family activities, before they settled down to serious talk. By then, Mel's nervousness had gone, and she felt foolish that she'd had the jitters earlier. After all, she reminded herself, Ron *is* a friend.

"I brought an updated copy," she said, handing him a résumé from her attaché case. "The one I sent you a while back doesn't include some grant proposals I've done recently."

"How's that going?" Ron asked. "Are you keeping busy as a freelancer?"

"Keeping busy is one thing; earning a living is quite another," Mel said frankly. "You know how it is with nonprofits. They're always scrambling for money and want you to do everything for next to nothing."

"That's the name of the game around here too," Ron said amiably. He scanned her résumé for a moment, and then took on a more officious demeanor. "I see where you've written proposals for the Task Force for the Homeless and the Neighborhood Assistance Project. How did those turn out?"

"There's not been a response yet. Both of those proposals went to the Woodruff Foundation, and it'll be a while before we know anything."

"Hmm."

"But I have an excellent track record for these types of things," added Mel, figuring she'd better speak up for herself, "and I'm confident that both agencies will get a good portion of what they're asking for—if not all of it."

"Well, you clearly have a real talent in proposal development and marketing, and I know that's largely what you did at the Chamber. And very successfully too." He let her résumé slide back on the table. "Problem is, things are really tight around here. Nothing has changed much since we first talked back in the summer. I'm sure you've read the paper. We're having a major reduction in force through attrition, and in some departments we're even laying off folks."

"I realize that, Ron," she said slowly. This was not what she wanted to hear. She needed to steer the conversation toward possibilities, not problems. Like a prudent attorney, she decided to concede a certain amount of ground first, then make arguments from her perspective. "I know that downsizing is the standard buzzword these days, and it's happening almost everywhere." She paused slightly. "But I also know that new opportunities are opening up, new ways of doing business. There's job sharing and other creative ideas to keep people working. And a lot of corporations are hiring part-time employees so they won't have to pay benefits."

She stopped short. She didn't mean to mention part-time options so soon. She had planned to wait until she had exhausted full-time opportunities, see if there was a possibility for a staff job, before proposing part-time consulting. But she had opened this can of worms, and she couldn't reseal it now.

"So you'd consider part-time work, then?" asked Ron, immediately picking up the bait.

"At this point, I'm open to anything. I need some consistent income." Damn, she hated to be this blunt, to show her vulnerability, but if Ron fully understood how serious things were, maybe he'd try harder to find something for her. Forget pride and ego,this was about survival. "I have a lot of skills that are transferable," continued Mel, "and what I don't know, I can learn quickly."

"Okay." Ron held up his hands. "You don't have to convince me. I know you're talented. I know you can do a number of things."

Mel kept quiet, waiting for the "but" to drop.

He cleared his throat. "I'm going to be honest with you, Mel. Even if we had some openings, and we don't right now, but even if we did, it'd be unlikely that we'd hire you in any capacity because of—well—because of what happened with Builder."

"What do you mean?" Mel asked

"I think you know what I mean. The lawsuit."

"The lawsuit? Builder's lawsuit?" Mel leaned forward. "You can't be serious. That was nearly a decade ago. Why should that matter now?"

Ron stretched back in his chair and arched his fingers into a steeple shape. "These things have a tendency to haunt you. It's a small world, Mel. Atlanta's a small town."

"But I don't understand," she said, incredulous. "That suit was against VRT—eons ago. And besides, it was determined that Builder was in the right—that he *was* discriminated against. I mean, what on earth does that have to do with anything here?"

"People talk," Ron said. "These folks run in the same circles."

"I don't get it," she said, genuinely confused. "What does that have to do with me? I mean, I could kind of see it if he had filed a suit and then come back years later and applied for a job. But this was against another company altogether. And *I'm* the one looking for a job, not Builder."

Ron looked away. "I know. Maybe I've said too much already."

"Said what?" Mel asked, exasperated. "You're not making sense."

He faced her squarely. "Certain corporations share information. You work for these companies, you get known. That can be good or bad."

It took a second for her to process the data. "Are you saying that because Builder filed a class action suit some ten years ago, I'm being blacklisted because I'm his wife? That's absurd."

"Look," Ron said. "Builder did some good work, was a top account exec, and all that. But once he filed that suit—" Ron shook his head. "He got a reputation as a troublemaker. He riled a lot of folks. And they don't forget."

Mel sat straight in her chair and put a hand on her hip. "Exactly who are we talking about here?" she demanded, tapping her forefinger on the table. "Who's the 'they' who don't forget? Why, half the people who were involved have probably moved on somewhere else, anyway. Who's doing this?"

"It's not that it's one or two people holding a grudge," Ron explained. "There are files and things—records. People remember names."

"This is unreal. It sounds like some kind of Mafia." A disturbing thought pushed its way through. "Could that be the reason why Builder keeps getting turned down for bank loans?" she asked. "Because of this lawsuit ten years ago?"

For a second Ron considered the idea, then dismissed it. "No, that wouldn't have anything to do with it. That's just, you know, banks being skittish about lending to small businesses, afraid to take a risk, that kind of thing."

"I don't know. I wouldn't put anything past anybody."

"Don't blow it way out of proportion," said Ron. "It's not as though someone is monitoring your every move, trying to make life miserable for you and Builder. Believe me, there's nothing sinister going on. It's nothing like that."

"Oh, sure," Mel said with hostility. "They just want to make it impossible for me to find a job."

Ron twitched his mouth. "I'm sorry now that I even brought it up. I just thought you should know—" He stopped short. "Like I said, certain corporations share information. That's all."

"Gentleman's agreement. Is that it?" Mel asked sarcastically.

Ron shrugged. "It's just the way things are."

"Well, *you're* vice president of personnel," Mel reminded him. "Can't you do something about it?"

"There's nothing I can do," he said meekly.

"You mean, nothing you *want* to do," she shot back.

Another BSJ. Ball-less, spineless jerk. The interview had turned into a disaster. What a waste of time. All she wanted was to get out of there. She felt like cussing Ron out, telling him how weak he was, telling him he could take his panoramic view of the skyline and $300,000 a year job, and screw himself. Here she was, desperately in need of a break, and he wouldn't lift a finger to help. And he's a so-called friend—a *friend!* He was pitiful—like so many black men who get a little bit of power and then don't know what to do with it. Scared to death to stand up to white folks, that's what it came down to. Scared that somebody white will say "No, nigger, you're moving too fast, you can't do that."

Mel stuffed her résumé into her case and rose to leave.

"Come on, now, sit down," Ron said, rising to his feet. "Let's talk about this."

"There's nothing to talk about," she said heatedly. "It's obvious you can't help."

"I'm just trying to tell you what the real deal is. I could have strung you along and all that, saying that maybe something would come through, but I figured you had a right to know."

"Fine, Ron, fine. So now you've told me. I need to go."

"All right, but wait a second. We've known each other too long for you to be this upset with me. Look—" He scurried to his desk and snatched a piece of paper. "I've written down a couple of names for you to contact."

Mel took the note from his outstretched hand. Home Depot and Federal Express were highlighted in yellow, with some writing under each.

"I've already talked to them so they'll be expecting your call," Ron said, in an effort to redeem himself.

Mel mumbled a barely audible thanks as she hurriedly left. The walk down the hall was interminably long, and it seemed as if the elevator would never come. Ron had some nerve. She couldn't believe it; she couldn't wait to get out of this place. She watched a man with a fat behind sashay down the corridor, balancing an overfilled coffee cup in his hand. He's probably making googols of money and doing nothing but taking breaks all day, she thought to herself. Someone who never had to struggle, never had to strain. It just wasn't fair.

In the lobby, several people were standing around the receptionist's desk, waiting to sign in or be escorted. Mel bypassed them, walking briskly to one of the revolving doors that opened to freedom.

"Just a moment, ma'am. Hold it, please."

A man's loud voice stopped her cold. Mel turned to see a security guard approach, his shiny black shoes crisply crossing the marble floor.

"You forgot to leave your visitor's badge," he said, pointing to Mel's jacket.

"Well, I—" Mel started. "Here, can't you take it?" She pulled the badge off her lapel, but in her haste to get rid of it, a sharp corner of the plastic braised her silk blouse, causing a pull. Damn! Her best blouse too.

"I can't take it," the guard said, speaking in a tone that indicated he was used to errant visitors attempting shortcuts. "You need to take it over there," he said, indicating the crowded receptionist's desk. "You also need to be signed out," he continued, unsmiling. "Isn't there someone with you?"

"No, I came down by myself."

"Well, you shouldn't have," he scolded. "What office were you visiting?"

"Ron Hamilton's—personnel," Mel blurted. Good! she thought. Maybe this would be a mark against Ron's perfect record. It would serve him right.

"Ah, Mr. Hamilton." The guard lightened up, as though his personal hero had been named. "Well, you can just sign yourself out then. When you return the badge."

Displeased, Mel cut her eyes at him, then reluctantly walked over to the receptionist's desk, feeling as though she had been spanked. Suddenly, she felt like Sasha during a moment of chastisement, and she immediately empathized with her daughter. She saw the guard return to his post where he occasionally glanced in her direction. Several people stood before her, waiting for clearance. Mel tapped her right foot impatiently. This is ridiculous, she thought. It's not as though I'm carrying classified Pentagon secrets. She walked up to the desk, plunked her badge down, and once again, quickly headed toward the exit.

"Miss, I need for you to sign out," said the receptionist, calling after her.

But Mel was halfway through the revolving door, and there was no way she'd turn back now. She vaguely heard another voice, a warning from the guard, gruff and agitated: "Ma'am, you need to stop. Ma'am!"

But Mel only moved faster; she wasn't going to stand for this. Out the door, she raced down the steps, lots and lots of steps, and had reached the third and final tier when her shoe caught on something slippery underneath. She fell on the concrete, bruising both palms and skinning her right knee. A circle of blood oozed from her leg and inched toward the hem of her skirt. Her pride was more damaged than her flesh. As she stood up to brush off her suit, she saw the guard sternly watching from the top of the steps, his arms folded in a satisfied stance, a martinet set in stone. Mel grabbed her attaché case and hobbled away, tears of anger streaking her face.

Rubbing it had helped, but the stain on her skirt was still visible. Mel didn't want to risk weakening the fabric, or further widening the water mark, so she tossed the damp paper towel into the trash. Looking in a full-length mirror at the ladies' room in the Radisson, she analyzed her condition: not good. She had been here for nearly an hour, trying to patch herself up, but with disappointing results. Her leg was still throbbing from the fall, her hands hurt, and although she had reapplied her makeup, there was nothing she could do about her eyes—they were still bloodshot from her outbursts of crying. Now, her stomach was getting into the act, turning queasy. A telltale sign of stress. Feeling sorry for herself, Mel had decided that since there was little she could do to retreat from this self-pitying mode, she might as well let it run full force.

Another chill ran through her legs; she was getting cold. She had taken off her panty hose and thrown them away. Bloodied and with a gaping hole, they were of no use anyway. To her dismay, she had discovered she didn't have enough money to buy another pair. After paying for parking at Landmark, all she had in her wallet was $1.63. How pathetic, she thought. She had meant to borrow a few dollars from Sasha this morning, but had forgotten to do so. She looked at her watch and walked over to the corner chair. She'd sit for ten minutes or so, and then leave.

She had debated going home and cleaning up, but knew if she did, she wouldn't venture back out today, not in this frame of mind. And she really should go to Humphrey. It was a special call meeting, an end-of-the-year evaluation of the Center's capital campaign, and all board members were strongly encouraged to attend.

A well-dressed brunette with shoulder-length hair walked up to the mirror. She gave Mel a curt nod, then tossed her head left and right, letting her dark mane shimmy back and forth. Another head flipper, thought Mel. Why do white women do that? And the habit started early too. Once, she had caught Sasha flinging her hair that way right after she had gotten a perm, and Mel had jumped all over her. "No daughter of mine is going to go around shaking her head like she's got marbles in it," Mel had said. "Are you doing the jerk or something?" Of course, she knew what it was. Sasha had picked up the gesture from some of her white classmates. But this was one habit that Mel would nip in the bud. There'd be no head flinging or swiping at the hair, no running through the hair with her fingers, then letting it fall—not in her house. "If you do that, I'm going to cut it all off," she had warned, but her threat was never put to the test. Sasha got the message.

A middle-aged woman came out of a stall, with nary a glance toward the sinks, and walked directly out of the lounge. Mel shook her head. How many times had she seen that—women not washing their hands after using the bathroom. Val had brought this to her attention a few years ago when the two of them had attended a play at the High Museum. Just for fun, during a fifteen-minute break, they had taken their own poll of the number of women who entered the rest room, used a stall, and washed their hands, versus those who didn't. Their tally: out of thirty-nine total, twenty-two washed, seventeen didn't. Subsequently, Mel had conducted her own survey at public rest rooms—at hotels, restaurants, airports, even when she was at the Chamber. Val was right. A whole lot of well-dressed women walked out without benefit of soap and water.

Let me stop, Mel thought. Enough criticizing. She eased out of the chair and braced herself for her next encounter—with a group of north-side business people who, unwashed hands or not, had no trouble paying their mortgage.

The meeting was being called to order when Mel walked in. Perfect timing. She didn't want to arrive early, and then have to submit to chitchat and possible questions about her "work." She had told them months ago that she was no longer at the Chamber, but she didn't feel like giving an update on what she was doing. Besides, up to now, no one had been forthcoming about suggesting job opportunities, so what was the point?

Humphrey was a small residential treatment center serving drug-addicted children. Most of the board members had been affiliated with the Center since it was founded well over a decade ago. By comparison, Mel was a relatively new member, having joined just the year before last.

She glanced around for Tom Dunkins, the only other black person on the board, but an infrequent attendee at meetings. He wasn't there, and if he came at all, would no doubt slip in late. She knew that Tom reinforced the stereotype that blacks operate on CP (Colored People's) time. Of course, any white board members who came in late were simply—late.

"I know everybody is busy with Christmas activities," Jan Rowland, the president, was saying, "but we thought it was important to assess where we are in the campaign as we prepare to close out the year." Jan religiously wore her hair in the same outdated but neat French twist. She called on the treasurer to present a report on the money raised for the capital campaign.

Here it comes, Mel thought. The money thing again. Always money, money, money.

The treasurer reeled off the financial figures. The campaign was proceeding well; more than 90 percent of their $5 million goal had already been reached. But there were still many outstanding pledges that needed to be honored, and it was hoped that several businesses could make those pledges by December 31. Board members were urged to make additional calls to their corporate prospects and nudge them to pay up by year's end.

"And one last thing," said the treasurer, "there are still a couple of board members who have not yet fulfilled their pledges."

Mel, who was doodling on a pad, perked her ears.

"Let me just say a word about that," said Jan, looking at no one in particular. "You know how we like to be able to say that we have one hundred percent participation from the board. It makes our case that much stronger when we solicit money from others. So I implore you, if you have not yet made your full commitment, please do so."

Tom Dunkins chose that exact moment to walk into the meeting and sit in the empty chair by Mel. She exchanged a smile and nod with him, then turned back to the gathering. All eyes were focused on the two of them. The picture couldn't have been clearer, she thought. Without naming names, the message rang out: that Tom and Mel, the two blacks, were the ones who had not paid their share into the kitty. Hadn't the treasurer said "a *couple*" of board members? Meaning two? Who else could it be? Except for Tom and Mel, everyone in the room was either retired and living off interest income, a high-salaried physician or corporate type, or somebody's pampered wife who drove expensive cars and hosted receptions at the garden club.

Perhaps if Tom hadn't come in at that particular moment, it wouldn't have been so obvious; the statement would have been one of many tucked into the overall minutes, a simple reminder to board members to make good on their pledge. But to Mel, the announcement boomed loudly, broadcasting her name. After all, she *was* guilty; she had paid only half of her five hundred dollar pledge, the minimum requested of board members. She knew that some members contributed up to $2,500 to the campaign, in addition to special gifts throughout the year. She wasn't anywhere near their income bracket, so that kind of donation was out of the question. But she did think the basic pledge was fair and reasonable, and she had fully intended to have paid it by now. She had made the first installment last year while she was still working at the Chamber. But things had changed, and the idea of coming up with several hundred dollars for a charitable contribution, no matter how worthy, when she was juggling just to cover basic bills—well, right now, it was more than she could manage. So she spoke up. Blame it on the botched interview with Ron, or Tom Dunkins's ill-timed entrance, or her assumption that everyone in the room suspected she was one of the culprits anyway. She couldn't let this go by unaddressed.

"I must say I'm really concerned about this money situation," she said, not waiting to be recognized.

"What do you mean?" Jan asked.

"I mean there's too much emphasis being placed on how much a board member can contribute monetarily. There are many other ways to be supportive."

"Oh, I think we all agree with that," Jan concurred hastily.

"Sure," someone pitched in. "Just look around this table, and you'll see examples of how people help out all the time. Tony's an accountant and reviews the books; Saundra gives us legal advice; Robert's been great with design ideas for the new facility."

"I know all that," Mel said impatiently, a little miffed that her pro bono promotional work on behalf of Humphrey had not also been mentioned. "My point is this: Since this campaign began, every single meeting has revolved around who has brought in how much money. I don't think that what we contribute needs to be itemized, line by line, like we're in some kind of contest. Some of us have different levels of resources than others." She paused, waiting for reaction. This wasn't coming out the way she wanted. She was beating around the bush. What she really wanted to say was "Look, right now I can't pay all the money I've pledged, and I don't need you to make me feel bad about that."

"I understand what you're saying," Jan said thoughtfully, "but I never saw this as a competition. More as an incentive, perhaps. I think if there's been too much emphasis on money, it's only because the campaign has taken on such a high priority, and we all want it to succeed. After it's over, I'm sure we can focus more on other things."

There were polite murmurs of agreement around the room.

But Mel had another point to make. "I'm also concerned about potential new members," she continued. "It's going to be hard to recruit new people if they have to make a substantial financial commitment. Realistically, we may need to revisit this whole diversity issue again, and what your expectations are of board members."

Mel was chair of the Board Development Committee, which had been asked to identify blacks and other racial ethnics willing to serve on the

Humphrey board. It was an embarrassment that out of twenty-four board members, Mel and Tom were the only nonwhites, while over half of the patient population at Humphrey consisted of African-American youngsters. Mel had pushed for the board to become more racially mixed, but soon realized that the job of identifying new members fell squarely in her lap. When she had asked others for recommendations, the old line, "We don't know any qualified blacks," had been hurled at her, although couched in somewhat different terms. Tom was no help; he was on the board in name only, viewing it as one more item to list on his résumé under "community service."

So it had been left up to Mel to do the recruiting. Several people whom she approached were already stretched to the limit with other volunteer activity. And she had received a cold shoulder from black folks with money, like Ron and Celeste, who, although they didn't say it, didn't consider Humphrey high profile enough to be involved with. They sat on boards that paid *them*. In fact, Mel remembered how, years ago, Celeste had once talked about the six hundred dollars she had received for attending a meeting at some major corporation, and that she'd used it for a one-day makeover, complete with a European facial and deluxe leg wax.

"I don't think anyone is saying that you have to contribute a certain amount of money in order to serve at Humphrey," said Jan. "That's not how we operate. We may make certain suggestions and have guidelines, but there are no financial obligations."

"Yes, but when you start saying that certain percentages haven't been reached, then somebody's doing some bean counting," insisted Mel. "The fact that people volunteer their time and talent should be worth something."

"Of course it is."

"But it appears as though the financial contributions are what's most appreciated."

"Oh, that's not true, Mel," Jan objected. "No one's saying that."

A raspy sound came from the center of the room. "For crying out loud, what's all the fuss about?" Avery Bernstein, growling his words, tapped a bony finger on the table. He was nearly eighty, a former pediatrician who continued to consult with Humphrey's doctors and counselors on occasion. Mel couldn't imagine him ever working directly with children, although he might have frightened a few into going straight.

"Making a financial commitment is a basic part of serving on a board," Bernstein said. "Everybody knows that. You're asked to join because of what you can bring to the table. *And that means money!*" He punctuated these last four words with a long index finger aimed at Mel.

"I'm sure I wasn't asked to join Humphrey because of my bank account," Mel retorted. "And I'm afraid people will be turned off if they have to make a significant financial contribution as part of their board responsibility."

"Oh, this is ludicrous," said Bernstein, throwing up his hands.

"Not really," Tom joined in. "A lot depends on what you'd call a 'significant' contribution. What I consider significant may be quite different from what someone else thinks."

"Exactly," Mel said with appreciation, although she wished someone other than Tom had backed her up. Now it looked as if she and Tom, neither of whom had paid their full due, were in cahoots, and that wasn't the case.

"This is hogwash," said Bernstein. "We have a fiduciary responsibility to this institution. That's why we're here!"

"I'm not denying that," insisted Mel. "I'm just saying that when you set goals and limits, some people can reach them a lot easier than others, on the basis of their financial status."

Jan stepped in, trying to calm the waters. "Perhaps another way to do it is to have each board member responsible for raising a certain amount of money, not that it has to come out of his or her personal pocket."

"I have a pamphlet called *Fifty Ways for Board Members to Fund-raise,*" said a voice from the rear. "I can make copies and distribute them to everybody."

There were a couple of chuckles, but then several people commented that it was a good idea.

"Obviously, we need to talk about this further," said Jan. "Let's put it on the agenda for next month. Mel, I certainly hope you'll be part of the discussion group to look into this."

Great, thought Mel. She should have kept her mouth shut. She had been upset about yet another demand for money; she hadn't meant for things to get to this point. And she certainly didn't need to be on a sub-committee with white folks talking about something they couldn't possibly relate to. But since she was the one who had raised the issue, she couldn't back down from dealing with it.

"All right. I'll work with the group," she said.

"Good." Jan looked relieved. "Any other volunteers?"

A few hands went up and then discussion moved to other business. Mel said nothing for the duration of the meeting. She was thinking about the comments she had made. They weren't really out of order; she fervently believed what she had said. But Avery Bernstein was right too. Humphrey's requirements for the board certainly weren't excessive. Maybe she was getting paranoid and too sensitive about the money issue. It was just that she was tired of hearing about it—everywhere she went. She needed to rest, to get away from it all. But it seemed there was no escape.

Maxx's white Lamborghini was parked in front when Mel pulled up. The windows of his car were so opaque that she couldn't tell if he was waiting inside or had walked around back. But as she turned into the driveway, he emerged from his car, with a note in hand.

"Thought I'd missed you," he shouted. "I was about to drive off."

Mel rolled down her window and stuck out her head; the cool December air rushed in. "I'll be around front in a minute," she said. She took her time easing up the long driveway and parking her car. Now what? she wondered.

Theirs was an odd relationship. The last few times she had seen Maxx, things had been strained between them. The last few years, in fact, they rarely met without getting into an argument. She'd vow to avoid one, but every time they got together, something happened to irritate her. The "something" inevitably revolved around his work, but there was a deeper, cryptic hurt. She would go on the attack; he'd present a lawyerly defense. And reconciliation would prove elusive.

There was a pattern to their meetings. Things would start off relatively well, especially when they focused on their common interest, Sasha. Mel knew that Maxx loved his only niece and expressed that love by showering Sasha with gifts and special treats. Often, he'd go overboard, buying items that were too flamboyant, like the sable jacket and muffler he gave Sasha last Christmas. Even though she disapproved, Mel would often hold her tongue, especially when Sasha was present. She didn't want Sasha to be drawn into the tension, into the volatile mix of the "something" that stood between her and Maxx. Inevitably, though, it would surface. It could be pushed down and held back for only so long.

This wasn't the way she wanted it, certainly not the way she had envisioned it. Maxx was her baby brother, her only sibling. Growing up, they were very close. Mel would alternate between the role of guardian sister and rough-and-tumble playmate—standing watch over him when needed, competing feverishly against him in neighborhood bike races and backyard track meets. Later, under Mel's tutelage, Maxx learned a respectable game of chess and a beastly backhand. But as adults, the four years between them seemed insurmountable, a breach beyond repair. Mel blamed it on a difference in lifestyle and values. But it was fueled by her placement upon her brother of a long-time culpability about their father—a culpability that, try as he might, Maxx couldn't shake loose, and from which Mel couldn't release him.

The house was cold and dark. Mel turned up the thermostat and opened the dining room curtains on her way to the front door. Maxx staggered in behind her, laden with Christmas presents and a lopsided grin.

"What's all this?" She followed him into the family room, where he deposited his load. "Let me guess," she said, pointing to the wrapped presents. "Sasha—Sasha—Sasha—and Sasha."

Maxx smiled. "Smart woman." He took off his gloves, surveying the room. "No tree yet?"

"Uh, no. We'll get it in the next day or so."

The only decorations in her house were the two-foot ceramic Christmas tree in the living room and a red-and-green-ribboned wreath on the front door. Normally, by now, the seventeenth of December, they would have their tree up. Early in their marriage, Mel had insisted on the fresh fragrance of a live tree, and over the years getting the tree had become a favorite family tradition. They would all three pile into the pickup and drive to the Farmer's Market. Laughing and in good humor, they'd inspect dozens of trees and nitpick the merits of the finalists, before selecting the winning Douglas fir. Always a Douglas fir.

Back at home, they'd make a fire, bring out hot popcorn and cider, and put on an old Johnny Mathis Christmas album. Then, the decorating would begin. Builder would untangle and hang the lights; Sasha put up the bulbs and crystal ornaments; while Mel served as overseer—making sure that the tree was straight, that not too many lights of the same color clustered together, that the Nativity scene on the mantel was properly centered, and that the Christmas cards were artfully displayed among the holiday bric-a-brac. That's the way things went—normally. But it had not been a normal year; and this was not a normal Christmas. With Builder putting in such long hours, they hadn't had a chance to get a tree. Mel told Sasha that if Builder couldn't break away, the two of them would take care of it. Life must go on, after all. But Sasha hadn't seemed too pleased.

"So, what have you been up to lately?" Mel asked. She sat on one corner of the sofa, Maxx at the other; the packages in between provided a temporary buffer.

"I just came from taking Nikki to the airport. She's spending the holidays with her sister in Houston."

Mel furrowed her brow, the name not registering. She had a hard time keeping up with Maxx's girlfriends. Most of his flings were just that—flings—short-lived and frivolous, so she had long ago stopped counting. "She must be pretty significant if you're taking time in the middle of the day to drive her to the airport."

"You remember Nikki," he said, picking up one of Sasha's smaller packages and playing catch with it. "In fact, I have you to thank for introducing me to her. She came to your party last Memorial Day. Frank Kirby brought her along. She's his cousin. Distant cousin."

"Frank's cousin?" Mel said, drawing a blank. "I really don't know who you're talking about. What does she look like?"

Maxx gazed up at the ceiling. "Oh, you'll remember her when you see her," he said confidently. He turned back to Mel. "Let's see—she's darker than you, a lot of hair, gorgeous eyes, and"—he paused, a smile forming—"let's just say she ain't no Twiggy."

Mel moaned when she realized who he was talking about. She started to say, "The bimbo!" then, caught herself. Of course, she remembered now, the buxom woman who was dressed in rainbow colors and acted kind of weird.

"*That's* Nikki? You can't be serious."

"Why not?"

"She's not exactly your type, is she?"

"And just what is my type, Mel?"

"Well, you know, someone with a little more—class." She didn't want to put the girl down, but, good grief, he could do better. He *had* done better.

"There you go, making judgments as usual. You don't even know her."

"True," Mel admitted. "And I realize first impressions don't tell the whole story. But she seemed so—out to lunch."

Maxx shook his head and chuckled. "You have no idea. Believe me, Nikki's got a lot going for her."

Mel responded with arched eyebrows.

"Seriously," said Maxx. "There's much more here than meets the eye. Nikki's very bright; she's a medical technician, works at Crawford Long."

"Well, medical technician or not, that's no testament that she's got her head screwed on right. I've met enough doctors and medical types to know that all kinds of people slip through."

"Give her some credit," Maxx said, getting antsy. "She's done a heck of a lot to turn her life around." He went on to say how Nikki grew up in a tough Houston neighborhood, put herself through medical school while taking care of her dying father, and, although only in her early thirties, had racked up numerous professional awards.

"Sounds admirable," said Mel, finding it hard to reconcile his description with the image of the spaced-out woman who visited her home last May. She watched her brother closely, waiting for him to reveal that he had set her up to believe something totally untrue, that this was a ruse to sharpen his legal skills, a dry run for his real life courtroom dramas. Like the time he had spun an elaborate tale about eloping with a woman in Vegas. It had sounded so believable; he had supplied such colorful details, had used the perfect pick of words. Then, after he had convinced her, he released an innocent, "I didn't mean any harm" admission that it was all a joke, something he had made up. *Why, I was just teasing, just seeing how far I could take it. Really got to you, didn't I?*

Yes, Maxx was good at dramatics, which was one reason he was such a successful trial lawyer. He could convert even the most hard-hearted. Mel wondered if he sometimes invented stories to support his own version of the truth, and in the process, subconsciously muddled the truth with fiction. Maybe that was his way of rationalizing why he defended the type of people that he did—the slick drug dealers and executive misfits. Maybe he had to convince himself that his clients had some redeeming qualities. So, to suit his own purposes and conscience, he rearranged reality.

Now, watching him talk about Nikki, he seemed sincere and honest, even to Mel's suspicious eye. If Nikki was all of these things, then maybe Maxx was right, maybe she had been too quick to judge. Still, her instincts told her that it was an infatuation based on lust, pure and simple, and would blow over in another month or so. She knew enough human psychology to realize that the more one objected to an idea and tried to convince someone of the error of his ways, the more entrenched that person became in his own point of view. She didn't want to push Maxx inadvertently further toward Nikki—so she decided to back off. To pursue it further would be pointless. He'd accuse her again of making a snap judgment, of being too critical. There was already enough dissension between them; they didn't need any more.

"Can I get you anything? A beer? Eggnog?"

"No thanks. I'll have a couple of these though." He scooped up a handful of paper-thin-shelled pecans, squeezing them in his fist.

Mel followed suit, except that she used a nutcracker.

"So what's up with you? Been out job hunting?" he asked.

"Not really," Mel said, selectively forgetting about the interview with Ron. "I had a board of directors meeting at Humphrey."

"Oh. Still doing volunteer work?"

"Yes," she said defensively. "And just because it doesn't pay, doesn't mean it's not worthwhile."

"Hey, did you hear me say anything? More power to you."

"Yeah right. I know how you think. Everything has a price."

"Come on, Mel, lighten up. You're too hard on me."

There was a brief silence as they both chomped on plump nutmeat.

"So how's Sasha doing? She all set for Christmas?"

"Well, she sure will be now. She'll have a fit when she sees these presents." Mel hesitated a beat. "Thanks for playing Santa."

"Hey, I have to look out for my girl." He wiped his hands free of nut debris. "I almost forgot." He reached into his breast pocket and handed her a slim red envelope, quartered by slivers of gold ribbon and a dainty bow in the center. "This is for you."

"How pretty," said Mel, impressed with the package. "Did you do this?"

"I have some talent."

"That's a lawyer's answer for you. Not a yes; not a no. Deliberately vague."

"I suggest you open it now."

"Really? I shouldn't wait until Christmas?"

"I wouldn't advise it."

Gingerly, she bared the delicate wrapping, which revealed two orchestra tickets to the *Nutcracker* at the Fox Theatre.

"Wow," said Mel, reading the small print carefully. "These are excellent seats. Right up front."

"When I talked to Sasha the other night, she told me you two hadn't been yet."

Mel hadn't been sure whether they'd get to go at all this season. Ever since Sasha was a toddler, mother and daughter had attended a Christmas performance of the *Nutcracker.* But this year, Mel had not made plans. It was one more expense she was trying to eliminate, although she knew she would have a hard time explaining it to Sasha. Now, thanks to Maxx, she wouldn't have to.

"These are great," she said, laying the tickets next to the bowl of nuts. "Thank you."

"Sure thing."

She didn't have any problem accepting gifts like this from Maxx—tickets to the ballet, clothes for Sasha. It seemed perfectly legitimate, aboveboard and natural, the right thing to do. But when it came to Maxx's giving cash to Builder, this she couldn't accept; she wouldn't accept. To her, the cash represented an attempted bribe for absolution, entrapping them in unwilling complicity with Maxx's scummy clientele, making them coconspirators in a circle of ill-gotten profits. Mel wanted no part of it. Maybe she was being hypocritical by not looking at this even-handedly. Certainly, the money Maxx used to buy the tickets came from the same source as the cash he lent Builder. But in her mind, there was a distinction between the shape and form of the transactions, a distinction, however subtle, that permitted her to receive her brother's offering.

"I leave for France day after tomorrow," Maxx announced, watching her out of the corner of his eye. "Flying to New York to take the Concorde."

"Lucky you," Mel said, a layer of sarcasm in her voice.

Maxx dismissed her brewing acrimony. "Next time, you should plan to come with me. It's been a long time since you've seen Mother."

"Yeah, well, as long as one of us goes—" said Mel, leaving the sentence unfinished.

"It's not the same. She wants to see you—and Sasha."

"Then she can come here," Mel snapped. She took a couple of the larger presents from the daybed and placed them in the designated corner of the room, where the Christmas tree, if they got one, would stand.

"You know how petrified Mother is of flying," continued Maxx. "It took a whole lot of nerve for her to make that last trip. Sasha was just a baby then."

"She was five, not exactly a baby."

"Even so, it's been a while. What—eight years?"

Mel didn't respond.

"That's too long, Mel. Besides, Sasha needs to get to know her. You shouldn't stand in the way of their relationship."

"I'm not doing that," Mel said sharply. "Sasha can write her anytime she wants. They exchange letters, they communicate. You act as though I forbid her to stay in touch."

"It's not like you're encouraging her," Maxx retorted. "Look, just think about taking a trip there, that's all I'm saying. I'd gladly pay for it. It's time you two put all this animosity behind you. She's your mother, for crying out loud."

"Let's just drop it, all right? When you see her, give her my best." Mel stood up. "Sasha just finished another present for her. I didn't get to mail it with the other things. Would you mind taking it? It's small."

She raced up the steps, eager to get away from Maxx and any further talk of their mother—Eunice Lincoln Brazeal. Usually, Mel referred to her in the third person—as she, her, or Eunice. Rarely Mother—and never with affection. In addition to Maxx's defense of the unworthy, their mother was yet another subject on which Mel and her brother did not see eye to eye.

A decade ago, Eunice had left her old life and friends and moved to the city of Nantes, where she soon married an Algerian who owned a bed-and-breakfast inn. Maxx had been there several times, usually making an annual visit during Christmas. But Mel had no desire to go, even though Maxx had raved about the gorgeous setting in the lap of the Loire River, and how their mother's current husband, a former chef, made exquisite meals. To Mel, none of that held any appeal. She was glad her mother lived so far away; the more distance between them, the better.

As Mel remembered it, the estrangement began when she was eight or nine, and she realized Maxx was her mother's favorite. At first, she noticed it in little things; then it became more obvious, more frequent, as her mother made no effort to camouflage her preference. Perhaps from her mother's view, these differences were minor. But lying unresolved in Mel's sensitive heart, they loomed ominously throughout her childhood.

It was Maxx who would get the largest slice of pie, more bubbles in his bath, a lingering hug at bedtime. It was Maxx who captured their mother's broadest smile, deepest pride, and heartiest laugh. When Maxx fell and broke his arm, their mother blamed Mel for not watching out for him. When Maxx was teased by older kids in the neighborhood, and came home crying, their mother punished Mel for allowing it to happen. Mel was expected to get straight A's; with Maxx, it was cause for celebration. On occasion, when Mel complained about the unequal treatment, Eunice would dismiss any differences as petty or nonexistent. "You're older and should know better," she would say. "Maxx is just a little boy." Painfully, Mel came to realize that, with her mother, Maxx would always be first. Mel felt she was never on equal ground, never given an even chance.

Her salvation was her father, bless his soul, who showed no preference in his children. "My chocolate M&Ms" he'd call them, bouncing them both on his knees. Mel loved her father, worshipped him, but she hated his having to work so hard and that he spent so little time at home. On the road three weeks out of the month, he hawked encyclopedias along the East Coast, leaving his precious M&Ms in the care of his domineering wife.

Thinking about her father, Mel swiped at a tear as she rummaged through Sasha's dresser in search of the beaded bracelet, a swirly V design of white and yellow beads that Sasha had made. She had finished it just a few days ago, custom-made for her grandmother, Mel's mother, a woman who, in Mel's view, didn't deserve a creation crafted with so much attention and care.

It angered her that Maxx dare suggest she cross the Atlantic to visit their mother. He had no idea what he was asking. It took every ounce of goodwill she could muster to maintain even minimal contact. She did it for Sasha's sake. Despite her own resentment toward Eunice, she thought Sasha should have some knowledge of her grandmother, should think of her as decent and fair. It was all Mel could do these past years not to poison Sasha's mind, not to tell of the loneliness in her childhood, how she couldn't go to her own mother for comfort, how she still blamed her for much of her pain.

Perhaps Mel would have gotten over her mother's hurtful slights. Perhaps her father's love would have been enough to assuage her insecurities. Perhaps by now she and her mother could have reconciled. Perhaps, perhaps, perhaps. But when her father died, the script played itself out to a tragic end. Devastated by the loss, her mother turned to her young son for solace, unaware that her daughter, the perceived strong one, possessed a fragile soul of unrequited grief. Mel was left to fend for herself, more isolated and alone than ever.

The last day of her father's life, Mel had rushed home from school, eager to see him after his long road trip. During his absence, he had missed her performance as Little Red Riding Hood, where she was the star of the fifth grade play. Just for him, she put on her crimson costume, all set to reenact her role. But Maxx had an agenda too. He wanted ice cream, right away. When their father suggested waiting until after Mel's show, Maxx threw a tantrum. Eunice, as usual, sided with her son. *What's the harm? He doesn't ask for much. Mel can wait a few more minutes.* There were other words spoken and details long since blurred, but this is what Mel remembered: her mother and brother locked in alliance; her dad, the mediator, rising from his chair, agreeing to get ice cream from Parson's Dairy, a few blocks over, tossing a kiss to Mel, promising to return quickly.

Moments later, there was a shriek of brakes and the loaded half-second of silence before a dreaded crash. *Daddy!* Mel ran to the door, her clammy hand unable at first to grasp the knob. Outside, she screamed at the sight of her father's beige Buick, horribly battered and scrunched on the driver's side. A hump of bloodied blue lay on the street, her father's face eerily twisted toward his back. A Parson's plastic bag flickered in the breeze, hemmed down by one of the large metal chunks of car that littered the street. Mel felt daggers on her shoulders and arms; it was her mother, trying to keep her from moving toward the immobile heap on the ground, the heap that used to be her father. *Let me go,* she pleaded, but her mother held firm, her tears mixing with Mel's onto the splattered glass at their feet.

Afterward, everything had moved in slow motion. Friends and neighbors trooped in, shaking their heads and whispering nervously. Uniformed police took notes, wearing the same shade of blue that Mel's father had on. A drunk driver ran a light, they said. Rotten timing. Such a shame. Mel's father and the other driver both died instantly. Mr. Brewster, who lived across the street, kept asking what he could do. In an odd voice, Eunice mumbled a short list of instructions, then Mel clearly heard—*vanilla, Maxx's favorite.*

The night her father died, Mel had watched her mother and brother eat ice cream. And for that, she had never forgiven them.

She closed Sasha's top dresser drawer filled with underwear and pajamas. The bracelet was nowhere to be found. Sasha must have moved it. Just as well, she thought. The bracelet was Sasha's gift; Sasha should send it. But as she walked out of the room, Mel noticed green and white tissue paper rolled in a ball on the edge of the desk. She picked it up. A name tag was tied around the middle. *Joyeux Noel* was printed in the center. Next to the "To" Sasha had written *Grandmere,* and next to "From" *Votre Petite-fille, Avec Amour.* They often wrote in French, exchanging postcards and letters, Sasha having to translate for Mel. Years ago when Sasha was given a choice of a foreign language, Mel had advised her to take Spanish. "You'll get more use from it," she had said. "Hispanics are the fastest growing ethnic group in this country." But Sasha opted to take French because her grandmother lived in France. To Mel, an appreciation for a foreign language was the one real asset her mother had given Sasha. And not much else.

When Mel returned to the living room, Maxx was flipping through a *National Geographic.*

"Thought you'd drowned up there."

"Nope. Just took a minute to find it. Here." She handed him the package. "Make sure she knows Sasha made it herself."

"Will do." He slid the magazine back into its proper place. "Guess I'll get out of here. I have a lot of work to finish before I split town." But he didn't budge from his seat. "Look," he started, "I want to talk to you about Builder and what's going on with the business. And about your job situation. I know things are pretty rough for you guys right now. I wanted to leave something for you."

Mel started to object.

"For the family," Maxx said quickly, "just to tide you over. Consider it a long-term, interest-free loan. I know you'll pay me back when you can." He reached into his breast pocket but Mel stopped him short.

"Absolutely not. No way am I going to take your money."

"Come on, this is just a temporary arrangement. Let me help you out."

"I said no, Maxx."

"But why not? You need money; I've got it to spare. Big deal. Families are supposed to help each other. You'd help me if I needed it."

"That'd be different."

"Why?"

"You know why. We've been through this before."

"Oh, so it'd be okay for me to accept money from you, but you have too much pride to take it from me?"

"Pride has nothing to do with it, and you know it. It's because of what you do."

Maxx opened his hands, palms up. "My conscience is clear," he said innocently. "I don't have anything to feel guilty about."

"Well, you *should* feel guilty, defending those sleaze balls that you call clients."

"You know you really need to get off this shtick. You act like I'm the sole person responsible for the drug problem in America. I may have one or two clients who—"

"One or two clients?" she said mockingly. "Now who's kidding who?"

"Look, people deserve a defense; that's what I went to school for. It's what I do for a living."

"That's no excuse and you know it. You're no public defender at the mercy of the court, stuck with the dregs of society. You've got your own practice, a *private* practice, and a very lucrative one at that. You can pick and choose the people you want to defend."

"You're right. And there's nothing wrong with defending people who get in trouble simply because they're involved with drugs."

"*Simply?* Listen to yourself."

"People make mistakes, Mel. Would you lock them up and throw away the key without even giving them a trial? What happened to all your wonderful, democratic ideals?"

"Remember what Du Bois said—if you're not part of the solution, you're part of the problem."

"Hey, I'm not the problem!"

"You're contributing to it," Mel insisted. "These people make their living off drugs, Maxx. You know that. And when you defend them, you might as well be selling drugs just like the guys on the street."

"Come on. Get serious."

"I am serious. The criminal justice system is a joke. You've said it yourself many times. Folks are barely even processed before they're out the door. Bail is set at what—twenty-five thousand dollars, fifty thousand, two hundred thousand? No problem. They've got the money in hand even before the ink's dry. And you're there making it happen. Just speeding the process along."

"*Me?* How'd I get in the middle of this?"

"That's what you do when you represent these people. You argue for lower bail, or you get them off on some technicality. It's all just a game to you. Meanwhile, people are dying every day over this crap."

"You act like I'm senior counsel to the Medellin Cartel," Maxx said with a smirk. "Believe me, the clients I deal with are small fry, and nothing at all like you've made them out to be. They only represent maybe twenty percent of my practice, at the most."

"I'm no fool, Maxx. The real number's probably closer to ninety percent."

"Nah, it's nothing like that," he denied. "Besides, like I've told you before, these folks are business people. There's a market out there, a need, and they're providing a service. Simple as that. Now, you may not approve of what they do—and I'm not saying I totally agree with it either—but they're basically decent, everyday people. And I bet if one of them walked in here right now, and started talking to you, you'd say, 'Wow, he's really a nice guy.' "

Mel snickered. "Hardly."

"You'd be surprised. Like one case I'm working on now. This kid named Lorenzo. He's nineteen years old, really a good kid. He got busted because he was hanging out with a group that was into crack. There was a bust in the apartment where he just happened to be visiting and, pow"
—Maxx smacked his hand—"next thing you know he's charged with possession and distribution. He was scooped up in the whole deal because he was at the wrong place at the wrong time. He swears he doesn't know anything about it; he was just an innocent bystander."

"Of course. Everybody's always innocent. No one ever sees or hears anything."

"He has a credible case."

"Surely you don't believe him?"

"The point is, a lot of people I see are in the same situation—first-time offenders, clean-cut kids who just took a wrong turn. They deserve a second chance."

"And here comes Righteous Maxx, ready to give it to them." She shook her finger at him. "Be honest. Most of the people you defend are hard-core dealers who've been at this for years, and when they get caught, they count on lawyers like you to get them off."

Maxx shrugged his shoulders. "Like I said, everybody deserves a defense."

"But do you have to sell out your soul along the way?" she asked, frustrated. "Every action has a consequence, you know." Her voice dropped lower. "Sooner or later, you'll have to pay the piper, Maxx."

For a moment, neither spoke.

"Are you still charging ten thousand dollars to give out your home phone number?" she asked suddenly. "Only for special clients, right?" Her voice drooled with sarcasm.

"Where'd you hear that from?"

"So it's true? You're not denying it."

"If people are willing to pay—so be it."

She looked at him with disappointment. "You know, Maxx, all your talent is just gone to waste. It's really sinful."

"So, what are you now—my judge, jury, *and* priest? Wake up, Mel. The world doesn't turn in black and white." He stood to leave, placing the green and white package inside his jacket. "Tell Sasha I'll take care of her special delivery. Have a good Christmas."

She followed him to the front door and watched him drive off. Why couldn't she make him see? He was so caught up in the seductive web of fast money that he could rationalize anything. And for what? It didn't have to be this way. If money was what he was after, he could make a good living being a corporate attorney. How much would it take to satisfy him? It's not as though they were *that* deprived when they were growing up. There were hard times, yes, but they managed. What was he trying to prove? It angered her no end to think of all the good he could be doing. Instead, he was heading straight for the sewer.

She was about to shut the door when the mail truck pulled up to the front yard. The mailbox was at the left edge of the lawn, but the white-haired postal carrier bypassed it, stopping at the mouth of the walkway. He got out of his truck to walk toward the house.

Probably another letter from a creditor, Mel thought distastefully. Something else to sign for.

She used to love going to the mailbox, getting unexpected samples of detergent or cologne, receiving notices from stores about a private sale for preferred customers. But during these last few months she had begun to hate the ritual of opening the mail. There were precious few gems to discover; instead, she received mostly white envelopes with windows, or curtly worded overdue reminders, and almost always, it seemed, some certified or registered packet that threatened court action if a debt wasn't immediately paid. Going to the mailbox had become her daily dread.

She stepped down from the porch to meet the mailman halfway. "If all you have are bills for me, then you can keep right on going," she said, trying to be cheerful. "Just pretend you forgot where I live."

"Aw, I can't do that," he said with a slow grin. "My boss would have my hide." He sifted through several envelopes until he found two that were tagged with the familiar green cards on back. "I have a couple things that need your John Hancock," he said, reaching for the pen behind his ear.

"A *couple?* Wow, I really hit the jackpot today." Her facade was breaking, and she could feel angry tears behind her eyes.

"You know what they say: When you're hot, you're hot."

"Yeah. And when you're not—" She let the sentence dangle.

The mailman held out a clipboard for Mel to sign for the first letter, from Peach State Doors and Windows, one of Builder's suppliers. Several of his creditors had tracked him down at his home address, evidently because correspondence sent to his office had gone unanswered. Mel hurriedly scribbled on the line for "agent," anxious to speed up the loathsome task.

The second envelope was addressed to both her and Builder. She glanced at the upper left-hand corner—Trent Academy. That was odd, she thought. Why would Sasha's school send the first semester report card by certified mail? Maybe it was a new school policy, an extra step to make sure parents saw their children's grades.

She walked back into the house, holding the rest of the mail in the crook of her arm, as she opened the letter from Trent. The stark black words printed on the crisp stationery jumped out at her.

Dear Mr. and Mrs. Burke:
It is with much regret that we must inform you that we will no longer be able to accept your daughter Sasha as a student at Trent Academy.

"What?" Mel cried out. She continued to read, disbelieving.

During this school year, three tuition payments which you submitted were subsequently returned for insufficient funds. While these checks were eventually paid, we can no longer allow this pattern of submitting bad checks to continue. Most recently, we received yet another check (see enclosed), which was also returned by your bank for insufficient funds.

You must understand that we are not in a position to subsidize any part of your daughter's tuition or to permit consistently late payments. The contractual agreement you signed when Sasha first enrolled clearly stipulates the financial obligations required of the parent or guardian to maintain a student's good standing at our institution.

We are sorry that it has become necessary to terminate your daughter's matriculation at Trent. Sasha is a fine young scholar, and we have enjoyed having her as a member of the Student Body. We wish her well as she continues her education in another academic environment.

You can be assured that we will expeditiously make Sasha's records available to whichever school you request.

> *Sincerely,*
> *Harvey B. Pryor*
> *Principal*

"Damn it!" Mel cursed. "Damn it! Who do they think they are?"

She flung the letter and the rest of the mail onto the dining room table, causing the crystal vase of tulips to overturn. She watched, immobile, as water ran down the center of the mahogany wood, and a spidery crack marred one side of the fragile vase. She picked up the letter and read it again, her hands shaking slightly. How could this be? She looked at the attached check marked NSF. Damn it, Builder, she accused. Why didn't you tell me? It was his responsibility to make the tuition payments, although since she had lost her job, Mel knew he was struggling like heck to carry the extra load. There had been a couple of late payments—but they had made the checks good. To kick Sasha out of school for something like that? What about all the years when they *had* been on time? Didn't that count for something? Poor Sasha. How would she take this? She loved Trent, felt comfortable there, and had her own set of friends. But now, they'd have to pull her out, make her change schools in the middle of the year, and send her to God knows where.

Feeling sorry for her daughter as well as herself, Mel distractedly opened several Christmas cards, not really reading them, just going through the motions, trying to keep her hands busy so her mind wouldn't have to work. The last card contained a greeting that was simple and direct. Beautifully embossed in bold silver letters stood the scripted word: *Peace.* Mel shook her head in denial. Not here, she thought. And not on the horizon.

CHAPTER 4

"Daddy, can't you *do* something?"

Sasha was on the verge of tears, her long legs stretched atop the faded tiger comforter on her bed, a matching tiger-striped pillow pressed against her chest. She landed pleading eyes on her father, looking to him for a way out.

Mel felt like the fall guy. Once again, she was the bearer of bad news. For the past half hour, she and Builder had been trying to explain to Sasha that, because of financial pressures, she would have to change schools. But Mel was the one who had actually spoken the words, who had delivered the hurtful blow. Now, Sasha looked to Builder, not Mel, for solace.

"Like I said, Baby, your mother and I agree this is the best solution. I know it's not going to be easy for you. But it's only a temporary situation, just till the end of the school year. Then, maybe you can go back to Trent and—"

"Builder, please!" Mel interrupted. "Don't promise her that."

He shot her a glance, but Mel stood her ground. The last thing their family needed was more deception, more unrealistic expectations. "We don't know how long it's going to be, Sasha," she said. "But it's not the end of the world. You'll meet new friends, and—"

"I don't want new friends! I like the ones I have."

"You'll still have those too," Builder assured her.

"But it won't be the same. I'll never get to see them, and we won't be able to do things together anymore and—Daddy, please! Don't send me to Duncan. I don't know anybody there."

Mel saw Builder's look of distress. This was as hard for him as it was for their daughter.

"Oh, you do know people there," Mel said cheerily. "There's Lauren Bolton from your Girl Scout Troop, remember? And Janis Price in your dance class. I saw her mother the other day, and she said Janis *loves* Duncan." Mel leaned closer. "I asked around, darling, making sure it was the best school available."

"The best school is Trent. And you're taking me out of there."

Mel pulled back. "We have no choice, Sasha. We can't afford it."

"What about Uncle Maxx? He has money."

Mel and Builder exchanged looks. Last night they had discussed this very thing or, more accurately, had fought over it. Mel made her usual argument, that taking money from Maxx, even for Sasha's education, would be condoning his drug connections. Builder said it was stupid to put Sasha through so much turmoil when they could borrow the money from Maxx on a short-term basis. Mel shot back that it wouldn't be short-term, that the other loans from Maxx, supposedly short-term, still hadn't been repaid. Besides, she had added, it was the principle that counted, and that as Sasha's parents, they were the ones ultimately responsible for their daughter's schooling. And so it went, back and forth. They did agree on one thing—that if asked, Maxx would readily pay the money to keep his niece at Trent. But it became a moot point. With Maxx away in France, and Mel unwilling to contact him at her mother's house, Builder reluctantly caved in. But he blamed Mel for making a bad situation worse.

"Uncle Maxx is out of the country," Mel said now to Sasha. "And besides, we can't turn to him every time we have a problem."

"He's at Grandma's, right?" said Sasha hopefully. "Just call him. I know he'll do it."

"This is a family problem," Mel spoke firmly, "and we'll solve it as a family."

"But Uncle Maxx is family too!"

"That's enough, Sasha!" Mel said sharply. "A decision has been made, and it's final." Then, she added gently, "You act like we're dropping you in some wild jungle or something. We wouldn't do that. Look, *I* went to public school. So did Daddy. We turned out all right, didn't we?" It was a lame reach for humor, and a failed one. Sasha immediately squashed all relevancy.

"Times were different when you were young. You've said so yourself."

Amazing how children can recall certain things at will, when it suits their purposes, thought Mel. She tried to sound upbeat. "Well, I'm convinced this is going to be a good move for you. Just give it a chance."

"But they have *guns* at Duncan," said Sasha, sounding what she knew would be a red alert. "A lot of kids carry guns and knives and all kinds of weapons."

Builder flinched at the image. "Mel, I don't know, maybe we should reconsider."

She ignored his comment, choosing to respond directly to Sasha.

"It's not correct to say 'a lot' of kids carry weapons. There were some problems in the past, yes, but I understand it was a handful of boys stirring up trouble, and they've been expelled. And there's a new principal over there who's made some wonderful changes in the school. You'll be just fine."

Knowing that her cause was lost with Mel, Sasha turned again to Builder. "But, Daddy," she protested, "I don't want to go. I know I won't like it."

"Look," said Builder, holding Sasha's chin. "We're a family here, okay? And that means, we have to stick together. What happens to one person affects everybody. Your mother and I will be there for you. Understand?"

Outnumbered, Sasha dropped her eyes and said sullenly, "Yes, Daddy."

Mel rose from the opposite side of the bed, where she had been sitting, and watched the two of them commiserate—Builder, trying to console the inconsolable. She looked at an oversized wall calendar where Sasha had carefully logged her after-school activities in the squared-off spaces marking each day: Tuesdays, flute; Wednesdays, gymnastics; Thursdays, glee club; Fridays, drill team practice. Mel swallowed hard. Her daughter's life certainly would change. Many of these activities at Trent wouldn't be available at the new school. Sasha would have a lot of adjusting in the coming months. Mel's eyes roved over to the right side of the calendar. Under Saturdays, Sasha had printed "ballet, 12:00." Well, at least that would remain a constant. Sasha had taken ballet since she was five, and Mel made a silent vow that nothing would interfere with those lessons.

"Everything was all right until *you* stopped working," Sasha suddenly blurted out in a hostile tone. "None of this would have happened if you had gotten another job."

Stunned by the accusation, Mel whirled around to face her daughter, whose red-stressed, teary eyes had narrowed with blame. From Sasha's view, Mel was clearly the culprit responsible for this upheaval in her young life.

"I've tried getting another job," Mel said, walking back toward the bed. "It's just not that easy."

"Yes, it is," Sasha insisted, wiping her eyes. "You just don't want me to be happy."

"Oh, that's ridiculous, and you know it," said Mel, losing all patience and empathy. "Nobody likes being in this situation. This is not my fault." She looked over at Builder for backup.

"Your mother's right," he said. "This isn't her fault. She's done all she could to keep things going around here." But his words sounded half-hearted, as though he doubted their veracity.

Mel noted how he referred to her as "your mother," rather than the more affectionate "your mom," which is what he usually called her when speaking to Sasha. When Builder used "your mother," it meant he was angry; and he was using that title a lot lately. "Your mother" sounded stiff and formal, like she was some cold-hearted distant person with whom he had no connection. She felt like an outsider in her own home, as though somehow she was the one who had incurred this fate. How could they stand as a united front when Builder didn't believe in his own gospel of "family"?

"There're a lot of reasons why things are really tight right now," Mel explained. "When I lost my job, that certainly didn't help our situation, but also, you should know that the business is not doing very well"—she paused, then decided that Sasha deserved to know more—"in fact, it hasn't been doing well for some time," she clarified, staring directly at Builder. If he wouldn't tell Sasha, then damn it, she would. She was not going to take all the weight for this. If it was anyone's fault, it was more Builder's than hers.

But Sasha placed the blame solely on Mel's shoulders. "You haven't been working in months!" she exclaimed. "If you would just get out and get another job—"

"Now just a minute," began Mel.

"All right now," Builder addressed Sasha. "You remember who you're talking to. You hear me?" His voice had a sharp edge.

Sasha surrendered a weak nod.

"Now apologize to your mother."

She heaved deeply and gave Mel a furtive glance. "Sorry," she said faintly, then buried her face into a linty tissue, sobbing.

"Now, now, it's all right," said Builder, melting. He put his arms around her, patting her back.

Mel pulled out a fresh tissue from a box on the night stand and laid it next to Sasha. "I'm going to start dinner," she announced. She recalled the adage that mothers are the glue of the family, the one who holds things together. How ironic, she thought. Right now, she wasn't doing much holding, by any measure. Sasha had designated Builder for that role, and he had totally acquiesced. Mel left the two of them, huddled.

She felt that sometimes Builder babied Sasha, that he was too sheltering and overprotective. As a consequence, Sasha had it far too easy, and frequently exhibited spoiled, self-centered behavior. Mel had seen evidence of brooding brattiness, especially in the past year. But this wasn't the time to bring that up. Certainly, Sasha had every right to be upset; she was, after all, about to experience a major change in her life that she had no control over. But for her to jump on the bandwagon with Builder and blame Mel for this predicament—that was all wrong.

In the kitchen, Mel rinsed carrots, broccoli, and celery, and vigorously chopped the raw vegetables. As she worked, she thought about her relationship with her own father, how much she revered him, how safe she felt when he was around, how lost when he was gone. They had a special father-daughter bond that no one could ever breach.

She knew that Builder and Sasha had that same kind of bond. She also knew it was important to Builder that Sasha not lose respect for him, that she saw him as the caring father who worked hard to provide for his family. And certainly, he was that. Yet, Sasha had no idea that the family's financial downturn wasn't simply a matter of being caught up in a storm of bad economic timing, as Builder had explained. It was also due to poor business decisions Builder himself had made—like using household money for business debt, and taking on more projects than he could handle, which stretched him too thin. If she had her way, Mel would have told Sasha the full story, or, preferably, would have had Builder tell her. It wasn't necessary that Sasha know specifics, but Mel thought Builder should at least own up to his part in this fiasco. "Making mistakes is a part of life," she had told him last night, "and we need to prepare Sasha for these kinds of things. She needs to know that you're not perfect, that no one's invincible." But it was as though he was afraid that if he were completely honest with his daughter, she would think ill of him, would think that he had let her down, and would love him less.

For her part, Mel went along with Builder's explanation—a bad economy—as the reason why Sasha had to change schools. But now Sasha was blaming *her!* and since her unemployment was the only tangible thing that had changed these past months, she could understand why. Sasha was a child, still, and didn't know any better. But Builder's lukewarm defense was inexcusable. To remain silent like that, not to speak up for her and not to admit his own goofs—that disturbed her more than Sasha's finger pointing.

She was straining to open a large bottle of apple juice when Builder walked in.

"Here, let me do it." He took the bottle from her and in one short twist, opened the lid.

"What do people with arthritis do?" Mel asked absently.

Builder sat at the kitchen table and ran his finger along the swirly grain of wood. "I got her quieted down. She'll probably be out for a while."

"Good. She needs to rest. At least now she knows. That part's over."

Builder pounded the table once with an open hand. "Damn! I hate having to take her out of Trent."

Mel carried two glasses of juice and joined him at the table.

"I tried reasoning with the principal," he said.

"Dr. Pryor?"

"Yeah. They told me he was on Christmas break, but I tracked him down."

"When was all this? What happened?"

"I saw him a couple days ago, right after you told me about the letter. He hemmed and hawed, said he was following school guidelines. The usual bull."

"These people want their money, Builder."

"I know that. And they're right—to a point. But they make exceptions when they want to. They do it all the time."

"So what did he say?"

"Oh, he was really into this holier-than-thou thing—laid back in his twerpy little suit, and there I was in my work clothes. I had just come off a job."

"Well, obviously, you couldn't come to terms with him."

"No. I even said I'd pay the rest of the year's tuition up front."

"How were you going to do that?"

"I don't know. I was just trying to buy some time. I would have gotten it somehow."

Maxx, she thought, but didn't say anything.

They sat there, silent, sipping tepid apple juice, and gazing at the walls, the table, the floor, as though searching for some outside intervention.

"Look," Builder said finally, "I know it doesn't seem like it now, but if you can just hang on a little while longer, just hang on, I'll turn this thing around. We're getting there, believe me, we're getting there."

"*Getting* there?" Mel asked incredulously. "How can you possibly say that?" It amazed her that he could remain in a state of denial, even in the midst of financial collapse. "We're worse off now than we've ever been," she said, wondering what it would take to shake him up and make him realize the seriousness of their situation.

"I'm telling you, just hold on. I've got a check coming from the Thomas job and I should be finished with the basement over on Flamingo any day now. I just have to set in a wet bar and do some trimming out. So, some money'll be coming in by next week. And I'll have enough to—"

"Builder," interrupted Mel, "just don't say it, okay? I'm tired of hearing it. It's always, 'next week,' 'next month,' 'next project.' But things never materialize. What about now? We need the money now!"

If only she could shake this man up! Open his skull and pour it in. Make him realize that his dream of having a viable business would have to be placed on hold, waylaid until better times. That they both needed to take some drastic measures to salvage what they had worked so hard for all these years.

"You've said it yourself," said Mel. "The only reason you've kept the business going this long is because I was able to cover the household. But I can't handle it anymore. Ever since I lost my job, everything's gone to pot."

Just talking about their problems made them loom larger than ever, and Mel wanted Builder to feel every bit of her pain.

"The second mortgage is way overdue. There's nothing left in Sasha's education fund; I had to use that money to keep the first mortgage current and make those back payments on the second. And we're still not caught up. The car insurance is due, the health insurance is due—I don't know how we're going to pay it all. And bounced checks are flying in here every which way."

She took a deep breath, thinking of all the money wasted on bounced check fees, money that could be used for food or utilities or to keep a roof over their heads. "I don't know why you insist on writing checks when you know there's no money in the account," she continued. "Why, we probably could have kept Sasha in school for all the money wasted on bounced check fees alone. Just in the past few weeks, we've been charged hundreds of dollars. That's absolutely ridiculous. It's killing us."

"I know, I know," he said quietly. "From now on, you handle all the checks for the house."

"You keep saying that, and for a couple of days, fine, you won't write any checks. But then you'll fall back into the same old habit. I don't understand it. I mean, how many times have we talked about this?"

"Look, I said I wouldn't write any more checks and I won't." He spat out the words, his full lips folding inward to form a thin, mean line. "What you don't know is, a couple of large checks I got from customers bounced on me, and that put all my shit out of whack. It makes me look bad. Now I've got people on my back screaming for their money." With an angry thrust of his fingers, he pushed away the half-full glass. "Those damn banks. Charging twenty dollars for a bounced check—that's highway robbery. It's a rip-off."

"Actually, they've gone up to twenty-two," Mel said, adding salt to the wound.

They said nothing for a minute.

"What about savings?" he asked suddenly.

"Savings?" Mel gave a sarcastic laugh. "What savings? What little bit we had is long gone."

"All of it?"

"Builder, I told you that some time ago, way back in the fall," Mel said, exasperated. "See, that's part of the problem. You won't even talk to me about these things, and when I try to, you don't listen."

He dismissed this latest salvo, dwelling instead on the state of their savings, or lack thereof. "I thought we had *something* left," he said. He grabbed the rear of his neck and wrenched his head back, as though in pain.

In an instant, Mel felt two conflicting emotions: an overwhelming compassion for her husband, knowing that despite his best efforts, things still weren't working, and at the same time, an unrelenting blame. After all, it was his poor business management and unwise use of their household money to pay business debt that had created their problems. And just as one contrasting emotion eventually yields to another, in this instance, blame overruled compassion. Watching Builder in his private torment, Mel thought of how his suffering, by its very nature, had sucked her into the undertow. His drowning had also become hers and Sasha's. And that, she found unforgivable.

Builder picked at a fleck of dirt beneath his nail. "I can't think about this right now. This stress is killing me. I can't even sleep at night, worried about how I'm going to pay this bill and that bill." He looked at her with pitiful eyes and released a deep sigh. "Why don't we give it a rest for now? Go on upstairs—cool out for a minute."

It was a backhanded way of saying "let's make love," but it was an invitation that Mel could not accept. Not with this heavy blame in her heart, not with her growing resentment of a man that she was quickly losing patience with.

"I've got to get dinner," she replied. "And besides, we can't gloss this over with sex. The problems are still going to be there. We have to deal with it."

"Fine," he said, irritated. "We'll deal with it. But what do you want me to do? Stop living? I'm working my butt off every day. I can't do any more. I can't bring it in any faster. You and I haven't been together in weeks."

"And whose fault is that?"

"Oh, so this is my fault too? It's all my fault that we haven't screwed, is that it?"

"It's after midnight when you come home, Builder. *Every single night.* By the time you get in, I'm half-asleep; I'm out of it. What do you expect me to do? Roll over and play the loving wife?"

His eyes narrowed into the same hateful gaze that Sasha had given her earlier. "You know something? Forget it. What do I expect from you? Nothing. Not a damn thing. I don't want anything from you." He leaned back in the chair, as though trying to move further away from her. "I don't know what your problem is, walking around here like you've got some chip on your shoulder. But let me tell you something. You haven't exactly been filling up the kitty lately. Or haven't you noticed? You're so busy looking at my shit and blaming me for everything. What about you? That part-time teaching job and a few proposals you're supposedly putting together—what's that about? It's not as though you're raking money in here in droves. And I don't see you out there sweatin' bullets to get a job. So get off this high and mighty trip. The only time you have two words to say to me is when you want to talk about some bill that's overdue or how something else needs fixing around here. Well, I'm not your damn repair man. I live here." At this last pronouncement, he hit his index finger harshly on the table.

The sting of his words pierced her to the core. Mel sat there, stunned by his ferocious tone, his ugly scowl. It was rare for him to speak to her that way. All of his resentment and frustration, built up over the past months, vented out in one mean swoop. She was the unlucky target, momentarily caught off guard, unable to put up a defense.

The phone rang, loud and penetrating. Builder was closest to it, but made no move to answer. Mel was grateful for the intrusion. She escaped from Builder's acute line of vision and walked behind him to pick up the wall phone.

"Hello?" She tried to sound normal, not wanting to give Builder the satisfaction of knowing that she was shaken by his harangue.

She listened to the person on the other end, then said calmly, "Just a minute. He's right here." She handed Builder the phone. "It's for you." Her voice was icy, even to her own ears.

He waved her off, getting up to leave. "I don't want to talk to anybody."

Mel stood in the doorway, blocking him. She held the phone at his chest, leaving him no room to ignore it. He wasn't going to walk out on this one, not if she could help it. A few minutes ago, she would have told the bill collector that no, Builder was not at home, and that she didn't know when he would be back. But not now. Not after the way he had treated her. He needed to be punished. He should be forced to listen to the bill collector, as she had listened so many times before. She had to get him back in some way.

"It's Simon Weaver, Atlantic Financial," she said, deliberately loud. "He's waiting."

Builder gave Mel a stony look, the two of them deadlocked in palpable dislike. Determined to win this battle, Mel continued her silent taunt, dangling the phone in her husband's face. For the moment, it was the only weapon she could wield. Finally, Builder yielded, snatching the phone out of her hand, taking as many steps away from Mel as the cord would allow.

"Hello," he said, brusquely.

Mel felt a twinge of satisfaction, but only a twinge. This ugly side of Builder was frightening, almost dangerous. She knew he had a short fuse, and although in their fourteen years of marriage he had never hit her, she could tell that this time he had come close. Just as frightening, however, was that a part of her almost wanted him to do it, dared him to do it. Then, she would have one more damning piece of evidence to hold against him. This whole thing was sick, that's what it was. Sick. What on earth was happening to them?

She walked to the sink, half listening to Builder's curt responses— "Yeah, I know it's late. Yeah, I'm working on it." He muttered something about making a payment next week. She shook her head, knowing it wouldn't happen.

A stray carrot that she must have missed earlier sat idly in the sink. Mel placed it on the cutting board and made quick jabs at the tough orange skin. Her hand slipped, causing the knife to gash her left thumb. She let out a cry of pain. Blood gushed onto the clear plastic of the cutting board and etched a path of red into the sink. She held up her thumb, surveying the damage. It was a deep cut, jagged, still oozing blood. How could such a small knife do so much damage? She wondered if she would need stitches. Behind her, Builder slammed down the phone. He walked over and put his index finger just inches from her nose.

"Don't you *ever* do that to me again, you hear?"

Flinching from the pain of her throbbing thumb, Mel was too surprised to respond. She saw Builder's eyes drop to her bloody finger, but his face remained unchanged. Then, for a second, she thought she saw a hint of pleasure, a gleam of triumph. Perhaps, to him, this was her just punishment, her rightful penance.

He stalked out of the kitchen, offering no words of concern about her injury.

Mel ran cool water over her bleeding cut and watched the pink swirl settle in the well of the sink. She reached for a paper towel to bandage her wound, her eyes smarting from the stinging shoots of pain. Even more hurtful, however, was the realization that, along with declining funds and self-esteem, her husband had lost his heart.

"And this one's absolutely lovely. I might even put it in the front window."

The manager of Sweet Seconds admiringly held a red velvet dress with puffy chiffon sleeves, the latest pullout from Mel's assortment of young girl finery. "Honestly, sometimes I wish I could pump up some of these clothes so they could fit *me!* They make the cutest things for children."

"Yes, they do," Mel agreed. But she was calculating what she might get for the large box full of fancy dresses and coats. They were mostly gifts from Maxx, clothes that Sasha had either long outgrown or hardly worn. They were in excellent condition, like the velvet dress, which Sasha had worn just once to a concert.

"Oh, this is gorgeous," gushed the manager, picking up a coat of white lamb's wool. She pushed her glasses toward her temples, peering closer at the label. "Great—it's a Sylvia White. And a ten too. A very popular size."

"Now, that's virtually brand new," volunteered Mel. "See, the tags are still on it. The winters are so mild here, my daughter never had a chance to wear it."

"Well, quite a few of our customers go to Vail for winter vacations or to the north Georgia mountains to ski. And it certainly gets cold enough there. A coat like this would be perfect for a little girl."

Mel smiled, pleased that she had thought of coming here today, glad that she had thinned out Sasha's overstuffed closet by removing years' worth of unused items.

"So, how much do you think I'll get for these things?" she asked casually, trying not to sound too anxious.

"It's hard to tell. We'll certainly put a good price on them. And as I said, I don't think there'll be any problem selling them." Her inspection complete, the manager pulled out an inventory sheet to record her new merchandise. "I'll need for you to fill out a contract," she added, writing busily. "Assuming that we sell some of these things in the next cycle, you can expect a check in about six weeks."

"What?" said Mel, feigning surprise. "Not till then?"

"Well, yes, that's the way things work. Even if something were sold today, we wouldn't be able to pay you for it until the end of next month. It's our policy."

Of course. The policy. Mel knew all about it. It was the way most consignment shops did business. She had called around and was told the same story, that it usually took several weeks after a sale before a commission check was mailed. She had decided, though, that she would take her chances at appealing to what she hoped would be the good business sense of the person in charge. She needed to get a payment on the spot. She wasn't sure how she was going to do it; she just knew she had to. She needed every cent she could put her hands on—fast. It was time now to go into her act. Lord, help me, she implored silently.

"Are you telling me it's not your policy to give an advance on certain items?" Mel deliberately sounded confused and flustered.

"Absolutely not. We never give advances. Read the contract there."

Complying, Mel scanned the designated portion that the manager pointed to. "But I was under the impression that you gave an initial payment for certain items that you know will sell right away."

The manager scoffed at the suggestion. "I don't know where you got that idea. No consignment shop operates like that. We couldn't stay in business if we did."

"But these things will practically sell themselves," Mel insisted, placing a hand atop the pile of clothes on the counter. "Surely you can work something out."

"I'm sorry, but that's not how it's done." She was sympathetic, but firm. "We don't give advances. Not ever."

Mel thought quickly. She wondered what Val would do in a situation like this. Probably pack up the clothes, act as if she couldn't possibly do business here, and threaten to take her things somewhere else. But where? There wasn't exactly a hue and cry for second-hand clothes, no matter how good a shape they were in. And trying to sell them at a flea market or garage sale wouldn't bring in nearly as much. Mel had heard that this store gave the best percentages in town. Located in Buckhead, it had a lot of bargain-seeking, quality-conscious patrons from around the city, and was the premier outlet for expensive castoffs.

"Do you want to leave them or not?" asked the manager, beginning to lose patience. She stopped writing and looked up at Mel. "They're very nice, and I'd like to have them, but, of course, it's up to you."

Suddenly the clothes had been demoted from "lovely" and "gorgeous" to simply "nice." People are a trip, Mel thought. Always out for as much as they could get. But then, that was her own mission for today, and she couldn't afford to fail.

"You *are* the owner of the shop, aren't you?" In negotiations, *play to the ego,* a lesson she had learned years ago at the Chamber.

"Actually, I'm the manager. The owner's out of town."

"Well, even so, you must have the authority to make such decisions."

"Of course, I have the authority," said the manager, raising her chin a notch. "But we have rules and regulations, and I have to honor them."

"I understand. But then, there are times when legitimate exceptions are made, right? I mean, surely the owner wouldn't want you to pass up all *this!*" Mel stretched out her arms above the mountain of goods.

The manager twitched her brow, indicating the start of a meltdown. Then, almost as quickly, her resistance solidified again. "No, it wouldn't work. We're on a designated computer program. We have over two thousand consignors. I couldn't possibly keep track of advance payments for that many people."

Mel saw an opening and grabbed it. "You don't have to keep track of two thousand," she said hurriedly. "Just one."

Another brow twitch. Not allowing time for a counterargument, Mel decided to pull out all the stops.

"I'll be honest with you. I need money. I've got a problem at home, and I have to come up with some cash right away. You and I both know you won't have any difficulty selling these things. So—what do you say?"

The manager was taken aback by Mel's frankness. "I—I don't know," she wavered. "Maybe if you were a longtime customer. I don't even know you."

Mel fished in her purse for her wallet. She retrieved several cards from plastic covers and plunked them on top of the lamb's wool coat. "Here's my driver's license—my voter registration card—my ID from my job" (never mind that it was no good). "I've lived in Atlanta for over fifteen years, I'm married, have one daughter, and my favorite color is red. What else do you need to know?"

The woman chuckled, then relented. "All right." She surveyed the counter full of clothes before her. "I can give you—a hundred dollar advance."

"I need at least two," pressed Mel.

"That's impossible," said the manager, stiffening again. "A hundred tops. No more."

An elderly customer, who had come in earlier, ambled toward the counter.

"I'll be with you in a moment, ma'am," said the manager. "I'm about to finish up here."

"Take your time, dear. I'm just browsing. Looking for something for my granddaughter." She peered inquisitively at the display of ruffled and lace dresses among Mel's collection. "Pretty," she said to Mel. "You have some lovely things there." She waddled over to a nearby rack.

Mel felt like kissing the old woman for her perfectly timed remark. With increased confidence, she looked at the manager, who had also heard the unsolicited validation.

Minutes later, Mel left the shop with three crisp fifty dollar bills. She had hoped for more, but this was better than nothing. Her persistence had worked, with a little boost from an unexpected source.

She climbed into her car and cautiously backed onto bustling Pharr Road. One down; one to go.

The waxy smell of polished guns assaulted Mel almost as heavily as the harsh overhead lights. She passed rows of typewriters, VCRs, and camcorders and stopped underneath a sign labeled "Jewelry and Fine Accessories." This time, her cache rested in a large black garbage bag, tightly tied by a twister of thick plastic. With one hand on the throat of the bag and the other on the bottom, Mel carefully hoisted the weight onto the smudged counter top.

"Ahhh, I see you're back." Thick fingers drummed across the counter, which was not quite tall enough to hide a massive stomach that moved like Jell-O, swishing from side to side. The wobbly stomach belonged to the owner, Otis Blake.

"How are you?" Mel asked, trying to maintain some semblance of civility.

"Beautiful, now that I've seen you. And what have you brought me today? More goodies?"

Two weeks ago when Mel first came here, she had never before stepped into a pawn shop. She had been uneasy about putting up valued possessions for cash, but Blake had seemed pleasant enough, and had made the transaction almost painless. Today, though, his manner was already grating, too familiar. Perhaps, Mel thought, it's because he now saw her as a "regular," and didn't feel the need for pretense. It was clear that this second trip was no fluke. Being here once again made her keenly aware of drowning deeper and deeper into a muddy pit that she couldn't escape. And, no doubt, Blake was aware of it too. Perhaps that's why, instead of the artificial charm of a fortnight ago, the first thing Mel detected today was Blake's macroscopic greed, as his lumpy fingers dug into her bagged treasure.

"Ahhh, what have we here?" He smacked his lips lasciviously. "More good stuff." One by one, he pulled out a tray, pitcher, creamer, and sugar bowl, the makings of a sparkling silver tea service.

Mel had stayed up until 1:00 A.M. this morning, rubbing and polishing the myriad crevices that had darkened under months of neglect. She kept the service in a recessed corner of a makeshift butler's pantry that Builder had made when they first bought the house. Twice a year, for Christmas and Easter, she always restored the tea service to its original gleaming glory. But this past Christmas, with the household in a less-than-festive mood, Mel had left it untouched, collecting more tarnish and dust in its hideaway. And so it had stood, until last night, when she prepped it for perhaps its most important showing ever.

"You sure you want to part with this?"

"I may come back for it," she said wistfully, knowing full well that this was the last good-bye.

"You know you have thirty days. Same as before. Your time's coming up soon on those other things you brought in."

"I know," said Mel, especially remembering the emerald ring Builder had given her for their fifth anniversary.

Blake set the silver pieces on the serving tray. "Okay," he said, sizing up the booty. "Let's see what we can do for you today."

Yeah, right, thought Mel. You mean, rip me off. She had an overbearing sense of déjà vu.

"Two hundred bucks. I think that's more than a fair price."

"I thought you said this was 'good stuff,'" said Mel, throwing his words back at him. It was a limpid stab at flirting, but she had to up the ante somehow.

"Two hundred is a generous price. Mighty generous."

He had totally missed the double entendre. She would need to try harder. "Ferguson's downtown offered me two fifty off the bat," she said with a straight face. She was stretching the truth again, a defensive tactic that she found herself using more and more lately. She criticized Builder for doing it, for being less than honest with creditors, yet, here she was, just as guilty. And in this pawn shop, this unsavory business, truth stretching—lying—seemed almost natural. Worse yet, she was beginning not to know the difference, much. Or care. When it came to money, everything was up for grabs. It was a game, with one person trying to beat out the other, a game where every player, however unwittingly, got suckered into making rash moves. Even the "kings" were really pawns of various types, playing into a larger master hand.

"Aw, now, you wouldn't be trying to scam me, eh? I know Ferguson; he's tighter than a witch's tit."

The expression is *colder than a witch's tit*, Mel thought smugly. But now was not the time to show off her broad-based knowledge. Blake would not be corrected by her on this day.

"I'm offering you a fair price here," he said, almost liltingly.

"Oh, I think you can be much fairer," said Mel, knowing she had little room to play with. She was up a barrel and both of them knew it.

She looked at Blake—with his thin lips, fat fingers, and red face. My God, she thought, has it come to this? Reduced to selling off bits and pieces of her life, trying to eke out a few more dollars. She watched Blake's lips move, justifying his price. He had no lips, really, just a straight line where a mouth should be. She imagined him as an auctioneer, and herself, a slave on the block. He was calling out numbers, fast and furious, in a hurry to make a sale. Except he was going down in price, not up. She stood there, vulnerable. But then, there she was, also in the crowd, a powerless and unwilling participant, bidding on her own stuff, bidding on her own life. She tried to raise the price, to shout above the fray, but when she opened her mouth, the words fell silent. No one could hear. She saw herself on the block—open, exposed. Two hundred dollars? Is that all? For this black woman of high? Surely, she was worth more than that. But there were no takers. None to be found.

"All right, tell me," said Blake. "What would you consider a fair price?"

For his part, Blake enjoyed the back-and-forth bartering, and intended to prolong it as long as possible. Most of his customers were men, rough-and-tumble types with ashy elbows and stained overalls, who brought in merchandise from questionable sources. Occasionally, he'd get college students looking to pawn or buy a TV or stereo. Rarely did women come. The few who did usually smelled of fried foods and cigarettes and sported Jheri curls plastered to the hilt. This one, though, was different. She had class. She was a real lady, he could tell. And what a looker! Like warm sweet honey fresh out of a comb. He wondered what kind of trouble she was in to be getting rid of so many things so fast.

Eventually, they agreed on a price, one that was in favor of Blake. Mel left feeling as though Blake's greasy paws had scratched away the last protective coating that shielded her from the elements. Each item, pawned and sold, represented another layer that was stripped off. That's ludicrous, she chided herself. *I came to him in search of a deal. I needed money; he gave it. It's business, pure and simple.*

With the money from the consignment shop plus the $275 that she had dragged out of Blake, she could put something down on the gas bill, which was scheduled for immediate disconnection. And she could make at least a partial payment on the auto insurance, which otherwise would be canceled tomorrow. She tallied up several other bills that needed to be paid—yesterday—and wondered what was left that she could possibly sell.

Mel returned home at midafternoon as dark clouds signaled an imminent storm. She couldn't shake the feeling that she had been violated, trespassed against. She turned on the radio, preset to a jazz station. She needed to hear something soft and cozy. She would make some tea with special herbs; perhaps that would help her feel better. But when she turned on the kitchen faucet, nothing came out. Nothing. She tried again, to no avail. With a knot in her stomach, she raced into the bathroom and tried the faucet there, but it too produced nothing. Damn it! Damn *it!* The water was off. That was one bill she had completely forgotten.

She marched into her small office and rifled through her overstuffed bills folder, held together by a wide rubber band. Yep, there it was, confirmed in black and white. The scheduled cutoff day was listed for January 21, last week. So, the city had probably granted these few extra days as some sort of magnanimous gesture of goodwill.

Mel shook her head, disgusted. *All these years of paying on time,* she thought, *and now, when we've got problems, they cut us off—over seventy lousy dollars. And yet, certain corporations can owe thousands of dollars in back payments for years, and nothing's done about that.* She caught herself thinking like Builder, reasoning that someone else was at fault, or that she should be given a break for no apparent reason.

Well, they *had* to have water. She'd have to make a payment today, along with paying the gas bill and the auto insurance. She didn't have enough to cover all of that. She'd write the checks and hope that, some-how, somewhere, some money would come through before the checks cleared the bank. She thought again of Builder and how he routinely employed a strategy of blind faith and hopeful stalling.

Her head spinning, she went back outside to a hostile afternoon, her glum mood a grudging accomplice to the dark sky overhead.

Standing in line to pay the water bill, Mel kept her head straight, try-ing not to attract the eye of a familiar face. City Hall bristled with activ-ity—a lot of comings and goings, but, she guessed, little productivity. It was said that if you can't get a job anywhere else, try the city. Like Mikey, the kid in the cereal commercial who eats anything, the city will hire any-one. How she wished that were true now. If so, she probably could have gotten a job here months ago. But recently, even the city had reduced its labor force, leaving those still on the payroll frantically projecting at least the appearance of work in progress.

The line was not moving. A man up front was disputing the amount of his bill, holding up everyone else behind him. Mel kept her head down, pretending to be engrossed in a little notebook in which she was simply jotting gibberish.

"Mel? Is that you? It's been ages."

Caught, Mel forced herself to respond politely to a woman in an impeccable yellow suit. She was a television public relations executive, a popular fixture at social occasions and someone who always seemed in-the-know about Atlanta's black elite, such as it was.

"It *has* been a while," Mel said, wishing she could dissolve into the marble tile. "Are you here to set up an interview?"

"No. I just came out of a meeting in the mayor's office. You know, Olympic stuff. Things are getting hot and heavy now."

"I can imagine."

"And what are *you* doing here?" Her eyes swooped down the line.

"Just taking care of some business," Mel replied.

It was bad enough to have to come in person to pay; she didn't need to have a witness. Most people who booted it downtown to pay their water bill did so out of necessity. Either, like her, their water was already turned off, or they were being threatened with an immediate cutoff. People with no overdue balances who had questions about their accounts usually made inquiries by phone. It was the poorer element, or the last minute, irresponsible ones, who paid in the flesh. Mel knew this, as did virtually everyone else.

"I missed seeing you at Celeste's and Ron's the other night. Great party."

It was a well-intentioned comment, nothing mean or malicious, an innocent conversational tidbit. But Mel felt as though a dagger had been thrust in her side. So, Celeste had had a party and hadn't invited her. Figures. Mel knew that her stock had declined in recent months, which made her a lukewarm commodity in Celeste's book. But to be ignored like that, not to be acknowledged at all—she deserved better treatment. And to hear about it second-hand added insult to injury. She thought that Celeste, despite her vanity, was a better friend. But there it was: official notice that she was no longer deemed worthy enough to be a part of, or even *around,* the so-called in crowd.

Being excluded was bad enough; what made it worse was that she cared as much as she did.

CHAPTER 5

The week-long deluge had converted the inclined sidewalk into a moving mud path. Drier ground was long since gone; slush and sludge overran every inch of concrete. Mel was sure that her knee-high boots, long, hooded raincoat, and oversized umbrella would provide ample protection against the pounding rain. But after slogging her way to the bus stop, just two blocks from home, she already felt the damp cold seep through.

Of all days for the car not to start. When she had turned the ignition this morning, the engine was silent. She had looked under the hood, not knowing exactly what to look for, but figuring she should at least go through the motions. She prayed that the problem was a dead battery and not a major electrical breakdown. *Lord, please, You know we don't need any more expenses; we can't handle the ones we have.* She had gone back in the house, scrounging for cab fare, rummaging through purses and favorite crevices used for storing extra money. Nothing. Even Sasha had no dollar bills in her stay-at-home wallet that usually held the remnants of her allowance. Mel's household search yielded only a handful of change, far short of what she'd need for a taxi. For a moment, she had considered scrapping the whole thing and not getting out in this torrential mess. But if she didn't teach her classes today, the persnickety chairman of the Business Department might dock part of her already flimsy pay, a prospect more depressing than the relentless downpour from above.

The rain assaulted her from all sides, aided by a fickle wind that changed directions at whim. Drenched and alone, Mel felt like the survivor of some natural disaster. The bus stop was in an area that had been razed for a new elementary school, so there was no canopy to offer cover, no sheltering trees to absorb the weighty rain, and no one else to share the misery.

Finally, sloshing through the water-logged street, the bus arrived. It almost bypassed Mel, an unfamiliar presence at this seldom-used stop.

"Rough out there today, ain't it?" The driver, in dire need of teeth, greeted her cheerily, perhaps to cover up for his near mistake.

Grateful for the warm, dry air, Mel sank wearily into a seat up front. She rubbed the face of her watch, which had clouded from the moisture: 9:15. She would be late for her ten o'clock class. With this weather and the nonrush hour bus schedule, there was no telling how long it would take to get there. Once she got to the West End Station, she'd have to take another bus up Stewart Avenue. Then, the long walk on campus to the Science and Business Building, where she would get soaked all over again.

She glanced around the near-empty vehicle. Only one other passenger was aboard. Most people who were going to work were already there. The sane ones, she decided, had stayed home.

At the next stop, the bus picked up a woman with two toddlers. Mel watched with interest as the woman maneuvered the children and herself into one row, then unloaded her drenched backpack and expansive baby bag onto the seat adjacent to Mel.

"Twins?" Mel asked.

"No. Thirteen months apart." The woman removed the raincoat from one child, and shook the water droplets onto the aisle. "This one here's the baby. He wants to keep up with his brother so bad, I think he's doing it just to spite me."

"You certainly have your hands full."

"Don't I know it!" She doused the aisle a second time with the other raincoat. "But they help me out a lot. Right, fellas?" She scrunched her face to elicit a smile from her children, as she wiped their chilled damp cheeks.

"It's a terrible day to have to bring them outside," Mel said, feeling sorry for the little ones.

"Yeah. I hate to do it, but I don't have no choice. It was hard gettin' 'em up this morning, too. They didn't wanna move at all. So I gave in and let 'em sleep late." She popped her gum loudly. "Usually we catch the six-fifteen."

"Six-fifteen!" Mel couldn't conceive of catching anything at that hour. "Where on earth do you have to go? Stone Mountain?"

She grinned a friendly smile. "Not too far from downtown. Over on Marietta Street."

"You must have to be there very early."

"Not till eight. But I gotta drop my kids off first and make sure they're settled in. Then I go on to work."

"You mean, you catch another bus after this one to get to your job?"

"Another bus and then the train. That's why I gotta get up so early.

These slow-behind buses take their own sweet time. They not moving us rapidly anywhere."

Mel made a knowing nod at the reference. Like most black Atlantans, she had heard the derisive phrase that was frequently used to describe the city's public transportation system. Officially, MARTA was the acronym for Metropolitan Atlanta Rapid Transit Authority; years ago, some anonymous punster substituted another series of words: Moving Africans Rapidly Through Atlanta.

"Are your children in a day care center?" Mel asked.

"Nah, I don't deal with day care centers no more." There was another crisp pop of gum. "I had 'em in one for a while, and seem like every week they came down with somethin'. Pickin' up all them germs."

"That can be a problem."

"Anyway, I couldn't keep 'em in a center now if I wanted to."

"Why not?"

" 'Cause they close at six. That won't help me none. I go to school three nights a week and sometimes I don't get home till after ten."

"You're in school, too? Wow, that's a tough schedule. It must be hard—juggling school and work and the children. How do you manage everything?"

"We manage. I keep telling myself it's just for a little while. I know better days are comin'. Like my mama says, 'It ain't about likin' it.' "

Mel nodded thoughtfully. "I suppose so. Is your mom able to help you with the children?"

"No. She and the rest of my family's back in Mobile. I'm the only one who's moved away. It's just me and these two." She pointed proudly to the slick heads of her sons, who had dozed off.

"So who keeps them for you?" Mel surprised herself by asking so many questions. She couldn't explain why, but she was intrigued by this amiable young woman, who, though rough around the edges, was strangely appealing. She had a "what you see is what you get" demeanor. No pretentiousness, just unashamed naturalness. Spirit! That was it. She had energy and spirit.

"This lady in the West End keeps 'em. It was a real blessin' to find her."

"I can imagine. It's a big relief when you know your children are well taken care of."

"You got kids?"

"A daughter. Thirteen. Her name's Sasha."

"Sasha," she repeated slowly. "That's pretty. Oh, my name's Tonya—

spelled Tonya—not *anya*—everybody makes that mistake. I been running off at the mouth all this time, and we haven't even properly met."

Mel smiled at the sudden bow to etiquette. "Glad to meet you, Tonya. I'm Mel."

"Mel? That's *it?*"

"That's it."

"Kind of a funny name for a woman, ain't it?"

Mel chuckled at her raw honesty. "Yes, I guess you could say that."

"Must be short for something."

"I was named after my father. His name was Melvin."

"So your full name is—what? Melvina?"

"No."

"Melvira?"

"Nope. You'll never guess." She was reminded of the name game in *Rumpelstiltskin.* "It's Melantha."

"Mel—*who?*"

"Quite a mouthful, isn't it? See why I keep it short?"

"Yeah," Tonya said quizzically. "Sure do."

"Actually," Mel volunteered, "I prefer my middle name."

"What's that?"

"Raven."

"Oooh," Tonya said approvingly. "Now, I like that."

So did Mel. Mainly because it was her father who had chosen it. When he first saw his firstborn, he wanted Raven to be her name. He was not one to pick out a child's name in advance, believing that you should fit a name to the child, not vice versa. His baby girl had a head full of black hair, and her teeny mouth, which opened and closed in a puckered way, reminded him of a delicate bird awaiting food. The name Raven seemed to fit her. But, as Mel found out later, Eunice had made up her mind long before her child was conceived that, if the baby was a girl, she would be called Melantha, which means "dark flower." Mel had never liked that name, which is why, even on official documents, she always used the shorter three-letter version. She wished that her father had been more forceful in standing up for his preference, but in his usual easygoing way, he had yielded to Eunice. "She carried you for nine months so she had the right to name you," he once told Mel. The compromise, then, was Raven as a middle name, and while her father had sometimes called her that, it got lost as the years went by, and disappeared altogether after he died.

When the bus emptied at the West End Station, Mel waved good-bye to Tonya and her small sons as they bravely confronted the pounding rain. She thought of how, when Sasha was small, she and Builder could afford to have Mrs. Hawkins come to the house. They never had to take Sasha out in weather like this.

She sighed deeply and adjusted the hood of her raincoat. Here she'd been feeling sorry for herself, yet this young woman—Tonya—a single parent, was raising two young children, plus holding down a job while going to school. And on top of that, taking the bus everywhere!

Suddenly, her own problems seemed much more manageable.

Her optimistic mood didn't last long. By the time she arrived at the college, she was a sloppy mess. A tractor trailer truck, bearing down hard on Stewart Avenue, had splattered her with gook and mud. She had been just a few steps away from turning off the sidewalk into the main entrance, but she couldn't move fast enough. The truck seemed almost gleeful to leave its dirty markings on Mel as she scampered unsuccessfully to get out of the way.

Once inside, she found a curt note in her mailbox from the chairman of the department, who didn't appreciate having to take over her 10:00 class. She felt like a disobedient child, slapped on the hand for being irresponsible.

She glanced at her watch: twenty more minutes before the period was over. No sense in going into the classroom now. Besides, she needed to clean up and get ready for her next class. And she needed coffee—badly.

A handful of students lounged in the cafeteria. A popcorn machine droned busily in a corner, and the hot buttery smell tweaked Mel's appetite. She surveyed the shelves' limited selections before deciding on peanut butter crackers to accompany her cup of caffeine.

"Eighty-five cents." The student cashier spoke dully, obviously not enamored with his work study job. Mel had never seen him before, but then, there were few faces here that she recognized. She taught only two classes twice a week at the junior college, and except for her students and a couple of faculty members, most faces were a blur.

A female student waited impatiently behind her, distinguished by a strong scent of jasmine, and titian braids piled a foot high. Mel moved aside the Styrofoam cup and packaged crackers. "Let me find some change," she said to the cashier, while digging in her shoulder bag. "Go on and wait on her."

"But I already rung this up."

"Then, cancel it," Mel ordered, using her teacher's voice. Why did everything have to be such a big deal? Couldn't he tell she was a teacher, a person of authority, deserving of respect? Not that kids cared these days.

The cashier grudgingly rang up the purchases of his next customer, the braided one, while Mel continued her search. Blindly, she felt for the tiny change purse that must have sunk to the bottom of her bag. She was about to dump the contents onto the counter when she touched the familiar beaded texture. At last! She let out a small cry of victory and held up the change purse like a lost treasure. Then she remembered. She had no car today. This was her bus fare back home. She had no other money.

She looked around for an ally, anyone from whom she might borrow a dollar or so. For a second, she started to ask the cashier, *tell* him, actually, that she'd bring in the money later. He had such a nasty attitude, maybe that was the only way people should relate to him. Give him back some of his own medicine. But it wouldn't be right to pull rank, and she couldn't defend a request for special treatment. Besides, a sign in bold black letters tacked on the wall quashed any notion of delayed payment:

CASH ONLY
NO IOU'S
NO EXCEPTIONS

Well, forget the crackers, but maybe she could at least get the coffee. Meticulously, she counted the change. Outside of the money for the bus, she had thirty-two cents—three cents shy from what she needed for coffee. Three cents! How pathetic. How ridiculously pathetic.

It was times like these that she longed for her former life at the Chamber. There, she would never have been subjected to diluted coffee and stale crackers, let alone have to pay for them! Among the many perks at the Chamber, taken for granted then, but sorely missed now, were the daily offerings of the company break room. Mel vividly remembered the large, open picnic basket that claimed center stage with a mixture of warm bagels, buttery croissants, and cinnamon rolls. Nearby, a glass bowl displayed plump berries, melons, and other fruits in a rainbow of colors. And off to a side counter, holding court on its own, was the coffee. Wonderful, glorious coffee! Always magically fresh, roasted to a deep mahogany with the perfect hint of almond.

"Hey, you want this stuff or not?"

Rudely snapped into reality, Mel gave the cashier a look of disgust. Who the heck did he think he was with his twerpy attitude? She'd find out his name and report him to the work study office, that's what she'd do. Would serve his butt right. But that wouldn't help her at the moment.

She flung her bag over her shoulder, and, allowing a smirk, pushed the crackers and coffee toward him. "You keep it. It's on me."

The rain had not slacked off much by late afternoon. Mel had ended up staying at the college longer than usual. She saw a flyer about an impromptu reception for a retiring faculty member, and although she knew neither the faculty member nor practically anyone else there, she had attended for one purpose only: to eat. She nibbled on celery sticks, barbecued wings, and petite cheese sandwiches. At various intervals, she unobtrusively placed several buffalo wings, miniature corn muffins, and raw broccoli spears into red cocktail napkins. She felt like a scavenger, scouring the table for scraps of food. But by the time she left, her shoulder bag contained several layers of carefully wrapped take-home portions. The refrigerator at home was sparse; this would serve as tonight's dinner.

During the musty bus ride back, Mel envisioned spending the evening by soaking in a warm bath with bubbles to the rim and sipping on a glass of wine for comfort. How she needed that! Maybe she would even put on a CD, something soft and instrumental, and burn some candles and incense. That would make her feel better. But as she walked toward her house, after getting off the bus, she knew another script awaited her. A ruby Mercedes was parked outside. She braced herself as she put her key in the lock.

"Mel! Gracious, look at you!" Relaxing in the living room chaise with several magazines in her lap, Celeste sat wide-eyed and amused at the sight of Mel in her dumpy raincoat. "What have you been doing out there? Swimming?"

"I've been walking," Mel said stiffly. "I had to take the bus." She removed her raincoat, shaking water onto the floor. "The car wouldn't start this morning," she added.

"We were wondering what happened."

"So, what brings you to this neck of the woods? Slumming today?" It was an unfair jab, but right now she didn't feel too kindly toward Celeste.

Before Celeste could answer, Sasha and Ashley rumbled down the steps, like a herd of horses responding to the whip.

"Mom, where've you been?" asked Sasha. "Look who's here."

"I see," Mel said, smiling at Ashley. "This is quite a surprise. How'd you two hook up?"

"They saw each other at a production this afternoon at the Civic Center," explained Celeste. "Hundreds of students from all over the city and these two spot each other in that huge mob. Personally, I think they conspired beforehand."

"We did not," said Ashley. "I told you, I recognized Sasha's blouse."

"It does stand out," Mel acknowledged. A deep purple with a wide collar, it was one of Maxx's many presents.

"Anyway," continued Celeste, "when I went to pick up Ashley, she insisted I bring Sasha too. So I signed a note for Sasha's teacher saying I'd be responsible for her. You don't mind, do you?"

"Of course not," said Mel. "I've always wanted the girls to get together, you know that." What she wanted to say was—*you* were the one who's kept them apart, not me.

Ashley motioned to her mother with a swish of her hand. "Don't you think you'd better head out now?"

Mel looked questioningly at Celeste, who had a sheepish grin.

"I have a hair appointment at Greenbriar. Remember Omar? I still go to him. I've tried a zillion people, and no one else can do my hair like he can. And there's an excellent nail technician in the shop too, so I thought I'd kill two birds with one stone. Anyway, since I knew I'd be coming in this direction, I told Ashley she could spend a little time over here rather than hang around the salon."

Mel gave a knowing nod. So that was it. Celeste wanted Ashley to stay here so she could be free to go about her errands unencumbered. Ashley was no problem, ever. But what bothered Mel was the sneaky, backhanded way Celeste had of doing things. Seizing the moment was her special talent.

"So, getting hair and nails done in a one-shot deal?" Mel asked wearily. She had to admit to being envious. Weekly manicures, shampoos, and occasional massages had long been eliminated from her routine during the first round of cutbacks.

"If I could, I'd try to squeeze in a facial," laughed Celeste. "But there's not enough time to do all that tonight."

"Too bad, isn't it?" Mel knew she sounded callous, but she couldn't help herself. "Heard you threw quite a party recently," she said, as the girls disappeared upstairs. She had considered not even mentioning it, but was curious as to how Celeste would respond.

"Oh, that. It was just a little get-together, a spur of the moment thing." Celeste gathered up the magazines, avoiding Mel's eyes. "I did try to call you but, uh, no one answered."

"Really? I can't imagine why. The machine's always on."

Celeste looked uneasy. "Well, you know how those machines are. Sometimes they act up, like when it rains real hard." Her words faded weakly in the face of Mel's direct gaze. She shifted positions in her chair, to accompany moving on to another topic. "So, how're you doing these days?"

"I'm doing," Mel said simply. She wasn't about to launch into a long-winded account of the family's current financial crisis. Besides, empathy would not be forthcoming here. She suspected Celeste already knew the big picture; no need to reveal the gritty details.

"Sasha told me she's going to Duncan now. Is she adjusting okay?"

"She doesn't like it, but then I don't think any school could live up to Trent in her eyes."

"That's only natural, isn't it? I'm sure Ashley would just *die* if we had to take her out."

"Yeah, well—it ain't about likin' it," said Mel, echoing the motto she had heard earlier from Tonya—the woman on the bus.

There was an awkward silence that loomed deadly. Mel broke it. "So, besides the party"—she couldn't resist one more jab—"what else have you been up to?"

"Up to my ears in this Olympic stuff, that's what. You know, we're one of the major corporate sponsors and—"

"You mean the company is one of the sponsors," inserted Mel, but the distinction was lost on Celeste.

"We're getting hit with all sorts of requests for speaking engagements. People want to know what's involved, and they're even asking us for blocks of tickets! Can you believe that? They're pretty brazen about it. I'm going to all kinds of receptions and luncheons and private dinners. It's a form of bribery, actually, but I'm enjoying it. It's nonstop. Ron says maybe if he files for divorce, he'd see me more often."

"Must be tough," Mel said coyly. Further evidence was not needed: She and Celeste were worlds apart. She didn't want to hear another word about the stressful demands of high corporate living. About "we" this and "we" that. About lunches and dinners and special favors. Please! She wanted Celeste just to go away. "What time is your appointment?"

"It's flexible. Anytime after six." She stretched lazily. "Guess I'd better get over there."

As Celeste stood to leave, Sasha's alarmed voice rang out from up stairs. "Mom! There's a tow truck in the backyard. They're taking the Honda!"

"What?" Mel stepped quickly to the rear of the house, with Celeste at her heels. "Builder must have come home and realized the car wasn't working," she mused out loud, reaching for some explanation. But even as she said it, that seemed unlikely. Builder rarely came home in the middle of the day, he hardly made it in at night! And even if had come home, why would he tinker with her car? He'd have no idea it needed fixing. And wouldn't he have left a note or something if he were having the car picked up for repairs?

She pulled the drapes back from the bay window in the dining room. A truck had backed into the yard, aligning itself in front of Mel's car. Mel knocked furiously on the window. "Stop that!" she cried out. "Stop it!"

Celeste looked at her as if she were out of her mind.

Mel darted toward the back door just as a powerful knock came from the front. For a second, she froze, not knowing which way to turn. Then, she raced into the living room, nearly bumping into Sasha and Ashley, who had descended the stairs.

"Mom!" Sasha said, breathless.

"Not now." Mel abruptly cut her off.

"But they're trying to steal the car!"

"What in heaven's name is going on?" asked Celeste, shadowing Mel once more.

"I don't know," Mel mumbled. "Have a seat while I get to the bottom of this." With a mix of nervousness and outrage, she roughly opened the front door.

A grizzled man, dressed in worn denim jeans and a motorcycle jacket, calmly waved some papers. "Evening, ma'am. We're here to claim your car."

"What do you mean 'claim'?" asked Mel, her voice shaky. She stepped outside and pulled the door shut, hoping to keep the conversation private. She could almost feel Celeste straining to hear on the other side. "Who are you?"

"I'm with TJ's Recovery Service." He handed her a bent card from his chest pocket. "We got an order here to pick up your vehicle. For nonpayment of notes."

"There must be some mistake." She knew she was behind on the car payments, and had received a couple of calls about it, but she didn't expect this kind of action. For them to come here and pick it up?

"No, ma'am, it's no mistake. You're Missus Burke?"

"Yes."

"And this here is three-one-two-eight Bramble Oak Drive and your car fits the description—green ninety-two Honda Accord." He looked up from his clipboard. "This is the right place. We've been watching you."

"Watching me?!"

"What I mean is, we've been here before but the car wasn't out. So we came back tonight."

"Oh, so you do your dirty business in the dark, is that it?"

He formed a lopsided grin. "It's not dirty business, ma'am. It's my job."

"I don't even know if this is legal. You're on private property, you know."

"Oh, it's legal, all right, ma'am," he said quickly. "We have authority to pick up the vehicle for overdue payments."

"Look," said Mel, formulating a lie. "I spoke to somebody the other day, trying to work out arrangements." She spoke softly, suspecting that Celeste was still standing just inches away on the other side of the door.

"I wouldn't know about any arrangements. All I know is, I got an order here for a repo and ain't nobody canceled it."

"But there must have been some mix-up," Mel insisted. "Arrangements were made to handle the back payments."

"I'm not the one to talk to about that. You got to take that up with your creditor, ma'am."

"Believe me, I will. I'm calling first thing in the morning. But in the meantime, just leave the car here. There's been a mistake, I'm telling you."

He gave a tired nod of the head, as though this defense was nothing new. "Ma'am, I'm not gonna stand here and argue with you. I got orders for the car, and I gotta take it."

"You don't *have* to take it," Mel said wildly. "Just—just tell them you didn't find anybody home."

He hesitated slightly, then chuckled. "No, ma'am, I can't do that."

"You can if you want to," Mel rebutted. "This will all be cleared up by tomorrow anyway. What's one day going to matter? Give me the benefit of the doubt."

He moved away from the porch, cutting off Mel's hope of making a deal. "We're hitchin' up your car right now," he said firmly. "If you've got valuables in there, you may want to get them out. I'll meet ya round back."

The grizzled figure disappeared amidst a phalanx of bushes outlining the house. As Mel opened the door, she was crowded in by Celeste and

the two younger witnesses. Sasha wore a look of distress and humiliation.

"Mom, you're not letting them take the car, are you?"

"Calm down, Sasha. It's a mistake, that's all. It's nothing I can't handle." She struggled to steady her voice.

"It'll be okay," consoled Ashley, patting her friend on the shoulder.

Celeste, her brow furrowed, tapped her nails against a flower stand.
"Are you really that far behind?" she asked.

Mel ignored the question, struck by the difference between mother
and daughter. Here was Ashley, a sensitive fourteen-year-old, comforting
Sasha, while Celeste had no words of support.

"I've got to get around back," Mel said flatly. She marched through the
house, her trio of witnesses following closely on her heels. She wanted
Celeste to stay put, to stay out of her business. She knew too much
already. Mel twirled around, confronting her. "It would really help if you
stayed inside with the girls," she said. "I can take care of this."

"Well, maybe I can do something too," Celeste insisted.

Outside, the rain had been reduced to a drizzle, but the cold wet air
refused to compromise. Without coats or jackets, the women and girls
stood shivering, arms folded, watching the tow truck driver switch a series
of levers and gears to move a giant hook within inches of the Honda's tail.
Assisting in the procedure, the grizzled one appeared between the truck
and the car, giving hand and voice signals to the driver.

Remembering, Mel cried out, "Wait a minute, wait a minute." She
dashed to the right side of the car and opened the door. She grabbed a
wooden tray of cassette tapes that nestled between the two front seats and
unlatched the glove compartment to retrieve insurance and auto documents. Amidst the clutter, a plain white envelope designated to hold
emergency cash, fell out—empty. Empty for months.

Damn. Who'd have thought she would ever be cleaning out her car for
the repo man? Had she known the car was in danger of being repossessed, she would have asked the Barkers next door if she could park the
car in their garage. They had a lot of extra space. Better yet, if she and
Builder had their own garage, that would have protected the car from
being taken, wouldn't it? The repo people couldn't just come into your
yard and open your garage, could they? Wouldn't that be considered
breaking and entering? She needed to know more about her rights; there
was so much legalese to sift through. When she and Builder first moved
into the house, they did have a garage. But it was termite infested and

Builder had torn it down with the promise to replace it. He never had. Another one of his good intentions stuck in the realm of the unrealized. *Damn Builder. Damn him for all of this.*

"Need help with anything?" Arms outstretched, Ashley was at her side.

"Yes. Hold these for me, will you?"

Suddenly, the grizzled one appeared at the door, causing Mel to jump. "We're also going to need your key."

"My key?!" She couldn't believe he said that. Why should she make it easy for him?

"Yes, ma'am, we need your key."

"But why?"

"We have to drive the car to a space on the lot, once we get it there."

"But the car doesn't even work. I couldn't start it this morning."

"You couldn't?"

"No."

He ducked his head and peeped inside. For a moment Mel thought she might have a reprieve. If he couldn't start the car, couldn't drive it, he wouldn't want it, right? Maybe they could work something out afterall.

He turned to shout to the driver, who was still making connections at the car's rear. "We'll have to park this one in a corner space."

Of course. How stupid of her. People's cars get towed all the time, for parking violations, for abandonment, for all sorts of reasons, and the truck operators don't have the keys. That doesn't stop them from taking the vehicles.

"I think it just needs a new battery," Mel said huffily, gathering her possessions. "It better not have anything seriously wrong with it when we pick it up." Her little warning rang feeble and pointless, but she needed to manifest some shred of ownership, however slight.

"We're not going to do anything to it," assured the grizzled one. "It'll be in the same shape as it is now. But we still need the key. You have to surrender it."

Another slap on the hand. Take away, take away, take away. Yet one more way to degrade her. "Sasha," she said, fighting to keep her voice steady. "Go get the car key off the extra set. In the ginger jar."

Standing several feet off to the side, Sasha stayed glued in place. The only thing mobile about her was her eyes, hurtful and disbelieving; eyes that moved back and forth between the car and the tow truck; eyes that forced her to be a reluctant observer of a legalized theft. Now she had to be a participant too?

"Go on, Sasha, get the key. Hurry up!"

Slowly, Sasha moved toward the house, every tortuous step representing her mother's betrayal and complicity.

Mel turned to Ashley, who was loaded down with the car's contents. "I think that's all. Put everything on the kitchen counter, okay?"

"Okay."

Slamming the door, Mel walked back toward the rear of the car, where the driver of the truck had finished hitching up his prey. The grizzled one signed a piece of paper, before handing it off to Mel.

"We're over in Douglas County. Near Six Flags. Map's on the back."

Mel glanced at the information silently. She felt beaten down, drained.

Celeste inched toward the grizzled one. "Tell me," she said, "you all just don't barge in and take people's cars for one little overdue payment, do you? I mean, at what point do you go to this extreme?"

Mel glowered at Celeste. She was so transparent. What difference should it make whether the car payment was two months behind or three or ten? She was just plain nosy, that was it. Looking for gossip.

"Each case is different, ma'am. It depends on the circumstances."

Mel was grateful for the generic reply.

The grizzled one walked over with his clipboard. "Just sign here, and that'll be it." He surveyed the expansive yard. "I gotta say, you're not exactly a typical case."

"What's that supposed to mean?" Mel asked.

He planted one leg on the truck, watching his colleague secure the hook. "Usually when we come out to pick up a car, it's from folks who are—you know, the riffraff type—the, uh, lower element."

"And I don't fit in that category, huh?"

"No, not at all."

"So that's supposed to make me feel better?"

"Oh, Mel, you know what he means," inserted Celeste. "It's a compliment."

"Humpf!" said Mel, angry at the implication and angry at Celeste for buying into the stereotype. "In other words because I live in a decent house and don't have six snotty-nosed kids pulling on my skirt, and don't have dirty curlers in my hair, or walk around on the back of my shoes"— she took a deep breath and gestured toward the tow truck—"I'm supposed to be *above* all this, is that it?"

"Mel!" chided Celeste.

"I didn't mean any harm," said the grizzled one. "I was just calling it as I see it."

Mel gave him a fierce look. The man honestly had no idea why his comments were offensive. If Val were here, she'd charge racism on the spot, would contact the company president, and probably end up getting *them* to pay *her*, due to racist remarks by an employee. But Mel didn't have the energy. All she wanted was for this episode to be over and for these intruders to go away.

She caught Sasha watching from the dining room. She seemed so small and helpless, dwarfed by the huge bay window and circumstances beyond her control. She had the look of a woeful waif who had lost her last friend. Mel motioned for her to come out.

Squeaky sounds from the tow truck turned Mel's attention back to the tethered Honda, which was being hauled onto the flatbed.

"Keep 'er steady, keep 'er steady," directed the grizzled one, as he and the driver communicated in their own sign language. In a minute, the raised Honda loomed larger than life, foolishly perched on the truck.

Ashley ran up with the key, which Mel reluctantly handed over to the grizzled man. Turning toward the window, she noted that Sasha had disappeared.

As the truck jiggled out of the driveway, Mel wondered how and when she would get the car back. Not only was there the immediate expense of making overdue payments and bailing out the car, but there would also be the repair costs, and no telling what that might entail. Builder had his truck, but she was left with nothing. She thought of the buses she had taken earlier in the day. Would she have to deal with that now on a regular basis?

"Too bad about this," Celeste said, watching her closely. "You'll get it out tomorrow, right?"

"Definitely. I don't intend to become a MARTA patron." But her words were for Celeste's benefit only. If she could get the car back within a week, that would be a miracle. She laughed weakly, massaging her temples. "God, what a day."

"Mel, if you'd only let us know how bad things are, I'm sure Ron and I could have done something."

To Mel, the words sounded insincere, offered up as bait for more information. "Well, thanks for saying that, but really, it's an oversight. I mean, we've sometimes been a few days late, but surely nothing to warrant this." Who was she kidding? Celeste knew what was happening. She may not have the specifics, but she knew enough. Why even bother with the charade?

Mel glanced up at the bay window. It was still empty, the way she felt inside. She turned to Ashley and put an arm around her shoulder. "I guess Sasha's pretty upset, huh?"

"Yeah, kind of. That's why I brought the key on out. But she'll be all right. I'll go on in and talk to her."

Celeste quickly intervened. "Oh, no. You're not going to stay now."

"I'm not?"

"No, not after—not under the circumstances."

"Why not?"

"Because, well, I don't think Sasha's up to having company right now."

"Celeste, it's no problem for Ashley to stay," said Mel. "The girls were looking forward to it. You go on to your appointment."

"Yes, Mother," Ashley concurred. "You go on."

"No, you're coming with me. That'll be better than having to make the trip all the way back here and—"

And be subjected to this mess, thought Mel. But she understood; she really did. She wished she could go away too, away from the bills and the debt and the hassle.

In the living room, Celeste hurriedly rushed Ashley to collect her things. It was as though she wanted to escape from the scene as quickly as possible before the Burkes' bad luck started to rub off.

"I need to say good-bye to Sasha," Ashley said, heading for the stairs.

"No," said Celeste. "Don't bother her now. She's probably resting."

"But it'll just take a minute."

"I said no. You can call her later." She practically pushed Ashley out the door. "I hope things work out. See you next time."

Whatever was left of their friendship went out the door with her.

Mel collapsed on the couch, one hand clutching her head, the other grasping her stomach. It was no surprise that her body had given out. It had let her down a lot lately, reacting with predictable churlishness to each new incident of stress.

She lay there for several minutes in eerie quiet. Then, the tears burst forth with a rush. She had held them back as long as she could in an attempt to put on a face of composure. She had held them back to protect Sasha, to hide her own humiliation from Celeste, to maintain a sense of well-being. But the bitterness and rage swelled up and broke through, and leading the slippery trail down her cheeks were tears of blame earmarked for Builder. So much of this was because of him. If it weren't for his business soaking up every single dime, putting them in such dire straits, this would have never happened. If she didn't have to scrape up money to pay other essential bills, she could have kept up with the car notes.

Each day seemed to bring a new crisis, one more demand for money that superseded an earlier need. Now, it was the car. She'd have to round up more money to get it back. But how?

She wondered what else she could pawn, barter, or sell. She took a mental walk through every room of the house, ending up lastly, here. She opened her eyes, resting them on the Romare Bearden sketch hanging above the fireplace. It was an original pencil drawing that she had won years ago as the grand door prize in an art seminar held at the APEX Museum. Bearden had whipped out the sketch in about two minutes, as part of his demonstration on the collage. Perhaps she could get several hundred dollars for it, maybe much more; she had no idea of its value. Now that Bearden was dead, his works were in greater demand. Why did that always happen to dead artists, to people in general? Appreciated most after they're gone. Maybe, Mel thought, she could ask her friend Anne, who was an art dealer in Seattle. Anne would be able to give an estimate of its value. She might even want to purchase it herself, or would certainly know tons of people who'd be interested. Finding someone to buy it wouldn't be a problem. The owner of the art gallery that had framed the sketch had mentioned that if she ever wanted to sell it, to let him know. Over the years, she had seen him around town, and he always asked about the Bearden sketch. *Want to make a deal?* he would inquire. *Never,* came her assured reply. *It's the only decent piece of art I own.* She would hate to part with it, but at this point, what choice did she have?

The loud chimes from the clock on the mantel startled her. Seven o'clock. She must have dozed off. Her face felt tight from her dried tears. Her stomach had calmed down but her head continued to throb. She needed to pull herself together and talk to Sasha, who was probably sulking in her room, still mortified at the sight of the family car being taken away. Her daughter was so sensitive, supersensitive, and in that way, very much like her.

Sleepily, Mel lumbered to the staircase and pressed her weight against the banister. "Sasha," she called out, "would you come down here?"

Several seconds passed. No response.

More volume was needed, more intensity. "Sasha! Did you hear me? I want to talk to you."

She waited to hear the creak of a door, or see a flash of light spilling into the hallway. But there was nothing.

It wasn't like Sasha to ignore her completely, even in her worst of moods. Was it possible that she just didn't hear? Maybe she had her earphones on or had fallen asleep?

Mel gathered the energy to climb the staircase, which consisted of fifteen high steps. It was one of the things she liked least about this house. On the landing, she heard no music from Sasha's room. The door was shut tight. Out of respect for her daughter's privacy, she knocked, but loudly. "Sasha, I've been calling you. Open up."

Nothing stirred inside. With growing irritation, she knocked again, this time jiggling the doorknob, which resisted her twists and turns. "Sasha!" she yelled. "Why is this door locked? Open up this instant! You hear me?"

Silence. Deadly, inexplicable silence. She had never known Sasha to lock herself in her room or be so blatantly disobedient. Could she have hurt herself? Had a fall or something or—oh, Lord, please. She waved away the thought. Sasha wouldn't hurt herself deliberately. No, it was unthinkable. She hadn't been happy lately, but surely she wouldn't . . .

Mel alternately banged on the door while frantically turning the doorknob. With a mixture of anger and fear, she repeatedly bellowed Sasha's name.

Finally, a small voice from the other side: "Okay. I'm coming." Sasha unlocked the door and cracked it by an inch, then quickly moved out of the range of fire.

Relieved yet fuming, Mel barged into the room. "What's the matter with you? Didn't you hear me calling? Why didn't you answer?" She looked wildly at her daughter, who had retreated from the barrage of questions to a corner of the bed.

Sasha said nothing. Buttressed by the wall against her back, she sought protection from a defensive line of pillows and stuffed animals, a makeshift fort against a powerful enemy.

"Don't you *ever* do that to me again!" Mel said. "When I call, you answer. Understand? I didn't know *what* was going on in here." Pacing back and forth, she scowled at Sasha. She was tired of her daughter's manipulative self-pitying antics. Everybody was supposed to cater to Sasha, to feel sorry for Sasha. Well, enough of that. It's time she snapped out of it.

Mel stopped at the foot of the bed. She stared at Sasha, as if looking hard would provide some answers. Before her was a girl with disheveled hair, brown eyes turned red, face drained white. She looked a sight, poor thing. Mel's heart softened. This was her daughter! Ashamed, she realized she had blasted away at Sasha because of her own insecurities and hurt pride. Sasha didn't deserve that. What she needed was motherly love, pure and simple, not someone who created even more tension. Mel felt guilty for slipping out of control.

"I didn't mean to scream at you," she said more calmly. "I was just upset. I'm worried about you."

Sasha maintained a hurt expression.

"What's going on with you?" Mel prodded.

"Nothing."

"Nothing? Don't give me that. Talk to me."

But she knew that was precisely what Sasha intended not to do. She had seen her play this game before. The strategy was to give Mel the cold shoulder, the silent treatment, disarming her from a counterattack. Avoidance psychology. Avoid the questions or give a cryptic, noncommittal response, eventually forcing the issue to recede, or the questioner (Mel) to back off. Sasha had learned this tactic from Builder, who frequently clammed up and shut down rather than share his pain. It was a self-protective aegis, designed to frustrate and immobilize. But Mel was determined not to allow it to work this time. Tonight, Sasha was going to talk. Too much had already been left unsaid.

"Just because things don't go the way you want, you can't lock yourself away from the world. And from me," Mel said quietly. "That doesn't solve anything. Right?"

Sasha curled a clump of hair around her finger.

"I know it was upsetting to see the car picked up like that. But I'm going to do everything I can to get it back as quickly as possible, okay?"

Sasha gave a faint nod.

"I'm worried about you. You seem so unhappy all the time. And for you to get this upset over the car being picked up—" She couldn't bring herself to use the word "repossessed."

"It's not just the car," mumbled Sasha.

An opening! "What, then?"

"It's just that—"

"What?"

"Nothing's going right."

"Nothing? That's an exaggeration, don't you think?"

No response. Mel didn't want her to retreat into silence again. "Let's see," she said quickly, "you saw Ashley today."

"Yeah, but just for a little while. She was supposed to stay longer." Sasha sat up straighter, her point proven. "See what I mean?"

"That was her mother's decision, honey."

"But it wouldn't have happened if they hadn't come for the car."

Mel could think of no rebuttal.

"I even beeped Daddy."

"You did? When?"

"When they were taking away the car. I thought maybe he could stop it. He didn't call back."

"He must have been tied up. If he knew it was you, I'm sure he would have made a special effort." Then, verbalizing an inner belief, she added, "He probably thought it was me." Those few words summed up the tenuous state of her marriage. Sasha immediately picked up on it.

"Are you getting a divorce?"

Mel bit her lip. "Why would you ask that?"

"Because you're always fighting. It's not like before. And Daddy's never home."

It was Mel's turn to be silent.

Sasha repeated her question, apprehension in her eyes. "Are you? Getting a divorce?"

"No. We're not."

"Promise?"

Mel hesitated. That was a word she rarely used. She knew how disappointing a broken promise could be. It was one of the things she constantly harped on with Builder: "Don't promise unless you can deliver." Years of experience had taught her that unexpected developments could unravel the best of intentions. So unless she knew she could absolutely deliver . . . But what absolutes were there in life?

"It's nothing for you to worry about, okay?"

"But if you *did* get a divorce," pressed Sasha, "who would I live with? You or Daddy?"

"Whom would you want to live with?"

"I don't know."

"Well, let's not even think about that. You've got to start thinking positive, happy thoughts. Okay?" She wondered if she and Sasha would ever recapture the feeling of those early years, when they were constantly together and had so much fun. They were close, as close as mother and daughter could be. What had gone wrong? How did they grow so far apart? How did it happen so quickly? Sort of like her relationship with Builder, and the way it was disintegrating, day by day. She reached out to smooth over part of Sasha's bangs but Sasha immediately drew back. "I was just trying to get the hair out of your face," Mel said defensively. It was this kind of touchiness that sometimes made Sasha difficult to love.

"Sorry." The statement was more of a dismissal than an apology.

"What *is* it with you?" Mel asked, her anger returning. "Aren't you tired of feeling sorry for yourself? Okay, it happens sometimes; we all go through it. But you've got to shake it off. This has been going on much too long. You've got to try to pull out of these negative moods. I know you can do it. Right?"

It was a pep talk to herself, as well as to Sasha. But it wasn't working for either of them. Sasha sat mummified.

"What's it going to take?" Mel asked, throwing her arms up. "How do I get some spark into you? Do I need to buy some batteries and wind you up?" She was trying to jolt a response out of Sasha, or at least drag out a half-hearted smile. She was not ready for her daughter's soft reply:

"I—I'm just all by myself. Nobody understands."

The plaintive comment jabbed Mel's heart. The words brought back painful memories of the time right after her father's death. She was around Sasha's age, maybe a year or so younger, when she had felt so abandoned and hopelessly lost. Her mother and Maxx could comfort each other; she felt she had no one. Her grief was further heightened by the innate ravages of puberty, that turbulent cycle of life where every emotion is magnified, every misstep a near tragedy. This was part of Sasha's problem, Mel realized. Timing. Lousy timing. Because even though Sasha was not going through anything as devastating as the death of a parent, the recent adjustments she had had to make, must seem, to her, monumental. The intense sensitivity of early adolescence, with its mixed-up rebelliousness and frantic search for self, left little room for clarity. Any additional pressures, piled on top, made the sorting out much more difficult.

"You're not by yourself, honey. I'm here. I understand."

Sitting on the edge of her daughter's bed, she put her arms around Sasha and rocked her. She rocked and rocked like never before. Without benefit of proper equipment, without the support of a pillow propped in the right position, or the kind of chair made for such purposes, and with her neck beginning to cramp—still, she rocked. She dared not change positions, dared not let go.

Sasha's taut body gradually gave in to the soothing, rhythmic motion.

Releasing tears and all resistance, the daughter allowed the mother to stroke her hair, ease her pain, and rock, rock, rock.

The house was dark when Builder arrived close to midnight. As he pulled his truck into the circular bend of the driveway, he immediately noticed the empty space usually occupied by Mel's car. He wondered where Mel might be at this hour. Could Sasha be sick? Could Mel have taken her to the hospital?

He hated this guessing game. For weeks now, he and Mel had barely spoken to each other, engaging in only the basic civilities, or talking almost exclusively about Sasha, their one common link. Withholding information, not sharing or communicating, was a weapon they both used. It was juvenile and immature, but also a method of self-protection. Builder had to admit he was probably more guilty of it than Mel. Things had gotten so sour between the two of them that he wondered if ever something was seriously wrong at home, whether Mel would even tell him. To keep him in the dark, to exclude him from involvement, she might choose to deal with it on her own. But surely she wouldn't do something like that when it came to Sasha? Would she?

He entered the house through the basement, not stopping to remove his muddy boots or dusty clothes. He mounted the stairs to the top floor quickly, and went directly to Sasha's room. She was sound asleep, snoring. He pulled the comforter close around her neck and kissed her on the cheek. She continued to snore, undisturbed.

He walked to the end of the long hall to the master bedroom, where he found Mel also asleep, her mouth lightly open, her head slumped against several stacked pillows. The remote control lay at her fingertips. A thick biography and a couple of days' worth of newspapers crossed the demarcation line to Builder's side of the bed. The only light in the room came from the television set, where the voice of Ray Charles crooned "Georgia on My Mind." It was the nightly sign-off for a local public television station and as Builder sank into his chair to remove his heavy boots, he watched the serene images of orange sunsets, luscious forests, and simple small town life. He sat mesmerized, savoring the peaceful interlude. But it was over all too quickly. The harsh static from the television abruptly ended the bit of tranquillity. Mel woke up.

"Hi," she said, almost by rote. She gazed at him sleepily and for a minute Builder thought he saw a hint of a smile, a flash of the old Mel, at the corners of her mouth.

"Hi." He switched on a painted antique lamp with a low-wattage bulb. Pale yellow light flooded the room. He walked over to the television, shutting it off manually. "Where's the car? You take it to the shop?"

The question jolted Mel into reality. Her large eyes almost instantly turned into two hardened spheres of burnished steel. She sat up straight, ready for battle.

"They took the car."

"What do you mean, 'took the car'?"

"I mean they came to the house and got it. Towed it away. It's been REPOSSESSED." She literally hissed the word at him, all the pent-up blame and hurt of a few hours ago returning with fresh vengeance.

"They took it?" he asked, unbelieving still.

"Yes," she hurled back. So much anger and venom in one tiny word. "For nonpayment of the notes."

"Shit." He walked into his closet, placing a barrier between himself and Mel's accusing eyes. He stayed there for a few seconds, trying to collect himself. He had to tell Mel something. He emerged with a strategy in mind. "I'm working on a couple of projects and should get a check in a day or two. I can probably get the car out then."

"If you say a day or two, that means at least a week."

Builder took a deep breath but didn't rebut. He'd hate to admit it, but she was right. His sense of time, of how long it takes to accomplish a goal, was frequently off.

"Meanwhile," she continued, "every day it's in there, it's costing money. Something like forty dollars a day for storage."

Builder balled up his dirty pants and threw them in a corner. "What a rip."

"You have no idea how humiliated I was," Mel said. "Celeste was here, of all people. She saw the whole thing. And poor Sasha, watching the car being taken away like that, right before her eyes. It's not good, Builder. It's not good."

He threw up his hands. "What do you want me to do? I can't work any harder or any faster. I'm doing the best I can. I don't exactly see you bringing any money into this house. All you do is sit around and complain all the damn time. Finding fault, placing blame—that's all you do."

"That's not fair. I'm working on several projects."

Builder snickered. "Like what? You mean that volunteer stuff? That's all well and good when you've got a job or some money coming in, but you can't afford to do that anymore. *We* can't afford it."

"I'm more aware than you as to what we can and can't afford," Mel said through tight lips. "You have no idea what I go through every day just to keep the lights on and food in the refrigerator. Just because I'm not out there hammering nails like you, doesn't mean I'm living the life of Riley." She sat up straighter, her eyes blazing. "What do you think I do, anyway? I work at the college, I'm writing proposals, I'm working on several reports. I'm making some money, but we have too many bills. We're behind on everything. It's out of control." She thrust her legs in front of her. "This is a heck of a way to live. We don't do anything anymore. We never go anywhere. We don't have any fun."

"You think I like it like this?" he asked cynically.

"Of course not. But if it weren't for you—"

"If it weren't for me, what?" He gave her a hateful stare.

"Never mind." She fumbled with the nearby newspapers.

"No, go on, say it," he goaded her. "Get it off your chest. If it weren't for me, what?"

"We wouldn't be in this situation in the first place. It's not because of *my* business or *my* mistakes."

"So it's all my fault, huh?"

Mel didn't answer.

"Fine, so it's my fault. I admit that. Excuse *me* for trying to make a business work."

Still silent, Mel raised her knees to her chin.

"It feels real good to know how much you support me," Builder spewed. "I'm out here getting no help from anybody, and then when I come home, *you're* all over my case. Whatever happened to taking the bitter with the sweet?"

"I think I've taken quite a lot of the bitter."

"You don't even know what bitter is. *This* little shit? Because of some overdue bills? Give me a break!"

"It may not be that much to you. But I'm the one who has to deal with these creditors and with people coming to my door. Having to put up with the nasty letters and phone calls. I'm sick of living like this. I'm sick of it!"

"If you feel that way, then why don't you just leave?" Builder said hotly. "Just go on and fuckin' leave. You're not doing anybody any favors by staying here."

Flailing his arms in disgust, he headed for the adjoining bathroom, and slammed the door behind him. Roughly, he flipped up the toilet seat and peed carelessly, sloshing his urine off the edge of the bowl. Let her clean it up, he thought. In the shower, he ran the water hot. It steamed the mirror and washed away his body funk, but could not remove his anger, which stuck to his skin like a tangled mess of matted hair that's impossible to budge. He talked aloud to himself, saying how he didn't need this crap, didn't need Mel, didn't appreciate the constant blaming. He wanted the echo to carry through the door so that she would hear it all.

When he came back to the room, Mel was curled up in a ball, the covers pulled high around her ears. She lay with her back to him, a defiant posture, and one that had become quite familiar.

Early in their marriage, they had vowed never to go to bed angry. They promised to fall asleep in each other's arms after passionate lovemaking, or at the very least, after a good night kiss, a real kiss, not some perfunctory peck on the cheek. For a while they had upheld that newlywed idealism; overall, their marriage had been good. But these days, their marriage bed had become a pyre of silence. When they did talk, their discussions deteriorated into arguments, resulting in the two of them sleeping with their backs to each other, several inches apart. Sometimes, after particularly nasty fights, and when even more space was needed between them, Builder slept in the guest room.

She probably expected him to do that tonight, he thought. No way. He wasn't going anywhere; he was sleeping right here. He was tired and frustrated and in no mood for accommodation. This was *his* house, *his* bed. And he was staying put.

He tossed fitfully, trying to get comfortable, assuring that she was not. His foot accidentally brushed against Mel's leg and she quickly pulled it back. Fine, if that's what she wanted, let her keep her stuff to herself. Did she think he was trying to cozy up to her? Not hardly. He didn't want to touch her, had no desire to. Why should he want to deal with a woman who'd jump ship at the first sign of trouble? Who needed that?

The sheets rustled as Mel slipped out of bed, taking her pillow with her. "I'm going to the guest room," she announced.

So, if he wouldn't go, she would. "Good," he mumbled spitefully.

After she left, he launched into a long soliloquy, at one point getting so worked up that he almost shouted down the hall, forcing her to hear, needing her to hear.

It was quite a while before he fell asleep in the cold bed his wife had shunned.

. . .

Mel sat in the corner of the den that she had converted into a tiny work area. Papers and books occupied every inch of space. Among the clutter was a report for Larson Cook that she had been working on, the last one she would probably do. She was on the phone now with Larson, and the news was not encouraging. From all indications, it was only a matter of time before his scraggly division at the Chamber was totally shut down, and he would be booted out. Previously, he had been able to shuffle a few freelance assignments to Mel, so he had called to warn her that "this cow's about run dry."

But, he stressed, he was looking. He was considering everything, including starting his own consulting firm. He also had something heavy in the works at ACOG, the Atlanta Committee for the Olympic Games. If he got in, he told Mel, he would do all he could to pry open a spot for her.

"I didn't know you had relatives at ACOG," she teased.

"I don't."

"But you must! Word is, that's the only way people get a job there. You've got to be somebody's wife, cousin, sister, or brother-in-law. Unless, of course, you're sleeping around with one of the vice presidents."

"A tad cynical, aren't we?"

"Realistic, that's all."

ACOG was one of the first places Mel had applied to after receiving her walking papers from the Chamber. She got as far as a couple of follow-up interviews, but nothing serious evolved. It irked her that several people whom she considered minimally qualified landed hefty jobs with seemingly no effort. They pranced around financially fat and satisfied, secure in the knowledge that they would have a job at least through 1996 when Atlanta would host the Games. And then, they'd probably still be employed there for another year or two, for it would surely require another bureaucracy in itself to close everything down and to prepare the myriad reports that would document the big event.

"So how much longer do you think you'll be able to stay at the Chamber?" she asked Larson.

"Who's to say? A month, maybe two. You know I'm raising Cain about it. But however it goes, I'll keep my eye out for you."

"Thanks, Larson." She knew he was a man of his word.

Theirs was an odd relationship—the vulnerable executive and his former right hand. Ever since Mel had lost her job, she and Larson had kept in frequent contact. The healthy respect that had always existed between them merged into a friendship of necessity. They were like bruised allies who have undergone an assault by a common enemy. Although Larson was still employed at the Chamber and had not endured nearly the number of battle scars, the inevitability of the approaching front lines evoked in him a growing empathy for Mel and her fight to stay afloat.

A loud knock on the door startled her. Mel hurriedly ended the conversation with Larson and went to the door. Through the peephole, she saw an unfamiliar man, the second white man on her doorstep within two days. Surely not another creditor? The car was already gone. What else was there to take?

"Who is it?" she called through the door.

"Simon Weaver. Atlantic Financial."

Damn! Atlantic Financial held the second mortgage on the house. Mel couldn't stand them. They were notorious for their exorbitant interest rates and inflexibility in working with customers. Builder called them legalized loan sharks. Be just a week late with a payment, and they'd slap a $50 penalty on top of their ridiculously high interest rates. More than anything, the decision a few years ago to take out a second mortgage on the house had turned out to be the single worst financial move that Builder ever made—and that Mel had reluctantly agreed to. Builder had needed an emergency infusion of funds into the business, and Atlantic Financial was the only company that would provide the money quickly. But the cost was high, and the Burkes had paid dearly, just in interest alone.

"What do you want?" Mel said curtly.

"I'm looking for Nathaniel Burke."

"He's not home."

"Missus Burke?" He didn't wait for an answer. "I need to talk about your account."

"What about it?"

"You going to open the door? We better do this face to face."

Mel hesitated. The last thing she needed was another confrontation. But how could she avoid him? He knew she was at home. She breathed deeply, promising herself not to allow this man to rattle her. She opened the door.

"That's better," he sniffed, rubbing his nose with a wrinkled handkerchief.

"You don't have any right to be here."

"Oh, yes, I do. When you ignore our phone calls and don't respond to letters, you don't leave me any choice but to come here. I have every right."

That voice, that sniveling, snarly, mean voice she had heard over the phone so often. How well it fit him. Simon Weaver: a real-life Simon Legree.

"I need a payment today," he said gruffly. "You're three months overdue."

"Three months!" Mel's heart beat faster. "That can't be right."

"Oh, yes, it is. And by next week it'll be four months."

Damn! How could Builder have gotten so far behind? This was *his* responsibility; they had taken out the second mortgage for *his* business. It was all she could do to handle the payments on the first mortgage. She knew they were already a couple of months behind on that. But to be almost four months back on the second? Would they ever climb out of this hole?

"I can't give you a payment right now," she said. "I can probably come up with something by next week."

"That's not good enough. You need to come up with something today. Right now. We're about to foreclose on you."

Foreclose! The word rang out ominously, and Weaver seemed to relish saying it. Mel felt like bashing that smug expression right off his face. She noticed him gazing beyond her at the interior of the house, as though taking inventory of the spoils in advance. She was determined not to give him the satisfaction of even thinking about it.

"You will not foreclose on my home," she said evenly.

"Unless you pay up," he sneered, "that's exactly what's going to happen."

"Never."

He grinned slyly. "I don't think you understand. You're three months behind."

"I heard you the first time."

He seemed miffed that she remained so calm. "Do you mind if I ask you a personal question?"

"What?"

"Explain something to me." Shamelessly, he picked his nose, dabbing the sticky mucus onto his handkerchief. "Why are you so laid back about this?"

There. So she had gotten to him. She wasn't screaming her head off or wringing her hands in distress, and that bugged him. What did these people want? For you to beg and crawl on your knees and plead, "Mastah, oh, mastah, please give me another chance!"

"Why should it bother you how I act?" she responded coolly.

His nostrils widened. "We can take your house, you know that?" He shook a chunky forefinger inches from her face. "We can take your house from you."

The bullying gesture infuriated Mel. How dare he point his foul finger at her! "Get out of here!" she screamed. "Get out of here now. Get off my property." She hollered him right down the walkway, her words pushing him toward his car.

"You're going to regret this," he threatened, scowling over his shoulder.

"Get out! And don't ever come back. Ever! You hear me?"

So much for calm composure.

Shaking, Mel returned to her cubicle of an office. Hands on her hips, she paced back and forth, alternately cursing Builder and blaming herself for being so blind. What a sorry predicament! Bills piled up to the ceiling and no way clear of paying them. Here she was, a college graduate, with a master's degree, no less, and all this so-called experience. What good was it doing her? Everything she had worked for these last few years was being threatened, was at risk. The family savings, Sasha's college fund—all of it wiped out. What did she have, really? A husband she couldn't count on and a drawerful of broken promises.

She opened a folder of freshly cut newspaper clippings and scanned the contents. Nothing even remotely interesting. But she couldn't afford to be picky; she had to take some action. The referrals that Ron had given her hadn't panned out. And there was nothing promising to hope for. No one was about to call and offer her a job tomorrow. She held up one of the half-inch advertisements:

Restaurant
Waitress Needed. Nights. Excellent Tips. Dunwoody.

No résumé or portfolio would be required here. No waiting around for a call back; no finger crossing in hopes of a second interview. Just a quick yes or no. Fine, thought Mel, give it to me straight. She dialed the number.

"Pinwheels."

"I'm calling about your advertisement in the paper."

"Call back tomorrow between two and four. The manager will be in then."

All right. That was a start. At least it wasn't an outright rejection. Be thankful for small favors, she told herself. With luck, she would get an interview in a day or two, and would drive out there to—wait, the car. She couldn't drive; she'd have to take the bus. All the way to Dunwoody. No telling how long it would take for them to get the money for the car. And they had to pay on the house. That was priority.

She covered her face with her hands. She couldn't rely on Builder; she just couldn't. He was working night and day, but it wasn't enough. And her little freelance projects just didn't cut it. They needed immediate, consistent income. At this point, she'd consider anything. *It ain't about likin' it.*

She picked up another half-inch ad and dialed the number. If she made enough of these calls, surely she'd get something. She'd work it out, somehow. She had to.

CHAPTER 6

The atrium at 100 Colony Square was packed with the professionally primped and polished. People scurried in and out, going to or coming back from lunch, or heading toward the next appointment. Builder boarded an elevator with a chatty group of three marketing manager types, who openly discussed their company's latest bid for an advertising account. Such comments were usually whispered amidst furtive glances or delivered in meticulous code to assure that no competitor might overhear. But clearly, Builder was considered "safe." He could tell that the group had quickly sized him up, taking note of his stained khaki pants, Benjamin Moore paint cap, and worn lumber jacket. In their circles, one must at least "look" the part, and they had concluded, by instant, unspoken consensus, that Builder was not a threat.

On the twenty-first floor, Frank Kirby offered a beefy handshake and ushered him into the office. "Good to see you, man. Good to see you." He vigorously patted Builder's back, then showed him to a chair.

"Thanks for working me in on such short notice," Builder said.

"No problem. I needed to skip lunch anyway. Can't you tell?" Frank laughed gustily and massaged his belly. "Maybe I should do what you're doing. Looks like you've dropped a few pounds."

"No, you don't want to do what I'm doing."

"Business takes its toll, huh?" asked Frank, reclaiming the seat behind his desk.

"The business is dying, man. Damn near bleeding to death."

Frank's fuzzy eyebrows dipped downward. "Jeez. I'm sorry to hear that." He skipped a beat, then, "Can you stop the hemorrhaging?"

"I've been trying, believe me. Things just aren't clicking. Seems like every time something good's about to happen, the rug's snatched from under my feet, like some invisible hand, deliberately tripping me up. It's tough as hell out there."

"Yeah. I got a buddy in Cincinnati who has a hardware store. Last I heard he was thinking about shutting it down. Been in the family for years. But the customers just aren't coming in."

Builder shook his head in sympathy. "I know how it is. I've been agonizing over this for months. At what point do you say, 'Enough is enough'? I mean, I can't keep putting my family through this, man. And for what? To hold on to some dream of mine or for some ego gratification of saying 'I'm in business'? Hah!"

"What about the banks?" Frank asked.

"Banks! They're a joke. You name 'em. I've tried 'em. Now if I want to go out here and borrow fifty grand for a top-of-the-line Mercedes, fine, they'll damn near throw it at me. But talk about getting some money for a business? They'll laugh in your face." He picked up a chocolate kiss from the candy dish on Frank's desk. "I got turned down just last week for an office renovation that was in the bag. I mean, in the bag! I could have done it blindfolded—gutting out an existing building and putting in a doctor's office. It was really more like a small clinic. The equipment people wanted me, I had met with the architects, even had a signed contract from the doctor." He narrowed his eyes and held his right forefinger and thumb a centimeter apart. "I was that close to getting it—*that* close. And sure enough, the bank comes back and says my financial statement's not strong enough."

"Oh, no."

"I told them it's not going to be *my* money; it's the doctor's money. All they need to be concerned about is whether I pay my subs on time— which I do—and whether I finish the jobs—and I have. I've never walked away from anything. My customers are satisfied. Ask any of them."

"I know. You do quality work, got a good reputation; I hear that all the time."

"But does it matter? Nah. These banks just don't want black folks handling that amount of money. Course, it'd be considered peanuts for a white guy."

"How much was the contract?"

"Two hundred grand."

Frank released a whistle. "Nice piece of change."

"Yeah, it would have cleared up all my stuff, believe me. There was a lot of profit in that job. It hurt not to get it."

"What about the doctor? Didn't he put some pressure on the bank?"

"Don't let me get started on the 'black doctor' kick. They're notorious for jerking folks around. But, nah, he wouldn't even return my phone calls. All he had to do was stand his ground and say 'This is the guy I want.' Or he could have shopped around for a loan somewhere else. There were a number of things he could have done."

"Sounds like a real weak son of a bitch."

"I've run into my share of them."

"So have I."

There was a pause as they both mentally identified several people who fell into that category.

"What's happening with this new bank?" asked Frank. "They're supposed to be targeting entrepreneurs and small businesses. You know, community banking and all that. Sounds right up your alley."

"They talk that talk but from what I've seen so far, they're about as bad as all the others." He inhaled deeply. "I don't have a whole lot of faith in any of this stuff anymore. I'm ready to throw in the towel."

"So, you'd really quit?"

"Either that or a bankruptcy."

"Ah, now, you don't want to do that."

"I may not have a choice. Even if I close everything down tomorrow, I'd still have tons of people to pay. Anyway, that's what I wanted to kick around with you. See if bankruptcy is my only way out."

"Damn, Builder. I'd hate for you to go that route. How far down are you?"

"About a hundred grand."

"Jesus! Is all that short-term?"

"Mostly. My lumber and painting accounts are up to the limit. Same thing with carpeting and windows. I can't put another dime on them. But some of it's personal debt too."

"You mean credit cards?"

"No. I mean my house. I fell behind on some payments, and the mortgage company's itching to foreclose."

"JESUS CHRIST, BUILDER! How the hell did that happen?"

Builder rubbed his chin as he delivered his confession. "I had to take out a second mortgage on the house a couple years ago, and I haven't been able to pay it off like I thought. Terrible mistake. Should have never done it. Should never have put my personal residence on the line for the business."

"Wait a minute." Frank leaned forward. "Are you saying—? Didn't you separate the business from your personal stuff? You're incorporated, aren't you?"

Builder sighed deeply again, opening and closing his hands. "Well, no, not officially."

"Come on. I know you're smarter than that."

"It's one of those things I kept meaning to do but never got around to."

Frank threw up his hands. "You should have come to me years ago. Or come to somebody!"

"I know that."

"I mean, a business bankruptcy is one thing. White boys do it all the time. Go out of business one day; open up somewhere else the next. Their personal assets are never touched—the house, the car—none of that's affected. But if you've got to take a *personal* bankruptcy, that'll mess up your credit for years. Plus, you still have to pay back mostly all you owe."

"I know," Builder said quietly.

They were silent for a minute, commiserating the state of things.

"Who's the mortgage company?"

"Atlantic Financial."

"Ump, ump, ump. I've heard some horror stories about them. They're low-down snakes, man. They'll take the shirt off your momma's back."

"Well, I'll tell you one thing," Builder declared, "they're not going to take my house. That's the bottom line. I'll do whatever I have to. If that means taking a bankruptcy, so be it." He reached for another chocolate kiss. "I tell you, it's the worst four-letter word in the dictionary."

"What's that?"

"Debt."

Frank seemed surprised, then nodded in agreement. "Yeah, you've got a point there." Builder looked so forlorn that Frank felt the need to reassure him in some way. "One thing about it, a bankruptcy will keep the wolves at bay and buy you some time. And that's what you need right now—time."

"So, you think you can handle this for me?"

"To be honest, Builder, I'd prefer if somebody else did. It's not really my area. I concentrate on divorce cases, custody suits, you know, domestic stuff. And from what I can tell, this wouldn't be a typical filing. You need somebody who specializes in bankruptcy law. I mean with all your business debt, plus your personal—and—hey, don't you still have that apartment duplex on Bankhead?"

"Yes, but I'm not making money off it. Just one tenant's in there. The guy on the right side disappeared about a month ago; knocked a hole in the wall and took the plumbing with him. Plus he stole the washer, dryer, refrigerator—everything's gone."

"Jeez."

"I've been trying to sell that place for some time. I wouldn't get any money out of it; at best I'd just break even. But I've got to get it off my back. That'd be one less mortgage payment I'd have to make."

"Had any interested buyers?"

"Not a one. People don't want to invest in that area. I'm telling you, man, none of my shit's working right now."

"Well, like I said, this wouldn't be an ordinary case. With the duplex and your business and all, you need an experienced bankruptcy attorney. Somebody who knows the judges and knows the system."

"Can you give me a referral?"

"Sure. There're a couple of names I can pass on. But, hey, what's the deal with Maxx? He should know some good bankruptcy attorneys. What'd he say?"

"He's been out of pocket lately. I haven't seen him in a while. Think he's working on some case in Miami."

"Miami, huh? He sure gets around. Which reminds me, I need to check up on him. Gotta make sure he's treating Nikki right."

"Nikki?" Builder echoed, not recognizing the name.

"Yeah, my cousin. From Houston. I brought her over to your place for the barbecue. That's where she met Maxx."

"Oh, yeah, right," said Builder, vaguely remembering.

"Evidently, things are heatin' up between the two of them," said Frank. "She said the best thing I ever did was to introduce her to Maxx."

"Really?" Builder asked, surprised.

"That's right," chuckled Frank, alluding to the possibilities. "Maxx and my dear sweet cuz. You never know." He pulled his Rolodex close to him, then tore off a sheet of memo paper. "Okay, back to the business at hand. I'm going to jot down several names for you, so hopefully somebody will be able to help you out—or at least steer you in the right direction."

"Thanks, man."

Builder sank deeply into his thoughts, as Frank flipped through the Rolodex, pausing intermittently to write down a name and phone number.

"Say, Builder," he began offhandedly. "Heard the one about the skunk?"

"Huh?"

"The skunk. When you file bankruptcy, it's on your credit record for years, right?" He looked up at Builder. "Well, they say at first it's like being a skunk; nobody wants to be anywhere near you. But after a while, the stink fades away, and people start coming around, bit by bit."

Builder gave him a pinched look. "Gee, thanks, man. You really made my day."

"Well, I thought it was a good analogy," said Frank, an apology creeping into his voice. He focused his attention back to the Rolodex. "Let me get a couple more names for you."

Builder stood to walk around the office. Several plaques and certificates lined the wall of documented legitimacy. Among them were gilt-framed degrees from Howard University (magna cum laude) and the University of Virginia Law School, and a bronzed plaque from the 100 Black Men of Atlanta, acknowledging Frank's outstanding service and leadership.

"Still active with the coalition, huh?"

"Yeah, you know how that is. Once you get tied in, you're hooked. It stays in your blood. But we're doing some good things. You ought to come on back to the fold, renew your membership."

"I'd like to, Frank, I really would. But right now I just don't have the time. I need every waking minute to try to keep this business alive."

"I hear you."

"Besides, Mel's always been the one who's big on volunteering, getting involved in this and that. Too much so, if you ask me." This last he mumbled under his breath.

"Speaking of my girl, how's she doing?"

Builder paused slightly. "Let's put it this way. We both might be in here to see you real soon."

"What do you mean?"

"You said you handle divorce proceedings."

"You and Mel? You can't be serious. You two are the Rock of Gibraltar."

Builder snickered. "This rock has a whole bunch of cracks in it. Big time."

"Aw, man, don't tell me that." Frank acted as though he had been wounded. "You've got to be kidding."

"If it's not happening, it's not happening. What can I say?"

"Well, I've got to believe you'll work it out. I mean, if you all don't make it, there's no hope for any of us." He handed Builder the list of names. "Good luck."

"Thanks for hearing me out," said Builder. "Appreciate your time." He raised the list in his hand. "I'll keep you posted."

"Do that. Let me know how it goes."

Builder pointed a finger at him. "Don't forget to send me a bill."

Frank made a stop sign of protest. "It's on me. You know that."

"You sure?"

"Absolutely."

"Thanks, buddy."

Frank Kirby closed his office door. Jesus! Builder was in knee-deep. And problems with Mel too. He'd had no idea.

He regretted making that crack about the skunk. He had only been trying to get a laugh, but it didn't go over well. Usually Builder had a pretty good sense of humor, but, in light of the circumstances, it was understandable that he wouldn't be in a laughing mood, no matter how good the joke.

Despite the depressing meeting, one funny thing did come out of it—Builder's comment about being in debt. It was definitely worth remembering. Somehow, thought Frank, he'd have to find a way to use it. He could see himself at the center of a cocktail party, setting the scene with a few embellishments here and there, and then, with proper timing, he'd put forth the profound philosophical question: What's the worst four-letter word in the dictionary? He imagined getting all kinds of responses. People would swear, curse, embarrass themselves. Finally, after much beseeching from his audience and in true dramatic fashion, he'd deliver the punch line:

What's the worst four-letter word in the dictionary? Debt.

Yeah, he'd have to remember that.

Builder could tell immediately that little had been done since he had left the job site. He had been gone a good two hours; after seeing Frank, he had picked up some lumber and run a couple of errands. As he drove his truck up alongside his customer's house, he noticed that only a few roofing shingles had been laid while he was gone.

Two day laborers, heads turned toward the late January sun, scrambled to their feet at the sound of the engine.

Builder hopped out immediately. "What the heck have you been doing?" he asked with disapproval. "I'm not paying you to sleep."

"Oh, we was just taking a break," the taller one said amiably.

"Where's Thomas?"

"He went up the street to get some cigarettes," the other one replied.

"Cigarettes, huh?" Builder said sarcastically. "How long's he been gone?"

The two exchanged looks; the taller answered: "Not long."

Displeased, Builder looked around at the scraps of shingle and debris that littered the lawn, and directed the two workers to clean it up. Unless someone was present every minute of the day, nothing would get done.

He had left Thomas in charge. Thomas was one of the best roofers he knew, fast and capable, but let him get hold of some weed, and it was anybody's guess when he'd reappear. No doubt, he was out somewhere getting fired up. Now, Builder would have to finish the roofing himself.

He had taken the job because he so desperately needed the money. It was a piecemeal project, requiring a couple of days' work, at the most. The roof needed patching and a trench had to be dug to create a runoff line for rainwater. A few years ago he wouldn't have thought twice about a project like this; there simply wasn't enough profit to make it worthwhile. He wouldn't have touched it. But these days, he was glad to get anything—anything—no matter how small. A piece here, a piece there. That's what his work had come down to. Fragments of bits and pieces.

But precious time had been lost today. He had planned to check in for a few minutes to make sure things were running smoothly, then go to East Point and drop off the lumber at a house where he was building a deck. But with Thomas gone, he had to stay. He had to bring home some money from somewhere today.

His jaw set, Builder took off his jacket to prepare for the climb. Had he known he would be on a roof, he would have worn different shoes. His construction boots were too heavy to maneuver well up here, but they had traction, and they'd have to do. The slope of the roof was steeper than it appeared from below, so he trod cautiously. A hammer and a box of nails lay next to a bundle of shingles near the section where Thomas had started patching.

Builder worked deftly, nails hanging from his mouth. One thing about this business, it had forced him to learn virtually every phase of construction: plumbing, wiring, carpentry. He could do it all. He had to. Too many times he had been in a similar situation as today, left stranded by people who didn't show up or half completed a job. Even the so-called good ones, the professional crews he used as subcontractors, often came up with the flimsiest excuses for not following through. So there was no choice but to do the work himself. He had received a good head start from his father, but these last few years of hands-on experience had acutely sharpened his skills.

"Mister Builder," came a voice below.

Builder grabbed the nails from his mouth and craned his neck to the side. "Yeah," he shouted back.

The tall worker came into view. "We done finished picking up. Want us to get started on the trench?"

"Yeah, do that. I'll be down in a minute."

The tall one pushed a wheelbarrow toward the opposite side of the house. The other one followed with a shovel and pickax.

Builder rarely hired people off the street. They had to be picked up, dropped off, constantly supervised. But he liked being able to offer employment to men who otherwise would not have work. That was one of the few benefits he received from having his own business—giving a chance to guys down on their luck. He knew that some of the workers squandered their earnings on bottles of MD20-20, five-dollar-a-hit women on Stewart Avenue, and the lottery. But others were really trying to make it happen, and the little money they made went toward putting food on the table. So, as impatient as he sometimes became with them, his own situation this past year provided a startling reference point from which he could see with new eyes. He had moved a step closer toward their brand of fragility, and while he hadn't exactly walked in their shoes, he had learned just how tough it is for some people to scratch out a living. *There but for the grace of God* ... If it was hard for him, these guys had barely a chance.

"I'm baaaaaaaack." Thomas appeared below, one foot on the bottom rung of the ladder, one arm waving sillily.

"Don't come up here," Builder scolded him. "You're high as a kite."

"High? I ain't been doin' nothin'. How can I be high?" He proceeded to climb the ladder.

"I'm telling you, Thomas, go on back down. You can't handle it."

"Oh, I can handle it all right. I started this job; I'm gonna finish it."

Thomas was on the roof now, and Builder could tell he had gotten hold of something during his hiatus. His movements were slower, and his eyes glazed. Probably marijuana. "Shit, Thomas, don't get up here and do something stupid. You'll have us both laying out on the ground."

"What do ya mean? I'm fine, see?" Thomas held out both arms, wobbled slightly, then regained his balance. "You go on; I can take it from here." He spoke to Builder like a parent shooing away a child. "Go on. I got it."

"Okay," Builder acquiesced. "But if you fall, it's on you. I don't have you covered, and I *know* you don't have insurance."

"Insurance? Who needs insurance? I prackly learnt how to *walk* on a roof."

Builder had to nod in agreement. Thomas *was* good. And if the truth were told, he was probably high most of the time he worked. It was inconceivable to Builder how he managed as well as he did. "Well, you're up here now, so—" He wasn't about to try to force Thomas back down. Doing so might result in both of them falling off the roof. He shook his head at the image. Wouldn't that top off everything? To be laid up in a hospital, totally out of commission.

"Hey, you hear the one about the hooker and the fried tomato?"

"No, and I'm not sure I want to." He had heard enough jokes for one day. He gingerly sidestepped some shingles on his way to the ladder.

"Aw, come on, listen up." Thomas made a cut to fit the curve of a gable. "It's a good one, man, I promise. Got it straight from Lazy-eyed Jack."

"Oh, yeah?" asked Builder, chuckling at the reference.

This was the way his days often went: dealing with unreliable workers, listening to vulgar jokes. He had to try hard not to slip into the crude demeanor and language so commonly used by the men. After all, he had a responsibility to his clients to maintain a respectable atmosphere. And so he would draw the line, stop a conversation, when he saw things get out of hand. Clearly, his "colleagues" were not students of Shakespeare, and their level of conversation hovered at the lower end of the creative spectrum. While the corporate arena was a prime target of Builder's disdain, there were some aspects about it which he sometimes longed for: an expense account to cover incidentals, the luxury of planning, avid discussions among sharp minds. His vision of owning his business had not included rooftop dialogue with a doped-up worker whose idea of a person worth quoting was some street corner guru named Lazy-eyed Jack. But, for the moment, this was his world.

"All right, Thomas," he said. "Lay it on me."

Thomas gleefully obliged. He was at home on top of a roof, one of the few times he was on top of anything. He told his joke with relish, and was rewarded with a big laugh by Builder.

The two men working below wanted to get in on the fun.

"You'll have to hear it from Thomas," said Builder, as he stepped off the ladder. He wouldn't do justice to the joke; besides, he didn't want to repeat the obscenities. Even though his crew was a motley one, it was still his job, however precariously, to try to hold them to a higher standard.

With her shoulder bag swinging from her arm, Mel rushed through Concourse A, glancing at the large clock over a ticket counter, which reminded her that she was late. She had let her class out early, but had gotten waylaid by a persistent student who disagreed with a grade. Anne's plane was scheduled to arrive fifteen minutes ago from Fort Lauderdale. As it was, there wouldn't be much time to talk, since Anne was taking a connecting flight home to Seattle.

As she reached the gate, almost cleared of passengers, she immediately spotted Anne, her legs comfortably crossed, reading a thick book. That was Anne, always cool and collected. She looked up and broke into a brilliant smile as Mel walked toward her, apologizing for being late.

Anne stood up quickly and gave Mel a hug. "I'm glad you could make it."

"You've cut your hair."

"Yes," said Anne, touching her shiny bob. "Like it?"

"Very much. Makes you look younger."

"Alston wouldn't want to hear that. People already tell him I look like his daughter."

"Wellll . . ." teased Mel. "Why should you be surprised?" Anne's second husband was nearly thirty years her senior.

"Well, let's talk fast," said Anne. "Why don't we walk on down to my gate?" She glanced at her watch. "I've got half an hour before my flight."

"You sure you can't stay over?"

"Next time."

"You always say that."

"Oh, hush. How have things been?"

Mel began to fill her in, skipping over the details of the last few months, but being honest about her strained marriage and her family's financial woes.

They met like this about twice a year, generally on the run, in between Anne's connecting flights from Florida, where she visited her mother, to Seattle, where she lived with her sixty-four-year-old husband, a well-to-do jewelry importer. Mel and Anne were roommates their freshman year in college. They had liked each other initially, but their friendship was officially born one October night, when, relieved that midterms were over, they celebrated by sharing a potent marijuana joint and a slew of personal secrets. Mel admitted to a suicide attempt after her father's death. Anne confided that at sixteen she gave up her virginity to a black boy, an exchange student from Zaire. Over the years they had maintained their friendship through Christmas cards, telephone calls, and quick airport visits.

"Mmmm. Let's get some of this. Smells delicious." Anne pulled Mel inside a miniconcession store and ordered two bags of popcorn. "It sounds to me like you need a vacation," she advised, after hearing Mel's updated synopsis.

"Let's see—where should I go? A month in Maui?" Mel said in jest. "Or perhaps Tahiti? Yes, that would do me just fine."

"How about Seattle?" They walked slowly down the side of the concourse, avoiding the main traffic, chewing their popcorn.

Mel looked at Anne quizzically. "You mean, your place?"

"Sure. I'd love for you to come. You need to come and play tourist. Or, if you want, you could hibernate at my house and eat bonbons all day."

Mel chuckled. "That sounds good too."

"Well then?"

"I'm tempted," Mel said thoughtfully. "But running away's not the answer."

"You wouldn't be running away. You'd be taking a break, that's all. You need some different surroundings, a new perspective. It's probably the best thing you could do for yourself right now. And for your marriage."

Mel raised her eyebrows in a "get real" expression.

"Well, you'd come back rested and refreshed," Anne continued, "and I'm sure Builder would appreciate you all the more."

"I doubt that."

They reached Anne's gate and strolled over to the window to watch the planes.

"Enough about me," Mel said. "How's your mom?"

Anne's face clouded. "Not well. I see her deteriorating more and more. She insists on staying in Florida, and regardless of what I say, I can't persuade her to come live with me."

"She wants to be on her own as long as she can."

"I know, but she needs help. She just won't admit it." Anne's eyes teared up. "It's so hard to see her just—fading away." She folded her popcorn bag, which was still half full. "What about your mother? Are you two getting along better?"

"I wouldn't say that. But she and Sasha have a pretty good relationship. They write regularly and—"

"What about *you*, Mel? I'm asking about you."

Mel took a deep breath. "It's different for you and your mom. You've always been close. But my mother and I—" She shrugged her shoulders and shook her head.

"You have to make an effort. Don't you want to patch things up?"

"To be honest, I'm glad she's on the other side of the globe."

"Oh, Mel! Make peace with her. Please. Do it soon." Anne gazed at a 747 creeping by. "She's not always going to be around, you know. And when that happens . . ." Her voice cracked as she looked out into the distance.

They stood at the window for several more minutes. Anne was the last to board the plane.

The distinct woodsy fragrance that always announced her presence caused Builder to look up from his cup of murky liquid.

"Val! How've you been?"

"Better than you, from the looks of things." She eased into the seat opposite him, placing her packages on the adjacent empty chair. "Are you waiting to meet somebody?"

"Yep. She's tall, blond, and frisky. Seen her?"

Val rolled her eyes. "Puhleeeze. Even Mother Theresa wouldn't look at you twice. Unless, of course, she thought you were one of the poor lost ones."

"That bad, huh?"

"Look at you!" Val admonished. "Bags under your eyes, looking all sad, wallowing in your tea." She peered closer. "That *is* tea, isn't it?" She shook her head, as though he was beyond help. "And those clothes have seen better days."

He seemed genuinely hurt. "These? These are my best work clothes. What's wrong with them? Everybody can't be like you and wear Gucci and Mucci all the time."

"Oh, stop it," she said good-naturedly. "But since you're at a mall, you might as well take advantage of it and do some shopping."

"No, I just had to check out a wall unit in Rich's. One of my customers wants one like it."

"Can you make one like it?"

"Pretty much. It may not have all the lines, but it'll be close enough. You know how much they're asking for that thing? Sixteen hundred dollars."

"Ridiculous!"

"I know. I can build it for a whole lot less, and with much better materials. Help my customer out and still make money." He said this matter-of-factly, without hint of bravado.

"It must be great to have that kind of talent."

He shrugged his shoulders and fiddled with his cup.

Val eyed him carefully. "Where's the Builder Burke that I know—strong, confident, full of spunk?" She spoke the words forcefully, as though trying to inject the adjectives back into his being. "Build-er," she called, looking under the table. "Oh, Builder."

"Builder Burke?" he asked, playing along. "Last I heard, he was beaten down so badly he swore he'd never show his face in town again."

Val made a tsk-tsk sound, shaking her head. "Such a shame. I rather liked the fellow. He was one of the few men I knew who wasn't a BSJ."

Builder had heard Mel use those initials before, but he didn't remember what they stood for. "A BSJ?"

"Ball-less, spineless jerk." Val pronounced the words with measured disdain. This was, after all, a phrase she had coined, and it deserved the proper amount of emphasis.

"So, I'm not a BSJ, huh? Guess I have some redeeming qualities."

"Yes, but you must act quickly before they disappear too!"

Builder took a deep, weary breath.

Val dropped the facade. "Is there anything I can do?" she asked sympathetically. "I know things have been tough lately."

"Yeah, well, it ain't been easy."

"I hear you haven't exactly been helping matters."

"What do you mean?" he asked suspiciously.

"Can I be really honest with you?"

Builder snickered. "Val, when have you ever not been? Why hold back now?"

She leaned forward and spoke seriously. "If you don't clean up your act, you're going to mess around and lose Mel. She's gonna walk."

The right corner of Builder's mouth twitched slightly. "If that's what she wants to do, I can't stop her."

"Of course you can."

"She's a grown woman. If she's made up her mind to leave—"

"I didn't say that."

"But she's thinking about it?"

Val leaned back in her chair. "She's not happy."

"Gee," he said cynically. "Like I've been jumping through hoops lately."

"It's this money situation, Builder. It's tearing her apart. I know that's at the center of all this, and—"

"It's more than the money. I'm working day and night trying to turn things around, and it's still not enough. When I come home, you'd think there'd be some appreciation, right?" He took a quick swallow from his cup. "When I go upstairs, she's either asleep or gives me an icy hello. I can't remember the last time we slept together. Now what the hell kind of marriage is that?"

"Builder, you're coming in at midnight or later. She's tired."

"From what? She hasn't been working for months. She sent out a few résumés but I don't think she's even looking anymore."

"That's not fair, Builder. I know for a fact that she's desperately trying to find something full-time. The job market's horrible right now. You know that."

"Okay, okay," he agreed. "But what I'm saying is that until she does find something, seems like she could help out in other ways."

"But she is."

"You mean those little freelance projects? They're not bringing in any money."

"Those 'little freelance projects' helped you all get the Honda back. Right?"

"Yeah," he had to concede. He took a swallow of his tea. "But I'm talking about real money. Something consistent. We've got some heavyweight bills and I can't carry them by myself. I've got to have some help."

"Maybe you will soon. You know we're talking about starting a black greeting card company."

"We who?"

"Mel and me."

"What?" he asked dully.

"She hasn't mentioned it?"

"I told you. We don't talk much."

Val let that comment slide. "Well, I've been kicking around this idea for a while. It's ideal for both of us. I'd do the illustrations, and Mel would handle the marketing end of it. And she'd come up with the words, too—she's good at that. It wouldn't have to be much. In fact, a lot of our cards would be blank inside. Most people like to write their own messages anyway. Don't you just hate it when you find a terrific-looking card, and you open it up, and it's got the wrong message?"

Builder shrugged. "I suppose so."

"Come on, Builder," she pressed. "Don't you think it's a great idea? You don't sound too enthused."

"I just know your friend is the corporate type—she loves that environment, thrives on it. I'm not sure she'd do too well in a small business, even her own."

"She has been a bit skittish about it," admitted Val. "She's heard stories about how good friends make bad business partners."

"That's something to consider. You two are about as different as you can be. You've got different styles and personalities. You're like night and day."

"That's true. For one thing, Mel gets along so well with white people. And you know me, I couldn't care less."

An attractive woman in a short leather skirt switched by and Builder took a sideways glance.

"Uh, uh, uh," Val scolded. "Naughty. Naughty."

"No harm in looking," he retorted. "I can't do anything else." He returned to the subject at hand. "So, where are you going to get the money to start this little venture?" he asked.

"We've got our sources," Val said mysteriously.

"I'm sure you know that Mel doesn't have one red cent to put into any kind of business deal."

"Neither do I."

"Then where's it coming from? Surely not the banks?"

She feigned shock. "How dare you even shape your lips to say that? No, actually I'm expecting a settlement soon. And this will be earmarked strictly for the company."

"Another one of your legal victories?"

"That's right. I've got to live up to my middle name."

"What's that?"

"Sue. Valencia Sue Bellinger."

Builder chuckled. "So what happened this time that you're getting a big settlement?"

"I didn't say 'big,' " Val clarified. "It's"—she reached for the right word—"respectable."

"Okay. So what happened?"

"Some little freckled-face pipsqueak at Electronic World called me a black bitch. He got upset because I returned some merchandise and wanted my money back. Can you believe that?"

"Nothing surprises me anymore."

"He kind of mumbled it under his breath, but I heard him."

"And I'm sure you took full advantage of the situation," said Builder.

"Oh, you know that. At first he denied it. Then, he said he didn't mean anything by it. So I called in his supervisor, and his supervisor's supervisor, and they told me this had never happened before and that I was overreacting."

"That's bull."

"Of course it is. I told them what if some black kid called a white woman from Dunwoody—bitch? They'd damn near lynch him! Anyway, they had the kid apologize, but I told them that wasn't going to do it, that they had to come up with a whole lot more. Last week they flew me to the corporate headquarters in Minnesota—to talk to the head man and his executive committee. Like I was supposed to be really impressed by that. They tried to appease me with a new refrigerator. A refrigerator! I told them I already had a damn new refrigerator." Her voice changed pitch. "I got one last year from Appliance Alley when *they* wouldn't act right."

Builder laughed. "Keep this up, and you'll run out of people to sue."

"They're asking for it. They have absolutely no respect for us. We do all the buying and then get treated like dirt. Anyway, I told them it was clear that they condoned racism and that I should be paid for public humiliation, mental stress—I named everything in the book. Made up some stuff, too. Said it would be a whole lot cheaper for them to compensate me than be faced with a possible boycott and get all that negative publicity."

"They'd be smart to work something out with you," Builder said. "A few thousand dollars is chicken feed to them."

"Of course it is. They have accounts all over the place to handle folks like me—nuisance accounts, they call them. Oh, and I did some research before I went up there. Found out the regional manager fired several black clerks for no reason whatsoever. So I mentioned all that. They looked at me like I was mad. Like 'How could you possibly know this?' But they listened. Oh, yes, they listened. They realized I can make a whole lot of noise."

"I'm sure they figured that out real fast," Builder said with a smile. He liked Val's crack-the-whip style. With her thick braids smartly coiled around her head, her eyes gleaming with high-spirited vim, she seemed ready to pounce on any adversary, to fight for any cause. She was constantly entwined in some sort of arbitration or legal maneuvering. And even though she had no legal training, the amazing thing was that she won most of the time. "Maybe I should hire you to plead my case against these banks," he said.

She didn't hesitate. "That's a great idea. You know I'd do it in a snap. We could hold a press conference, maybe get a few other black businessmen to talk about their problems—there'd be folks lined up for blocks."

"Val, I was only joking."

"But why not do it? You should make a fuss, a big fuss. It's a shame that a person with your skills and experience can't get the right backing. And all this money we pour into these banks. We've got to call these crackers down on it."

"Well, I guess my attitude is that if you push them into a corner, they'll still get around you somehow."

"Good grief, Builder! Don't go pulling an Uncle Tom."

Builder laughed. "Me? Not a chance. No, I agree with what you're doing. And I say more power to you. Lawsuits and that whole legal thing—it can be very effective. I did it myself a few years back, remember? But now my situation's different. I mean, I don't want to get a business loan or line of credit as a result of being known as someone who pressures folks or from some forced quotas. I want my work to speak for itself."

"And that's the way it should be, but that's not how it happens." She straightened up in her chair. "What's with you, anyway? You and I were always the loud, militant types. Have you gone soft on me?"

"I don't know. I guess I'm just damn tired. I'm tired of fighting and of bustin' my ass every day and gettin' peanuts in return. Right now, I feel like saying, 'Y'all take it, just take it all. You won.'" He pushed his hands into the air.

"Well, we can't have any of that." She pulled her large purse close to her and removed a legal-sized sketch pad. "What you need is some optimism, some faith. Where's your faith, Builder?"

"It's worn out too."

"Can I borrow this for a sec?" she asked, reaching over to pluck a pen that peeked out from his breast pocket. "You know, sometimes if you can just picture yourself in a certain situation"—she drew on the pad as she spoke—"if you can imagine where you want to be, then it's easier to get there."

"If only it were that simple."

"I'm serious. There's actually a name for it. Some kind of psychological technique that you can use as a form of meditation."

"As far as I'm concerned, if I can't see it, touch it, or smell it, it doesn't exist."

Val shook her head in disappointment. "A typical male response."

"What can I say?" Builder said innocently. "I am what I am."

For a couple of minutes she concentrated on her pad; he cooperated with his silence, watching the passersby in between slurps of lukewarm tea.

"There! It's rough, but"—she tore off the sheet and handed it to him—"you get the point."

Builder looked at a caricature of himself, sporting a ridiculously huge smile as he sat atop a massive truck. Surrounding him were several stick figures with elongated arms holding out stacks of bills in his direction. In the right corner, another figure stood behind a video camera, propped up by a tripod, and next to it stood a truck with *Eyewitness News* on the side. At the bottom of the sheet, in large capital letters, were the words: "Builder Burke: Banking on Bucks."

"Hey, this is great." He smiled admiringly. "You're good at this."

"Thanks. You sound surprised."

"Well, no, I knew you had artistic ability. I just thought it was more of a hobby." He looked again at the drawing. "This is really good."

"Thanks. It keeps a roof over my head."

"Not interested in working with an ad agency or anything?"

"I wouldn't last two minutes with an agency, you know that. I couldn't be tied down. I've got to have space, do things on my own terms."

"Yeah, I understand."

"We both like the independent life, Builder."

"Except you're a lot better at it than I am."

"That'll change. I guarantee it." She nodded toward the paper. "Just look at that every day, and you'll start feeling the power."

"The power, huh?" He looked at the drawing again, this time with skepticism. "Is there a mantra or something I need to chant as I gaze upon this?"

"That's up to you," said Val, ignoring his sarcasm. "It can't hurt. But for this to work, you've got to have the right attitude. You've got to become a true believer."

"A believer in what?"

"In your own power! That's why I made the sketch with your pen. It represents you and your energy. The power is already within you, you just have to—" She opened her palm dramatically, signaling him to finish the sentence.

"Bring it out," Builder supplied.

"Exactly."

"Lord, she's gotten religion."

"How do you think I deal with these crazy white folks all the time?" She lowered her voice conspiratorially. "I vis-u-a-lize." She spoke the word with satisfaction, slowly enunciating each syllable. "I see them in a closed room, sweating it out. Judgment's being handed down, and they have to come up with the cash. Lots of it. They know they're wrong, and now they have to pay. Sometimes I see them with nothing on but their underwear. And that's a terrible sight, I can tell you that. But it makes me strong; oh, it makes me strong."

Builder considered this for a second, then smiled devilishly. "So all I have to do is visualize naked women, is that it?"

Val groaned in disgust. "You're hopeless, you know that? Hopeless!" She gathered up her things in an exaggerated huff.

"Where're you parked?" he asked, rising to leave. "I'll walk you to your car."

"But I haven't finished shopping yet."

"Sure you have." He took charge of her packages. "You get all this money from white folks, and then you hand it right back to them. That's *your* weakness."

"Well, at least I have something to show for it," she retorted.

"Yeah, yeah, yeah." He escorted Val and her boxed bargains out of the mall. Carefully tucked under his left arm was the rolled-up sketch of himself, grinning broadly in the face of monied success. He had already committed the image to memory.

CHAPTER 7

In its heyday, the restaurant was a watering hole for local politicians, where deals were cut more easily than Brie, and favors swapped for votes with nary an eye blink. But as commercial development sprouted in the more affluent, northern end of DeKalb County, the politicos took their money and trading partners to spiffier environs. To combat a bloated mortgage and dwindling clientele, the restaurant adjusted its personality—downward. Pinwheels became a favorite haunt for a seedier crowd, mainly spillovers from the strip joint next door that served up alcohol and flesh, but no real food.

This was Mel's third week. She worked from seven to eleven, on Tuesdays, Wednesdays, and Thursdays, and by the time she finished, it was after midnight when she arrived home. So far, there had been only one close call—the night when Builder had come home, and Mel was still in the shower, scrubbing away any smoky evidence that she was working in a restaurant/bar where the mostly male patrons possessed smelly cigarettes and gluttonous eyes.

She hadn't yet told Builder that she was working at Pinwheels, partly because she wanted to present him with a handful of crisp bills, in a dramatic gesture to prove that, indeed, she was doing her share to bring in what money she could. But the other reason was to reserve the information as ammunition for the next attack. She envisioned an argument, typical of their talks these days, where he'd blame her for not doing more to support the family financially. She would then reveal that she had been working at Pinwheels to catch up on the second mortgage, to pay the sixteen hundred dollars that was overdue, and that she had done so without his knowledge. It would make him realize how out of touch he was with the family. It would make him get off her case. And it would make him feel bad. Good!

She knew it was only a matter of time before Builder found out. She'd have to tell him soon; if not, Sasha would beat her to the punch. All she had told her daughter was that she was working on a special project, but she couldn't use such a cryptic excuse much longer. Sasha was curious about her mother's mysterious nightly absences, and might innocently mention them to Builder. Clearly, Mel would have to disclose her whereabouts soon, or risk having someone else do it for her.

"Is there anything more I can get you?" she asked pleasantly. She laid her receipt book on top of her empty tray.

"Oh, I can think of a coupla things," slurred one of the men. He landed two bloodshot eyes directly at her cleavage, accented by a ridge of scalloped black lace. He and his companion laughed drunkenly at this latest sexual come-on. After two hours and several beers at Pinwheels, they showed no hesitancy. Mel continued to hold her smile, reminding herself she was here for a purpose and would not be deterred.

She didn't know which was worse, the cigarette smoke that brought on a nagging headache the instant she set foot in the door, or the sloppy behavior she had to endure from customers' lack of class. Such behavior was tolerated, even considered appropriate here at Pinwheels, where the management's selection of "uniforms" for the waitresses set a tone completely opposite from the pristine. Mel detested her flimsy outfit. Everything about it was a contrived attempt to exude sexuality—from the short black leather pants and fishnet hose to the tight, low-neck top that pushed out her mammary glands and gave her goose bumps from exposure. Mike, the manager, frowned on short hair, not sexy enough in his opinion, so all the "girls" wore shoulder-length tresses, either homegrown or artificial. Mel's hair wasn't quite long enough to meet the standard, so she bought a cheap black wig of wavy, cascading curls. The finishing touch was an oversized pink satin hair bow, designed to add a hint of girlish charm to the overall effect of slut. She felt ludicrous and humiliated in the getup.

After the first hour of the first night, she was ready to quit, until the manager pulled her aside. "Look happy out there," he had advised. "Flick those lashes, show some teeth. Make it worth your while." And so she had forced herself to smile at men whom she would totally ignore on the street, to shut her ears to the raunchiness that punctuated the mealtime conversations, and to fling her fake hair, the way white women do, in reply to an off-color remark.

The manager was right: Customers were more generous when their egos were stroked. Each night she averaged over a hundred dollars in tips. Sometimes, she'd call up her affected Southern accent, and let it run loose for the night. Or she'd pretend she was an actress playing a role—anything to psych herself up, to help her get to the end of the night when she could count her money, and mark off one day fewer that she'd have to be here. She convinced herself she could smile a little bit more for a little while longer until her mission was accomplished.

Now, with everything in her, she leaned forward provocatively to put the receipt in the center of the table. "Here's the *real* test of your manhood," she teased, knowing full well neither man was looking at the bill. "I enjoyed waiting on you. Come back soon. Okay?"

"We sure will," one of them replied, licking his lips. "And you take real good care of yourself, hear?" He slipped her a crisp ten dollar bill.

"Why, thank you."

She headed toward the bar to get drinks for customers at table 12, when she saw him. She nearly stopped in her tracks, and glanced from left to right to see if there was another route to take. Ron! Of all people! He was with a group of men in business suits, being seated at table 14, *her* table!

Quickly, she crossed to the opposite aisle, holding her tray upright to obscure her face. She took refuge at the rear of the bar, where she could see without being seen. Ron and his companions grinned broadly at Angelique, the perky hostess, who was passing out menus and probably telling them at this moment that "Raven" would be their waitress.

Mel felt her stomach gnarl. This is crazy, she thought. Pull yourself together. You've got a job to do; go on over there and do it. But she couldn't move. She stayed rooted to the spot, wishing she could dissolve into the floor until Ron and his crew left the premises.

She had deliberately chosen this restaurant to avoid a situation like this. Of all the restaurants where she had applied for a job, Pinwheels was ideal because it was farthest away from the beaten path, farthest from the places that most of the people she knew hung out. But she should have known better. Despite all the talk about being a big international city, Atlanta was still a small town. Too small.

Maybe she could get one of the other waitresses to take the table, she thought. She had done a couple of favors, surely someone could help her now. With a hopeful eye, she looked around for a substitute, but spotted no one; no one, that is, except the bartender, who had discovered her sanctuary and was heading her way.

"What are you doing way back here? Hiding from the wolves?"

"Uh—no," Mel sputtered. Was it that obvious? "My stomach's a little queasy, that's all." That was it! She would feign sickness for a little while—she really *didn't* feel well—maybe hang out in the ladies' room until Ron left. That would still give her time to work a couple of hours before closing.

"I got something that'll straighten you out, pronto. It's a magic potion made from celery," said the bartender. "If it'll cure Montezuma's revenge, it'll cure anything."

He trekked to the front of his domain just as Angelique came up to the bar. Mel saw them huddle for a second before he thrust his thumb in her direction. Angelique scurried on back.

"Not feeling good?" She reeled on without waiting for a reply. "Things are getting hectic out there. You've got a table full of hungry men on fourteen. And ten is asking for the check."

"Okay. I'll be there."

"Sure?"

"Yes. In just a sec."

Turning to go, Angelique mimicked the manager's voice. "Remember to switch those hips, jiggle your stuff, and make all of us some money." It was a phrase that the manager used ad nauseam to instill pep and enthusiasm among his "girls."

Before, Mel had always recoiled at the words, which she considered degrading and antifeminist. But perhaps because she had heard them so often, or because Angelique said them so mockingly, this time they didn't seem as offensive. Rather, they jarred her into action.

She strutted to the front of the bar and asked for four glasses of water. The manager was partially right—not about the switching and the jiggling, but about money. Money was why she was here. Money was why she endured the lascivious looks, the silly wig, the too-tight clothes. So what if Ron saw her? She wasn't doing anything illegal or unethical. She had nothing to be ashamed of. She was making money for her family, damn it. Desperately needed money. *It ain't about likin' it.*

"Here, this'll straighten you right up." The bartender set a glass of greenish liquid in front of her.

"Thanks," she said, taking a few sips out of deference. Her nerve up, she took a deep breath, preparing to go into her act. No need to make a big deal out of this, she reminded herself. Just stay cool. But as she approached Ron's table, her resolve melted and her knees wobbled. She imagined herself collapsing to the floor from the weight of the water glasses and the fear of discovery. But she made it to the table standing erect, her chest pumped up, and her inlaid dimples made prominent by a pressed smile. "Good evening, gentlemen. I'm Raven, your waitress for tonight."

There was no hint of recognition from Ron. He laughed and joked along with his companions, even flirted with her a bit, par for the course on a boys' night out. Mel avoided looking at him as much as possible, and when their eyes did meet, she detected no double takes that might indicate he suspected her. So far, so good, she thought. Ironically, the wig and outfit and heavy makeup, all the things she hated so much, provided a fortuitous disguise. Of course! Ron didn't expect to find her here, so why would he? People often don't see what's right in front of them. Besides, Ron was used to seeing her in business attire or casual wear, not a sleazy makeover like this. So since she didn't look like Mel to him, she wasn't Mel. She was Raven, right?

She had pulled Raven out of the mothballs when Mike the manager had asked her to invent a sexier alias. "Mel is too masculine," he had said distastefully. "You need something playful and exotic." For a moment, Mel had been at a loss, trying to come up with a name comparable to Angelique or LaShaundra or Alexandra, the manufactured monikers of the waitresses at Pinwheels. Surely Betty or Sue wouldn't do. So, ending the search close to home, she had proposed Raven, of which Mike approved. To the folks at Pinwheels, that's who she was. And to Ron, she now reminded herself, that's who she was: Raven, not Mel. All that panicking for nothing.

By the time she brought out their sirloin steaks, Mel had begun to relax. She kind of enjoyed watching Ron play naughty host to this group of bawdy white men from out of town. It was a role that he seemed very comfortable with. Earlier, he had evidently obliged his guests' request for a taste of nude Atlanta and had taken them next door. From what Mel overheard, he had enjoyed the girlie shows as much as anybody. She wondered what Celeste would say if she found out that her ever perfect husband, who she believed was totally enamored and satisfied with her, had laid aside marital righteousness for slinky relief at a nude bar. Her own secret, Mel concluded, was safely under wraps. But then, somebody asked for the Worcestershire sauce.

"Lay it on me right here, doll, will you?" His hands occupied with a knife and fork, the man tapped the center of his steak.

Following directions, Mel moved in toward the table, leaning over to apply the sauce. It must have been the angle at which she was standing, or the curve of her arm that caused a shift in her cleavage. Ron made a gagging noise of stunned recognition, his eyes locked onto the raised mole that peeped out from the tip of Mel's lace bodice. Once, during a pool party, he had teased her about that mole, when he was out of Celeste's earshot, and giddy from a couple of gin-and-tonics. He had said it was the luckiest mole alive, strategically lodged between her breasts, the next-best place where any man worth his salt would love to be. And now, it was this same unmistakable mole that gave her away.

"Mel!—Is it?—I thought you looked fa—" He couldn't finish the sentence; his mouth hung wide open.

Mel stiffened; the chill of discovery crept all the way down her spine. "I'm Raven," she insisted through tight lips. "I must look like somebody you know."

"Baby," one of the men at the table said loudly. "I sure wish you looked like somebody *I* know."

Mel tried to laugh it off. She avoided Ron's gaze and moved to the opposite side of the table.

"Sounds to me like ol' Ronald's confused," someone teased. "Like maybe he can't keep his lady friends straight."

"Not me," protested Ron, keeping his eyes locked onto Mel.

"Aw, 'fess up," another piped in. "There's nothing like a little dish on the side, right?"

"Yeah," someone laughed. "As long as you don't get the appetizers mixed up with the entree." He described how, in a moment of hot tub passion with his wife, he screamed out his girlfriend's name.

As Mel left the table, she felt Ron's eyes pierce her back.

The rest of the evening was endless. At one point, Ron went to the rest room and cornered Mel at the side of the bar.

"What are you doing here?" he asked stupidly. "What's with this Raven bit? And the wig and all?"

"I'm working," she said defensively. "Isn't it obvious?" She spoke with resentment, angry that he had found her and was forcing her to face her real identity. As Raven, she could hide behind the facade of a floppy waitress; but Ron's presence was an instant reminder that she was Mel Burke, former successful Chamber of Commerce executive, reduced to waiting tables in a place of questionable repute.

She thought she had prepared herself for this possibility, if someone she knew should walk in and recognize her. She had formulated a ready-made explanation: that she was gathering research for a client who wanted inside information about the restaurant industry. Now, she realized how ridiculous that would sound. Who did she think she was kidding? She wouldn't convince Ron or anyone else that she was here under some investigative ruse. She wasn't that good an actress. And lying required a hell of a lot of effort. Besides, at this point, what did it matter?

"You been working here for a while?" Ron asked.

"Long enough."

"Damn. And Builder knows about this?"

"What do you think, Ron?" she said, irritated.

She wanted to imply that of course Builder knew about it. Answer a question with a question, avoid a direct response, and people might assume what you want them to. Then, move on to something else before they have time to follow up. "You'd better get back to your buddies," she said, nodding in the direction of his table. "Looks like they need you to keep them in line."

"Oh, they're harmless. We're just having a little fun." His tone turned more serious. "Uh, listen, Mel—you won't mention this to Celeste, will you? That you saw me here? She'd get all bent out of shape. She wouldn't understand."

So, he was concerned about his hide, about what dear Celeste would think. He evidently didn't know that she and Celeste hadn't spoken in weeks, not since the car was repossessed.

"Why should I tell Celeste?" she asked innocently. "You don't need her permission to come out at night. You're a big boy, aren't you?"

Relief spread over his face. "I really am going to see if there's something I can do about finding you a job. I'll make a few calls, touch base with some folks who owe me a favor."

It was a lame attempt to appease his conscience—and to thank her in advance for not ratting to Celeste. Mel didn't expect anything to come from it. In fact, she could virtually guarantee that by the light of day, Ron would have forgotten all about his pledge, made under duress in a third-rate restaurant where neither of them was supposed to be.

"*Ooooh, child, things are gonna get easier; ooooh, child, things'll get brighter. . . .*" It was a favorite oldie, and this morning the song seemed directly aimed at her. It was a message Mel needed to hear, the soothing lyrics assuring her that, yes, things will get better. But when? she thought. When?

She flipped a giant pancake and watched the beige batter swell from the heat of the skillet. This was a long-standing ritual, making pancakes on Saturday mornings. When Sasha was younger, Mel used to serve her pancakes in bed, a once-a-week childhood indulgence allowed as a reward for good performance in school. Now, instead of watching cartoons in bed, Sasha came to the table with a book in hand. But throughout the years the menu had remained the same: whole wheat raisin pancakes with nutmeg and cinnamon, and a glass of orange juice.

The DJ was making an earthy appeal for the radio station. " ... so get out those checkbooks and give it up. We need your support here at WCLK. And I don't wanna hear no loose change. This is Youngblood asking you to dig deep. Real deep. I know you won't let me down."

"Sorry, bud, not this time," Mel talked back. "I need to get on the air and ask for money for *me*."

"You say something?" Sasha asked absentmindedly, not looking up from her mystery.

Mel slabbed a couple of butter squares onto the mound of pancakes. "I said breakfast is ready."

"Got enough for us?"

Startled, she twirled around to see Maxx coming through the kitchen door. He was not alone. Clutching his hand was Nikki—whom Mel hadn't seen since last year's party.

"Uncle Maxx!"

"Sasha!" he rejoined with equal joy. "How's the most beautiful girl in the world?" Releasing Nikki's hand, he opened his arms to his niece and gave her a generous hug. "You really ought to keep this door locked," he said to Mel, in mock rebuke. "*Anybody* might walk in."

He looked good. His eyes were bright and sparkling; his smooth skin enriched by recent flirting with the sun. He had been in Miami for several weeks, the lead attorney on a major drug trial that involved several defendants, and obviously during that time he had managed to sneak in some R&R. But Mel was most surprised by Nikki; not only was she here with Maxx and hanging on to his every word, but physically she was a woman transformed. Her hair, a raspberry red last summer, was a toned-down auburn, russet. And her clothes were light-years from the tacky outfit she had worn at the barbecue. The tan safari pants, black tie-up Enzo Angiolini boots, and tailored plaid shirt looked hand-picked from a Saks display window. Courtesy of Maxx, no doubt.

Addressing Sasha's barrage of questions, Maxx explained, while avoiding Mel's gaze, that, yes, he did win his case. Not surprisingly, he was sketchy on the details. Sasha had no inkling that her dear uncle was a drug dealer's best friend, and the sad part, thought Mel, was that Maxx himself didn't see it that way. In his own mind, for his conscience's sake, he simply viewed his clients as entrepreneurs who happened to handle risky merchandise, and, like anybody else who was accused of wrong-doing, deserved a legal defense.

But now was not the time to reheat that cup of soup. Maxx was back, Sasha was happy. And sitting at the kitchen table, gloating over her man, was the made-over Nikki.

She mentioned how she had visited Maxx for a weekend several weeks ago and since then had flown numerous times between Atlanta and Miami. "Till finally I said, 'What the heck, I'll just stay with him till he finishes the case,'" she giggled.

Mel wished that Nikki had not been quite so open about her relationship with Maxx, since Sasha was taking in every word. "What about your job?" she asked. "How could you take so much time off?"

"I took a leave of absence."

"Wow," Mel said enviously. "They must really like you at Crawford Long. Good jobs are hard to come by these days."

"So are good people," inserted Maxx. "They know a good thing when they see it; they're not going to let her go." He stroked Nikki's hair. "And neither am I."

"Oh, Maxx," she said coyly.

"Think we should tell them?" he whispered, loudly enough for everyone to hear.

"Tell us what?" Sasha asked eagerly.

"We're going to get married," they announced in unison.

"MARRIED?" screeched Sasha, her voice going up an octave.

"You're kidding!" Mel blurted, then immediately regretted having spoken so bluntly. She turned to Nikki, trying to clean it up. "I mean, what do you possibly see in this guy? He's hopeless."

"Oh, I see a lot of things in him," Nikki responded sweetly. She interlaced her fingers with Maxx's, moving inward and outward, performing a dance of passionate touch, using their raised elbows on the table as the dance floor.

Stunned by their announcement, Mel watched her brother and his bride-to-be engage in digital lovemaking. She had never seen Maxx so affectionate before. He was always a love-'em-and-leave-'em playboy, with his fast cars and worldly women. But here he was—sitting at her kitchen table, making finger love with the bimbo.

The bimbo. No, she'd have to stop thinking of her in those terms. It was Nikki—Nikki. Her future sister-in-law. Lord knows, it would take some getting used to. Maxx, her urbane Ivy League brother marrying this earthy Texas girl.

She's all wrong for you, Maxx, all wrong, thought Mel. You need a woman who's more mentally challenging, who'll stand up to you and speak her mind. All the sophisticated clothes in the world can't give Nikki that. Those kinds of assets have to come from within. Don't you know that? Can't you see?

She wanted to tell him all of these things; to prevent him from making a mistake. But what did it matter what she said? He wouldn't listen. Once upon a time he might have, back when they were close, before he got into the drug business and when her opinions as his big sister carried some clout. But that was years ago. As he became entrenched in his way of life, she became more judgmental, and the schism between them grew ever wider.

Still she had such hopes for Maxx, and had often thought that the woman he married might somehow help turn him around, make him see the light and straighten out. But Nikki? Forget it. It was clear that she'd just go along with the program, would blindly accept whatever Maxx dished out. Was that all that men wanted—a woman at their beck and call who espoused an "anything you say, dear," attitude? She wondered how much Nikki knew about Maxx's law practice, the nature of his clientele, and why he went to Miami so frequently. Did she think it was all on the up-and-up? Surely, she wasn't that naive. Was she?

"When's the wedding?" Sasha asked excitedly.

"June." Nikki said dreamily. "Just a few months away."

"Why the rush?" asked Mel, a tinge of criticism in her voice.

"Rush? You're one to talk! Didn't you and Builder get married after about six months of seeing each other?"

There. He had her.

"Uh, it was longer than six months," Mel floundered.

"Hardly. Maybe six and a half. Seven, tops." He turned to Nikki, and stroked her chin. "If I had my way, we'd already be married. One night we almost went to a justice of the peace."

"This all just seems so—unlike you," Mel said, flustered.

"Can't you tell?" he said, grinning broadly. "I'm in love with this woman!"

It must be, Mel had to admit to herself. He had never come close to claiming his love for any woman. *Like,* yes. But love? The word had never crossed his lips—not that she could recall.

"Can I be a bridesmaid or something?" inquired Sasha.

"Sasha!" Mel reprimanded. "You don't ask to be in a wedding; you're invited. Besides, you're too young to be a bridesmaid."

"We'll find a special place for you," Maxx said assuringly.

"We certainly will," Nikki said cheerily. "Maybe you can be the flower girl."

"She's a little old for that," snapped Mel.

Sasha looked crushed, and Mel felt like biting her tongue. Why was she being so nasty? It was as though she couldn't control herself.

Nikki turned to Sasha. "Maxx is right. We'll find something extra special for you to do. You could be a junior bridesmaid. Maybe carry the Bible. Would you like that?"

"Sure."

"And we'll have so much fun shopping for a dress for you," Nikki added. "I've already decided. My colors will be lavender and pink."

Mel resisted the urge to roll her eyes.

"Nikki has a special request," Maxx said, nudging her elbow, like a parent pushing forth a bashful child.

"Well, I—" Nikki began haltingly. "I don't have much family. Just a sister. And—I'm not really into going to church and all that. I mean, I believe in God," she added quickly, "but Maxx and I—we decided we didn't want a formal church wedding. And—" She looked to Maxx for help.

"Go on," he urged, smiling.

"Well, to me, hotels are just so impersonal—you know, for a wedding. So I was wondering—could we get married here?"

"Here?" Mel repeated, hoping she had misunderstood.

"Well, actually, not in the house. In the backyard. I love your yard—I remember from last summer—with all the flowers, everything smelled so wonderful. And all that space. And I like being close to nature. It would be a wonderful way to start our marriage."

"And would you have the reception here too?" Sasha asked eagerly.

Nikki nodded hesitantly. "That's what we were thinking. I never thought it made much sense for people to go to a wedding and then pile back into their cars and drive all the way across town for the reception. This way, we could have the marriage ceremony and the reception in the same place. And it would all be outside, so there'd be room for people to move around."

"Like a garden wedding," said Sasha.

"Yes. That's the idea."

"But what if it rains?" Mel asked. The question sounded silly and insensitive, but it was all she could think of. Nikki's request had taken her completely off guard.

"If it rains, we'll move it inside," Maxx said plainly. "Or we'll set up a tent. No big deal. I'll take care of all the expenses."

Mel could tell he was irritated by her unenthused response. It was just that this was a lot to absorb at one time. First, their unexpected announcement of plans to marry; now, their wanting to use her house, or more accurately, her backyard. The last thing she felt like was having a big festive party. With her and Builder barely on speaking terms, and the rest of her life in such upheaval, she didn't need the stress of hosting a wedding and reception and all that that involved. Sure, Maxx would pay for it, but there would be a zillion arrangements to make: food, music, flowers. Damn Maxx for putting Nikki up to this. He should have asked her himself, in private, should have given her time to sort it through, given her a way out.

"So what do you say?" Maxx asked, a slight edge to his voice.

They were watching her expectantly. What choice did she have? Maxx was her brother. And as much as she disapproved of the way he made his living, and his selection of a bride, she did love him. She wanted him to be happy. How could she say no? "Sure," she said, straining a smile. "Have it here."

"All right!" Maxx slapped his knee like a kid just granted permission for dessert. "See, baby," he said to Nikki. "Ask and you shall receive."

"Thanks so much," Nikki gushed.

"How about a toast?" Maxx proposed.

As Mel went to the dining room to get glasses, she heard Maxx, in a low voice, ask Sasha about school. Sasha responded that she didn't like it, that the kids were unfriendly and too rough.

"Well, I'll see what I can do about getting you out of there."

From the corner of her eye, Mel saw her brother and daughter glance at her in a furtive way, to make sure she was occupied. Pretending not to hear, she created more movement than necessary in retrieving the glasses from the china closet.

In a louder voice Maxx asked, "Where's Builder? Is that man never home?"

"Hardly ever," Sasha answered with a shrug. "He's out working, where else?"

"Well, tell him to dust off his wing tips," Maxx joked. "I want him right there at my side to hold me up."

Mel returned to the table with a tray of petite cordial glasses. "Will cranapple juice do?" she asked. "It's still morning, and we have an under-aged person present." She thrust her head toward Sasha.

"Oh, Mom!"

They toasted to eternal love and a long, happy marriage. Seeing Maxx and Nikki laughing and touching, Mel realized anew how far removed she and Builder were from any semblance of such tenderness. Deep down, if she were to admit the truth, part of her resistance to the wedding was knowing it would serve as a painful reminder of how married love—good married love—should be, yet how little of it existed in her own home.

The beeper went off again and this time Builder put down his hammer. Whoever was calling was persistent. Or maybe it was several different callers. His beeper had been going off like crazy for the last half hour. People expected him to stop whatever he was doing immediately and call them back. But that wasn't always possible.

He moved a four-by-six off to the side and surveyed his work. The deck was coming along nicely. His customer would be pleased. The smell of fresh cut pine punctuated the warm spring air. Builder inhaled deeply as he wiped his forehead. He was working alone today and seemed to have gotten more accomplished than with a crew of men who would have had to stop for lunch, take numerous breaks, and then be driven home. So far, there had been no interruptions. Only the beeper.

He pressed his pager, revealing a series of phone numbers. One he recognized as his lumber supplier. But the others were all the same unfamiliar number with a 753 exchange, somewhere close to home, and with three zeros at the end, the family code that the call should be returned ASAP.

He went inside the house, shouting to his customer that he was using the phone, and vowing to himself that he would buy a phone for his truck as soon as some extra money came in. Extra money, ha! Who was he kidding? Luckily today he was working at a place where he didn't have to search for quarters and a public booth.

"Duncan Middle School."

Duncan? So it was Sasha who had called.

"This is Nathaniel Burke," said Builder. "I believe my daughter's been trying to reach me. Sasha Burke. Do you know anything about that? Is she all right?"

There was a slight hesitation. "Just a minute, please."

He heard rustling in the background, and then,

"Daddy!"

"Sasha! What's going on? Are you okay?"

"I—I was in a fight," she sniffled.

"A *fight?*"

"Yes."

"You're not hurt, are you?"

"No. But they won't let me leave until you come get me. The principal wants to talk to you and Mom. I tried calling her, but she's not home." She became more agitated as she spoke.

"Okay. Calm down. You sure you're okay?"

"Yes. Hurry, Daddy."

The parking lot at Duncan was nearly empty when Builder drove up in his truck. A group of students, congregated out front, expounded loudly the fate of one of their own.

"Yeah, he got caught feelin' up some girl last night."

"Say whaaad?" someone asked.

"Happened in the gym. Right after the game."

Good Lord, Builder thought, as he passed by. *This* was where Sasha was going to school? No wonder she didn't like the place.

His construction boots created a pounding echo as he walked quickly to the principal's office. Sasha sat in the outside reception area, her head and shoulders bent, as though she were dragged down by some immeasurable weight. When she saw him, she immediately ran up and flung out her arms, seeking protection.

"It wasn't my fault, Daddy, it wasn't."

"Okay, baby, I believe you. Just tell me what happened."

"Mr. Burke?"

The gray-haired bespectacled receptionist twirled around from her computer and pointed a bony finger in the direction of the principal's office. "Miss Wright has someone with her, but she needs to talk to you. She'll be with you shortly."

"Thanks."

Builder escorted Sasha back to her seat and pulled up a chair facing her. He touched his daughter's tear-stained cheek and gave her a handkerchief from his back pocket.

"So you didn't start it?"

"No, Daddy. Honestly."

"Well, what was it about, Sasha? Who'd you fight?"

"Bernadette Perkins. She never has liked me. She always calls me stuck up and that I think I'm cute and that I act white—things like that."

Builder shook his head.

"She thought I was talking to some boy that she likes. Daddy, he's not even her boyfriend! She likes him, but he doesn't like her. And anyway he was just asking me about homework, that's all. But she got mad and jumped me."

"*Jumped* you?"

"Yes. She started fighting right there in the hallway. Pulling my hair and everything. Right in front of the lockers."

"Sounds like you didn't have much of a choice."

"I didn't. But now I'm the one in trouble. They say you can get put out of school for fighting. And that's going to mess up my records and everything." She dabbed at her eyes. "Now I'll never be able to go back to Trent."

Builder sighed deeply. Was she still holding on to that hope? It was probably his fault for letting her think that might happen. Initially, he thought it would. Much as he hated to admit it, Mel was right again. He had promised too much and failed to deliver.

"Let's not worry about your records and all that. As long as you didn't start the fight—" he said, seeking her assurance one more time.

"I didn't, Daddy," she insisted.

"Then that's all that matters."

They were quiet for a moment.

"You don't look too worse for the wear. Who won?"

"I did."

His heart skipped a beat. So, Sasha had beaten the bully. She had stood up for herself and fought back. He was sorry that she had been forced into that situation, but it sounded like she had handled things well. He was proud of her. Real proud.

The office door opened. A tall brown-skinned girl emerged, flanked by a woman with a scowling expression. Behind them, standing at the door, was Miss Wright, the principal. The girl's face had track marks running down both cheeks; reddish welts were evident even through her dark skin. Her face was all scratched up! My God, thought Builder, had Sasha done that? The girl was almost six feet, nearly as tall as he. She gave Sasha the evil eye but said nothing. Her mother was doing all the talking.

" . . . and I swear I ain't coming back up here no more, having to get off my job to bail your butt out. Next time, just don't even call me."

"Hopefully, Mrs. Perkins, there won't be a next time," said the principal. "Right, Bernadette?"

Bernadette stared stonily at the floor, then mumbled, "Yes, ma'am."

"This is Mr. Burke," the receptionist announced, by way of introduction.

Builder stood and shook hands with the principal and Bernadette's mother. Sasha also stood and Builder placed his hands on her shoulders.

"I guess things got a little out of control," he said to Mrs. Perkins, out of sympathy for her daughter's damaged face.

"I'll say. Look at her. Her face look like it been through a meat grinder." She turned to Sasha. "You who did this?" she asked incredulously. "Girl, you got some nails on you. You must have dug in and held on for dear life."

Sasha meekly cupped her hands together, and for the first time Builder noticed the even line of dirt beneath her nails. Dirt from Bernadette's face.

"I hope there won't be no lastin' scars," Mrs. Perkins said.

"I'm sure they'll heal in time," inserted the principal.

"I can't believe you let her do that to you," Mrs. Perkins said to her daughter. "She not even half your size." She turned back to Sasha. "I don't blame you. I know it was Bernadette's fault. She always pickin' fights."

"But she won't anymore," the principal said firmly. "We have an agreement. Remember, Bernadette: three-thirty next Tuesday with the mediator."

"And what do you need to do now?" Mrs. Perkins prodded.

Bernadette stood defiantly.

"Go on, chile. Out with it."

"Sah-ry," she muttered, glancing quickly at Sasha. The word slid out of the side of her mouth like something vile.

"That ain't good enough," her mother said. "Say it like you mean it."

"Sorry." This apology didn't sound genuine either, but it was louder, more distinct.

Sasha nodded. "I'm sorry too."

After Mrs. Perkins left, still berating Bernadette as they walked down the hall, the principal invited Builder and Sasha inside. The meeting was brief, an acknowledgment that indeed, according to several witnesses, Bernadette initiated the fight. But Miss Wright warned that Sasha also needed to learn how to deal with conflict in ways other than resorting to violence.

"I don't know what else she could have done," Builder said, irritated that the principal was placing part of the blame on Sasha. "You can't expect her to just stand there and let the girl beat her up. I'm sending her here to get an education, not to be somebody's punching bag."

"All I'm saying, Mr. Burke, is that even in situations where a child may not be the aggressor, it helps her to learn how to defuse a potential argument or fight. That's why I also want Sasha to meet with the mediator next Tuesday. To talk about conflict resolution. She and Bernadette have to learn how to get along. And this is one way to start addressing that."

Sasha turned to Builder. "Do I have to?"

"Actually, it's school policy," Miss Wright said firmly. "Either that or suspension."

"Suspension!" Both Builder and Sasha spoke the word simultaneously.

"But it wasn't even my fault," protested Sasha.

"I know you didn't start it. But the problem won't go away by itself. You and Bernadette will have to work this out."

Again, Sasha turned to Builder, but he conceded to the principal, "You've got to follow the rules, baby." Then addressing Miss Wright, he said pointedly, "She'll be at the counseling session. Whatever it takes."

"Good." Miss Wright rose from her chair and smiled kindly at Sasha. "Who knows? You and Bernadette might end up being the best of friends."

"She hates my guts," Sasha said sullenly.

"Well, she learned an important lesson today. And, frankly, I don't think you'll have any more trouble out of her."

As Sasha went to her homeroom to retrieve her books and jacket, the principal slowly walked with Builder to the front of the school. He liked her firm, direct manner, which exuded a quiet toughness. She was attractive, fortyish, and very petite, standing just over five feet in her heels. She clearly knew her stuff. It made him have a bit more confidence in the Atlanta Public Schools.

"You don't exactly have an easy desk job, do you?" Builder said.

She shrugged her shoulders. "Oh, like anything else, there are ups and downs. Today was actually a good day. There were only two fights and neither one involved a weapon of any type. Maybe that's progress."

Builder let out a deep groan.

"It's a different world than when you and I were in school." She pushed her glasses to the bridge of her nose. "Thanks for coming out," she continued. "Some parents wouldn't have made the effort."

"Oh, I had to be here, no two ways about it. I just wonder why Sasha's the one who was picked on."

"Who knows how these things get started? She's a new student; she's pretty; she's smart. I think it was jealousy. Bernadette acts out sometimes in order to get attention. Her mother means well, but she has her hands full with six children. And her father's a truck driver and is hardly ever home."

"Must be tough."

"Yes. So many of our kids don't get the support they need from home; they think the world's against them, and—well, you know the story." She paused a moment. "Your daughter's lucky to have two caring parents. I met your wife when she registered Sasha for school. And, of course, she's been up here several times helping out in the classroom." Miss Wright stopped walking and looked up at him. "How can we get *you* involved, Mr. Burke?"

"Me?"

"You sound surprised."

He was embarrassed, actually. He realized he should be much more involved with Sasha's life and her activities. There was so much going on with her that he didn't know about. Was it because she was a girl? Would it be different if she were a boy?

When Mel was pregnant, he had promised himself that he would treat his child the same, male or female. And in the early years he did do his part: changing diapers, feeding Sasha dinner, reading bedtime stories. He even took her to several Hawks and Braves games. But when he started his business, his demanding work schedule left him with fewer hours to spend with her. As in other areas, Mel picked up the slack, shouldering most of the school activities, like the gift wrap fund-raisers, the field trips, the PTA.

Now, confronted with his lack of involvement, he confessed to Miss Wright that he was remiss and would do better. She nodded briskly, then asked what he did for a living. When he told her he was a self-employed contractor, she immediately suggested how he could contribute. Perhaps by holding a demonstration on basic carpentry. Or by participating in the upcoming Career Day.

"I'm not sure Career Day is such a good idea. My business is hanging on by a thread."

"All the better," she said, not missing a beat. "Students need to hear about the pitfalls as well as the successes. We teach reality here, not fantasy."

Yes, he liked this woman. She was sharp, to the point.

"So—I can count on you then?"

He paused a moment. Then—"I'll be there," he committed.

"Good. And one more thing, Mr. Burke."

They had reached the front doors, and she rested an arm against the metal jutting. "I've looked at Sasha's records. I'm sure you know she was an A student at Trent. But her first report card here was not that good."

He hadn't noticed. He hadn't noticed much of anything lately, so absorbed was he in this debt thing.

"It's always difficult adjusting to a new school," Miss Wright continued, "but I know Sasha can do better. I have to ask, are things stable at home?"

Builder felt his face flush. How could he lie to this woman, with her intelligent eyes, and creased brow of concern? "It's not the best of times," he acknowledged. "I mentioned the business. There've been pressures." He left it at that, his voice dropping.

"I see. Well, we do have individual counseling available and—"

"Counseling?"

"Yes. When students don't perform to their capability, there are usually underlying reasons for that. Sometimes it helps them to talk with someone outside the family. For a more objective point of view."

"You think that's necessary for Sasha?"

"I think she'd benefit from it. Of course, I can't force her to go. It would be completely voluntary. Perhaps if you and your wife talked to her, she might be more receptive."

"But wait a minute. She's already going to see this mediator, right? On Tuesday."

"That's a separate issue—that's about the fight."

Builder shook his head.

Miss Wright laughed softly. "It's not as bad as it sounds. Sasha's a good student. She's just going through a bumpy time right now and whatever we can do to help her—" Seeing Sasha approach from the hall, she ended the conversation.

Outside, the same group of students who had huddled earlier still maintained their semicircle of gossip.

"There she go," someone announced, seeing Sasha. In one concerted motion, the others turned toward her too.

A tall boy with a red basketball jacket called out loudly, "Yo, Miss Holyfield." Curling his long fingers, he dragged them down through the air, making a high-pitched catlike sound.

"Way to go," someone else shouted, holding up a V for victory sign. Two students punched each other in a mock fight.

Builder shot them a look of disgust and hurried Sasha to the truck. Great, he thought. Just great. So his daughter was now a heroine. By tomorrow she'd probably be one of the best-known kids at Duncan. Her claim to fame? Not some outstanding scholarly achievement or first-place finish in a sport. No—Sasha would now be known for having scratched up the face of a girl who was nearly twice her size.

Builder folded the sports page and tossed it with the rest of the day's paper. It had been ages since he had taken time to read anything, and in a way he enjoyed this little respite. But enough was enough. He glanced at his watch. Where could Mel be? It was almost five, and she still wasn't home. He wanted to talk to her about what the principal had said about Sasha. He didn't want to leave Sasha alone, but he had to get moving. He had already missed several hours of work when he went to the school, and he had a lot of catching up to do. With each passing minute went the opportunity to make money and climb out of this hell of a debt hole.

The phone rang. Mrs. Hawkins.

"My nephew's on a new shift today, and he can't bring me over there. So I was wondering if you all could pick me up."

"What time are you supposed to come over?" asked Builder.

"Same as usual—six o'clock."

Same as usual? Mel needed a sitter on a regular basis? What the heck was going on? He pressed Mrs. Hawkins for details—how often did she come, for how long, and where did Mel say she was going? But, perhaps sensing that her phone call might have precipitated a domestic spat, Mrs. Hawkins was diplomatically evasive and requested that Mel call her when she arrived.

Builder did some mental detective work, trying to figure out what Mel could possibly be up to. For Mrs. Hawkins to come over, it must mean that Mel was away from home for several hours in the evening, because if it were only an hour or two, Sasha would generally stay by herself. Builder remembered how last year Sasha had declared herself too old to need a sitter at any time, but Mel had insisted that she'd feel better knowing someone was at home with Sasha, for any long length of time after dark. So, Builder mused, if Mrs. Hawkins came at 6:00, it was likely that she stayed late into the evening. What could Mel be doing for all that time on such a regular basis? He didn't like what he was thinking.

When Mel rushed upstairs into the bedroom a few minutes later, Builder was fuming.

"Where the hell have you been?" he thundered.

Mel's mouth dropped open, surprised that he would use such an ugly tone. She answered his question with two of her own: "What are you doing here? Is something wrong?"

"Oh, so I can't be in my own house unless something's wrong, is that it?"

"It's not that. It's just that you're never home at this hour. Did something happen at work?"

"No. But something happened with Sasha."

Mel looked alarmed. "What? Where is she?"

"In the bathroom, taking a long hot bath. She needs it. She was in a fight."

"A fight?" The whole top half of Mel's face raised up.

He gave her the barest of details, skipping over the part about his resolution to be more involved at the school. Rather, he emphasized that the principal mentioned how Sasha's grades had fallen and that she needed to have counseling. He made it sound worse than it really was, almost as if Sasha had some mental disorder, that she was nearly expelled from school, and that it was Mel's fault that she didn't have a better handle on things. He was into the blame game again. She played it; he played it. It was unfair, and he knew it. But he couldn't help himself. He couldn't stop the stream of hurtful words. The more he spoke, the more vindictive he became. Mel sat silently, taking it.

" . . . and all the while I'm out there bustin' my butt, I thought you had things under control here. Where were you today? Sasha tried to reach you repeatedly. It's like you disappeared off the face of the earth. And I was waiting for the building inspector to come by a job. I totally missed that appointment. Now I'll have to make another one, and there's no telling when I can get him out there. Which means I'll have to wait longer now to get paid for the job."

Mel let out a deep sigh. "I'm sorry about that. Any other time, and I would have been here."

"So, where were you?"

"I—I had some things to take care of."

"Like what?"

"Just things, Builder," she said, becoming agitated.

"What things?" he insisted fiercely.

"What difference does it make?" Mel rose from the bed. Now it was her turn to vent. "You make it sound like this is all my fault. Well, it's not. The one time Sasha calls from school, I wasn't home. Sorry. What else do you want me to say? You act like I committed a crime."

"I want to know what was so damn important that kept you out all day?"

"It wasn't all day. I ran a few errands, okay?"

"Like what?"

"Builder, I'm not going to account for every minute of my time."

"I wonder why. Mrs. Hawkins called and said she's supposed to come over tonight. And that she's been coming here a lot lately. What's that all about?"

Mel became visibly flushed. "I just have—things to take care of."

"What about taking care of this house? What about taking care of your daughter? No wonder Sasha's in trouble. You've been out gallivanting at all hours and leaving her here alone."

"She's not alone. Mrs. Hawkins has been here. Sasha's been fine."

"Obviously not. She got into a fight today, remember?"

"That has nothing to do with anything."

"Oh, it doesn't? It's not important, then?"

"You know what I mean."

"No, I don't know. But I promise you this, I'm going to find out what the hell is going on around here." He paced back and forth, and threw her an accusing look. "Tell me something. You running the same errands during the day as you are at night?"

"What do you mean?"

"You screwin' some nigger behind my back?"

"Oh, please. You must be kidding."

"No, I'm dead serious. You been dealing with someone? Is that why you're never home?"

She put a hand on her hip and rolled her eyes. "I'm not even going to answer that."

Her nonchalant response infuriated him. He took three quick strides across the room. He whipped her arm off her hip and roughly pushed her onto the bed. "You damn well better answer me, Mel. Don't play me for a fool." He pressed the weight of his body against hers and pinned her tightly by the wrists. "Our thing is bad—real bad." His eyes flashed in anger. "It's been about nothing for months. But I swear, if you're dealing with somebody else—*Are* you? Huh?" He shook the bed. "Are you?"

He felt her squirm underneath him, struggling to get loose. But he tightened his grip on her wrists, causing her to flinch.

"You're hurting me," she gasped. "Get off. I can't—breathe."

"Answer me, Mel," he insisted. "Are you seeing someone?"

She turned her head back and forth, and snarled out an angry "No."

He pulled back, satisfied he had gotten the answer he wanted. But what else could she say, really? In that position, she would tell him whatever he wanted to hear. He had left her no alternative. He was no closer to the truth than before.

He watched as she sat at the edge of the bed, massaging her wrists. She gave him a frightened, tearful look. But there was something else too—hate. He mumbled an apology, stepping away from her. He had never laid a hand on her before, never could understand how a man could resort to physical dominance in any way against a woman. When things get that bad, he had always said, somebody ought to leave. Now, he was startled by his own use of force. In just an instant, he had lost control. He retreated to his La-Z-Boy, disgusted with himself.

"You want to know what I've been doing?" Her voice was low and deep, full of a viper's spit, rising up to strike back. "I went to Atlantic Financial today. Trying to get more time to pay on the second mortgage. Guess what? It didn't happen. They said no way. They said that *you*"—she pointed her finger at him—"have gone back on your word too many times, promising to make a payment, and then not following through. Now, I wonder, why on earth would they make a statement like that? Anyway, when I tried to make a partial payment, they wouldn't accept it. Didn't even want to talk to me. Said they've already moved ahead with foreclosure."

He wanted to ask questions, to get more information. But Mel's strange commentary held him back. She was, after all, providing him with what he had demanded—a narrative account, although cynical, of the happenings of her day. She spoke calmly, tightly, with a surging tide of sarcasm. Builder sat mute.

"And after I left there," she continued, unzipping her purse, "I went to the drugstore because I needed some of *these*." She tore open a package of black fishnet pantyhose and dangled them at him like lurid bait. "You see, my other pair has a big run in them, all the way up the left side. And that just won't do, you know. Oh, no, not at all."

She walked to the closet and retrieved a worn pink and white tote, an old ballet bag of Sasha's. She heaped the contents onto the bed, then picked over them, one by one. "It's just so gratifying to know you have such faith in me. Why, some men might suspect that I've been laying up with somebody. Can you imagine? While all the time I've been holding down a job at night. That's right. A j-o-b! And guess what it is? Wait-ressing!" She shrieked the word, as she held up her tiny uniform. "Oh, yeah—and guess *where* I've been waitressing? None other than lux-urious, first-class—Pinwheels—where for some reason, men of every size, shape, and color think I should be privileged to have them paw all over me."

She was into it now, gaining steam and momentum, moving faster, getting angrier as she talked. "Let's see here." Scornfully, she picked up the black mop of curls. "I get to wear this number. Cute isn't it?" She threw it back down into the despicable pile. "Oh, and this ridiculous pink hair bow—charming, don't you think? And look—I just love these spike heels; they make my feet feel soooo good."

Tears of anger and hurt all merged into one heavy outburst. "*Why* do I do this?" she asked, nearly screaming. "*Why?* To bring in money, of course. To do my part. To help pay on the second mortgage that *we* had to take out in order to pay *your* business loans that got us into this damn mess in the first place." She balled up the skimpy outfit along with the fishnet hose. "Here, take a closer look." She flung the clothes at him across the room, but they landed in the middle of the floor. "You think I'm out all the time, having fun? You think I'm with some man? Ha! Think big, Builder. I'm with a *lot* of men. Hey, if I'm going to do some-thing, I go all the way." She pitched the garish pink bow at him, which got no further than the other end of the bed. Then she picked up one black high heel and hurled it hard at him.

"Are you out of your mind?" he cried, raising an arm to protect him-self. The shoe hit his elbow, then dropped to his feet.

She threw the other shoe at him, but this one missed the target com-pletely, toppling over a lamp instead. "I hate you," she blurted. "I've had it!" She left the room in a tearful fury.

Builder remained in his chair for a long time, surrounded by Mel's black and pink artillery, and wondering what in the world had happened that his marriage had gone so wrong.

CHAPTER 8

Seated in the rear of the courtroom, Mel focused on a prominent feature of the bankruptcy judge: his sharply pointed chin. Not a good sign. For some reason, people with pointed chins always seemed manipulative and sly, even sinister. Her experiences with those with severely angled jaws had not been positive—from her strict fourth grade teacher Mrs. Turner, who resembled the wicked witch of the North, to the college date who had spiked her orange juice with vodka in an effort to get her high. She recalled that a particularly lewd customer at Pinwheels had sported a pointed chin, as did Simon Weaver, the detestable bill collector. And now—this judge.

So far, his behavior had proved Mel right. He seemed overtly sympathetic to the few white people who had come before him, gently berating them for falling into debt, sending them off with best wishes for the future. But with the black debtors, Mel noticed subtle differences. He put on a more stern demeanor, asked more probing questions, and kept them on the stand nearly twice as long.

Mel fidgeted on the hard bench and glanced again at the list of debtors scheduled for a bankruptcy hearing this afternoon. She and Builder were down for 3:30 P.M.; it was now after 4:00 and there were two more cases before theirs. Their attorney had suggested that they come early, so they would know what to expect and not be intimidated by the process. But the longer Mel waited, the more anxious she became, and the more she disliked this judge, who was currently giving a young black man a hard time.

"I need some water," Builder whispered. "Want anything?"

She said no, a typically spartan response. The less said to him, the better, she thought. He barely spoke to her these days, so why should she to him? Anyway, every time they had said more than two words to each other, the talking deteriorated into a fight. She was still full of resentment that his actions, his long-standing business debts, had forced them to file bankruptcy exactly one month ago, and had brought them to this courtroom today for the creditors' meeting. The bankruptcy filing had staved off the foreclosure on their home, but it was only a temporary reprieve.

The court still had to approve their petition, and this was the first step in that process. Their attorney, Karen Henry, had warned them to expect several creditors to object to the filing.

"How are you holding up?" Karen asked now good-naturedly. She had been sitting on the other side of Builder, going over some papers. She slid toward Mel now, reducing the gap between them.

"I'll be glad when it's over," Mel said.

"So will I. At this rate it'll be after six before I get home. I have another case after yours. My husband is not going to like it." She winked knowingly, but Mel couldn't relate. It had been a long time since she had been eager to go home to be with Builder. First of all, he was never there, and even if he were, they would both choose to spend their time on something else, rather than each other.

In their first meeting, Mel had learned that Karen was a newlywed, when she had happily pointed to the framed wedding photograph on her desk. Mel recalled how shocked she was that Karen had snared such a handsome, physically fit guy. Looking at the radiant couple in the photo made her confront her own biases. Of course, she realized that fat people could be sexually attractive and lead enjoyable, fulfilling lives. However, coming face to face with that reality somehow seemed—odd. Karen wasn't just fat; she was huge—at least 300 pounds. But despite her massive weight, which some would consider a tremendous liability, Karen was professionally secure and personally fulfilled with a husband eagerly waiting to love her. While Mel, thin and attractive, was jobless and in debt to the gills, and living with a man with whom she barely spoke. You sure can't judge a book by its cover, she thought. From her perspective, for the moment at least, Karen definitely had the better index.

She inched toward Karen, filling the remainder of the empty space left by Builder. "He doesn't seem too fair," she whispered, pointing her head toward the judge. "Kind of racist, isn't he?"

Karen shrugged. "Aren't they all? It's just a matter of degree."

"How do you think it'll go for us?"

"It's hard to tell. Actually, he's one of the better ones."

Mel groaned. "That's not encouraging."

"Don't worry about it."

Mel glanced at the papers in Karen's lap and could tell immediately that they had nothing to do with her case; another client's name was scribbled on top. She started to ask Karen if maybe they should go over some materials one last time, but thought better of it. That would be insulting, wouldn't it? They had hired her, hadn't they? She was their attorney, highly recommended by Frank Kirby, who had lavishly praised her as extremely capable and well-prepared.

Karen had explained that theirs was no run-of-the-mill bankruptcy. With all of Builder's business debt, plus the small rental duplex that they owned, it made for a complicated filing. As a favor to Frank, Karen charged only her routine up-front fee of $200 with the balance of $550 to be paid out in the bankruptcy plan. Mel was grateful for the discounted fee, but on top of that she and Builder also had to pay $120 just to file their case. Declaring bankruptcy was no cheap proposition. She thought of all those who had lost their homes simply because they couldn't afford to file.

A young white couple now sat in the petitioner's box, and once again, Mel noticed that the judge seemed to emit rays of kindness. He nodded sympathetically, smiled at various points, and wrapped his legalistic comments in coddling paternalism. The couple's assets included a $150,000 house and a new Jeep Ranger.

"You're trying to do too much too soon," the judge scolded mildly. "Rome wasn't built in a day, you know." He told them it was probably good that this happened now, because if they learned from their mistakes early on, they shouldn't have any more financial trouble. As they stepped down, he cheerily wished them well.

The clerk belted out the next name but then someone announced that case had been postponed. The clerk referred to his list. "NATHANIEL AND MELANTHA BURKE," he boomed.

Mel jumped. After the long wait, it was suddenly their turn, but she was caught off guard.

"Let's go," said Karen, heaving as she rose.

"But Builder's not here!" Mel said, panicking. "He stepped outside for—"

"Get him," Karen ordered.

Mel dashed out of the courtroom, her heart pounding. Of all times for him to leave! Where was the water fountain? She rushed to the side hallway and saw the fountain at the other end. But he wasn't there. Surely, he wouldn't have gone downstairs to the cafeteria? Karen couldn't stall that long. She ran up to two men in deep conversation near the elevators. "Where's the men's room?" she gushed.

"The men's room?" one of them asked.

"Yes."

"I—don't know," came the slow response.

"Try around the corner," the other suggested.

Mel scurried in that direction and as she turned the corner, almost collided head-on into Builder. "Come on," she said angrily. "They've called us."

The judge was waiting impatiently, his forehead fixed in a frown. Karen, standing at the attorney's table toward the front of the courtroom, motioned for them to come forward. Mel and Builder were sworn in and sat side by side in the petitioner's seat. The questioning began.

"You have a payment to the court?" asked the judge.

"Yes, I do," Builder replied. He removed a $500 money order from his back pocket. "Do I give it to you?"

"No, no," the judge said curtly. "To him."

The clerk came up to accept it.

"And you need to give the clerk any credit cards that you have," the judge said tiredly. "Cut them in half and surrender them to the court."

"I don't use credit cards," answered Builder.

The judge raised his eyebrows in surprise. "And *you?*" he asked, peering at Mel over granny-rimmed glasses.

"I—I didn't realize I had to give them up," Mel said, confused. "Credit cards aren't our problem. I've never misused credit cards."

She knew she sounded snobbish. But the way she saw it, she wasn't here because she'd been buying clothes and VCRs and other items on credit. She was here because her husband had been in search of the American Dream, trying to establish his own business. That's what got them in trouble. Why should she be penalized in the same way as someone who irresponsibly charged all kinds of things on credit?

"It doesn't matter what brought you to this point," the judge said. "The fact is, you're here. And when you file for bankruptcy, you must surrender all credit cards."

"But I use them mainly for identification," she protested.

"Just turn in the cards," Builder hissed in her ear.

Earlier, she had seen other people surrender their cards, but she honestly assumed it was because their bankruptcy resulted from credit card misuse. She hadn't thought to ask Karen if she had to do the same thing. And Karen hadn't mentioned it.

"Your attorney should have advised you," said the judge, peering down from his high perch. "While you're in bankruptcy, you cannot take out any new loans. You cannot sell or buy property. And you certainly cannot have any credit cards."

His pale transparent eyes showed no emotion, no feeling. He spoke in a condescending tone, like explaining to a child for the umpteenth time a lesson that should have been learned long ago.

Mel threw an angry glance at Karen, who looked sheepish.

"I need your cards, ma'am." The clerk eased a pair of scissors onto the front ledge of the bench where Mel sat.

Shakily, she pulled out her wallet, and put three plastic cards on the walnut ledge: one from Rich's, one from Neiman-Marcus, and, most painfully, her VISA.

"Cut them in half," the judge directed.

Reluctantly, Mel obeyed. This was part of the ritual, part of the punishment—to cut your credit cards in front of a courtroom of strangers. Designed for extra humiliation.

Mel huffily sat back onto the hard bench, assessing the damage beyond the mutilated cards.. She had to admit that her little protest hadn't helped; if anything, it had further alienated the judge. What was she thinking about? It was clear from the beginning that he didn't treat black people fairly. Why add fuel to the fire? She looked at the judge with renewed dislike. He was a small man, nearly devoured by his high-backed brown leather chair. He probably has a Napoleonic complex, Mel thought. She was familiar with the syndrome: short men trying to exert power, to compensate for their lack of physical stature.

"I see you're in the contracting business," he said to Builder.

"That's right."

"For how long?"

"Going on eight years."

"Looks like you've tallied up quite a string of debts along the way."

Builder shifted in his seat. "Business was good at first, but these last couple of years have really hurt."

"I'll say." The judge picked up another sheet of paper and studied it. "You're about a hundred thousand dollars in the red." There was no sympathy, only contrived bewilderment. "This is a repayment plan that you're petitioning for," he said haughtily. "If business is so bad, how are you going to make payments to the court?"

"Your honor, if I may," interjected Karen. "I'd like to—"

"Just a minute, Miss Henry," he rebuked. "I want to hear directly from"—he looked at the file again—"Mr. Burke."

What an asshole, thought Mel. So blatantly prejudiced. He hadn't asked questions like that of the previous couple. She saw Builder fold and unfold his hands in his lap. For the first time in a long time, she felt like reaching out and holding him.

"It's not that I'm not making any money," Builder explained. "It's just that the level of these bills takes everything I earn. If I can pay out what's due over a period of time, then I can keep things current. Plus handle the court payments."

The judge raised his eyebrows and took a deep breath, as if he didn't believe Builder. He wasn't satisfied. Far from it. He shuffled through more papers. "I see here that you're surrendering a rental property."

"Yes."

"You fell behind more than four thousand dollars in that mortgage."

Why is he so specific? thought Mel. He hadn't mentioned that kind of information about anyone else. Why all this microscopic attention to our case?

"And your personal residence. How long have you been living there?"

"Fifteen years."

"And your arrearage is"—he flipped through a couple of pages—"two thousand, two hundred dollars. I see that you have a foreclosure pending on your house, which is why you filed bankruptcy, right? To stop that." He set his mouth in a smug way, as though genuinely pleased that their financial situation was so perilous.

"And you," the judge addressed Mel. "Are you currently employed?"

"Not at this time," she replied, feeling her stomach tighten. "My job was terminated last year."

The judge scrutinized her from above. "What have you been doing since then? Catching up on the soaps?"

Nervous giggles rippled throughout the courtroom. Mel swallowed hard to compress her anger. "I've been working on several part-time projects," she said, trying to keep her remaining dignity intact. "I develop business plans for small companies, and I've been teaching a couple of classes."

She omitted the waitressing. It was too recent, too raw. It hadn't lasted long anyway. Besides, she wouldn't give this judge the satisfaction. No telling what nasty comment he'd make if he found out she had worked at Pinwheels.

He peered out from his lofty perch. "How many objections do we have to this case?" he asked. "How many creditors?"

Representatives of several companies stood and identified themselves. There were attorneys for a large lumber company, a floor and tile company, and several other businesses with whom Builder either had

204 FAYE McDONALD SMITH

accounts or long-standing bills. Mel noticed that there was also a representative from Atlantic Financial, although not Simon Weaver, thank goodness. He was probably out harassing someone else, she thought.

After listening to the objections, the judge thumbed through the stapled papers before him. He made several notations on his pad and entered numbers into a calculator. He pored intently over the papers while tugging his pointy chin. Mel visualized him dragging that chin down—dragging it down, down, down—stretching it vertically until it reached the floor, finally descending into a grotesque contortion, with the rest of his body snaking out behind him.

After a few minutes, he swiveled in his chair, directly facing Karen. "Miss Henry, we have a problem."

Karen, who had been relegated to silence, immediately stood at attention. "Yes, Your Honor?"

Inwardly, Mel sneered at the title. There was nothing honorable about this man.

"According to my figures, this plan goes beyond sixty months, which doesn't conform to Section thirteen-twenty-two (c). Now, I don't know what kind of new math you're using, but it's not getting past first base with me."

Mel looked over at Karen, who was shuffling through some papers. What did this mean? Was the judge denying their petition?

"I wasn't aware of any inconsistency in that regard," Karen said, collecting herself. "We can re-configure—perhaps reduce the plan by a couple of items and pay those creditors directly. I'm sure we can make any adjustments that might be needed."

"That's a lot of adjusting," the judge said. "My objection stands." He referred again to his pad. "And there's another problem."

Mel saw Builder stiffen. Her own stomach churned again.

"Under this plan, unsecured creditors will receive less than they would in a Chapter Seven liquidation. We can't have that. That's a direct violation of Section thirteen-twenty-five (a) (four). And this court won't allow it." He fired off a series of questions, popping them out like bullets, barely giving Karen a chance to respond before releasing the next salvo.

Mel fidgeted. Karen had told them previously that she expected several creditors to object, but here it was the judge himself, the person who had to approve the petition—their trustee—who found fault with the plan. What fair chance did they have now? Her palms grew clammy. She tried to follow the legalese exchanged between Karen and the judge, and although she didn't understand specific bankruptcy codes and sections, one thing was clear: They were not winning.

She had come today angry and resentful that they were forced to file bankruptcy, but now, it looked as if it might not even be approved! So what did that mean? Would they lose the house after all? Would getting another lawyer make a difference? Was Karen just not competent?

The judge announced he would put his objections in writing and told Mel and Builder to step down.

You bastard, thought Mel. Aren't you going to wish us good luck? She felt like screaming.

Karen gathered her papers and headed out the side door. Mel and Builder followed, full of concern.

"What the heck happened in there?" Builder demanded.

"We're not going to lose our house, are we?" This was Mel's main concern, and she needed reassurance fast.

"No. The stay against the foreclosure is still on. They can't touch the house," Karen said.

"But what about all the objections?"

"What I'll have to do is go back and run the numbers again." Karen seemed flustered and embarrassed. "I don't know, they can't be off by that much."

"So what does that mean exactly?" asked Builder. "What's the next step?"

"Well, the judge is objecting on two points. I'll have to rework the numbers in a way to satisfy those objections. So we'll have a response and a new plan in time for your confirmation hearing next month."

"Is it often that they turn down a petition?" Mel asked.

"It happens. And I'm sorry it happened to you guys. But as I told you, you have a complicated case."

It sounded like Karen was trying to find some breathing room, making a defense for herself. You've been concentrating too much on that new husband of yours, thought Mel. Maybe if you had spent more time working on our stuff . . .

"You never can tell how it's going to turn out until you get into the courtroom," Karen continued. "A lot depends on the judge you get and the mood he's in on a given day."

"I knew it the minute I saw him," said Mel. "Remember, I told you how he was prejudiced?"

Karen nodded wearily.

"He sure jumped into our business with both feet," said Builder.

"That's part of his job. He's not there to rubber-stamp everything. But I don't want you all to worry."

Right, thought Mel. Easy for you to say. Your home isn't at risk.

"What about the five hundred I gave them?" asked Builder.

"That counts as your first payment in the plan."

"But, hell, if they're not going to approve this thing—"

"I'm pretty sure they'll approve it."

"But if they don't," he persisted, "I want to make sure I get my money back. I can't afford to have five hundred bucks lost in some bureaucracy."

"I hear you."

Builder scratched his head in frustration. "Damn! Why is it that nothing ever goes smoothly for me? Can't even file bankruptcy without some hang-up. I mean, is it a jinx or something?"

"Don't take it personally," said Karen. "I think they'll eventually approve the petition. We just have to jump through some extra hoops, that's all." She looked at Mel contritely. "I'm sorry about the credit cards. I could have sworn I had gone over all of that with you."

"I wish you had. I sure would have done things differently."

Like applied for a duplicate VISA before filing bankruptcy, thought Mel. And leaving it at home before coming here today. You can't tear up what you don't have, right? In court, the clerk had asked her to submit the cards that she had. She could have interpreted that to mean just the cards she had on her person, not necessarily ALL the cards she possessed. If she had a card tucked away at home, she wouldn't have been able to turn it in. At least she'd have one smidgen of control left. Not that it mattered anymore. The cards were gone. Too late to do anything about it now.

"Are you sure you can work this out?" Builder asked Karen, obviously needing affirmation.

"Yes," she said with confidence. "You'll get a letter in a few days about the objections. Don't be alarmed by that; it's routine. Meanwhile, I'll be working on things from my end. And if necessary, I'll call in another attorney just to make doubly sure the numbers pan out."

If you had done that the first time, this wouldn't have happened, thought Mel, and then she felt bad for thinking it. It wasn't all Karen's fault—it was that scoundrel of a judge. He was out for blood today, and they were his unlucky victims.

• • •

"If it weren't for Sasha, I'd have gone a long time ago."

"No, you wouldn't have."

"Yes, I would."

Val's living room was packed with Afrocentric art and sculptures, along with an eclectic mix of the contemporary and the traditional: antique chairs, Tiffany lamps, nude oils, delicate watercolors—evidence of Val's prowess at estate sales, outlets, and old-fashioned in-your-face browbeating. A tall pile of expensive art books stood neatly stacked in a sweet grass basket next to the fireplace.

There was a touch of the quirky. Keeping company with framed prints by James Vander Zee and P. H. Polk, and cuddling next to candles and ginger jars, were miniature bulls made from soapstone, clay, and wood. Val was a full-fledged Taurus, and collected any make and manner of the bovine figurines that paid homage to her astrological sign.

Coming here was always an adventure for Mel. Each time she visited, she saw not just one or two new items, but several additions, picked up from Val's latest "negotiation." Sometimes whole rooms of furniture would be rearranged.

For the past hour, Mel had talked incessantly of her frustration with Builder, the lack of money, today in court. The more she talked, the more she wanted to say. It had been a long time since she had so openly shared her feelings, feelings that she had kept inside, partly as a way of denial and partly because talking about them with Builder further aggravated the problem. But like a revolution ready to erupt, by being denied and pressed down, these feelings, once stirred, gathered even more steam.

Val had been a good listener, commenting briefly here and there, playing the supportive friend. But this latest pronouncement from Mel jolted her into action. "You can't let a few financial problems get in your way. You've been married—what? Fourteen years?"

"Fifteen," Mel corrected her.

"So you're going to hightail it out of Dodge when he's flat on his back?" She shuddered. "That's cold."

"The marriage is cold," said Mel. "It's dead. It's not just the money situation. It's at the point now where I don't feel anything for him; I just don't care. I mean, I might as well be married to"—she groped—"the mailman, for heaven's sake. There's no emotion. None. And he feels the same way about me. Or doesn't feel, I should say."

"I don't believe that. I know Builder loves you."

Mel continued as if she didn't hear: "It's like we're zombies, walking around lifeless. We don't go out anymore. We don't have any fun. There's no money. He blames me for not bringing in anything, and then when I do, he insists that I stop working, talking about how"—she took a breath before launching into an imitation of Builder—"'This is really beneath you. Surely you can do better.'"

"You know what that's about. Ego. He doesn't want you parading around in next to nothing with all those men breathing hot and heavy. I think it's admirable he took that position."

"Admirable? Humpf. Money is money. I didn't *enjoy* working at Pinwheels. But he acted like I had a slew of choices. I mean, he of all people should know how tight the job market is. But then he looks at me like somehow I'm not trying hard enough. I'm sick of it, just sick of it! I've had it up to here with Builder and being broke and all of it."

Val picked up a Bosc pear from a bowl piled high with fruit. She spoke quietly. "I remember so well what you said a while back, right here in this room." She thrust her index finger downward. "We were watching the news, remember? People in Somalia were dropping like flies, children *dying* from no milk and no food."

Mel was mute, knowing what was coming next.

"And the little baby, remember? That poor little baby, scratching at his mother's breast, because, you know, *nothing* was coming out. People barely able to walk—they were so weak. And I remember what you said."

"I know," Mel replied sheepishly.

"You said, 'If I ever complain about anything again in my life—'"

"Shut me up," Mel chimed in. She took a deep breath. "Yes. That's true."

"Soooo?"

They were both silent for a moment.

"Look," Val said. "Think about all the good things about Builder. He's a decent man. He's up and about every day, working hard. He's not strung out on gambling or drugs or women. He's a good father; Sasha worships the ground he walks on. I mean, you can't ask for much more. He's given you all a beautiful home—"

Mel gave her a look that demanded inclusion.

"Okay, *together* you made a beautiful home."

"A home we almost lost, I might add. And still might."

"That won't happen," Val said, with a wave of her hand. "Okay, so he's made some mistakes in his business. At least he's *got* a business. That says a lot in itself. Do you know how many black men are scared shitless to even *try* something like that? Why, they don't even go to the bathroom without asking permission." She pressed her hands together in mock prayer. "Oh, Mr. Boss Man, is it okay for me to pee now?"

Mel laughed in spite of herself. "You're crazy, you know that?"

"At least Builder's out there trying to make a go of it. Unlike my dear beloved ex, who thought his office was this couch. Till I tossed his raggedy tail out."

"Yes," confirmed Mel. "He was a bona fide BSJ."

Val shook her head. "Why'd it take me so long to wise up? Why didn't you tell me?"

"I did. You just didn't listen."

"Yeah. I sure was snowed under. Me! Can you imagine?" She shook her braided head in disbelief. "Well, at least there was no commingling of funds. Lord knows where I'd be today if we'd had a joint account and all that. What was his was his and what was mine was mine. I had enough sense to keep all that separate."

"I wish I could say the same. If only I'd known then what I know now."

"Well, you got married in the Dark Ages, dear," Val teased. "Back then, that's the way people did things—pooled everything into one. The ultimate merger, you know."

Mel was reflective. "I didn't tell you this, but—a few months ago I went to the safe deposit box because I needed to cash in some bonds, and—he had cleaned out everything."

"*What?*" Val said, sitting straight.

"That's right."

She remembered the day clearly. It was last fall, on a chilly October morning, and she had gone to the downtown office of Sunbelt Company Bank. She needed cash to stave off the predators, and, as a last resort, had decided to use some of the assets from the safe deposit box. In the box, she and Builder had placed several envelopes with various headings: Emergency Cash, Sasha's Education, Savings Bonds. As Mel pulled out envelope after envelope, she was shocked to find that they were depleted—totally. Later, when she angrily confronted Builder about it, he said he had cashed in some bonds to buy materials for a project, so that he could finish it and get paid. He swore that he would replace everything soon, and was sorry that she had to find out about it that way. It was yet one more deception, one more barrier of distrust.

"Well, clearly he's not the best money manager," Val said now. "But you really wouldn't walk, would you?"

"Oh, you don't know," Mel said. "I'd fly out of there if I could! Like I said, if I didn't have Sasha, I would have been gone."

"I don't believe that. Sasha's not exactly a two-year-old. And if it were really that bad, you'd have skipped a long time ago. Come on. It has to be something else."

"Yeah, like money. How can I get out here and keep a household going on my own? With no job? Now I know why women who are abused stay with their husbands."

"Oh, please. You're hardly abused."

"Abuse comes in all kinds of ways, Val."

"Well, I think the reason you haven't gone off and done something foolish is because deep down you know you can't chuck your whole marriage because of a few bad times. Besides, you and Builder have too much history. You can't stop now. I mean, what if I had stopped midway in my 'negotiations'?" She stretched out her arms to the room. "I wouldn't have half the stuff in here."

"That's a different situation."

"Not really. It's about staying power. You know what some cracker said to me the other day? He said, 'How many more are out there like you?' Like I'm grooming an army of crusaders or something. They can't stand it when you look them straight in the eye, when you stand up to them, and you're fearless. They don't like that. Makes them nervous. But you know what? He gave me an idea. That's exactly what I should do—groom an army of people who'll stand up to these crackers. They'll suck your blood any way they can." She wrapped the remains of her pear in a napkin. "You know, it might be to your advantage that you don't have credit cards anymore."

Mel snickered.

"Seriously. Credit cards, bank accounts, they're just ways for white folks to keep tabs on us. They already know too much as it is. Down to the kind of douche you use—raspberry or cinnamon."

"Val, really!"

"I don't trust any of them. I use cash, that's my policy. And never, ever give out your social security number."

"I don't. I know that much."

"I don't give out diddly-squat. In fact, I have two or three social security numbers. I just transpose the digits."

"That's illegal!"

"Get with it, Mel. You've got to stay a couple steps ahead of these people, I'm telling you. That's why I'm pushing so hard to get these greeting cards up and running."

"How's it coming?"

"Well, I've started some sketches. Want to see?"

They moved to the back of the house into Val's workroom. Unlike other parts of the house, where every nook was filled with bizarre bric-a-brac, where brilliant colors screamed from the walls and audacious art vied for attention, this room was a stark study in beige and white. Severely underfurnished, it held a drawing table, gooseneck lamp and stool, a telephone, and a lone throw rug woven from muted beige. Val had carefully designed this sparse space. She wanted nothing to distract her, nothing to pull her imagination where she might not want to go. She wanted her ideas to rise out of a faceless womb of creativity, pure and untainted by outside influences.

She opened a broad flat portfolio and set out several large sketches for Mel's review. "This is the tip of the iceberg. I can really get moving once my ship comes in."

"What ship?"

"You know, the settlement from Electronic World. I'll use that money to get things started here. It should be happening soon. You need to decide whether you're coming on board with me or not."

It had been put on hold, by Mel at least, this idea of starting a greeting card company and working with Val. She had resisted for two reasons: She didn't know how a business partnership would affect their friendship, and she needed income *now*. She couldn't afford to invest a lot of time and energy into something that, at best, wouldn't yield any profits until several months down the road.

"You can always get started on the business plan or the feasibility study," prodded Val. "Although I already know it's feasible. All we have to do is put the cards out there. They'll sell." She stood back to survey her work. "What do you think?"

Mel nodded approvingly. Val had used a mixture of bold lines and geometric shapes to create images of people and activities; some abstract, others more defined. The sketches projected an immediate interpretation, but after the first glance, other variations emerged, allowing for a range of possibilities.

"Everything's just rough pencil right now," Val said. "Color will make a big difference. And words—that's where you come in. Although I think we could have two versions of the same card. One with words, the other without."

"Hmmm," said Mel, half listening. "I really like this one." She had focused on a sketch of two images, strangely androgynous yet distinctly male and female. They were joined at the waist, merging into one.

"What comes to mind when you look at that?"

Mel paused for a second. "*Not* Builder and me."

They laughed.

"You've gotten too cynical. Let's see." Val viewed it critically. "I think it could mean anything from 'thank you for a wonderful time last night'—to—a wedding card."

Mel groaned. "The wedding! Don't remind me."

"You mean, Maxx and uh—"

"Nikki."

"Right. How's it going?"

"Slowly. Let's just say I don't need the hassle."

"Don't people elope anymore?"

"Fat chance of that. No, Nikki wants 'the towering oaks and the wisteria, to be close to nature.' " Mel rolled out the words, accompanied by fluttering eyelashes, à la Nikki. "Sometimes I wonder what she loves more—Maxx or my backyard."

"Well, she sure got herself a heck of a prize."

"Honestly," said Mel, exasperated. "Every woman has a soft spot for Maxx. Even you. I don't understand it."

"You shouldn't understand it. He's your brother." She flicked a speck of dust from her blouse. "What does Nikki have anyway to make him want to tie the knot?"

"Big boobs and big legs. That's all I see. I thought Maxx was deeper than that."

Val chuckled. "He's a man, honey. He's got that thing between his legs, you know." She said this as though surely that should explain everything. "So, you're not thrilled about this little union?"

Mel shrugged. "Weddings are supposed to be happy and joyous. I don't feel any of that. I guess part of it is that I don't think Nikki's right for Maxx. I mean, she's all right, but I just can't get very excited. And I've got to get the house in order; everything's kind of been dumped into my lap. And then, Eunice is coming—"

"Oh," Val said with interest. "Is that definite?"

Mel's face clouded. "Yeah. She hates to fly but she wouldn't miss this for the world. Maxx is her heart."

"Hmmm." Val eyed her carefully. "So I'll finally get a chance to meet her. She's staying with you, right?"

"Heck no," Mel said strongly. "She'll be at Maxx's. That's one of the things I'm going to get straight tonight. I'm going over there later."

"Sounds like you're beggin' for a fight."

"What do you mean?"

"Your mother's flying all the way from France. I'm sure she expects to stay with you."

"Oh, no. She's coming for Maxx's wedding, not to visit me. She'll breeze in as the proud madam of the groom, spend a little time with Sasha, and then fly on back to France and her life. Good riddance." Mel nearly spat out the last two words.

"What's with you two, anyway? I never really understood."

"It's simple. We don't like each other. Maxx has always been her favorite; that's no big secret. He could do no wrong. Me? I could never do anything right. She nagged, nagged, nagged. Constantly."

"Well, you're the only girl and the oldest. Maybe she tried too hard. Seems like she's trying to make up for it. She's always sending Sasha things for Christmas and her birthday, right?"

"Oh, she and Sasha have a great relationship. When she calls, we'll talk for a minute but then I hand the phone over to Sasha. She's the one Eunice wants to speak to anyway."

"And what's with this first name bit?"

"What?"

"You always call her Eunice."

"That's her name."

"You know what I mean. You don't call her Mom or Mother?"

"Rarely."

"Does Maxx call her Eunice too?"

"I'm surprised Maxx doesn't call her God."

"Maybe you're not giving her a chance, Mel. People change, you know."

"She and I are worlds apart. Literally."

"The problem is you're probably too much alike."

"Alike?" Mel was insulted. "I'm nothing like her."

"I don't know. The apple doesn't fall too far from the tree," Val teased. "It sounds like she's a perfectionist, and Lord knows you certainly are. When folks don't live up to your ideal"—Val made a squishy sound, mashing her thumb into the palm of her left hand—"you don't want anything to do with them."

"I'm not that way at all," Mel objected.

"Face it. You can be pretty cold-hearted. You can cut people off without batting an eye."

Could part of what Val said be true? Was she too unforgiving, too judgmental? But that didn't make her the same as her mother—did it?

Sometimes Mel was amazed and frightened at the ease with which she severed relationships. This was especially true when she was younger. She could be terribly enthusiastic about someone, and then, one wrong word or gaze askance could result in an instant and permanent turnoff.

True, she was disgusted with Maxx and his career choice and disappointed with Builder because of his business mistakes, but she didn't think she defined her relationships with people by the fallacies of their ways. After all, she had put up with Builder's stuff for a long time, and while she abhorred Maxx's connection to drugs and all that it represented, the two of them still maintained a relationship. No, there was no comparison to her mother. None.

Throughout her childhood, Mel always thought that her mother showed obvious favoritism to Maxx, which had carried over into adulthood. Mel couldn't let go of the hurt and sting of that rejection. Nor had she let go of the undercurrent of blame that she harbored for her mother's indirectly causing her father's death. How many times had she replayed that scene: her brother's request; her mother's insistence; her father's ill-timed trip to the store. *If you had just let Daddy alone!* But it was Eunice, her mother, who had pushed for Maxx to have his ice cream; Eunice, who had said, "Mel can wait a few more minutes." That's the way Mel remembered that fateful night of her father's death, and on many other occasions. It was always "come back later" to Mel, "another time" for Mel, "Mel can wait." But with Maxx, Eunice granted everything immediately, on the spot.

At times, she almost hated her mother. How could Val possibly suggest that she was like her? She had it wrong, very wrong. God, no, thought Mel. I'm nothing like Eunice. Nothing at all.

Nikki flitted around the dining room table, picking up the remains of dinner. Three centerpiece tapers flickered lazily, giving off a rosy haze to the room.

"That was great," Builder said. "I don't know when I've had a meal like that."

"Oh, now, stop," Nikki beamed. "You're making too much of it."

"Are you sure I can't do something?" Mel asked. She suspected that this offer, like her earlier one, would also be rejected, but it felt like the polite thing to say. "I can at least help clear the dishes."

"No, you don't," came Nikki's predictable reply. "Just stay put and relax. You're guests tonight, and I want to do this all by myself."

"Never argue with a determined woman," Maxx said, winking at his bride-to-be.

"I can't see you two ever arguing at all." Builder looked at Mel in a not-so-friendly manner, his comment a put-down of her as much as a compliment to Maxx and Nikki.

They had been at Maxx's for over an hour, firming up arrangements for the wedding and partaking of Nikki's specialty, spaghetti, laden with chili, oregano, and Builder's rave reviews. Mel was getting tired of Builder's obsequious narrative to the effect that Maxx had seemingly found the perfect mate in Nikki—an excellent cook, an affectionate lover, and most especially, a supportive partner. *Yeah, and she'd be great at licking boots too,* thought Mel cynically.

"Let me say it again," Builder continued, nibbling a piece of garlic bread. "Dinner was fantastic. You keep laying out meals like that, and Maxx's tailor can retire. Comfortably."

He had said more tonight than Mel had heard him say in the past several weeks. It must be the reprieve from the creditors. It was a temporary reprieve, a false one, but it allowed for an inch of breathing room. Even though the bankruptcy hadn't been approved today, there was the expectation, the firm hope, that it would be. So the albatross, while still present, was not clutching quite as tightly.

"Let's talk about Mother," Maxx said suddenly.

Mel took a deep breath. She knew what was coming.

"I think it's best that she stay with you," Maxx proposed.

"I think it's best that she doesn't," Mel said quickly. "It's going to be pretty hectic right before the wedding."

"All the more reason. She could help out. She's good at things like that."

"Well, I think she'd be more comfortable here," insisted Mel. "And besides," she said, appealing to his ego, "she'll want to spend as much time as possible with you."

Maxx moved smoothly to his next argument. "The thing is, some of Nikki's folks are coming in, so between her place and mine, we're going to be filled up."

"My sister and a couple of cousins," Nikki volunteered.

I'll trade you my mother for them, Mel wanted to suggest. Instead, she said lamely, "There *are* hotels," knowing how selfish that sounded.

"You don't put family in hotels," Maxx said. "Not if you can help it."

"A hotel? For your mother?" Builder glared at Mel. "That's insane."

"No, I didn't mean her," Mel said lamely. "I meant—" But she didn't finish the sentence. What did it matter? He had already misunderstood.

"What's the big deal anyway?" Builder spoke through a frown. "We have room. She can stay with us. Period." To him, the decision was simple; to discuss it further was absurd.

"There's more involved here than you realize," Mel said, simmering.

"You always make things more involved."

Just stay out of it, she wanted to shout at him. She had expected to have this conversation with Maxx, not with Builder. Why was he so interested in Eunice all of a sudden? What did it matter to him where Eunice stayed? He knew that the two of them didn't get along. All these years, he had never said much about it. Why butt in now? Just to rile her, that was why; to illustrate that this too was Mel's fault, to hammer in the notion that their marital and financial problems stemmed from her unwillingness to cooperate and that this was a pattern of behavior.

"If you don't mind," Mel said sharply, "this is something Maxx and I need to work out."

"Fine." Builder balled up his napkin and thrust it on the lone plate remaining on the table. "She's your mother. It's just that it makes no sense that you wouldn't want her to stay with you when she comes for a visit."

"Like I said—it's a matter of comfort."

"Whose? Hers or yours?"

Mel sighed. She was losing the battle. And to an opponent she hadn't anticipated. That's all she and Builder needed, something else to divide them. Maxx had said little. And why shouldn't he? His brother-in-law had taken up the gauntlet.

"Sasha's told me she's excited about her grandmother coming," said Nikki. "Bet I know where she wants her to stay."

Great, thought Mel. Now Nikki has joined the bandwagon, with the unspoken implication that Mel might be depriving her daughter of a grandmother's love. She should have talked about this with Maxx, alone. One-on-one she could handle, but three-on-one? "All right," she conceded, "she'll stay with us."

"Good!" Maxx snapped his finger. "It's the best way to go. You two can catch up on a lot of lost time."

Mel rolled her eyes. Maxx was trying to orchestrate some miraculous reconciliation that would never happen. He had no idea of the bitterness she felt toward their mother. It would be an effort, a great effort, just to be civil to her. And at this moment, Mel wasn't sure she could manage even that. Builder mumbled how he didn't see what all the fuss was about anyway.

Nikki brought in a huge glass bowl brimming with grapes. "This should tide you over till dessert."

"Dessert! Ahhh—where would I put it?" fawned Builder. "There's no room."

"Make room," she ordered jovially. "Mississippi mud pie with fresh whipped cream. Coming right up."

"I can't stand it!" Builder said appreciatively.

Maxx made a smacking sound and rubbed his hands together.

Mel, however, had zoomed in on the newest addition that had been set before them. "California table grapes," she blurted. "Don't you know there's a boycott on?"

Nikki looked puzzled. "A boycott?"

"Is that still happening?" Maxx asked. "I thought it was resolved some time ago."

"Oh, no. The boycott's still on."

"You mean, on these?" Nikki pointed to the bowl.

"Yes."

"But why?"

"Because the growers in California treat the workers like dirt," Mel explained. "No benefits, virtually slave wages. Besides, they have them spray the grapes with all kinds of chemicals and pesticides. A lot of the workers have gotten cancer and some of their children have been born deformed. With no legs and no arms."

Nikki winced. "That's horrible."

"For God's sake, Mel," Builder said gruffly. "Do you have to turn everything into a damn forum for some cause?"

"Well, it's the truth. These grapes aren't good for anybody. They have too much crap on them. And we should respect the boycott. For the farmworkers' sake."

"Excuse my ignorance," Maxx said with humor. "I plead guilty." He bowed his head and tapped his chest. "Mea culpa, mea culpa. I'm the one who bought them."

"It's too bad," said Nikki. "I love this kind. And they don't have any seeds."

"There're plenty of other kinds that are fine to eat," said Mel. "Like the

Concord grapes from upstate New York. And muscadines. That's what I buy. You can find them at health food stores and lots of other places in town. And then there are certain types of black and red seedless grapes that are okay."

Nikki looked at the glass bowl suspiciously. "I guess I should get rid of these, right?"

"Of course not," said Builder. "They're here; let's eat 'em. You throw them out, and then you'll be accused of wasting resources." He scowled at Mel. "If you ask me, grapes are grapes." Defiantly, he tore off two limbs and cupped them in his hand, ready to eat.

You asshole, thought Mel. They exchanged glares.

Maxx stood up quickly. "Look, bro, why don't you come on down-stairs—shoot a game of pool."

"What about dessert?" wailed Nikki.

"We'll get it later, baby." Maxx walked over and planted a kiss on her lips. "You're something else, you know that?"

Nikki flashed a smile. "Think so?"

"Indeed, indeed." He grabbed a couple of beers from the refrigerator and nodded to Builder on his way to the lower level. "Come on down. I'm setting up."

Nikki announced that she'd hold their dessert until later, and disappeared into the kitchen.

Still fuming at Mel, Builder munched on the contested grapes. "Satisfied?"

"About what?"

"You think everybody's got to deal with your agenda all the time, don't you?"

"I don't know what you're talking about."

"Don't give me that. You know damn well what I'm talking about." He lowered his voice, speaking through clenched teeth. "What you just did to Nikki. And this thing with your mother. Your know-it-all attitude. Like you've got some high moral ground, some superior intellect, that nobody else can touch."

"Hey, Builder!" Maxx's voice shouted from below. "Come on down here and get beat."

Builder angrily pushed back his chair. "Sometimes you can be a real bitch."

Before she could respond, he turned away from her and took to the staircase to join Maxx.

For several minutes Mel pondered over what had happened. Was what she said really so terrible? She had just spoken the truth, that's all. Why was Builder so bent out of shape? She listened to the faint sounds of the cue stick smashing into balls, of the muffled voices of her brother and husband, of Nikki puttering in the kitchen.

Nikki reappeared, carrying two plates of pie, smothered with waves of whipped cream. "I figured we'd go on and have ours. It'll give us a chance for some girl talk." She slid Mel's dessert in front of her.

"Looks good," said Mel. But she felt nauseated.

Nikki settled into her chair and looked at Mel with sisterly closeness. "There's so much I want to ask you," she said.

"Like what?" She probably wants to know about some of Maxx's boyhood antics, thought Mel, not eager to go back in time.

With the curve of her fork, Nikki neatly pierced her pie. "Well, you've been married for a while, so I thought you'd know—how do you keep a man happy? I mean, *really* happy?"

Builder leaned over the pool table, his taut body positioned for his best bow and arrow ground shot. "Number four, left pocket." He pushed the cue forward, sending the cue ball sailing across the felt, which in turn smacked into a striped enemy that nudged the number 4 ball close to its target, but not inside. "Damn. Almost."

"Almost is not good enough, bro," Maxx teased. "You're too tight. You need to loosen up." Smoothly, he sidled along the length of the table, eyes narrowed, picking his shot. Decision made, he tapped the rim of the table with his ring. "Seven in heaven. Right here. Come to me, baby." He ripped a powerful shot, zigzagging the ball back toward him, where it found its intended home in the brown leather pocket.

"Nice," Builder conceded.

Maxx continued to play, hitting with precision and familiarity. "So, have you cooled off yet?"

"What do you mean?"

"You and Mel. You were close to searing each other at dinner. Thought I might have to pull out my fire extinguisher. What's with you two, anyway?"

Builder took a swig of his beer. "What's with us? The same thing that's been with us for a long time. Nothing. I can't say two words to her before she starts jumping down my throat." He paused, checking himself. "I know she's your sister and all, but—"

"Hey, you're not telling me anything new. I know how critical she can be. She's still on my case about what I do."

"Eleven on six, six in the corner," Builder said, this time getting his shot in. "You lucked up with Nikki," he told Maxx. "She's sweet, mild-mannered, someone who'll really work with you."

"Can you believe it? A few more weeks, and I'll be a married man." Maxx let out a jungle yelp and pounded his chest, Tarzanlike.

"I wish you well, bro, I really do. You and Nikki will probably be all right. But I tell you, as far as I'm concerned, being married is about the most unnatural state you can ever be in. I mean, you compromise to the nth degree, make all kinds of sacrifices to the point where there's nothing left of *you* anymore. And all your individuality gets sucked down the tubes." He tried to concentrate as he prepared for his next shot.

"I know it's not easy. I read the other day where something like half of all marriages end in divorce. And that's supposed to be an improvement from previous years. Pretty discouraging, isn't it?"

"Well, that won't happen to you," Builder said forcefully. "I can tell already."

"So, what are you—the voice of experience?"

"Hey, I'm your best man. My job is to keep your spirits up, not bring you down. Can't have you picking up on my negativity and backing out of the wedding. Besides, haven't you heard? Misery loves company." He aimed for number 14, but used too much force, and scratched

"Finesse, bro, finesse," teased Maxx, surveying the table. "Let me try something here." Aligning the cue ball in front of his yellow and white target, he placed the cue behind him, arched backward, then nudged the cue forward. The number 9 ball rolled slowly, obediently, into its designated pocket.

Builder whistled.

Maxx gave him an "it's nothing" grin. "What can I say? I'm good, bro. I'm damn good."

"Well, if I were living in the lap of luxury and could come down here and practice two or three hours a day, I'd be damn good too."

"Two or three hours a day! I haven't touched this table since the last time you were here, and you know how long that's been. I'm just good, bro. You've got to admit."

They played intently for a few minutes, before Maxx broke new ground. "I talked with Mother last week. She wants Sasha to go back with her—after the wedding."

Builder absorbed the news. "Really?"

"Yes. For the summer. Sasha's never been there, and it'd be a good chance for Mother and her to get to know each other. What do you think?"

"Well, I—I don't know. I guess my first reaction is it sounds good. If that's what Sasha wants."

"Are you kidding? She'd love it. You all haven't made any plans for her for the summer yet, have you?"

"No, not that I know of."

"I mean, you haven't put down a deposit for a summer camp, or anything like that, have you?"

"I don't think so, Maxx, but, you know, Mel handles that kind of stuff. But I'm pretty sure she hasn't put down any deposit anywhere because there hasn't been any deposit money."

"Look, this would be my gift to Sasha. The trip to France. I'd love to do this for her."

"I appreciate it, Maxx, I really do. But—"

"But what?"

"There's a lot to consider. Mel, for one. You have to convince her. I doubt that she'd be too keen on the idea."

"I know. Anything involving Mother is an automatic turnoff."

"It's going to be a hard sell. I can tell you that already."

"Well, you give the go-ahead, and I'll handle all the logistics. Does Sasha have a passport?"

"No. She's never needed one before."

"Okay, get me her birth certificate, and I can send off for one. They process them really fast in Miami. And do me a favor, will you? Don't mention this to Mel yet. I really need to think it through, try to figure out the path of least resistance."

"Okay, but don't wait until the last minute. She doesn't like surprises."

"I know. On the other hand, if I've made all the arrangements, and am holding Sasha's airplane ticket in my hand—" He waved his right arm to illustrate.

Builder responded with a "have it your way" shrug.

"How're her grades?" asked Maxx, trying to cover all the bases. "She's still doing okay in school, isn't she?"

"Pretty good. It hasn't been her best year."

"Maybe by next fall she can go back to Trent. Or go somewhere else."

Builder was silent.

"I'd like to do that for her," Maxx said.

Builder stood up straight, delaying his shot. "You do more than enough already. I could never repay you for all that you've done."

"It's not about repaying me. Sasha's my niece; I've got to look out for her."

"Yeah, but she's my daughter; she's my responsibility. Mel's and mine. That's one thing we do agree on. We can't have you paying for trips to France and private education. We're the parents here. When money's tight, then we all have to make adjustments. As a family."

"That's true, to a point. Meanwhile, you've got to live."

"Well, right through here I've had to put living on hold."

"But you need to get *some* enjoyment out of life, or you'll go crazy. When was the last time you played golf, even?"

"It's been a while."

"Not since last summer, I bet. Right?"

No response.

"I don't know anybody who works harder than you do. Sixteen-, eighteen-hour days. But you can't keep up this pace, bro. You're playing with fire."

"I've got to keep it up. At least for a while. I don't have any choice." He moved to the other end of the pool table, steadying his cue for a delicate maneuver. "Number two, right pocket." Upon impact, the ball skidded toward the appointed goal, but en route, brushed against the 8 ball, which followed it, magnetized, all the way home. "Awww, shit!"

"Tough break," said Maxx, with fake sympathy. A winner by default, he laid his cue on the table, signaling the end of play, for the moment. It was more to give Builder a respite than himself.

They removed the balls from the pockets and racked them, then sat side by side on the carpeted steps, nursing their beers.

"Tell you what," said Maxx. "When Sasha goes to France with Mother—"

"*If* Sasha goes."

"*If* she goes, it'll be a perfect time for you to take some time off. And Mel too. You both need a change of venue. That's why you're at each other's throats all the time. Go on a cruise or something. Take a second honeymoon. It'll do you a world of good."

"I'll tell you what'll do me good, and I won't have to go anywhere. Just getting these debts off my back. That's all I want. But damn it's hard. Seems once you get behind, it's hard as heck to catch up. The harder I try, the worse it gets."

"Maybe you're trying too hard."

"What's that supposed to mean? Am I supposed to roll over and play dead?"

"No. Just—play differently. You've got talent and drive. There's no reason in the world why you shouldn't have contracts coming at you from all directions."

Builder snickered. "Where're they going to come from, Maxx? The sky?"

"I think the problem is you're dealing with the wrong folks."

"You mean, my customers?"

"Yeah, partly. You've got to get into those neighborhoods where new houses start at half a million. And you need to circulate. Forget this Lone Ranger stuff. In your business, you've got to network."

"Yeah, I know I should do more of that."

"More? You don't do *any*. You didn't even call me when you should have. *Me*—your brother-in-law. You didn't have to take the bankruptcy, Builder. You should have called me, man."

"We were about to lose the house. I didn't have any choice."

"But there might have been another way out. There's always other ways. You should have told me what was going down. I would've helped out."

"I can't come running to you every time I get into a bind. Besides, at the time, you were down in Miami, focusing on some big case. You didn't need any distractions."

Maxx grinned sheepishly. "I was already distracted. Nikki was with me, remember?"

They each had their own image of what that meant.

"I still say you should have called me," Maxx repeated.

"No, you've bailed me out a zillion times. It's got to stop somewhere. I already owe you—what? Over twenty grand?"

"I told you not to worry about that. I know you're good for it. Besides, I consider it an investment in your business."

"Well, I'm going to pay you back. And soon. I'm committed to that."

Maxx took a swig of his beer. "I met this contractor in Miami you might be interested in talking to. He's planning to set up an office here in Atlanta, in Norcross, I think, and wants to expand throughout the Southeast. He does corporate headquarters, mostly commercial stuff. But he needs a minority partner to bid on a lot of the projects around here. I told him about you."

"Oh, yeah? What's his name?"

Maxx snapped his fingers, trying to recall. "Gilbert? Gilchrist? Something like that. I've got his card upstairs. Might be worth giving him a buzz."

"Sure. I'll call him."

"Good. I didn't know how you'd feel about working with someone else. You've got your own style and way of doing things. Getting involved with other people means having to dance to their tune."

"At this point I'll dance to damn near any tune with just about anybody. I'll do the Watusi if that's what it takes. What I've been doing so far sure hasn't been working."

"Who knows? If the two of you click, it might be the ticket to some big bucks."

"What do you know about him?"

"Not much. Seems nice enough. We had a couple drinks at a bar one night. Typical white guy with long money, inherited most of it from his family. The usual story."

Builder shook his head. "It comes so easy to them."

"He's made millions and is looking to make more," Maxx added. "But he needs a minority partner to tap into some of the new deals coming down. So he's got to at least give the *appearance* that the money's being spread around."

"He's not on the take, is he?"

Maxx chuckled. "You're starting to sound like Mel—like everybody I hang out with has blood dripping from his hands."

"You know me better than that."

"Well, he seems legit. But you'll have to check him out for yourself. We didn't discuss details. I mean, we're talking about a possible joint venture here, not saving souls."

"Course, it's possible that both can coexist," said Builder.

"I agree. But try telling that to your wife."

"Not me," Builder retorted stubbornly. "She's your sister. You've known her longer." He didn't want to talk about Mel anymore tonight. He had decided long ago that there was an unbridgeable gap in the way they viewed such matters. He stood up to stretch, and raised the last of his beer to his lips. "I'm ready," he said, moving determinedly to the pool table.

"You mean, you haven't had enough?" Maxx asked. "You want to lose *again?*"

"I don't intend to lose. I'm about to hit my stride now." He reached for the chalk to prepare his cue.

"Bro, you're dreaming!" Maxx teased. "Talk about lost causes. Why don't you just give it up?"

"Nope," Builder said, poised for the break. "My luck's *got* to improve." He smashed the cue into the nose of the triangle, scattering balls helter-skelter across the table.

CHAPTER 9

Dragging the vacuum into the living room, Mel noticed the layer of dust that clung to the baby grand. It represented one more task she hadn't counted on, one more chore that would take up precious minutes in an already crowded day. She had just dusted the piano a couple days ago, waxed it, even; yet it looked as though it had not seen the soft folds of a dust rag in some time.

She took a deep breath, berating the loaded breeze coming in from the screened windows that transported remnants of pollen and swarms of mites. Keeping the dust under control was a constant challenge. Normally, she would bypass the piano, letting its layer rise higher. But today she couldn't ignore it. Eunice would be here this evening, and everything—everything—had to be perfect. As perfect as possible for Lady Perfect.

It bothered her that she still cared what her mother thought, that she still sought her approval and aimed to please. She added dusting to her mental list of things to do and was about to plug in the vacuum when the phone rang. Another interruption! She'd be able to get things done if not for the continual phone calls. With the wedding just a week away, people were steadily calling with questions about directions, or dropping off gifts. Then, the caterer wanted to confirm part of the order—was it a gross of smoked oysters or roasted oysters? The florist had reported that a new shipment of birds of paradise was due next Thursday and would Mel want to substitute those for the peace lilies?

Now what? she wondered. She left the vacuum in the middle of the floor, her stomach and head starting to react to the stress at hand. "Hello?"

A perky female voice greeted her, asking about the annual Memorial Day bash at the Burkes. "Did I miss your call? You usually get in touch with me way before now."

That was the problem with traditions: Do something the least bit different, and people will call you down on it.

The voice rambled on. "I didn't want to come all the way over there if you're not having it this year. I ran into Celeste, and she said she hadn't seen you in months. Are you okay?"

Of course not, Mel thought, I'm bankrupt. There's no way we could afford a party, like in the past. Even a few bags of chips and some soda would be a strain. She assured the caller that, yes, she was fine, but that there would be no party this year since she was hosting her brother's wedding in a few days.

"Oh. That explains it. My goodness, we've been coming to your house on Memorial Day for so long, I don't know what we're going to do."

Gee. If only I had that problem, thought Mel. But the call reminded her that a whole year had passed since last Memorial Day, when the downfall had begun—the decline into debt, the deep descent into a lifestyle of fiscal restraint and daily cutbacks.

One thing about coordinating the wedding that Mel did enjoy was being able to spend money again, even though it wasn't hers. Maxx had not given her a budget—"Whatever it takes," he had said, "whatever you and Nikki come up with"—so, given free rein, she had enjoyed ordering the best food, the most exotic flowers, the jazziest band—all without concern about the bottom line. She used to do things like that frequently; how lucky she had been, without even knowing it.

She had barely hung up the phone when the irritating ring whined again. She started not to answer it, but knew that wasn't the solution.

"Mel. Glad I caught you. I need a favor." It was Maxx, sounding rushed and speaking fast. He had been called into court unexpectedly and wanted her to pick up their mother. The flight arrived in an hour.

"You've got to be kidding!" Mel cried. "I can't. I'm not ready."

"What do you mean 'not ready'?" Impatience slipped into his voice. "What's there to do? Just get in the car and pick her up."

"But you don't understand. I haven't finished cleaning and—"

"Mel, come on now." His voice was firm, almost angry. "She's been flying for hours. You've got to be there to pick her up. She's your mother, for God's sake."

Damn! If only she *hadn't* answered the phone. Maxx would have handled it some way. Left a message for Eunice to take a cab. Or gotten one of his assistants to pick her up. Or . . .

He quickly gave her the flight information, reminding her to go to Concourse D for international arrivals.

"What about dinner?" Mel asked weakly.

"Oh, er—I think I can still manage that. Just get her there and get her settled. I'll come over as soon as I can. See you later." He hung up.

Mel screamed at the phone.

Why did Maxx always put her into these situations? Why this? Why now?

It was bad enough that she'd have to endure her mother for ten days. But she hadn't expected it to start this soon. The plan had been for Maxx to pick her up from the airport and for the two of them to have some private time at a downtown restaurant. After a long dinner, he'd bring her to the house, they'd all visit for a while, and then, exhausted by the long trip and evening, Eunice would be ready for bed. Mel wouldn't have to be alone with her. One night down, nine to go. So much for best-laid plans.

Now, she wouldn't have the four or five extra hours she needed to finish cleaning house and tend to the final details. She wouldn't have time for the long leisurely bath she had looked forward to, to prepare herself mentally and physically to meet Eunice. She tore the scarf off her head and looked around wildly. Where to begin?

The guest room! Not remembering if everything was in order there, she scurried in for a last-minute once-over. All seemed ready. Fresh cut gladiola stood tall in a lead crystal vase on the dresser. The newly washed and Downy-ed bedspread lay wrinkle-free across the large four-poster. The television was angled just so, to assure the best viewing stance from both the bed and the adjacent chair. Easy listening music drawled softly from the radio on the night stand. Vanilla potpourri released a light, delicate scent. The room smelled good, looked good; it was clean, uncluttered, inviting. For sure though, her mother would find fault with something. She always did.

A colorful "welcome" banner that Sasha had made was draped across the door. That's it, Mel thought. Sasha! She'd be a big help.

Mel glanced at her watch, moving quickly as she thought. She'd have to hurry. She couldn't go like this, not in these funky jeans and sweater that she had cleaned in all morning. She'd have to at least take a shower and then pick up Sasha from school on the way to the airport. It would be close, but she'd have time. She'd make time. She needed Sasha.

It was a shame. Here she was, a grown woman, about to use her daughter as a shield against her own mother.

There was never a good time to go to the Atlanta airport, but a Friday afternoon before a holiday ranked as one of the worst. Mel and Sasha were stuck in a long line of cars waiting to enter the short-term parking lot.

"We're so late," Sasha lamented. "Can't you do something?"

"Honey, there's nothing we *can* do. I can't exactly jump over these cars, now can I?"

"Oh, hurry up, hurry up." Verbally, Sasha moved the cars along, to the accompaniment of a modified thrusting motion from her seat. But it would take more than words and willpower to budge this line forward. "Why don't you pull over to the side and double-park or something?"

"I can't do that. You see that policeman? He'd ticket me in a minute. And anyway, it's jammed over there too."

"Oh, brother!" Frustrated, Sasha crossed her arms and pouted out the window.

Mel shook her head, at a loss as to how to deal with Sasha's adolescent mood swings. A few moments ago, her daughter was ecstatically happy, excited about seeing her grandmother, delighted that Mel had retrieved her from a boring science experiment. Now, detained in a car, she allowed a glum darkness to overtake her.

"Look, why don't you go on in and see if you can find her?" Mel proffered.

Sasha brightened. "Yeah!" Then, her face gave way to a puzzled expression. "But how will I know her? I mean, what does she look like?"

"She looks like her pictures, of course." Mel lightly brushed aside the questions, but they lingered with her several minutes after she had given Sasha specific instructions to meet by the baggage claim exit.

How will I know her? What does she look like?

The small voice of doubt in Sasha's voice tugged at Mel's conscience. Even though she and her mother weren't close, too much time had passed since Sasha had seen her grandmother. Seven years, nearly half of Sasha's young life. Letters and photos, though important, were poor runners-up to personal contact. It was sad, really. In essence, her daughter was going inside the airport to meet a stranger, a woman with whom she had corresponded and talked to by phone, a woman whom she called Grandma, but a stranger nonetheless. The last time the two were together, Sasha was so young that her memories of Eunice were vague and ill-defined.

But the last several years since Mel had seen her mother had only further cemented her negative remembrances. And there were many. Like the time Eunice embarrassed her in front of her junior high school class by announcing to all present, boys included, that Mel was only ten years old when she started her period. Working as a nurse at a nearby hospital, Eunice had been asked by Mel's teacher to speak to the class on health, hygiene, and puberty. In giving an example about how bodies develop differently, she had mentioned that some girls begin to menstruate in their mid-teens, while others are as young as nine or ten. And then she had used Mel as an example of an early starter. Mel was mortified. When, in tears and self-righteous anger, Mel later lashed out at her, Eunice replied that she had meant no harm and had only mentioned Mel by name because her classmates knew her. It was her way of making the abstract real. "Besides," she had said innocently, "menstruation is a fact of life, dear. It's nothing to be ashamed of." But for Mel, that day at school was the equivalent of a public flogging—administered by the hands of her own mother.

There were other bad memories, other humiliations, always unintentional and misunderstood, according to Eunice. But Mel viewed them as deliberate and mean-spirited.

A pimpled airport attendant appeared, yelling that the ticket machine to the parking lot didn't work. People tried to back up and drive around, but there was nowhere to go, no room to move. Horns honked discordantly, and short tempers, previously held in check by good manners and a bow to Southern civility, suddenly let loose, as, dominolike, irritation puffed up into anger, vented through a barrage of cussing and swearing.

All around her swirled discord and growing panic. But in a strange way Mel welcomed the chaos. She was still not ready to face her mother and this was another way to gain time. Legitimately. She sat there in resigned serenity, probably the only one amidst a sea of drivers creating neither sweat nor curses nor a nicked bumper.

She has to go through customs, so that will take time, Mel reminded herself. Still, she estimated that by now, Sasha and Eunice had found each other and were waiting for her on the other side. Ten minutes passed. Fifteen. She watched a petite young woman struggle with a Louis Vuitton pullman, picking her way through the jumble of cars, stopping every few paces to change sides, as she dragged the heavy luggage.

Finally, the airport police officer, who had been ticketing illegally parked cars on the side, attempted to untangle the logjam. "About time you did something, you bastard," someone shouted stupidly, prompting the officer to go over to the car and reprimand the driver, contributing to even more delays. Eventually, cars began to inch forward, and Mel meticulously maneuvered her way to the prearranged meeting site.

Initially, she didn't see Sasha and Eunice in the press of people. But Sasha spotted her, waving her arms furiously. It was impossible for Mel to get to the curbside, so Sasha and Eunice, one carrying a hat box, the other rolling a loaded luggage cart, stepped carefully through the maze to reach Mel—and refuge.

"Mom! What took you so long? We've been waiting forever."

Ignoring Sasha's complaint, Mel looked directly at Eunice, who, despite the long flight and subsequent wait, appeared fashion crisp in her dark shades and navy and white pantsuit.

"Mel, dear. It's so good to see you."

They hugged awkwardly, the broad brim of Eunice's hat interfering with the embrace.

"It's been much too long," Eunice said, smiling a smile that showed still perfect and all-natural teeth.

"Yes, it has been too long. You look great."

She did. Eunice's smooth rich skin, the beneficiary of the best that French cosmetics had to offer, belied her sixty-four years. Despite deepening circles under her eyes and more streaks of gray than Mel remembered, Eunice was still markedly attractive. Her salt and pepper hair was cut in a short, sophisticated style. She had maintained her trim figure with regular aerobics and a weekly dance class. A former nurse, Eunice was conscientious about getting sufficient exercise and eating a proper diet. And it showed.

With the luggage deposited in the trunk of the car and her passengers buckled up, Mel veered cautiously out of the crowd of cars. She was glad she had to keep her eyes on the road. It felt strange, having her mother here, sitting next to her, after so many years.

Eunice chatted easily. About Sasha—how tall she was, how bright. About her flight—long but restful, and giving her a chance to read a biography. About Atlanta—she had forgotten that there were so many trees, and how, from the sky, the city looked like a forest.

"We have a lot of things planned for you," Sasha said excitedly.

"You do?"

"Yes. There's the King Center. The Botanical Garden. Stone Mountain. Underground. The Carter Center. Lake Lanier—"

"My goodness," Eunice interrupted joyously. "How am I going to do all that?"

That's the idea, thought Mel. To keep you busy, to keep you active, to fill every waking minute of your day. Then there would be less time for talking about the past and personal hurts, and less likelihood of an argument.

"And, of course, there's the wedding," Sasha said, finishing her list. "That *is* the main event, you know."

"Yes indeed. And I can hardly wait. Did you get a new dress?"

"Yes. From Uncle Maxx and Nikki. I'll show it to you as soon as we get home. It's lavender with white satin bows."

"Oh, I know it's pretty," said Eunice.

They lapsed into a dialogue of broken French, punctuated by giggles of error and a few English words. But they managed to keep the conversation on track, just the two of them. Mel understood little of what they were saying. Once again, with her mother around, she felt like an outsider, on the periphery. Only this time, it wasn't her mother and Maxx; it was her mother and Sasha.

Out of the corner of her eye, Mel could see that her mother was addressing her. "What?" she asked, turning quickly to her right. "You talking to me?"

"Oui."

"Oh, Grandma! Mom doesn't know French."

"That's right," Eunice said, snapping her fingers. "I had forgotten. It was Maxx who took French."

Maxx, of course. Always Maxx.

"Now I remember," Eunice said. "You took Spanish, right?"

Mel nodded. Four years in high school and two in college, she wanted to say. But it didn't matter now. Didn't matter how many years of Spanish she had taken. Didn't matter if she was a Spanish expert. The main thing was she hadn't taken French.

"Well, then, we should stop talking in French, Sasha. It's not very polite, you know, since Mel doesn't understand."

"Oh, don't worry about me. You all go on. Sasha needs the practice."

"No, it's not polite," insisted Eunice. "Besides, we'll have *plenty* of time to talk French." She winked at Sasha, who broke out in a smile.

Coming up the deck two steps at a time, Maxx nearly knocked Eunice over with a generous hug. They laughed and joked and kissed, a genuine mother-son reunion. Mel couldn't help but compare his lively greeting with her lackluster one a few hours earlier. There was a difference in Eunice's response too, all of which did not go unnoticed by Sasha.

"You act like you haven't seen each other in years," she said. "It's only been since Christmas."

"Hey, that's still a long time," Maxx said. "This is my favorite lady, you know."

"I thought I was," Sasha said with fake jealousy.

"You're my favorite *girl*. There's a difference."

"And where does Nikki fit in?" Sasha baited.

"Eh," he looked from side to side, searching facetiously. "Guess I'll have to fit her in somewhere."

Eunice rapped him on the shoulder. "Aren't you naughty."

They all three laughed, as Mel busied herself with pouring iced tea for Maxx. They were out on the deck rather than in the family room because Eunice had a problem with the potpourri in her room. It was too pungent, she had said, giving her a headache and making her wheezy. She had requested that not just her room but the whole house be "aired out" because the scent, though slight, had traveled everywhere.

Mel watched her mother closely. With her hat and sunglasses off, and in the presence of her favorite child, she looked completely relaxed and even more youthful. Seeing her brother and mother together for the first time in so many years, Mel was struck anew at how much they resembled each other. The two of them always did favor—the same high cheekbones, flashing dark eyes, bronzed complexions. Maxx was undeniably Eunice's son. Mel, on the other hand, looked like her father—lighter with broader features.

Maxx proposed that Sasha join him and Eunice for dinner with Nikki. Mel protested, saying Eunice needed time alone with Maxx and his bride-to-be.

"Oh, let her come; it's no big deal. It's nothing formal. You should come along too."

Mel shot him a "you know better than that" glance, but under Eunice's watchful gaze, said simply, "Thanks, but I need to take care of some things around here."

As Eunice and Sasha left to change clothes, Maxx put up his feet and nursed his tea. "Guess it takes a wedding to bring a family together."

"Either that or a funeral."

"Aren't you cheerful."

"Just speaking the truth."

They were silent for a minute.

"She's glad to be here. You know that, don't you?"

"She's glad to see *you*. And Sasha."

"She's glad to see you too. Can't you tell? You've got to give her half a chance. She's mellowed out a lot."

"Look. I know you're hoping for some grand reconciliation. But Eunice is Eunice. Always will be. We're just very different people, that's all."

Maxx sighed deeply, deciding to move onto another track. "I've been meaning to talk to you about something concerning Sasha."

"What about her?" Mel asked suspiciously.

He spoke slowly, deliberately. "I want to do something really special for her."

"You're always doing something really special for her."

"I mean something she'll remember for a long time." He took the plunge. "I think it'd be great for her to go to France this summer. To stay with Mother."

Mel stiffened. "What did you say?"

He put his feet down and set his glass on the table. "Think of it. A chance to go to France. She can help Mother and Alfred at the inn, and see how a business is run. She can bone up on her French, maybe take some lessons while she's over there. Imagine how much she'd learn! I mean, how many kids have an opportunity to do something like that? At her age?"

"There's no way in hell I'd let Sasha go over there."

"Why not? It's a perfect opportunity. She can fly over with Mother when she leaves."

"I said no, Maxx. The answer is no. I don't want Sasha in that kind of—environment." She spoke the word with pure displeasure.

"*Environment?* For God's sake, you act like Mother's some kind of monster or something. When are you going to get over this crazy grudge you're holding against her?"

"I'm not holding a grudge," she said firmly, forgetting that the open windows throughout the house made for easy listening of raised voices. "If Sasha wants to get to know her, to write to her or talk on the phone, fine. I've never interfered with that. But going halfway around the world and living with her?" She shook her head. "No way." She walked over to the railing, putting distance between him and his idea.

"She's her grandmother, Mel—her *grandmother*. The only one Sasha has. Besides, it's just for a visit, for a few weeks, even. It doesn't have to be the whole summer, if that'll make you feel better."

"No, that won't make me feel better. The answer's no. Period. It's not a good idea."

"Mother thinks it's a great idea."

Mel jerked around accusingly. "You talked to her about this?"

"Yes, before she came. And I also talked about it to Sasha. But only a little," he added quickly.

Mel's eyes blazed; her lips quivered. "You had no right, Maxx. No right. Going behind my back like that."

"I wasn't going behind your back. I was just trying to check out a few things first. No sense telling you about it if Mother had plans for the summer. In case she might be traveling or something. But it's fine with her. She'd be delighted if Sasha could come. And I mentioned it to Builder. He thought it was okay."

"He did, did he? You talked to Builder too?" Mel reproached. "Who else knows? The mailman? The paper boy?"

"Aw, come off it, Mel."

"No, *you* come off it. We're talking about my daughter here. *My* daughter, Maxx. Not yours. You seem to have forgotten that. You're making plans for her, left and right, checking in with everybody else except me—her mother. You've gone too far this time."

Maxx released a long breath, accepting the criticism. There was no arguing with Mel when she got this emotional. An otherwise rational person, she was closed to hearing anything remotely positive about Mother. It was like there was this huge mountain that she couldn't traverse. And the more Maxx pushed her to cross over, the more she resisted.

When he spoke again, it was with lawyerly calm, an attempt to rattle Mel's misplaced self-righteousness and invoke her sense of fairness. "So, you're telling me that you'd deny Sasha the opportunity of a lifetime because you and Mother don't get along. Is that it?"

Unmoved, Mel looked at him with hostility. "Interpret it any way you want."

She went inside, leaving him to wonder what else he could do to get her to change her mind.

"Here, use this."

Sasha shook her bent head, tears continuing to flow down her face.

"Take it," Mel insisted, pressing the handkerchief into Sasha's palm. She looked around self-consciously, aware that others in the tiny café were witnesses to this sad little scene. A bearded young man, seated at the next table, made a point of raising his newspaper parallel to his head, preferring the travails of the world over the conflict at hand. Two middle-aged women, however, between bits of conversation and Danish, kept steady eyes on Mel and the sobbing Sasha.

It infuriated Mel when Sasha went into one of her self-pitying episodes. Once started, they had to run their course, and nothing seemed to stop the torrent. In fact, the more Mel protested or tried to shame Sasha out of it, the more prolonged the crying sessions became. So she had learned to back off, and let the pattern unfold: first, the sniffing; then, shoulders heaving; and finally, full-blown tears.

"See, you just proved my point. How can you expect to go to another country when you act like a two-year-old just because you can't get your way?"

"But why not? Why can't I go?"

"For a lot of reasons. It's just not a good time right now. You're too young, for one thing. And there's the money it'll cost."

"But Uncle Maxx said he'll pay for everything," protested Sasha. "He already bought the airline ticket."

"Well, he'll just have to get his money back," Mel said sharply. "He jumped the gun and was way out of line. He should never even have mentioned this to you. Should never have put the idea in your head."

Sasha dabbed at her red eyes. "It's because you don't like her, isn't it? Isn't that why?"

They say the truth eventually seeps out, somewhere down the road, sooner or later. It may emerge immediately on the spot or after years gone by. It may come in the form of old diaries rediscovered, of whispered secrets revealed, of missing links found. Covering up the truth is not always bad, if done to protect the innocent or alleviate hurt. But no matter how noble the intent, the truth cannot be hidden. Ultimately, it will show itself.

As it did now. With her mother living so far away, it had been easy for Mel to pretend to Sasha that theirs was a normal relationship. What made it easy was that Eunice was never around to attend family dinners and birthday celebrations, the school functions or recitals. It's on such occasions that relationships are stretched and tested, where there is no escape behind polite letters or phone calls, where one is forced to confront the present. But Eunice was always in France, always distant, beyond reach. Since she had come to visit, however, the truth had no place to hide. Despite Mel's best efforts to camouflage her real feelings, Sasha keenly felt the chill in the house.

Mel looked around the café, feeling duped into coming here. It had sounded like a good idea; Sasha had happily proposed that they come to the Oxford Bookstore, long a favorite pastime, while Eunice and Nikki went out for a get-acquainted lunch. It was going to be Sasha's treat, using money saved from her allowance. They used to come here frequently, browse for an hour or so, then end up at the café for dessert and hot chocolate. It was a tradition that had gotten waylaid in the past year, along with a series of other things in Mel's former life, when money was not a problem, and the constant pressure of making ends meet was not foremost in her mind. So when Sasha suggested coming here today, Mel had welcomed the chance for a little respite and an overdue mother-daughter chat. She didn't expect, though, that Sasha would harp about the trip to France—would plead, cajole, and now, finally, cry—upon hearing Mel's adamant "no."

"It's because you and Grandma don't like each other that you won't let me go," Sasha insisted. "It's not fair."

Put that way, it did sound petty and juvenile and unfair. But Mel couldn't help herself. There was too much to overcome, too much to lay aside. "Maybe when you're older," she said. "When you're sixteen. That might be a good time."

"I may not live to be sixteen."

"Oh, Sasha, stop it!"

It bothered her whenever Sasha spoke in fatalistic terms. Was this a simple adolescent rebuke or the veiled warning of a serious problem? It was hard to tell the difference. Mel was well aware that parents often wrongly dismissed such language as insignificant, as Cassandralike cries of pending disaster. She didn't want to do that with Sasha. From her own experience, she knew how devastating such a misjudgment could be. Better to be overly safe than sorry.

"Why would you say something like that?" she asked quietly.

Sasha shrugged her shoulders. "You're the one always saying that nothing's guaranteed."

"Well, that's true, but—" She looked at her daughter, hunched over, forlorn and hapless. Was she being too hard, too unreasonable? Was she making Sasha pay the price for her own resentment toward Eunice? Could Maxx be right, after all?

Several minutes passed before Mel spoke again. "Does it really mean that much to you?" she asked.

Sasha's head shot up. "Yes!" she said, a glint of hope in her eyes. "Oh, please, Mom, it'd be great, I just know it."

Mel exhaled heavily. "I'll think about it." It was as close to a "yes" as she would ever come. But it was all that Sasha needed.

"Oh, thank you, thank you, thank you!" She clapped her hands with glee, her tear-stained face breaking into a smile.

"I said I'd think about it," Mel clarified, already regretting that she had relented this much. But as far as Sasha was concerned, the decision was made.

"There's so much to do," she rambled. "I need to get my clothes together and pack. Uncle Maxx was right."

"Right about what?" Mel asked coldly.

"Oops." Sasha put her hand over her mouth, realizing she had exposed the setup.

"What does he have to do with this?"

"Well, uh——" She had a sheepish expression.

"It was his plan to come here, wasn't it?"

"Well, yes, but—I mean, I wanted to come here too. He just thought of it first, that's all."

"Yeah, I'll bet he did." So this was Maxx's doing. One of his under-handed out-of-court maneuvers. Have Sasha butter her up, cry the croc-odile tears, and then—voila!—get a reversal. After all, if Sasha couldn't change her mind, who could? He had probably even coached her, helped her prepare her arguments. Well, the strategy had worked. Without even making an appearance, Maxx had won his case. Mel had fallen for Sasha's emotional appeal.

"France is a long way to be by yourself," Mel said, pondering the impli-cations of the journey.

"Mom, it's not like I'll be alone."

"You know what I mean—without your father or me. If ever there's a problem of any kind, call me. Understand?"

"Okay."

"Promise," Mel pressed.

It was usually Sasha who asked for that extra assurance; "promise" was a word that Mel shunned.

"I promise, Mom," Sasha said seriously.

On the way out, Sasha stopped to peruse several books on conversa-tional French.

"The language you can handle," Mel muttered under her breath. "It's your grandmother I'm worried about."

When Sasha asked what she had said, Mel told her never mind.

The bed was littered with clothes, many of them out of season and inappropriate. In the process of selecting what to wear to the wedding, Mel had virtually emptied her closet, and was becoming increasingly frustrated. Her wardrobe consisted mostly of tailored business attire, acquired during her years at the Chamber; there was little that could be described as festive and gay.

Dissatisfied, she surveyed the few items in contention: a solid teal shirt dress with breast pockets, a paisley ankle-length skirt and matching top, and a yellow linen suit. None of the finalists was outstanding; each would simply "do." That seemed to be the status of her life lately. Barely getting by, just making do.

She had slipped out of her jeans and was pulling her sweatshirt over her head when Eunice tapped at the open door.

"Hi. Got a minute?"

"Uh, sure. Come on in." Standing in her bra and panties, Mel reached for the shirt dress and unbuttoned it.

"I see you've been busy." Eunice cleared a spot on the bed, choosing to sit there rather than the corner chair. "Cleaning out your closet?"

"Just trying to decide what to wear on the Big Day." Self-consciously, Mel stepped into the dress. "How was lunch?"

"Wonderful. Nikki is such a delight. She has a childlike innocence that you don't usually see in young women these days. But I can tell she's smart. And funny too. I'm glad Maxx found someone with a sense of humor."

How would you know about that? Mel thought. But she only concurred that, yes, Nikki was sweet and seemed devoted to Maxx.

Eunice leaned back on some piled-up clothes, like a chummy roommate eager for girl talk.

You were never willing to talk when I needed you most, thought Mel. And you certainly weren't willing to listen. Why start now?

How often had she longed for an intimate mother-daughter relationship, especially in the years after her father's death. And how much she had envied her friends who seemed to be able to tell their mothers anything. There were so many times when she wanted to confide in her mother and talk openly about the confusing feelings of a teenager bursting into maturity. When Mel needed her most, however, Eunice had seemed indifferent and unapproachable. So Mel kept her feelings inside and boarded up. Seeing Eunice now, all comfortable and settled amidst the thrown-about clothes, Mel wanted her to leave, to go back to the guest room, or read quietly in the den. To be anywhere except here.

"Goodness, dear, have you lost weight? That dress is literally hanging on you."

It was true, the dress just hung there, shapeless and without form. It had always been somewhat roomy, but now it nearly swallowed her. Mel hadn't realized it, but she must have lost weight. This past year, she had not partaken of regular business lunches, complete with dessert and B&B brandy, which often served as the backdrop for all manner of negotiations. Since she had lost her job, she usually had only yogurt or fruit and crackers for lunch, or skipped it altogether. And, no doubt, the constant stress about money had also taken its toll.

"It's good that you've kept your figure," Eunice said, "but you don't want to get too thin."

She was right. And Mel knew she was right. But still, the words smacked of familiar criticism. She was in no mood for Eunice's advice or personal judgments. She tried to steer the conversation in a different direction, asking Eunice about her husband Alfred, about their bed-and-breakfast inn—anything to get the focus off her.

But her mother seemed to recognize the attempted detour and worked her way back to Mel. "When was the last time you had a physical? I'll bet your energy level is way down. You look tired and worn out."

"Even if I do, I don't need you to remind me of it," Mel snapped. They were falling into the same pattern, biting and scratching over insignificances.

"Don't take everything so personally, Mel."

"How else am I supposed to take it? You're talking about *me*, right?"

Eunice widened her eyes innocently. "I'm just telling you what I see. I'm not trying to hurt your feelings. Like I've always said, if *I* can't tell you certain things, who can?" She shifted positions on the crowded bed. "I didn't realize you were still so—touchy."

Just shut up, Mel wanted to scream. Shut up. She turned back to the mirror, and evaluated herself in the paisley two-piece. She primped excessively, tying the fabric belt this way and that, hoping that, if she ignored Eunice long enough, she would get the hint and just go away. But her mother remained curious about a lot of things.

"I don't mean to pry, but—is something wrong between you and Nathaniel?"

"What gives you that impression?" Mel replied coolly.

"Well, I've only seen him once since I've been here. I know he's working a lot, but—it's a feeling I've picked up. That the two of you are having problems."

"Very perceptive," Mel said bitterly, then regretted her caustic tone.

Eunice didn't deserve that. Even though Mel didn't understand her mother's professed newfound interest, sarcasm was uncalled for. Maybe Eunice really was concerned.

"I was just wondering if maybe there's—someone else."

Mel almost laughed. Builder with another woman? As tired and funky as he was when he came home at night? "No, that's not the problem," she said assuredly. He was too exhausted to even heat up dinner, let alone light the fire under some frisky young thing. And depending on the project he was working on, he often smelled like a musty attic, or was covered with particles of sawdust amidst his grimy work clothes. Hardly the modus operandi of a man who had just left a lover. On the other hand, there was a whole lot of time during the middle of the day when she didn't see him, and had no idea where he was. So if being with another woman was what he wanted . . .

"I know how easily it can happen," said Eunice. "Your father wasn't exactly a saint, you know."

"Daddy?" Mel asked, surprised.

"Mmm." Eunice folded her arms, assessing Mel closely. "It just doesn't have enough punch."

"What?"

Eunice pointed to the paisley.

"Oh, this." Mel looked down at her outfit.

"It's too drab. Not quite right for the hostess of a wedding. You need something more alive. With pizzazz."

Suddenly Mel didn't care. She was more interested in the troubles that Eunice had alluded to. "You and Daddy had problems?"

"What marriage doesn't?" She ran over Mel's question, holding her hands parallel like she was framing a picture. "Maybe with the right earrings, something to jazz it up." She quickly nixed her own idea. "No, jewelry won't do it. What else do you have?"

"That suit there." But Mel wanted to get back to this business about her father. "Did Daddy have a—girlfriend?" It was strange to think of her father in those terms.

"Girlfriend*s* is more like it," Eunice said, sitting up straight and removing the suit from its hanger. "I found out later that it had been going on for years. He was a rolling stone, all right. Couldn't keep his eye in his socket and his thing in his pocket."

Mel was shocked. She had never heard her mother, always so dignified and aloof, speak so loosely. But even more shocking was the revelation about her father's philandering. "Daddy and other women? I find that hard to believe."

"Believe it. It happened. A lot." Eunice handed over the skirt.

"And you stayed with him throughout all this?"

"We had an understanding. Besides, he was a good provider and an excellent father. And you and Maxx needed him. Especially you."

Mel pulled the yellow skirt over her hips, pondering the truth in that statement. "Yes," she said wistfully, "I did need him."

The alliances had been drawn early: she and her father versus her mother and Maxx. They seldom operated like a cohesive family, more like sets of twos. Mel regarded her mother as cold and callous and never understood why her father stayed with her. Often, she had wished that she and her father could live somewhere else, not far, maybe down the street or a few blocks away, but separate and apart from her mother and Maxx. That way, she'd have more time with her father, without Maxx's pesky interference or her mother's ceaseless demands. It was an unrealistic dream, based on a little girl's jealousy of her father's love.

Hearing this secret about her father, Mel felt a slight sense of betrayal, that her love as a daughter wasn't enough. But neither, evidently, was her mother's. He needed more, if not from his wife, then from another woman, or several women. Perhaps that explained Eunice's coldness, at least, partially, Mel mused. Maybe she was unresponsive because she knew her husband was with other women, and he was with other women because she was unresponsive. And so the cycle continued. Mel looked at her mother with an unfamiliar glint of sympathy. It must not have been easy for her.

"You said this went on for years. So, you knew about it all along?"

"I guess I suspected from the beginning. But I never really had any proof. Then, finally, when I confronted him, he admitted everything. 'Fessed up,' as they say."

"When did that happen?" She was trying to picture herself at that time, and recall images or experiences that might have contained some clues. "Was I still small then?"

"Oh, no. You were a big girl. It was just before—about a week before he died."

"A week!" An involuntary chill rattled Mel's spine.

"It was a terrible time—your father dying in that horrible accident. I was grieving for him, yet I was so hurt by his affairs with other women. Part of me felt that the accident had been an act of vengeance and that it was the price he had to pay for his betrayal." She looked at Mel with apology. "I know that's a terrible thing to say, but it's how I felt. I had so many different emotions. And then, I was trying to be strong for you and Maxx. I didn't want the two of you to see me fall apart."

Mel remembered how odd it had seemed, and how heartless, that her mother didn't cry the night of the accident, during the days that followed, or at the funeral. She had never seen her mother mourn her father, which convinced her all the more that Eunice was an uncaring, unfeeling woman, and which further deepened the division between them. Had she known all this, maybe it would have made a difference. Maybe.

"Is that why you sent me away?" she asked now. "Because you couldn't handle things?"

Eunice picked up an oblong scarf on the bed and began folding it. "That was a mistake," she said. "You don't know how many times I regretted it." Her eyes focused on the scarf, avoiding Mel. "I should have kept you at home. With Maxx and me."

"Why? Why did you do it?" The old hurts, simmering below the surface, rose up anew. The momentary kinship she had felt with Eunice, when hearing about her father's quest for love outside the home, and that neither one of them could hold his heart, that brief connection with her mother just an instant ago, had vanished. In its place, back in full force, were the long-held feelings of resentment and distrust.

"You have to understand. At the time, I thought I was doing the right thing. I couldn't reach you; I couldn't talk to you."

"You didn't even try. But you could reach out to Maxx, couldn't you? No problem there. You could talk to him. You always could."

"That's because he let me talk to him," Eunice said slowly. "It was easy to do. But with you, there was always this—barrier—between us. I don't know, I always knew that you and your father had this special bond. Maybe that was it. That's the way it is in some families."

"And what about you and Maxx?" Mel hurled. "What about *your* special bond?"

Eunice didn't deny it. "That doesn't mean I loved you any less. I never made a difference in the two of you."

Mel made a noise of disbelief. "How can you sit there and say that? You can't possibly believe that."

"You were two very different children. But I loved you both the same."

"Right. You loved me so much that you sent me away."

"I didn't know what else to do. I was—scared and frightened."

"*You* were scared and frightened?" Mel challenged. "For goodness' sake, I was the child; you were the adult, the parent. I looked to you for comfort. I needed to know that things would get better. But I didn't get that from you. No, you had all kinds of time for Maxx, but you couldn't wait to ship me off. Out of sight, out of mind."

"That's just not true. That's not the way it was."

"Wasn't it?" Tears of anger framed Mel's eyes. "Then why'd you send me to Dexter?"

The question stunned Eunice with its vitriolic force. For a moment she was silent, then gave the only answer she could. "At the time, I didn't know how to handle you. I didn't have any other choice."

"That's a cop-out if I ever heard one."

"It's what the doctors recommended too," Eunice said in defense. "After your father died, you shut out everybody. You weren't eating, you weren't going to school. And then—when you took those pills—"

The phrase hung in the air, a throwback to a time that Mel fought to suppress but which had never completely dissolved. *When you took those pills.* Did that explain it all for Eunice? Was that the basis for her action? If anything, Mel needed her mother even more after the botched suicide attempt, after the night of ingesting twenty aspirin and eight Midol. Yes, twenty-eight pills. She had counted every single one. Her heart had ached so much for her father, she had felt like slicing it out of her chest, anything to ease the pain. If ever there was a time she had needed Eunice, it was then. She needed her mother to put loving arms around her, to tell her how much she knew it hurt, and that she understood the pain. But Eunice didn't do that. Or couldn't do that.

"I thought if I didn't get some kind of help for you, then you *would* end up killing yourself," Eunice said now in defense. "I thought if you went away for a while, you wouldn't be reminded so much of your father and— of what happened. And that it'd be easier for you to accept things."

"You act like it was nothing," Mel said, fuming again at the memories. "It was for ten whole months. Nearly a year! You just tossed me aside and didn't give a damn. How do you think that made me feel?"

"But, Mel, that wasn't my intention at all," her mother protested. "You needed good psychiatric care, and Dexter was the best center around for teens with problems. And when you came back, you seemed fine."

"But I wasn't fine. I came back worse off than when I left. I was raped while I was there." The words tumbled out like so many sordid secrets revealed in the heat of assigning blame. "You didn't know that, did you?" There was a hint of satisfaction in Mel's voice, validating her belief that her mother had been so removed and distant that she wouldn't suspect anything was wrong, least of all that this most awful of violations had been perpetrated on her daughter.

"Raped?" Eunice sputtered the word. "Why didn't you tell me?"

"Because I was a child, remember? I wasn't sure what to do. He threatened me, and I believed him. He said if I ever told anyone—" She let out a long breath.

"Who was it? Not one of the doctors?"

"It was a counselor. On a camping trip. To enjoy the great outdoors," she added mockingly. "We were looking for baby turtles, and I got separated from the group. Next thing I knew someone grabbed me from behind and pushed me to the ground." She rubbed her shoulder as though trying to stop a shudder. "His name was Terry, and he worked part-time. He had a cracked front tooth. I remember it was on a Thursday. I remember it hurt."

Eunice cringed at the image. "Oh, Mel! You never told anyone? You dealt with this all by yourself?"

"I was so mixed up. I felt it was my fault for straying away from the group." She looked at Eunice with hard eyes. "I couldn't tell you because I blamed you for what happened."

"Me? Why?"

"Because you were the one who sent me away. If I had been home— I'd have been protected, and it wouldn't have happened."

"Oh, God." Eunice sat humbly, taking the weight. "I'm sorry. I am so, so sorry."

It was the apology Mel had wanted for so long. An admission by her mother that she had fallen short and had sorely let her down. That her favoritism toward Maxx and her absorption in her own problems had made her oblivious to or incapable of dealing with her daughter's pain. But to hear Eunice say she was sorry, finally, after so many years, was anticlimactic and insufficient. It wasn't enough.

"Maybe I'll be a better grandmother to Sasha than I was a mother to you," Eunice said.

God, I hope so, Mel thought. But she just nodded in agreement.

"I wanted to thank you for letting her come to France this summer. She's thrilled about it."

"Well, there're still quite a few things I need to iron out."

"I'll take good care of her," Eunice said firmly. "You won't have to worry."

Their eyes locked in a voiceless pact. This would be a test of sorts, this summer with Sasha. It would be a way for Eunice to begin to make up for all that she had done wrong with Mel. It also represented a big shift for Mel—being willing to allow her mother at least to walk on the road to redemption.

Mel turned toward the mirror and patted down the yellow suit. She turned sideways, not liking the frontal view. Even though she was thin, in this outfit she looked boxy, too corporate. Maybe if she wore a gardenia in her hair, it would lighten things up. Or a pair of summery flats. Or . . .

"If you don't mind my saying so," Eunice began carefully, "that color doesn't do much for you. You have a lot of yellow in your skin as it is, and it makes you look kind of washed out. You have anything else?"

"Nope. This is it," Mel replied, her irritation rising. "It'll have to do."

"Wait a minute. I have something that will work perfectly. I'll run and get it."

"No, that's okay," Mel said quickly. "This'll be fine."

But Eunice was already out of the room. "Be right back," she said, excited.

Mel wasn't keen on wearing anything of Eunice's. It wasn't that her mother didn't have good taste—she dressed exquisitely—but wearing something of hers would bring her too close. Even though they had crossed a hurdle today, there remained a vast wasteland of misunderstandings and hurts yet to be forgiven, let alone forgotten.

Eunice returned, smiling broadly, holding an opaque dress bag close to her chest. "You're going to love this," she said, unzipping the bag on top of the cluttered bed. "I got it at a little boutique that was going out of business. It was such a great deal, I couldn't pass it up." She pushed back the plastic, revealing a delicate cotton eyelet. The tag was still on the dress. The original price of $525 was crossed out and underneath it in red ink was scribbled "$265." "It's one of those dresses you can do all kinds of things with—blouse it up, wear it off the shoulders—it'll look fabulous on you." Eunice shook out the dress, along with a wide matching piece of fabric. "And you can wear this around your waist or use it as a head wrap."

In the next few minutes, Eunice became fashion directress, turning Mel this way and that, fluffing the dress off the shoulders, on, then off again, experimenting with the excess cloth. "That's it," she said, snapping her fingers at the final result. "It's you. It's perfect."

Mel looked in the mirror. The dress was pretty. To use Eunice's word—

perfect. And it *had* been so long since she had worn anything new. Still, it belonged to Eunice. "Aren't you planning to wear this?"

"To be honest, I packed it because I couldn't make up my mind. It was either this or another dress I brought. Well, now that decision's made. This has your name written all over it. I want you to have it."

"But I can't—"

"Don't be silly. It's yours."

Mel protested further, but after much back and forth, finally accepted her mother's peace offering. Maybe it was true that people mellow with age, she thought. Eunice sure seemed to be trying hard to make amends for the past. But it would take a whole lot more than a new dress for her mother to begin to make up for all the suffering she had caused over the years.

CHAPTER 10

"The ring, please."

The minister dabbed at the clear pearls of sweat on his forehead, as Builder fumbled in his pocket for the velvet-covered case. Even at 5:00 P.M., it was swelteringly hot, and the flowered canopy under which the wedding party stood offered little protection from the thick humid air.

Cool and collected, Maxx received the ring from Builder and slid it onto his bride's finger. Nikki looked radiant in high-necked Victorian lace. There was the exchange of vows, a prolonged kiss, the minister's booming introduction of the new husband and wife.

Just like that and it's over, thought Mel. After all those weeks of preparation. And now, phase two.

The five-piece combo tuned up, a signal for the guests to shed their layers of formality. Some of the men loosened ties and flung jackets over their shoulders. A young woman wriggled out of high heels, preferring to sink her stockinged feet into the fresh-cut grass.

"Did you see the size of Nikki's ring?" Mel overheard someone say.

"I know," came the response. "It's a headlight. Just about blinded me."

Throughout the backyard, the furious fanning, which had been suspended during the brief ceremony, began anew, as delicate Chinese paper designs stirred up welcomed relief.

"Lord, it's hot. If somebody sues you for heat stroke, don't call me."

Mel turned to see a flushed Frank Kirby waving a folded program across his face.

"I know this wasn't your idea," he huffed. "You're too smart for this."

Mel smiled, stepping to the defense of her new sister-in-law. "Oh, lighten up, Frank. Nikki wanted tradition—with a contemporary twist."

"Yeah, but *outside?* In *June?*"

"Well, you know it's where she and Maxx met. She thought it'd be nice to get married here. Like coming full circle. Where's your sense of romance?"

"Gone with the heat—and with my first wife. She took everything." He laughed good-naturedly, admiring her in the dress bestowed by

Eunice. "You're looking awfully spiffy, as usual. You're one pretty woman, Mel."

"Why, thank you." She felt herself blush. "That's nice of you to say."

"Beauty obviously runs in the family. Your mother's very attractive."

This time, Mel didn't respond.

"And that Sasha," Frank continued. "She's coming right along. Going to be a knockout, for sure. You'd better get ready."

"Please," Mel groaned. "I've got enough to worry about."

"Builder told me she's going to France for the summer."

"Yep," she said curtly.

"That's great. Be good for her to get away. And good for you two to spend some time together, speaking of romance." He clucked his tongue and gazed over at Builder. "The ol' guy looks pretty dapper today, doesn't he?"

He did. It had been a long time since she had seen Builder out of his grungy work clothes, and the rented black tux was especially becoming. "Clothes do make a difference," was all she said, and then excused herself to check with the caterer.

She and Builder still hadn't talked much. These past days leading up to the wedding were like so many others; his coming in late, her being asleep or pretending to be. And when they did talk, out of necessity about Sasha or household concerns, it was brisk and tense, a dreaded task to be disposed of as quickly as possible. They rarely talked about money; discussions on that topic inevitably deteriorated into name-calling and blame placing, and made the fragility of their marriage frighteningly more obvious. So, by unspoken agreement, they avoided the subject altogether, electing to ignore the major source of their discontent.

At the request of the caterer, she had another table set up, conferred briefly with the band leader about the timing of the toast, and made sure that the wedding gifts had sufficient space. She was reviewing the names in the guest registry, checking to see if everyone had signed, when Sasha rushed up in a bloom of lavender.

"Mom, we're waiting for you. You haven't been in any of the pictures."

Mel smoothed down Sasha's bangs. "Well, honey, I'm not officially in the wedding party. You go on back and finish. I have a few things to check on."

"But Uncle Maxx sent me to get you. And Grandma said she wants a family picture."

"Oh, I see," Mel said slowly.

Sensing her reluctance to move, Sasha took her by the hand. "Come on," she prodded.

Like a dutiful child, faintly reprimanded for nonparticipation, Mel followed her daughter's lead.

"So, how'd I do?" Sasha asked. "Did I walk okay?"

"You were great. Carried that Bible as steady as a rock. Like you'd done it a thousand times."

Sasha beamed. "Grandma said my ballet training helped me stay balanced and poised."

"That's probably true."

"Uncle Maxx didn't seem nervous at all, did you notice? But Nikki was shaking like a leaf. Grandma said it's good luck when you're nervous on your wedding day."

Mel sighed. Grandma said, Grandma said, Grandma said. Was there no end to it?

They worked their way toward the center of attraction. Several guests, sensing that the photographic session was nearing an end, had edged closer to congratulate the bride and groom. Maxx, Nikki, Builder, and Nikki's sister, who served as maid of honor, smiled broadly under the late afternoon sun. The photographer directed them to freeze.

"That's a good one. Hold it right there." He snapped alternately from two cameras hanging around his neck, and was setting up the next pose when Maxx spotted Mel.

"There you are. Come and get in on this." He scanned the crowd. "Now where'd Mother go? *Mother!*" he called out.

"Here I am." Glamorous in her peach chiffon dress and matching hat, Eunice was relishing her role as the groom's mysterious mother, who lived in a quaint French town with a well-to-do Algerian. She ended her conversation with one of Nikki's co-workers and took her place next to Maxx.

The photographer clicked away, rearranging them into several poses and smaller groupings, with Eunice stationing herself to the right of her son. They took the "original" family photo that Eunice wanted of herself and Mel and Maxx. And then, immediately afterward, Eunice made another request.

"Just of me and Maxx," Eunice said, wriggling her son's ear. "Of this handsome groom and his very proud mother. You don't mind, do you, dear?" she asked Mel.

"No, of course not." Mel moved away, leaving the two of them to pose and smile for a picture that would no doubt become the blown-up crowning glory of Eunice's photo collection, to be expensively framed and set in an obvious place, maybe even on a pedestal of its own, for any and all to see. She knew her mother so well.

She watched as Eunice literally glowed beside Maxx, her fine son who had graduated from Harvard magna cum laude and become a successful Atlanta attorney. What more could a mother want?

If only you knew what he really does for a living, Mel thought. If you knew about his corrupt clientele and how he uses all that education. Would you be so proud of him then?

So often Mel had been tempted to tell her, to burst that bubble of maternal pride that Eunice seemed to hold in exclusive reserve for Maxx. How would she feel if she learned that her darling Maxx was the defender of drug dealers and organized gang lords? That he defended people who were responsible, directly or indirectly, for the crime on the streets that makes them less safe to walk? That he used his sharp legal mind not in some noble pursuit of justice, but to manipulate the system, to plea-bargain for racketeers so that they need never serve a day in jail, to argue on flimsy technicalities, resulting in cases being dismissed.

What would you say, Mother, if you knew? How much of a difference would it make?

"Mel, everything's gorgeous—the yard, the flowers," Nikki gushed gratefully. "You've done a wonderful job arranging all this."

"Thanks." Mel looked at her new sister-in-law. She was indeed a beautiful bride. "I'm glad it turned out the way you wanted."

"Oh, even better than I dreamed."

"I never did give you a proper hug," Mel said. "Welcome to the family—Sis."

They embraced delicately, out of respect for Nikki's dress and the muggy air. "So, how does it feel being Mrs. Maxximilian Lincoln? For all of"—Mel glanced at her watch—"twenty minutes?"

Nikki shut her eyes and inhaled deeply, a spattering of perspiration glistening on her forehead. "It's marvelous. Absolutely marvelous. I just love him so much." She looked over at Maxx, who was laughing and posing with Eunice. He caught her eye and pointed downward at his side, indicating for her to return.

"You're not finished yet?" Mel asked. "You need to start enjoying this reception. That photographer will keep you tied up forever."

"I know. But I think your mother wants to take a picture with me. She said it was a special request."

Eunice and her special requests. First, a picture of herself with Maxx.

And now, with Nikki. But not a word about Mel. No special request for her.

It shouldn't have mattered to Mel, but it did. She thought she was beyond such slights, but she wasn't. She wandered into the crowd, playing the busy, gracious hostess with a yard full of people to look after. She was startled when Builder suddenly appeared, holding two glasses.

"Here, take this," he demanded, pressing a glass of champagne into her hand. "I'm about to give the toast."

"Looks like you've already gotten a head start," Mel said, then was sorry for being critical. Could they say nothing kind to each other, even on this wedding day, when they could at least hope to get swept up in the momentary atmosphere of goodwill?

Builder clanked her glass with such force that some of the champagne spilled over. "This is a wedding, haven't you heard?" he said. "You're supposed to drink to the bride and groom." He slurped his champagne and then cornered a passing waiter, insisting on a refill.

Mel was amazed—Builder was borderline drunk! Except for a couple of beers now and then, he seldom drank, so to see him like this, on the verge of losing it, seemed so out of character. She had a jarring sense of déjà vu—remembering when Lenny, Builder's worker, came to the yard drunk, demanding money. Only this time, it was her own husband threatening to explode. How did he drink so much so fast? He had seemed fine earlier. Maybe it was because he wasn't used to it, that it had affected him so quickly. And with the heat, and all. Lord, please, she prayed silently, don't let there be a scene today.

"You've had too much to drink," she said carefully. "I think maybe you should go in for a while."

"Go *in*? Are you crazy? I'm the best man. I've got a job to do." He sauntered toward the mobile stage where the band leader was directing the combo in a flourish of dramatic musical beats. This was the prelude for the toast, Builder's cue to go on.

The band leader handed the microphone to Builder, who at first looked at it like an alien object. He announced that it was time for the toast, and told everyone to make sure they had something to toast with. He invited Maxx and Nikki to join him at the center of the portable dance floor.

Mel held her breath as Builder began.

"Maxx, my man, I know you and Nikki will have a fantastic marriage." He held up his glass in tribute to them, and then turned to the audience, adding, with a devilish smile, "Unlike some people I know." There were ripples of uncertain laughter and several furtive glances in Mel's direction.

"Now," he continued, addressing Maxx, "you and I have had many a conversation about this marriage thing, right?"

Maxx nodded good-naturedly.

"And you know that I warned you not to do it, in fact, I *begged* you not to do it. But"—Builder took a couple of gulps from his glass as the crowd waited expectantly—"seeing as how you went on and *did* it anyway"—he paused—"at least you picked yourself a fine woman to *do* it with."

His phrasing and intonation made his words almost vulgar. Some people were becoming increasingly uncomfortable.

"Now, everybody knows that the role of the best man is to give advice," he continued, "and, I thought about this and thought about this 'cause I wanted to tell you something really profound, you know?"

Mel felt her stomach tighten. Why couldn't he just give a regular toast and be done with it?

"Well, finally I came up with something. And, based on my personal experience, mind you, the best advice I can give to you is"—he looked out at the audience, like he was about to deliver a gem—"when the going gets rough—run to the nearest exit!" He laughed with extreme exaggeration, as though he had just made the funniest statement imaginable.

Disgusted, Mel wanted to get as far away from him as possible. If he made a fool of himself, so what? Right now, she didn't care. He was beyond help. She was tired of making excuses and playing clean-up lady. Fall down on your face, for all I care, she thought. Let Sasha see. Let the whole world see. Let them all see what I have to deal with.

Sensing disaster, Maxx gingerly took the microphone from Builder in order to prevent further damage. "Man, this is a dangerous weapon in your hands," he said laughingly. "You're going to get me in trouble before I even start my honeymoon."

He went on to thank Builder for his "wonderful vote of confidence," adding that while some of the folks there might not understand, he knew that Builder often meant the exact opposite of what he said. "So with that in mind, I sincerely appreciate your enlightened words of wisdom, which certainly get top honors for originality."

It helped save face for Builder and deflected attention away from him. It was also a demonstration of Maxx's infectious charm. No wonder he was so effective in the courtroom, Mel thought. He was good at smoothing over rough edges, Builder's as well as his clients'. Just as he worked this crowd here, Mel could see how he talked his way into the hearts of jurors, convincing enough of them that his clients were innocent victims gone astray.

Debonair and in charge, Maxx tipped his glass in a salute to the guests themselves. "Nikki and I want to thank all of you for coming and being a part of our special day." There were cries of "here, here," and "all right," as the guests soaked up the compliment. "And I want to thank my brother-in-law here for serving as my best man."

He put his arm around Builder in camaraderie, but partly, Mel knew, to steady him. Maxx recognized Eunice, Sasha, and Nikki's sister. "And last, but not least," he continued, "a big thank-you to Mel for all her work in putting on such a tremendous spread. Thanks, Sis." He lifted his glass to her amidst a spattering of applause. "So everybody eat and drink up because we plan to be here till the wee hours of the morning!" He gazed seductively at Nikki—"Well, *almost* that long, right, darling?" Tilting back her head, he gave her a devouring kiss on the lips, which evoked a rising wave of wolf calls.

The band played "You Are So Beautiful," the pre-arranged signal for Maxx and Nikki to dance for the first time as man and wife. As they swirled around in the center of the makeshift floor, Mel hurried down front, intending to escort Builder to a less populated area. He was standing off to the side, watching the dancing newlyweds along with everyone else. But Mel didn't want to risk his making some loud, inappropriate comment, disrupting the magic of the moment, so she made her way to his side just as the band leader signaled others to join in the dance.

"Come on," he said gruffly when she appeared at his elbow. Before she could object, he led her onto the portable parquet and pulled her tightly to his chest.

"You're holding me too close," she complained. The buttons of his tux pressed against her midriff.

He released his grip slightly, but not by much. "Better?" he asked in a brusque tone.

Mel watched other couples glide by, caught up in the wedding bliss that comes with the promise of new love. The well-intended vows of faithfulness and caring temporarily touch even the most cynical, and create a hope that such idealism might be possible still. Why couldn't she and Builder feel some of that rebirth too? She saw the closed eyes and tender touches of surrounding couples, swaying in the romantic spillover that emanated from the center of the floor. She dared not look at Maxx and Nikki, the source of that hopeful promise. How much more of a reminder did she need that her own marriage was immune to such idyllic overtures, and had dissolved into an out-of-sync two-step on this hot, sticky day.

Builder still held her so tightly that Mel could feel her dress creasing; she'd definitely have wrinkles across her top by the time the dance was over. Builder's hands were callused and rough from working too many carpentry jobs, and as he repositioned his right palm across her back, a hangnail caught the fabric of her dress.

"Doggone it," he said. "Something's—"

Glued to her, he tried to disentangle himself, but as he pulled his hand away, Mel felt more of a tug across her back.

"Stop!" she nearly screamed. "You're making it worse." She imagined a wide rip along the middle of her back. The beautiful dress from Eunice was flawed, if not irreparably ruined.

Val, dancing next to them in a whirl of blue taffeta, stopped to lend a hand. She freed Mel's dress from further torture and laughingly admonished Builder that he needed a moisturizer.

"It's a snag, but you can't tell too much," she assured Mel, patting the material. "You've got a string hanging that needs to be cut. Want me to help?"

"No," Mel said, not wanting to further disrupt Val's good time. "I'll manage." She walked off the dance floor, with Builder following behind.

"Sorry about that," he said in a low voice, suddenly appearing more sober. "Let me see."

"Never mind." Irritated, she brushed him off, wanting him just to leave her alone, but he stayed close at her heels.

She knew it wasn't his fault. It was never his fault, in that it was not intentional. But still, the fact could not be denied: Builder was increasingly a liability. The snagged dress was just a small example. It seemed everything he did contained negative offshoots that also affected her. Regardless of his best efforts, nothing was going right. Was he working through some kind of bad karma, that she, as his wife, had to go through too?

Close to tears, she was anxious to go inside to see the extent of this latest injury. Not that it mattered, really. She wasn't going to change her outfit. She'd snip the string and be done with it. It was ridiculous to get upset over something so insignificant, she told herself. *Remember the starving children of Africa. The orphaned babies with no loving arms to rock them to sleep. Put things in perspective!* But even this strategy didn't work. The accumulation of hurts and disappointments rushed to the surface, giving even more weight to Builder's faux pas.

The huge yard, which she loved so much, seemed to conspire against her. She had staged the reception toward the rear of the yard to take advantage of the preponderance of the purple and white wisteria; now, she wished she had set things up closer to the house. The walk back seemed interminable.

"Whoa, hold up. Where're you going?"

Mel whirled around to face not only Builder closing in on her, but also Maxx, who was right behind.

"What's the hurry?" Maxx called. "If I didn't know better, I'd say you two were skipping out for a rendezvous."

Mel glared at him. His wedding day or not, she was in no mood for Maxx's antics. "I'm going inside to fix my dress," she snapped.

"Okay, well—take this in with you." Maxx reached in his back pants pocket and pulled out a folded gray envelope. He took Mel's hand and placed the envelope in her palm. His distinctive capital "M" was written in red on the upward side of the envelope.

"What's this?" Mel asked.

"Take it. It's yours."

"But wha—"

"It's a gift," Maxx interrupted. "From Nikki and me. Let's just say it's our way of thanking you for making this day really special for us."

Mel opened the unlicked envelope. Inside were two five-hundred-dollar bills and a check made out to her for nine thousand dollars.

"Oh, come on, Maxx," she said, trying to hand the envelope back to him. "I can't accept this. There's ten thousand dollars here."

Builder whistled.

"Sure you can accept it," Maxx said casually. "I told you, it's a gift from Nikki and me. I put part of it in cash because I didn't want you to have to fill out a form at the bank. You know, anything ten grand and up, you've got to document. I didn't want you to have to go through all that."

Refusing to accept the envelope back, Maxx put his hands in his side pockets and rocked on his heels as he talked. Mel held the envelope awkwardly, uncertain what to do with this gift horse that had come to her so unexpectedly. A subdued Builder stood by as a witness.

"I don't want your money, Maxx," she said, sounding firmer than she felt. "I'm sure that you—and Nikki"—she was careful to add, since he had made such a point of saying the money was from both of them—"can find plenty of ways to use this."

"The point is, we want you to have it," he insisted. "You put a lot of time and effort in this, finding the right band and the caterer and—"

"But *you* paid for everything!" Mel blurted. "Not a dime came out of my pocket. There's no need to give me any money."

"Well, the way I see it, I'm still coming out ahead. It would have cost a hell of a lot more if we'd had the reception at some hotel. I'd much rather give you the money than the Marriott or the Ritz."

"I don't know," she said, weakening. "I just don't see how I can accept this."

She could feel Builder watching her closely. How many times had she criticized him, lambasted him, for taking money from Maxx? Of course, she could rationalize that this was different. For one thing, she hadn't gone to Maxx and asked for a loan, as Builder had done numerous times. No, Maxx had come to her, had presented her with this money in appreciation for coordinating his wedding. And then too, this was a joint gift from Maxx *and* Nikki, something Maxx had repeatedly stated.

But in truth, Mel knew this was all Maxx's doing. She suspected that Nikki had no idea he was even making the gesture in her name. No matter. The problem was not who was giving the money—Maxx alone or Maxx and Nikki—the problem was the source of the money. It always came back to that. Because, as hard as Maxx might try to camouflage it, any money from him was related to drugs, indirectly perhaps, but related no less. And if it was wrong for Builder to take money from him, wasn't it equally wrong for her?

"Look," Maxx said, "just accept it for what it is, okay? A simple gift of thanks. That's all. Besides, I know how tight things have been since you lost your job. I'm sure you could use the extra change."

Change? To him, ten thousand dollars was *change?* Clearly, when it came to money, she and her brother were on opposite ends.

The band broke out into a jazzy version of "You're One in a Million." Maxx said he needed to get back to the dance floor, as he had promised Eunice he'd dance with her to her favorite song.

"Talk to her, bro," he advised Builder, about Mel. "Get her straight." Then, as he scurried to rejoin the crowd, he turned around with a suggestion. "You can always put some of it toward Sasha's education."

Mel shook her head at the sly remark. He certainly knew which buttons to push.

"What are you going to do?" asked Builder, walking with her toward the house.

"I don't know," she replied honestly, her animosity toward him temporarily neutralized by this new dilemma.

Maxx had a knack for forcing her to confront the harsh realities. Was it deliberate on his part? Was this another attempt, perhaps subconsciously, to prove that, despite her high-sounding rhetoric, her moral compass was not one iota stronger than his? Was he a charming devil in disguise? Or was she making all too much of this?

Why couldn't he be a physician who worked in an inner city clinic with indigent patients? Then it would be easy; his income would be from honorable sources, from the caring art of healing, not destruction, and she wouldn't have to agonize over whether to accept money from him. Of course, if that were the case, he probably wouldn't have discretionary money like this to fling around, either.

She let her thoughts flow over the reality of her situation. Simply put, she needed money. Her brother had just handed her ten thousand dollars as an outright gift, no strings attached. It's not as though she had to lie, steal, or cheat for it. Was she holding on to some naive code of ethics? In a way, the clients that Maxx represented were bolder and more honest than the suited-up businessmen who defrauded people through so-called legitimate enterprises and whose hands were never sullied. All money, to some extent, is tainted, right? Nothing is ever really pure. Is it?

What if Maxx worked for a major corporation? It could be argued that his income from there was contaminated too. What if the corporation manufactured products in Third World countries, where it was known to pay next-to-slave wages and provide unsafe conditions for the workers, all in the interest of cutting expenses and being competitive? Wouldn't that money derive from exploitative sources? Would she even think twice about it?

Of course, there was the option of just doing nothing. She didn't have to cash the check; she didn't have to spend the money. Or, as Maxx had proposed, there was always Sasha's education fund to consider, which, Lord knows, had long been depleted. Realistically, though, she most immediately needed to put the money toward their mountain of bills, which desperately needed to be cut down.

Deep in thought, Mel wearily entered the house to put up the envelope, forgetting all about removing the wayward thread that still hung from the center of her back.

The loud rummaging downstairs startled Mel out of a deep sleep. Half awake, she suspected a burglar, and jolted up in bed, her heart beating too fast from the clutch of fear. She had to do something, but what? Call 911?

By the time the police got here, anything could have happened. Should she load the gun that Builder kept in the closet? *Builder.* She rubbed her eyes to see better in the dark. The space next to her was flat and smooth. Of course. It was Builder making all that noise.

Relieved, she sank back on the bed, feeling foolish for suspecting an intruder. She should have known that no thief would dare make such a racket, especially not at—she looked at the clock on the end table—3:34 A.M. What on earth was Builder doing at this hour? Faint mumblings now accompanied the movements, although she couldn't make out what he was saying.

She concluded that he must still be drunk, probably in worse shape than at the wedding. He must have really gone overboard this time. After Maxx and Nikki left for their honeymoon, he had gone out with Frank Kirby and a couple other guys from the reception who wanted to "continue the party" at a billiards hall in Midtown. No telling how much he had drunk while there.

Mel burrowed her head into the pillow, trying to force herself back to sleep. The best she could hope for was that he would eventually calm down and sleep it off. She considered going into the guest room, but then remembered her mother was there. Oh, Lord, she thought, don't let him wake her up. She could see Eunice now, emerging with sleepy-eyed concern, asking, "What's wrong?" and "What's going on?" That's all I need, thought Mel—more questions about the state of my marriage.

There was a loud clanging of glass. Mel pulled back the sheet, deciding to investigate. She descended the stairs silently, barefoot and without a robe, dressed in a short sleeveless gown. At the entrance to the kitchen she gasped. The careful clean-up after the wedding might well have never occurred. The kitchen table and counters were covered with canned goods, pasta containers, spices, foil wrappings—virtually every item that had been in the pantry. In the middle of the floor stood two big cardboard boxes of empty glass bottles that Mel had saved for the recycling bin. A shopping bag stuffed with folded brown bags leaned against the refrigerator. Even the popcorn popper and coffee pot, usually perched on a side shelf off to themselves, were uprooted. Builder had stripped the pantry from top to bottom and created a monumental mess in the kitchen.

A grunt came from the pantry as Builder backed out, pulling a huge box filled with Mikado dishware that Mel rarely used but liked to keep close at hand.

"What are you doing?" she asked, with an equal dose of curiosity and anger. She knew that she'd be the one who'd have to put everything back in place.

He straightened up, his face flushed from too much wine and exertion. "Ho!" he said cheerily, waving her into the kitchen. "Come on and help me find it."

"Find what?" she asked, remaining where she was.

"The Perignon. Dom Perignon."

She sucked in her breath in disgust. "You mean, you pulled out all of *this*"—she waved her arms disjointedly—"looking for a bottle of *wine?*"

"Not just *a* bottle, baby. *The* bottle. Perignon 1985—vintage year. Remember? Maxx gave it to us a while back."

"I don't believe it," Mel said, surveying the chaotic kitchen anew. "You did all this just for—look at this place!"

"Don't worry. I'll clean it up. But we've got to have a proper toast. See, here—I already got out the glasses." He pointed to two engraved goblets that sat perilously close to the edge of the counter.

"Builder, it's late," Mel said, not at all amused. "I don't want anything to drink. And you certainly don't need any more."

"But we gotta have a toast," he insisted. "I've been saving that bottle for something really special. Well, this is it. I mean, it's not every day that Maxx gets married. *And,*" he emphasized, "we get ten thousand dollars."

"Ten thousand dollars?" Mel repeated. "So, that's what this is all about."

"Yeah. That deserves a Perignon, don't you think? Come on, don't just stand there. Help me find it." He opened the cabinet above the stove, where a punch bowl and other glass items were stored.

"I know it's not in there," Mel said quickly.

"I've been thinking," he said, continuing to search nonetheless. "There's a couple of ways we can go with that money. If we put at least five or six of it on business bills, that'll help me get to the next deal with—"

"No way," Mel said firmly. "I'm not putting any of that money into the business."

He looked at her like he had been spanked. "Why not?"

"Because I can't afford to take that kind of risk. I'm not dumping more money into—"

"Dumping?" he said, offended. "Is that what you call it?"

"Builder, we have absolutely no savings," Mel stated. "There're basic things around here that have to be covered."

"I know that. And this'll get us there that much quicker. All I need is about five or six grand to cover some upfront expenses on a couple of these projects. And then when I get a big draw later on, I can put that money back and then some."

"It never works out that way," Mel said coldly. "That's why we're in the situation we're in."

His mood turned ugly. "Why are you always puttin' a damper on things? Always so negative?"

"I'm not negative. I'm just trying to be practical. Somebody has to be around here."

"Oh, so now I'm not practical, huh?" he said, his anger rising. "I guess it's not practical for me to want to put some things together for this family—to get us out of this hole."

"What you're proposing is not the way to do it," Mel said. "We've gone down that road too many times before. I'm not going to let it happen again."

"Oh, you're not, are you? So now you think you can call all the shots, is that it?"

Mel blew out a breath. "That money was a gift to *me*. Not us. I think I have a right to say how it should be spent."

"Right?" The word infuriated him. "What about *my* rights? I have a right to some fuckin' support around here."

She took a step back, not liking the snarl on his face. "Look, enough's enough. It's four o'clock in the morning and—"

"So what?" he growled. "It could be six o'clock or eight o'clock. What difference does it make?" He stood in the middle of the kitchen, hemmed in by the clutter he had created. "Help me find it," he demanded, referring to the Perignon. "It's gotta be here somewhere."

Mel watched him with disdain. Maybe if he had another drink, that would lull him off to sleep, and stop him from ransacking her kitchen.

"There's all kind of wine left from the wedding," she said, trying to appease him. "Why don't you open one of those bottles on the counter?"

But the suggestion only fueled his rage.

"That inferior shit? You think that's all I deserve? Second best?"

Funny how alcohol affects people differently. Mel remembered the times her father drank too much. He would quietly slip over to a corner chair and sleep it off. But Builder seemed to grow more hyper and excitable. Was it because he so rarely drank that he was reacting this way? He generated a type of motorized energy that was spinning out of control, running off course, destined to crash.

His eyes latched onto a pair of lower cabinets, which he opened forcefully. He pulled out neatly stacked Tupperware containers and let them tumble willy-nilly onto the floor. "Where is it?" he said, kicking everything in sight.

"Stop it!" Mel ordered. "You're making a mess. It's not in there."

"Then where is it?" he shouted. "Where'd you put it?"

"Me? I didn't put it anywhere. Maybe you drank it sometime ago and forgot all about it."

"No," he lashed out. "I would've remembered, damn it." He accused her forthright. "You put it somewhere. Trying to hide it from me."

There was no reasoning with him in this state. She refused to deal with it anymore. "I'm going back to bed," she announced. She turned on her heels to exit, but in one quick step, Builder grabbed her by the wrist.

"You're not going anywhere," he snarled. "You're gonna help me find it."

"Are you out of your mind?" For the second time in twenty-four hours, she struggled to free her wrist from him, entrapping it further by her resistance. "Let me go!"

Unlike before, however, Builder gripped even harder. "Who are you supposed to be? Miss Untouchable or something? You think nobody can even *breathe* near you?" His eyes speared her with a viciousness she had never before seen.

If she'd been smart, she would have pacified him in some way, maybe stop struggling, say something to comfort him, certainly not say anything to provoke him. He was drunk, after all, and not rational. And even though he was reeling out of control, she still could have reined him in, calmed him down; perhaps even gone through the motions of looking for the damn Perignon. A few more minutes, and he probably would have collapsed on the downstairs sofa, overcome by too much wine and the search for more.

If she'd been smart. But she had reached her limit too. As sober as Builder was drunk, she was wound up and stressed out from the interminable months of built-up resentment and unresolved blame. The financial strain, the marital coldness, the secrets laid bare. She could no longer accommodate, cover up, or pretend. And perhaps too, in a deep, deep part of her, there was the diabolical motivation, the twisted incentive, to flirt dangerously with the outer limits, to push him closer toward the punishment she felt he deserved. Perhaps, subconsciously, she wanted him to say something or do something that would make him forever sorry, beholden to her in an unrelenting mode of contrition.

But illusions played out in the mind, those images projected and imagined, often appear antiseptic when acted out on a real stage. Not burdened by emotion, they dissipate into mirages, which keeps them separate from the truth. Perhaps, if Mel had realized this, she would have understood the difference and not have said what she did.

"You're crazy! You know that?" Her eyes squinted from the pain of her throbbing wrist, but her voice rattled with self-righteous scorn. "You're crazy. Crazy. Crazy!"

The words enraged him. "Shut up!" He slapped her on the cheek, then muzzled her mouth and half pushed, half dragged her into the living room. "Don't you call me that, ya hear?" Like discarded trash, he flung her down on the sofa. The back of her head grazed the armrest and her legs dangled over the cushions. He thrust all of his weight on top of her in a deliberate press of strength.

Mel tried to push him off. Vainly, she tossed and kicked in a effort to get free. But she was no match for him. With physical dominance and fierce will, he pinned her down; his powerful body suffocating her, imprisoning her, rendering her immobile.

"Get off," she managed to say, but the words were lost in an avalanche of rough kisses. She hadn't realized he was so strong. His body felt like a block of concrete, firm and solid from all that hammering, from all that damn building.

"Give it to me," he hissed. "Come on."

His hand pressed hard against her thighs, pushing aside the thin layer of lace that made up the crotch of her panties. His fingers pried open her legs and clumsily reached for the inner prize that was hers to give, not his to take.

"Open up, damn it." A drunken demand, focused ever so sharply on one singular goal.

With everything in her, Mel fought back, knowing that struggling only made matters worse and prolonged the ordeal. Her resistance empowered him, increased his determination. But she would not give in. It was all she had left, all she could hold on to. She would not yield to him; she could not allow him that satisfaction.

"Give it up!"

Oh, Lord, she prayed. Help me! Help me! At this moment, she hated Builder. Hated him more than she had ever hated anyone in her life. This can't be happening, she thought. Not again! Only this time it was worse. This time it was her own husband.

She squeezed her pelvic muscles in a last stand against the onslaught.

But Builder's weight and probing penis quickly flattened her feeble fortress. He pushed himself inside of her, furrowing up a hostile tunnel, moving deeper and deeper toward top dead center—the furious explosion that, when reached, was devoid of any semblance of love. Married or not, it was rape.

Finished, Builder withdrew from Mel, stood and adjusted his clothes, and looked down at her with contempt, as though he had tried on the merchandise and rejected it, not pleased with the way it fit.

He reached into his pants pocket and tossed a handful of coins on her violated body; his way of showing how little he valued her, that she was hardly worth the bother. "Thanks for nothin'." He left the room, and after a moment, Mel heard him start his truck.

Gingerly, she sat up and rubbed the soreness on her arms, consciously avoiding the despicable wetness smeared on her stomach and down her legs. She stayed there in the dark for a long time, too shocked to move. She was anxious to take a shower, a hot, hot shower, and scrub away Builder's markings. But she couldn't get her limbs to work. Intertwined with her anger and shame was the paralyzing disbelief over what Builder had done. *How dare he! How could he?* This from a man who had vowed to love, honor, and cherish her. She didn't deserve this. No woman did.

She and Builder may not have had the most affectionate relationship, but they managed to maintain a modicum of respect for each other. Now, he had destroyed even that. There was nothing left. Nothing.

Resolved, Mel collected her thoughts and her bruised body and began the task of cleaning up: herself; her kitchen; the rest of her life.

"Look, Val, if you can't do this for me, then fine. I'll call a cab." Mel was terse and cold. She was no candidate for an eleventh hour conversion, much to Val's chagrin.

"I just don't see why you have to go traipsing off to Miss Anne's." There was sarcasm in Val's voice. And a hint of betrayal. "You could just as easily stay here with me."

"Thanks," Mel said, less harshly. "But you're too close. I need distance. I'd go to Hong Kong if I could."

"I still think you should give Builder another chance. His life has been hell lately and—"

"Don't start," Mel interrupted. "I've heard enough." She coiled the phone line around her hand and adopted a businesslike tone. "My plane leaves at 1:30. Shall I call a cab?" She had lost precious minutes rebutting Val's objections, and it was critical that she get back on track.

"No, don't call a cab," Val said unhappily. "I'll take you."

"Good." Mel hung up quickly, cutting off further protests.

There was nothing more to do but wait. She was sorry now that she had called Val. She should have just taken a cab, as was her original plan, and either call or write to Val once she had left the city. But Val was her good friend, her best friend, and that seemed like a cowardly way to handle things. So Mel had told her the barest of details, only that "something had happened" between her and Builder, and that she needed to get away. She didn't mention specifics. It was bad enough to think about that horrible night, let alone actually describe it.

Mel glanced at her bags, positioned at the front door. This would be her second trip to the airport for the day. Just this morning she had taken Eunice and Sasha to catch their plane to New York and then on to Paris. Now that it was her time to go, the seconds clicked away at a snail's pace.

Somehow, she had managed to get through these last few days. The main problem was dealing with Sasha, trying to explain to her why her father wasn't home. Mel suspected that Builder was staying at his office—it had a half-bath and a rollaway stashed in a closet—but she didn't know for sure, and she couldn't have cared less. She just knew he wasn't coming back in the house, not as long as she was there. And if he did, then she would leave, so determined was she not to be around or have any contact with him.

She hadn't even answered the phone, in case he might be on the other end. But she knew he had called Sasha, wishing her bon voyage. She had overheard Sasha tell Eunice how Builder had explained that married people have problems sometimes and that this was one of those times. But Sasha was confused. She didn't understand what had happened to cause her father to stay away. She had sense enough, however, not to badger Mel with questions, discerning her mother's hard line.

To her credit, Eunice also didn't pry, although the "morning after" she said she thought she had heard a ruckus downstairs and asked, "Did that have anything to do with it?"

There were moments of awkward silences and tense pauses. At each inquiry about Builder, from people who called or stopped by, Mel had instructed Eunice and Sasha to simply say, "He's out." But they were unwilling coconspirators, and every repetition of that two-worded half-truth seemed to punctuate all the more the cover-up at hand.

Finally, this morning arrived, and Mel saw them off. Another burden lifted. Not that she considered Sasha a real burden, but caring for her, making arrangements, the daily routine of parenting, had taken its toll.

As a survival tactic, Mel had shifted into a discarding mode, peeling off people like layers of clothing. Each layer removed made her lighter, more free, not so weighted down. First her husband, now her daughter. It was providential that Sasha had a place to go—and ironic that it was Eunice who made it possible. By taking Sasha with her for the summer, Eunice had opened up for Mel a whole new path of exploration, a type of freedom she hadn't known for years, where she could move unencumbered. And given her the gift of time to make adjustments.

Thank you, Mother, for something.

She meandered into the living room, where, out of habit, she sat on the sofa. Then instantly, she sprang up, repulsed by the site of the crime. This used to be her favorite spot, her reading corner and haven. But Builder had marred it irreparably. Just as he had marred her life.

She paced aimlessly around the room, and looked with disdain at the framed poster of a landscape scene which now hung above the mantel. It was a poor substitute for her beloved Bearden, which she had painfully sold weeks before. And for what? she berated herself angrily. To raise money to help pay bills that Builder couldn't take care of because his precious business sucked up every red dime. And he had the nerve to call *her* selfish and self-centered! How dare he—after all that she had done over the years to show her support. She should have left a long time ago. And then for him to force himself on her like that, ranting about some damn "wifely duty" and how—

A loud knock at the door startled her. Val!

She opened the door eagerly, but was met by the lopsided smile of a young man holding a stunning flower arrangement.

"Are you Mrs. Burke?" he asked brightly.

Mel was hesitant. "Yes," she said, noticing a white van parked out front with the name Finley's Florist painted on the side.

"For you, ma'am." He held out a basket brimming with thunder lilies, like a master of ceremonies bestowing first prize. "Guess this is your lucky day," he pronounced.

Awkwardly, Mel took the shellacked basket of flowers, mumbled thanks, and shut the door. Under normal circumstances, she would have tipped the driver, but to do so now would have validated a gift she wanted no part of.

The note, in his own handwriting, said simply, "Love, please forgive me." It was signed with the initial B.

For Bastard, she thought. Oh, he was clever. He knew how much she loved flowers, like some women love pearls. But did he really think this could make up for what he had done? Could even *begin* to?

She ripped the card into tiny pieces, letting them fall, confettilike, onto the floor. She went into the kitchen, removed the lid off the trash, and ceremoniously dropped the flowers, basket and all, into the deep plastic grave. Denied water and light, they wouldn't last long.

There was no flinching, no reaching down to salvage a stem or two. She saw the flowers not as a beautiful bouquet, but as a symbol of him, a reminder of that terrible night. Which made the killing-to-be easy, deliberate. And cruelly satisfying.

Out front, a car horn beeped. Val, for sure.

Liberation at hand, Mel Burke left her house with purposeful abandonment, not caring if she ever returned.

The water lapped against the boat in a rocking motion. Minnows darted to and fro, unsure where to swerve to avoid this latest intruder. Larger fish frolicked in a game of cat and mouse, seemingly unconcerned that a hook to the jaw might suddenly end it all. They were right to swim with ease. The fish for this boat had already been caught. Thirty-six feet long and resting, *The Best of the Lot* bobbed gently in the heart of Puget Sound.

Mel inhaled deeply, taking it all in—the mist on her face, the fresh air of the sea, the life beneath her feet. "There's nothing like the water, is there?"

"Nothing," agreed Anne, next to her.

"Thanks again for all—"

"If you thank me one more time, I'm throwing you overboard."

Mel laughed at the image.

She had been in Seattle for a week, the guest of her friend Anne Creighton and her husband Alston. It was a good decision, coming here, far removed from the problems in Atlanta. Each day put more distance between that world and this, and today, sailing in Alston's boat, she had almost entirely forgotten about her other life, her real life. She was going to ride out the fantasy for as long as she could.

"Tack time, mates, tack time." Alston appeared, moving quickly to the stern, as Mel and Anne reached for their appointed lines.

They all three pulled, heaved, and belayed, nudging *The Best* on a course to reap the benefit of the starboard breeze. Mel enjoyed these frequent intervals of crewing. Working the sails made her a part of this wholesome environment of wind and water, made her more deserving to be here.

"So, while I've been slaving down under, you two have righted all the wrongs of the world, right?" Alston asked.

"Nope," Anne said perkily. "And what's worse, we haven't even tried."

Mel watched closely as Anne and Alston chatted amiably, engaging her in conversation, making her feel at home. Alston had been so gracious about her coming. When she showed up last week, he acted as though she were some long-lost friend of his, even though she had seen him only once before, when he and Anne lived in San Francisco, and Mel had visited them while she was there attending a conference. He owned a diamond import/export company that required frequent travel overseas. He told Mel he was glad she could spend some time with Anne—to keep her company and (he had added facetiously) out of trouble.

Mel doubted that Anne would ever be in trouble, whether of her own making or someone else's. She possessed an aura of equanimity that, to Mel, bordered on the angelic. She had always projected a serene demeanor and wise maturity that seemed well beyond her years. Mel recognized it immediately when they were roommates in college. Anne would talk about her family's horse farm in northern Connecticut, not in a pompous, boastful way, but out of a respectful bond with the land and the animals. And when Mel went home with her once during spring break, she saw the same kind of near-palpable peace among the rest of the family.

Unspoiled by money and privilege, Anne was different from other rich white girls on campus. To them, Mel was there "by accident," because (the word had gotten out) of her father's insurance money. But such distinctions didn't matter to Anne, and it was out of genuine egalitarianism that their friendship had blossomed.

Now, with the aid of binoculars, Mel raved over the magnified scenery as Alston pointed out the majestic sights: Mount Rainier, dipped in white, the peak of the Cascades; and over there, Mount Olympus, a silvery stretch of splendor.

"I've never seen anything like it," Mel marveled.

"On a clear day like this, it's truly fabulous," said Anne.

After several minutes of gazing and another round of tacking, Alston said he needed to check on the salmon "to make sure the sauce doesn't burn." Whistling, he headed toward the galley below.

Mel shook her head in amazement. "I still can't believe he's actually cooking down there."

"It's what he likes to do best: cooking and sailing. It relaxes him. Put the two together, and he's in his world."

"You really do have it all, don't you? Not only a husband who'd give you the moon, but he's an excellent cook too!"

Anne dismissed the comment with a downward flip of her hand and toss of the head, but Mel felt a rare case of envy coming on. Seeing Anne and Alston together, so comfortable and content, made her starkly aware of what she didn't have. And like a bilious cloud blocking out the sun, the realization suddenly changed her mood.

Through dark sunglasses, she looked sideways at her friend, half resenting her for the good life that she enjoyed, had always enjoyed. Anne knew nothing about having to struggle or think twice about things financial. She was a paradigm of the rich getting richer; both she and Alston came into their marriage with money and privilege. And even though Mel was here now partly because of that money and privilege—was a temporary and appreciative beneficiary—still, feelings of resentment swelled up. How many black women have that kind of opportunity? she thought. To be bred with money and then to marry someone with even more?

Maybe Val was right, Mel thought. Maybe she should have stayed with her until things cooled over with Builder, until she decided what to do. At least she and Val operated within the same realm of reality. There was a commonality of economic status that intrinsically bound them, connected them. With Anne, there was no such tie.

Anne sensed the tension. "Everything all right?" she asked, after several minutes of silence had passed.

"Yeah, sure." Mel kept her eyes straight ahead, focused on the glistening blue. "Just thinking."

"About Builder?" The question was timid, cautiously probing.

"No. And I don't want to think about him. It'd destroy this beautiful view."

Anne took a deep breath and nodded, backing off from further intrusions. "I think in time you'll get back together," she said. "You have too much going for you not to."

You have no idea what we have or don't have going, Mel started to say. But just as quickly as her foul mood had descended, it lifted, almost magically, allowing a new interpretation of the well-meaning comment. How like Anne—always the optimist, always having something good to say. Mel wondered what was wrong with her that, for even a minute, she could have harbored ill feelings toward Anne, of all people. Dear Anne, the friend who had kept in touch through the years, and had opened up her home. It wasn't possible to feel estranged from her for long.

"You're still going with me to the showing tonight, aren't you?"

"Oh, I don't know. Maybe."

"Maybe? How about an unequivocal yes!"

Mel smiled weakly. "Aren't you tired?" After being out on the water for several hours, she was looking forward to crawling under the silk sheets in the guest bedroom, and crashing on solid ground. Sailing was exhilarating but exhausting.

"Once we get home and freshen up, you'll be ready to go again," Anne said confidently. "Besides, you won't want to miss this man's work. It's exquisite."

For Anne, one of the most enjoyable aspects of being an art dealer was to find and promote obscure artists. Her latest "discovery" was an elderly Native American carver whose woodcuts she had bought at a local crafts festival. She tracked him down on a reservation and persuaded him to submit several pieces to a gallery.

"Say you'll come," she said, like an excited schoolgirl.

Mel agreed to go. How could she refuse? Especially after all that Anne had done for her these past few days. Besides, this was Anne's bailiwick, and tired or not, the least she could do was show some interest.

Alston came up, bearing steaming plates of grilled salmon, which made Mel even more agreeable. Eating the succulent fish, she leaned back in the arms of *The Best* as it passed luxurious estates against the backdrop of the mountains. Beyond geography, Mel was as far away from home as she'd ever been. Which suited her just fine.

She heard him before she saw him. The gallery was otherwise quiet with the hushed murmurs of the favorably impressed, but a distinct baritone separately charted its own wavelength. As Mel rounded the stained glass pane at the entrance, she saw that the voice belonged to a sweater-clad figure who was describing the meaning of a wood sculpture.

"Well, well!" said Anne, a small smile forming on her lips.

"You know him?"

"Yes. He's—" She stopped in midsentence, her focus shifting to the gray-haired Indian artist who stood on the opposite side of the room. "Come on, I'll introduce you."

The old Indian, gracious in words and manner, extended a roughened hand to Mel. Gingerly, she sandwiched it between her own hands, feeling an unexplained reverence for the weathered fingers that had created so much beauty in the room.

Shortly, they were joined by "the voice," whom Anne hugged vigorously. She introduced him as Xavier Lightfoot, photographer, and was surprised to learn that he was the maternal grandson of the gentle Indian carver.

"Such a small world," Anne said. "Who'd have guessed?"

"And here I was wondering about this white woman who had corralled my grandfather to come to the big city. I figured I'd better check it out. Had I known it was you, I wouldn't have worried."

"So you say," Anne said teasingly, "but I know you can never relax around us pale faces."

The gallery owner approached, wanting to talk to Anne and the old man. Left by themselves, Xavier volunteered to walk Mel through the exhibit. She was glad for the personal tour. At each piece, he had a story to tell, recounting the tales passed down by his grandfather; how the piece was formed, what it represented, when it was made. For Mel, the wood carvings seemed to come alive, embellished by Xavier's rich melodic voice and obvious pride. The most dominant carving was a painted five-foot totem pole, which Xavier, as a boy, remembered his grandfather working on many years ago.

"He's so talented," said Mel, admiring the chiseled details.

"He says people are making too much of a fuss. All he wants to do is cut his wood and be left alone."

"You mean, he doesn't recognize the value of all this?"

"To him it's just a hobby. There're truckloads of pieces like this back at the village. And he says that's where they should stay. I tried for years to get him to show his work. He wouldn't do it. Evidently, Anne must have reached him in a way I never could."

Mel nodded knowingly. "She has that way with people."

The tour over, Xavier continued to talk to Mel at intervals throughout the evening. When not at his grandfather's side, he was at Mel's, bringing her a drink, making sure she was comfortable, introducing her as "Anne's friend" to some of the people he knew. He offered to show her around Seattle whenever Anne might be occupied. And Mel already knew she would accept.

Often, in gatherings like this, people say things in an effort to make a visitor feel at home. This is especially true after a drink or two. They propose to show you around town, take you out to dinner, demonstrate their hospitality. Their offers are well-intended and legitimate, but by dawn of the next day, long forgotten.

Intuitively, Mel knew that Xavier would follow through. Perhaps mostly out of allegiance to their mutual friend Anne. But also, Mel suspected, because he seemed to genuinely enjoy her company. And when he did call, she'd answer. He was personable, charming, and knowledgeable about the area. Best of all, he was a friend of Anne's, which certified him as A-OK.

Once, though, Mel saw Anne watching them intently and thought she detected a hint of disapproval. But the look vanished as quickly as Mel dismissed it. Hadn't Anne told her in passing that she was glad Xavier was taking her under his wing because that freed her up to concentrate on the art patrons in attendance?

During the drive home, Anne declared the reception a success. She was thrilled at the turnout, and confident that write-ups in the local press would bring well-deserved recognition to Xavier's grandfather. "And speaking of recognition, you certainly received your share, didn't you?" She gave Mel a sideways glance.

Mel found herself blushing. "What do you mean?"

"Xavier, naturally. You two were in a huddle most of the night."

"I'd hardly call it that. But I did enjoy talking to him. He's quite interesting."

"Yes, he is." She pushed in a tape.

"He told me you met three years ago?"

"That's right. He's had several exhibits, mostly nature photography. But I hear he's moved into commercial modeling—magazine covers, things like that. I'd kind of lost touch with him."

"He offered to show me around the city."

"Did he?"

"You don't mind, do you?"

"No, why should I?"

"Well, you and Alston said you had all these places you wanted to show me, and—"

"We can still do that."

"What if Xavier has some of the same places on his list?"

"You'll just have to see them twice," Anne said, attempting to sound dictatorial.

Mel chuckled, then fiddled with her seat belt. "So, he's safe to hang out with?"

"Safe?"

"You know what I mean. He's not an ax murderer or anything like that?"

"Not that I've heard."

"Gee, why do I get the feeling you're not telling me something?"

Anne inhaled deeply. "Xavier's fine. He's an interesting guy, just like you said. It's just that—"

"Yes?"

"He can be very—disarming."

"Meaning?"

"Meaning nothing, maybe. But when you're vulnerable—" She kept her eyes straight ahead on the road.

"I see. You think that just because he shows me a few sights, I'll be so grateful that I'll jump in bed with him. Honestly, Anne!"

"I didn't mean it that way."

"Well, that's the way it sounded."

Anne shifted in the driver's seat. "Let's face it. Xavier's a very attractive man, and you're in a"—she reached for the right words—"fragile position. I wouldn't want to see you get involved in something that could complicate matters."

"*Involved?* For heaven's sake, I'm just going to Pike Place. How involved can you get at a seafood market?"

They both laughed, and the conversation turned to other topics. But Mel had the nagging suspicion that Anne knew a lot more about Xavier Lightfoot than she was willing to share.

Two days later, Mel saw much of Seattle through the front seat of a Mazda convertible. It was a gift, Xavier said, from an eccentric millionaire who had requested a photograph of his beloved dead dog—in a coffin. Other photographers had scoffed at the idea, insulted that they were asked to squander their high-priced skills on such a subject. Curious, Xavier not only took the photo but had stayed to console the bereaved with a sympathetic ear. For taking the time, he received his $400 fee plus a "bonus" in the form of a spanking new Mazda that was later delivered to his door.

He recounted other stories that were equally outlandish, keeping Mel in stitches throughout most of their drive-by tour. She couldn't remember when she had laughed so much or felt so carefree.

It was a cloudless day, tailor-made for sightseeing. Xavier bypassed many of the tourist spots, preferring the back roads and hilltop views that only a native would know.

"I thought Atlanta had trees," said Mel. "But this!" She swooned over the giant evergreens and cedars imprinted on street after street, amassing an army of mini forests that pulled rank over the urban cement.

At an outdoor café he introduced her to *latte*—best with vanilla, he recommended—and over their second cups, revealed that he was divorced after a seven-year marriage. At his urging, Mel talked a little about Sasha, even less of Builder, mentioning only that she and her husband were "reconsidering things." He nodded with understanding, saying that he and his wife had gone through two separations before finally making the break.

Toward dusk he proposed a picnic in the park, ordered take-out from a deli, and spread out the wide blanket that had been stuffed into the Mazda's tiny trunk.

They set up camp on a high embankment with Lake Washington at their feet.

"A wonderful ending to a wonderful day," said Mel, taking in the cool evening air.

"It *has* been great, hasn't it?" he agreed. "But you'd probably think the backside of a molehill is beautiful. You were overdue for a vacation—anywhere."

She laughed agreeably. "*More* than overdue."

They devoured a meal of turkey sandwiches, Russian potato salad, and pickled artichokes. Xavier unscrewed the tops of two bottles of beer made from a local micro brewery. Mel took a sip, surprised at the light taste. "I'm usually not a beer drinker, but this is delicious."

"I thought you'd like it."

They sat on the blanket, Indian style. Mel was glad that her consistent yoga practice enabled her crossed legs to lie parallel to the ground, not sticking up toward the sky, like two stiff stumps.

She savored the moment, the quiet, the serenity. And the attention. Xavier seemed to know exactly what to say and when to say it, in a manner that made her not at all uneasy. Was this what Anne meant when she described him as disarming?

"How do you have all this time?" she asked. "I thought you were a working person."

"I am. That's one advantage of working for yourself. You have a lot more flexibility and can set your own schedule."

Mel thought of Builder and how the opposite was true for him. He put in long hours all the time, and still it wasn't enough. Why was it so hard for him yet seemingly so easy for others?

"Actually, I'm working now," Xavier said, in that deep bass voice.

"Sure you are," Mel said in jest.

"It's true." He cocked his head, looking at her from a new perspective. "Mind if I ask a personal question?"

"You've been asking all along."

"Yes, and you've chosen to ignore what you don't want to respond to. Don't think I haven't noticed."

"So why the preamble?" Mel teased, taking another sip that seemed to embolden her. "If I don't like the question—" she shrugged her shoulders, leaving the sentence dangling.

"Promise not to slap my head off?"

"Slapping's not my style."

"All right then." He paused deliberately. "Exactly how many moons *are* you?"

Mel sucked in her breath. "That's an interesting way of putting it."

"Are you going to answer the question?"

"How old do you think I am?"

"Oh, no. I'm not going to play that game. I might really get into trouble."

"I told you. I'm not the slapping kind."

"Well—" He donned an investigative tone. "I know that you and Anne were once roommates. So, unless you were a child prodigy who started college at age ten—"

Mel released a smirk to indicate that was clearly not the case.

"I'd say—thirty-four?"

She pointed her forefinger upward.

"Thirty-five?"

Again.

"Thirty-six? Thirty-seven?"

Mel continued to shake her head and point to the sky.

"Not thirty-eight?!"

"Bull's-eye."

"Really?" His baritone voice rose to near tenor pitch.

"Oh, don't act so surprised," she said. "You've obviously been calculating all along, adding up the years in your head. I could almost see it."

He had to laugh. "It's just incredible. Thirty-eight! You look ten years younger. Easily!"

"Sure," she joshed, not believing it for a minute. "I think that's a *little* exaggeration."

"I mean it." He cupped her chin in his hand, his eyes animated at the subject up close. "You don't look a day past twenty-five."

"It's a black thing," she teased, in a husky voice. "You wouldn't understand."

People always thought she was younger than she was. Part of it was because she had kept her weight down, she knew that helped. But she had the type of face that belied her age. People often mistook her for Sasha's older sister. At carnivals and state fairs she liked going to the booth where they'd guess your age or your weight. She would always have them guess her age—and they were always way off. Sasha had a shelf full of stuffed animals from the people that Mel had stumped over the years.

Xavier released her chin. "Have you ever done any modeling?" he asked.

"Never. Unless you count charm school when I was thirteen."

"You modeled in charm school?"

"If you could call it that. My mother was horrified that I was becoming a tomboy. 'I'm not raising some uncouth hoyden,' she used to say. So she enrolled me in this prissy charm school. Its motto was 'making today's girls tomorrow's ladies'—or something like that. I hated it. Anyway, I won first prize in their beauty contest and was in a photo layout for a teen magazine. Can you imagine—'before' charm school and 'after' charm school. It was absurd."

Xavier chuckled. "I'll bet you were cute. A cover girl at thirteen!"

"Hardly."

"But see, you have the look, no doubt about it. They recognized it even back then." He unfurled his legs, and sat on his haunches, facing her directly. "I have an idea I've been thinking about for some time. And today you've really inspired me. Want to hear about it?"

He talked about his work, his photography. How he had always been attracted to the elements of nature, to the land, and animals, and how even when he started to focus on people, he preferred to take pictures of people in their most natural state—unfinished and unposed. He lamented that so much of commercial photography was artificial and painted on, with the subject's underlying beauty never fully recognized. He wanted to create a book of photos highlighting the natural beauty of women over thirty, and he had been on the lookout for someone who would be the lead model; someone whom he would photograph in different expressions and lighting; someone to illustrate that energy and youth are timeless. Someone, he said, like Mel.

"We live in a youth-crazed society," Xavier said. "Not that thirty-eight is ancient, mind you, but in this business—"

"It's not exactly the time to be starting out," Mel finished for him.

"That's my point. Everybody's after the eighteen- or nineteen-year-old ingenue. But, heck, most everyone looks good then. You expect it to be that way. The thing is, at that age women are sexy, but they're not sensual. Know what I mean?"

Mel raised her eyebrows at the fine-tuned distinction.

"There's a difference that comes with having a certain amount of wisdom and maturity from just living life," he continued. "It shows up in the face. It's a kind of quiet beauty that doesn't scream at you. It's not cheap, and it's not made up. It's strong and it's real."

"Sounds almost poetic."

He dismissed her compliment with a shake of the head. "I'm not a man of words. But I do have an eye for beauty. True beauty." He looked at her intensely. "Are you game?"

"Game for what? I'm not sure what you're asking."

"I want you to be my model. My lead model. I want to take some pictures of you, lots of pictures. I want people to see what I see—a beautiful, vibrant woman who looks years younger than she really is. That's the kicker, right there. That'll be the drawing card. I want to use your photographs for promotion, along with the press releases, when things get to that point. So people can clearly see what the book is all about."

Mel furrowed her brow. "So this'll be a collection of photographs of—different types of women?"

"Yes. Of real women who've taken care of themselves in a natural, wholesome way," explained Xavier. "They don't need plastic surgery or extensive cosmetics to boost them up. And because of that, they look much younger than they are. Like you."

"Thanks for the compliment, but I'm a firm believer in makeup. I say if there's help out there, use it."

"The problem is most women overdo it—with two and three different foundations, changing their hair color every week—even their supposedly natural look comes off fake." His long hands whipped through the air as he spoke. "But you—it's hard to find someone like you. Believe me, I know. I'm looking all the time."

"This is all very flattering," Mel said. "But as the song says, 'a pretty girl comes a dime a dozen.'"

"It's not about being pretty. I'm talking about something much more—a concept. Women with natural good looks who look younger than they are. Representing different ethnic backgrounds. I think people would be interested in that and would want to see that. And I'd feature you because you'd have such broad appeal. It's hard to typecast you."

"Oh, you mean, the black/white thing, is that it?" asked Mel. "I don't have distinctly African features, but on the other hand, I'm clearly not white. I have this kind of indefinable, generic look, right?" She winced at this disparaging self-description that often made her uncomfortable, like she never quite fit in.

"You have a beautiful look that's distinctly your own," Xavier said evenly. "That's why you'd be terrific on the cover and as the lead model. You'd be perfect for this. Perfect."

That word again. One of her mother's favorites. It had always made Mel feel that she was reaching for some unattainable standard that Eunice had set and only Eunice could meet. But somehow, when Xavier said it, it didn't seem far-fetched or contrived. Perfect seemed very—*natural*. Amazing how the same word, from separate people, elicited such a different response.

"Well, it'd be fun to think about," Mel said.

"Do more than think about it," he urged. "Trust me. You'd be great."

"I'm not even sure how long I'll be here."

"At least a couple more weeks, right?"

"Probably. It's kind of open-ended."

"I'll pay you well for your time." He skipped a beat. "And your body."

She blushed at the double entendre. "I thought it was my face you were interested in."

He smiled coyly. "I like things open-ended too."

They settled back on the blanket, cradling heads in hands, studying the brilliance overhead. Xavier flipped part of the blanket on top of them, providing a layer of coverage as the night air turned brisk. He talked of his childhood, recalling the stories that his grandfather told about the Indian ancestors who graced the skies. His deep voice dropped to a sacred hush that nearly lulled Mel to sleep.

But out of nowhere, an involuntary tremor rippled through her body, snatching her back to reality.

Was she out of her mind? It had been barely a week since she had left Builder and here she was, a married woman lying on a blanket with a man she'd known all of two days.

For a moment, she felt a pang of guilt for having such a good time. She thought of Builder and all of his hard work, trying to make a go of the business. But she pushed back any images of him. The wounds were too fresh, the hurt too intense, for her to feel guilty for long.

She told herself it was all right to be pampered, to be paid attention to, and to feel at ease here. Besides, after what Builder had done, she owed him no allegiance. Wasn't he the one who had breached the vows, who had scuttled the commitment, and put their marriage on the edge? She had done all she could to hold things together, hadn't she? Who could blame her for having some fun? What was wrong with that?

A new star appeared before her eyes. Maybe it was a sign that she should take a different course, a new direction. A sign that she *was* in the right place. She snuggled deeper into the blanket. Yes, this was what she needed: relaxation, time to reflect, and—she looked over at the man lying next to her, including him on the list—time for Xavier.

"What happened? You run out of drug dealers in Atlanta and had to come all the way here?" Confronting her visitor in the giant library, Mel leaned back against the cathedral glass doors, making sure they were shut tight.

"There you go. Thinking the worst of me, again. I told you. I'm here on business."

"Yeah, I bet." She walked the length of the room, hands on hips. "You're checking up on me, right?"

"No," he insisted. "What does it take to convince you? I'm here on business, that's all. And since I knew you were in town—"

She glared at him, unconverted.

He raised his arms outward, feigning a hurt, puzzled pose. "I thought you'd be glad to see me."

In a way, she was. But she couldn't say that to him. Not yet. He was too much of a reminder of a time and place that she'd rather not think about right now. But what really bothered her was that a half hour ago he had showed up totally unannounced at Anne's front door, bearing a plump attaché case and a silly Cheshire grin.

"You could at least have called before coming, Maxx. It's a matter of courtesy. This isn't my home, you know."

"Oh, calm down. Your friend Anne didn't seem to mind."

That was true. When Maxx had arrived so suddenly, Mel noticed that Anne didn't seem to think it the least bit odd. With his witty conversation and impeccable manners, he had charmed her just as he charmed everyone, proudly showing a packet of 4 x 5 wedding pictures. Anne was duly impressed that he would take time to visit Mel during a hectic business trip, commenting on how sweet that was. On the surface, it appeared innocuous enough—that Maxx had dropped in just to say hi. But knowing her brother, Mel knew that, despite his denials, this visit to her was his main mission and not some side activity.

"Anyway," Maxx was saying, "if I had called beforehand, I'm sure I would have gotten the 'she's not here' routine. I hear lately that's the only message you have for people."

The reference was to Builder, who had often called during the past few weeks, but whom Mel refused to talk to. Maxx was right. Had he called, he probably would have received the standard announcement that was delivered to Builder. Anne's housekeeper, Estelle, had received strict orders to obtain the identity of any callers for Mel before she would say whether Mel was available. Only Xavier Lightfoot had an automatic green light.

"So you still haven't talked to Builder?"

"No. And I don't plan to."

"Why not? You can't just ignore him. Whatever problems you have, you've got to at least talk it through."

She grew testy. "Maxx, back off, will you? You don't know the half of it."

"What I do know is that if you keep ignoring him like this, eventually he'll stop calling altogether."

"Great. Maybe he'll finally get the message."

"Are you saying it's over? Is that what you really want?"

She didn't answer. She wasn't sure anymore what she wanted. It used to be she knew almost intuitively what decisions to make, about her job, her family, her home. Now, everything was a struggle.

"I went by the house the other day," Maxx said, gauging her reaction. "He looks like shit."

"Is that so?"

"Yes. He's still working like a dog—half eating. He said you didn't even tell him you were going away. You didn't leave a note or anything. He had to find out from Val."

"Well, he's always been good at finding out what he wants to."

"What's that supposed to mean?"

"I don't want to talk about Builder, okay?" She was exasperated. "In fact, now that you've seen me, you can report back that I'm fine, and I'll be getting in touch with him soon."

"How soon? You've already been here a month. How much longer do you need?"

"I don't know. Whatever it takes."

A tap on the glass door interrupted their conversation. Anne ducked her head inside. She had restyled her hair and changed into a linen pantsuit.

"I have a few errands to run," she said. "Need anything while I'm out?"

"No, I'm fine."

She smiled at Maxx. "It was great seeing you. Sure you won't stay for dinner?"

He glanced at Mel before responding. "Thanks, but I really do have plans."

"I probably won't be here when you get back," Mel said to Anne.

"Why am I not surprised?" Anne spoke in her usual friendly way, but with a underlying curtness that Mel's keen ear picked up.

Then and there, Mel made a mental note to sit down and talk to Anne—really talk. They hadn't spent much time together since Xavier had embarked on his whirlwind sightseeing rounds. And when she and Anne were together, Anne adroitly kept the spotlight on Mel, curious about what she had seen, and where she and Xavier had been. Mel wanted to focus more on Anne. Something wasn't quite right with her—she had seemed on edge and smiled a lot less than when Mel had first come. Mel suspected that it might have something to do with Alston's long absences (he was away now in Tokyo), which had put more of a strain on the marriage than Anne might want to admit. This morning, over a late breakfast, Mel was about to ask about that when they were interrupted by Maxx's arrival.

"Remember," Anne said now to Maxx, "my other offer still stands."

"I'll keep that in mind."

After Anne left, Mel returned to her most immediate mission—getting Maxx to follow suit.

"When's your flight?" she asked him. "You've got a new bride at home, and I'm sure Nikki misses you. Surely you have other things to do than hang around here."

"Just can't wait to get rid of me, can you?" He admired a jade bookend fashioned into a lion's head. "My flight's tomorrow evening. This is a long way to come and have to turn right back around. I'm going to stay at least overnight."

"As long as you don't stay here."

"Why not? You heard Anne. She offered."

"She was being polite."

"This place is certainly big enough."

"Not here, Maxx!" Mel was adamant, her eyes shooting daggers.

"Relax," he said, amused at her outburst. "Don't get so bent out of shape. I'm at a downtown hotel."

"Good."

"Why are you so paranoid?"

"I'm not paranoid. I just don't like surprises like this, that's all."

Here she was, acting footloose and fancy free, doing her own thing—when out of the blue, Maxx pops up. Not that she had anything to hide—but, damn! The world just wasn't big enough.

From the cherry wood bookshelf, he retrieved a leather tome of illustrated Shakespearean plays. "Know what I think?" he said, lugging the hefty volume to a table. "I think you're going through a midlife crisis, feeling the need to get away and spread your wings." He flipped a few pages, alternately looking at her and the works of the Bard. "It's the kind of thing men have been doing for years, and since you're a 'new age' woman, I guess it's only natural that you picked up on that pattern. Equal opportunity and all."

Mel shook her head in bored interest. "Thanks for the two-cent analysis."

He took in the surroundings with a sweep of his hand. "So, you have a boyfriend tucked away somewhere to go along with this package?"

She sucked in her breath. "You know, Maxx, you've got a hell of a nerve; making all kinds of assumptions—and wrong as usual." With her narrowed eyes and tart response, she projected the stance of the wrongfully accused, the righteously indignant. But inwardly, she quivered that he had come so close to the truth.

Over the last few weeks, she and Xavier had been virtually inseparable: ferry rides to countless sites, listening to jazz on a Vancouver pier, day-long adventures that brought new discoveries. All the while he had snapped pictures, setting up some shots, shooting others "as is." And in the many shared hours between them, during the dawn of day and under the cover of night, over brunches and lunches and dinners—throughout all this—they had become more than working partners. Did she consider Xavier her boyfriend? Not exactly. Not quite.

Maxx shut the Shakespeare book with a solid clap and a serious expression. "I'm worried about you. And I'm worried about Builder. I don't want to see you break up."

"There's really nothing you can do."

"Sometimes it helps to have a mediator."

"You're offering your services?" Mel asked, somewhat amused.

Maxx shrugged. "I can try."

Mel pressed her lips together. "I appreciate your concern, I really do. But this is something Builder and I have to deal with on our own."

"How's that going to happen if you don't even talk to each other? How much time do you need?"

"I don't know. However long it takes."

Sometimes, late at night, before falling asleep in Anne's guest bedroom, she had wondered how things would be had she stayed in Atlanta, whether she and Builder would have worked it out by now. She would berate herself and question her own behavior. She had married for better or for worse, hadn't she? But then, the images of sinking deeper and deeper into debt, the mountains of mistakes by Builder—all of that would emerge anew, and she would reassure herself that she was right to leave. Lord knows, she had given it her best shot. How long should a person try to save a dying marriage? Ironically, Builder's assault that night in Atlanta had created the excuse she needed to go, and had provided her with a way out that was timely, convenient, and necessary.

Maxx, in need of a new strategy, blurted out a surprise proposal. "Come back with me tomorrow."

"What?"

"It's a long flight. I could use the company."

She had to smile at his attempted levity. "Look, I appreciate all this brotherly concern. I really do. But as you can see"— she raised her shoulders, and exposed her palms—"I'm doing fine here. I'm really okay."

"Seems that way. But what about Builder?"

"What about him?"

"He's still your husband, isn't he?"

She sighed, tiring of the conversation. "Just tell him that I'll be in touch."

"When, Mel? *When?*"

"I don't know when," she said, irritated. "Frankly, the thought of going back to Atlanta is—depressing. I'm not ready. That much I do know." Her voice took on a hard edge. "I don't want to talk about this anymore."

He was silent for a moment, then, "Okay. Next subject." He turned to face her directly. "What about Sasha?"

The question startled her. "Sasha?"

"Have you talked to her lately? Or have you written her off too?"

"Come on, Maxx, be fair."

"Well—have you talked to her recently?"

"Of course. I call every week. She's doing fine."

"No. She's not doing fine."

Her heart skipped a beat. "What do you mean? Of course she is."

He smiled broadly. "She's doing *great*. Absolutely *great*."

Mel looked at him with suspicion. "What are you trying to say, Maxx?"

"She loves it over there, she's having the time of her life. Evidently she's made several friends. She and Mother get along well, and she's happier than she's been in a long time." He paused precipitously. With Maxx, everything was about timing. "She'd like to stay there and go to school."

"You can't be serious."

"She didn't think you'd like the idea, so . . ."

"So you're asking for her, is that it?" She shook her head. "My own daughter can't even talk to me."

"It's not that. She just thought you'd automatically say no. She wanted me to sound you out. That's all."

"I'm sure Eunice has a hand in this."

He shrugged. "She knows how emotional you can get."

"This is my daughter we're talking about. I have every right to get emotional."

In her last conversation with Sasha and Eunice, they had both hinted about Sasha's staying longer, that there was still so much to do, so many places to see. Mel had assumed they were referring to Sasha's staying closer to the opening of school, returning the last of August rather than early in the month, as was originally planned. But for them to think she would even consider allowing Sasha to go to school in France for a whole year? No way. Eunice should know better than to encourage such an idea. Familiar pangs of resentment started to ferment.

"Look," said Maxx. "There could be some real advantages to this. You and Builder are going through a tough time, and whatever you decide, there'll be a period of adjustment. Do you want Sasha in the middle of that?"

It was a rhetorical question, and not expecting an answer, he moved to his next point. "Sasha and Mother get along great. And regardless of your feelings about Mother," he said hurriedly, "Sasha *is* her only grandchild. You wouldn't want to deny them this chance to really get to know each other, would you?"

She started to tell him that she had heard these arguments before, and that, upon Sasha's pleading, she had finally agreed to let her spend the summer with Eunice. But beyond that? No. Enough was enough. She didn't verbalize any of this, however, as Maxx relinquished nary a pause for rebuttal. Talking fast, he was intent on thoroughly laying out his case.

"And look at the school situation. You have to admit that Sasha had a rough year at Duncan. She hated it there; she never really felt comfortable."

"She won't be going back," Mel countered. "She'll be starting high school in the fall."

Ignoring that comment, Maxx pressed ahead. "There's this terrific international school not far from Mother's," he said excitedly. "Think of what Sasha would gain from that! The people she'd meet, the experiences. Come on, Mel. She's already there, why not let her stay? This is a once-in-a-lifetime opportunity. You can't just let it slip by."

"It was a so-called once-in-a-lifetime opportunity for her to go for the summer," Mel inserted tartly. "I think that's enough opportunity for a while."

Maxx disregarded the rub. "Mother said she'd pay for the school. Although I told her I would gladly—"

"No," Mel resoundingly objected. "Absolutely not. I'm not accepting money from her. And certainly not from you."

Her response was no surprise. "There's another thing to consider," he said, saving his strongest argument for last. "Mother especially wants Sasha to stay because—of her condition."

Mel frowned suspiciously. "What condition?"

Maxx slowed his pace. "She didn't want you to know. She has a form of lupus. It's controllable now, but—"

It was hard to believe. Elegant Eunice? Dressed to the nines, smooth-skinned, *perfect* Eunice—sick? It didn't seem possible.

She was diagnosed over a year ago, Maxx said. The doctors said she might live another five years, ten years—it was hard to predict. Medication and diet helped to some degree. But a big portion was relegated to luck.

"She looked so healthy," Mel said, thinking back. "I wouldn't have guessed in a million years that anything was wrong."

"She's fine right now. She has her strength and her energy. A few years down the road, though, she might not be in such good shape; she might not be able to—" his voice cracked. "Don't you see? She's worried that she won't have years ahead to spend with Sasha. She's afraid she'll miss out. She wants to make the most of this time."

They were silent for a moment, each thinking about the mortality of their mother and the consequences thereof. But for Mel, another thought worked its way through. *She didn't tell me. She told Maxx, but she didn't tell me.* Even in the midst of the disturbing news about her mother, she realized, once again, how Eunice and Maxx had this special "thing," this heart-to-heart bond that carried them through joys and adversity. And once more, she was not a part of it. It had been over a year, he had said. For over a year they had both known but had not bothered to tell her.

"She didn't want you to worry and feel sorry for her," Maxx said now, as though reading her mind.

No. It's because she doesn't love me the way she loves you, Mel thought. She never has, and she never will. No matter how much progress they had made when Eunice stayed at the house, no matter how well-intentioned their resolve to patch up the past, the years of misunderstanding could not be erased within a few days or by tearful confessions. The undeniable, painful fact was that her mother loved Maxx much more. She always did, and she always would.

Somehow, that harsh reminder became an all-consuming thought, outweighing her concern for her mother's health, taking her totally and errantly off track, causing her even to question whether Maxx was telling the truth, or if his "news" was just another tactic to sway her. She didn't put anything past him. She was familiar with his courtroom antics: sliding through every loophole, stretching any conceivable technicality, using whatever drama was needed. Could Eunice's suddenly acknowledged illness be a dramatic attempt to win the case?

And so, partly from the sting of years of being an outsider, of being removed from the closeness between Eunice and Maxx, and partly out of a suspicious respect for Maxx's unorthodox tactics, she asked a question she shouldn't have:

"You wouldn't be pulling my leg, would you?"

He looked at her with bugged eyes. "You mean, lie? About Mother? I wouldn't joke about a thing like this."

No. Of course he wouldn't. It was stupid of her even to think it, let alone say it. But the damage was done. Maxx got upset.

"How self-centered can you get?" he asked. "Can't you ever think about anybody but yourself? I just told you Mother might be dying, and all you can think about is that I'm trying to trick you!"

"That's not exactly what I meant," Mel said lamely.

Maxx would hear none of it. "You think she needs your sympathy? Let me tell you something, she wouldn't want it. Because it wouldn't be worth a pot to piss in."

"Now just a minute," Mel intervened.

But Maxx was on a roll. "I don't know what your problem is, but you're screwing up. I can tell you that. You've got a husband who needs you now more than ever, and you act like you don't give a damn. Sasha and Mother asked me to talk to you because they feel like they can never get through. Everybody has to be so careful around you—like walking on eggs. Otherwise, your precious feelings might get hurt."

"I think you've said enough, Maxx," she warned him through tight lips.

"No, I haven't said nearly enough. That's part of the problem. You're always on everybody else's case, you can't even see your own faults. And you've got plenty of them." He looked around the room extending his arm. "What are you doing here, anyway? Is this supposed to be some kind of hideaway or something? It's like you're living in a fantasy. You expect everybody to put their lives on hold and wait until you get your act together?"

"I *have* my act together," she said, her ire matching his. "And you have some nerve coming here and talking to me like this. *You* of all people, lecturing *me*? If anybody lives in a fantasy, it's you. You're always denying how what you do really doesn't hurt anybody, and—"

"Don't change the subject," he broke in harshly. "We're talking about you here."

"Well, I don't want to talk about me 'here,' " she said stubbornly. "As far as I'm concerned, this conversation's over." It sounded childish, even to her, like the kid who, not liking the way the game is turning out, takes his ball and leaves in a huff.

"You'd better wise up, Mel. Real fast. You need to bring your ass on back home."

"Get out of here," she seethed, thumbing toward the door. "Just leave!"

He did, without another word.

From the massive front windows of the library, she watched him sit in his rented Pontiac for several minutes, twiddling his fingers on the steering wheel, probably debating whether to come back in. If he tried, she wouldn't open the door, she decided, and was about to give Estelle the housekeeper those very instructions, when Maxx started the car.

Her eyes followed the vehicle for as far as they could see, watching Maxx drive off the grounds and out of sight. She needed to tell Estelle to add his name to the "hit list," in case he tried to reach her by phone.

Her head hurt and her stomach was jumpy. The nerve of him, upsetting her like that. The news of her mother and of Sasha had compounded an already testy situation.

Maybe if she took a long bath in that marble whirlpool tub she had come to know, she might relax. With this goal in mind, she climbed the winding staircase to the guest room suite.

Maxx was right about one thing. She had to make a decision soon. She couldn't continue to leave things hanging. She *had* been living a fantasy— no responsibilities, no concerns. But she couldn't stave off reality any longer. Something had to give.

The ride from Anne's hilltop home in Bellevue to the restaurant in downtown Seattle took only fifteen minutes. Mel was seated at a table nearly a half hour before she was to meet Xavier. He was running late, according to a message left for her, so to occupy her time, she ordered an appetizer, then a glass of wine, followed by another.

By the time Xavier rushed through the door, Mel was feeling quite mellow. Maybe it was the two glasses of wine, or more accurately, the three for the day, since she had had one shortly after Maxx left. She managed a lazy smile as Xavier apologized for his tardiness. "You have a little catching up to do," she said, tapping her glass.

Xavier grinned. "I'm good at catching up." When he turned to signal the waiter, she got a whiff of his cologne. He reached into his breast pocket and slipped a folded twenty dollar bill into her hand. "This should cover your taxi."

"Oh, no," Mel put the money in the center of the table. "After all you've done for me? I can pay my own cab fare."

But he insisted, placing the bill back in her hand. "I was supposed to pick you up, remember? This is on me."

"Everything's always on you."

In the weeks they had been together, he had paid for all their meals and activities. They were legitimate business expenses that he could write off, he once said, and even on occasions like tonight when there were no photos taken, no semblance of "work," it helped set the stage for the next go-round, or so Xavier explained. At first it didn't bother Mel; but lately, maybe because of the passage of time, she felt like she was freeloading, staying at Anne's, the outings with Xavier, and paying for none of it. How much longer could she continue to take, take, take—and not pay her share?

"If you'll feel better about it, we'll call this a working dinner," said Xavier. "To be continued at my place," he added, watching her carefully.

"Your place?"

"Right. I have something to show you."

Immediately, she realized the import of his words. "The photos?" she asked excitedly. "Are they ready?"

He released a sly smile. "You'll have to wait and see."

She had been to his place only once before. And that was a short visit. He had forgotten a new filter that he wanted to experiment with, so en route to the sightseeing tour of the day, they had made an unscheduled stop at his condo. She was there just long enough to have a glass of lemonade, see his darkroom and studio, his camera paraphernalia, and files of photos neatly cataloged. She was glad that the visit was brief. Too much temptation lurked within.

Normally, their outings were just that—outings. Outside activities, photo shoots, ferry rides, day cruises. And with lots of people around.

Tonight, though, was different. Mel felt an intimacy that she had not experienced before, and, she surmised, Xavier felt it too. Even the sparsely populated restaurant contributed to their closeness, as though the two of them were alone in an oasis, while most people, on this gray Wednesday evening with thunder overhead, chose not to venture out.

They ordered a selection of appetizers in lieu of entrees, by unspoken agreement that dinner in this manner would be quicker. Both of them, for their own reasons, were anxious to finish: Mel to see the photos; Xavier to see her reaction. Pushing them along was a wave of intensity that would inevitably have to be reckoned with.

A couple entered and was seated at a table directly in Mel's line of vision. The young woman—tall and beautiful—laughed a bit too loudly at the comments of her companion, a paunchy, fiftyish man who clearly enjoyed his status for the night. Nearly sitting in his lap, she teasingly nibbled his ear, then held up a menu to hide their activity beyond. But the "cover" was transparent: Mel knew exactly what was going on. Obviously a paid prostitute, the woman was "tonguing" him, as Builder would say. Her job was to make him feel like king of the hill. And he was lapping it all up.

Mel had often witnessed such liaisons. In years past, when she and Builder frequented restaurants, long before their financial woes, and even when she traveled for the Chamber, she would see couples like this, couples who stood out like a sore thumb. The women were scantily dressed and fawningly attentive. The men were aging mid-America types from places like Vincennes, Indiana, and Kearney, Nebraska—small town, church-going conservatives no less, who, when on a business trip or attending a convention in a big city, acted as if they were suddenly let out of a cage, free to roam in an untamed wilderness. They owed it to themselves, they no doubt reasoned; and so, they paid for it, doing things with their nubile partners that they had only fantasized about. Afterward, they would return home to unsuspecting wives, and assume their traditional head-of-household roles in upstandingly moral fashion.

Yes, Mel had laughed at them. But now, she wondered, was she that different, that far removed from the man in the corner who was getting his throat jammed? Was she here in Seattle, as Maxx had implied, desperately trying to live out a fantasy, let loose from her own cage? Was it as obvious to others that she and Xavier were similarly mismatched, together only for prurient reasons?

She glanced at Xavier, who smiled at her from across the table. No, she assured herself. It wasn't like that at all. First of all, nothing sexual had happened. Not really. Just a few light kisses and casual hand-holding—hardly torrid sex. Secondly, and most important, theirs was a real friendship, a relationship that grew naturally out of Xavier's professional interest. They weren't using each other but genuinely liked each other. What harm was that?

It was after nine when they drove to Xavier's, the top of his car pulled back in homage to the stunningly violet sky after the rain. Inside, he led her directly to the den-turned-studio, teasingly admonishing her to keep her eyes closed, further prolonging her anticipation. He stopped at the doorway to flick on subdued track lighting before finally agreeing to let her see.

She let out a sigh of amazement. The room was transformed into a photographic museum, with herself as the lone subject. There were photos of her everywhere: huge, enlarged photos on easels, propped along the baseboard, and most noticeably, suspended from the ceiling in blown-up formats.

"This is—remarkable." She could barely speak, her wide eyes doing the talking for her. She hadn't expected anything like this! She knew Xavier was developing the pictures himself and wanted to show them to her all at once. But she thought they would be in an album. And certainly not so many.

"I don't believe you did this!" she exclaimed, realizing all the work involved.

"Presentation is everything," he said, beaming.

"Is that me?" she asked sincerely, settling in on a hanging photo which showed a striking woman with windswept hair and a face that looked almost mystical.

"Yes. It's definitely you."

"Wow. You made me look *too* good!"

He laughed, pleased at her delight. "The camera doesn't lie."

She glanced around the room, awed by the different looks and moods that Xavier had captured. It would take hours to study all the photos the way she'd really want to. She threw up her arms. "There's just so much here."

"I know. I'm going to have a heck of a time deciding which ones to use. Come here," he said, reaching for her hand. He led her to the opposite end of the room to an easel holding an 8 x 10 black and white on pale yellow poster board. He gazed fondly at the photo. "This is my favorite."

Mel looked into the face of a woman with unfathomable eyes and a hint of a smile. As though she had a secret all to herself. Mel had felt that way before—when she found out she was pregnant with Sasha, before she had told anyone. But she didn't know that that was the look; was that how she had looked *then?*

"I wonder what I was thinking."

"Remember when this was taken?"

"No." She turned to him for help. "Do you?"

"It was the day we went to Mount Rainier. We were right at the foot."

"Yes," she said wistfully. "That was incredible." Then, her mood changing, she spanked him lightly on his hand. "I can't believe you took so many pictures I wasn't even aware of."

"That was the whole idea."

She focused again on the photo. "My hair looks so dark. Almost jet black."

"It's the shadows. Besides, I might have tweaked the lighting some."

"So you do perform magic."

"Not really." He smoothed a wayward strand around her temple. "Your hair's naturally black, isn't it?"

She made a facial twitch. "Is this going to disqualify me?"

"What?"

"If I confess that I lighten my hair?"

He laughed. "Of course not."

"I told you, I believe if there's help out there, use it." She turned back to the photo. "When I was younger, my hair was dark like this. In fact, my father sometimes called me Raven. That's my middle name."

"Raven," Xavier repeated tenderly. "I like that. But then, I think I'd like anything that's yours." His eyes danced with excitement. "We could call you Raven in the book of photos. What do you think?"

"Hmmm." Mel tilted her head, pondering. "Perhaps." It would certainly do more justice to the name than its last outing as the Pinwheels waitress.

"This is really going to work," Xavier said. "I see all kinds of possibilities."

"Who knows," Mel teased, "years from now, you might be putting out the umpteenth edition: *Eighty-Year-Olds Who Still Look Thirty.*"

He chuckled at the thought.

"And then," she added, "in parentheses, there'll be the subtitle, '*Please Don't Tell Them Otherwise.*'"

They both laughed; Mel was as excited as he about the potential for success.

"Don't move," he said. "I'll be right back."

He returned with two glasses and a bottle of champagne. He gave her the glasses to hold while he manipulated the corkscrew.

"To a successful new venture," he toasted. They clinked glasses and sipped.

"To Raven—your resurrected name," he added. They clinked and sipped again.

"And to the most creative photographer ever," Mel said, taking in the surroundings. "Everything's beautiful."

"You're beautiful." His rich voice deepened with affection.

Suddenly, his lips were on hers, oozing sweet champagne into her mouth, champagne made sweeter by first being in his. Made ready by him, the honeyed liquid flowed into a shared space of mutual consent. A small amount trickled onto her chin; he gently absorbed it with his lips, moving them rhythmically down her neck.

"It's time, Mel," he whispered. "It's time."

She was a lot like her father, her mother so often said, in a not-so-complimentary way. Now, she and her father had something else in common: infidelity.

Mel turned on her side, unexpectedly coming face to face with the shiny object atop the black lacquer night stand next to Xavier's bed. Earlier, she had taken off her wedding ring, with some difficulty. Her fingers must have swollen slightly over time, as she had a hard time sliding the ring over her knuckle. It was a perfect fit the day Builder had put it on, and she had removed it only once, for a cleaning.

Taking it off tonight was a symbolic gesture, and a silly one, really. She had seen a woman do it on a television drama, during one adolescent summer when she had passionately watched soap operas nonstop, with so much vigor and intensity that the overload eventually cured her addiction. But she vividly remembered that scene, the removal of the wedding band, because she had cried out to the character not to do it, not to forsake her marriage in favor of a man who was not her husband. At the time she had spoken with the idealistic purity of a romantic teen. But now she understood. The ritual was a needed preparation—a conscious reneging of vows, an act of closure to a previous life.

She thought about her last time with Builder, when he was unbearably rough and abusive. So, so different was Xavier—tender, sensitive, with no need of guidance or direction, touching her in the right crevices, the right way, making love like a man in love. It was as though he knew her body from long ago, knew it better than she did, knew how she felt and what she wanted, even before it birthed within her.

Xavier stirred next to her, massaging her shoulder, caressing her thigh. With his warm breath on her ear, he invited her to merge with him once more, to continue the hours-long lovemaking that neither was willing to let go.

Readily, Mel accepted the invitation. Closing her eyes to the discarded ring, she turned to face her waiting lover, who was primed to erupt again.

CHAPTER *12*

Builder flipped through the pages of an *Ebony* that Eunice had purchased when she was there. It was another annual issue on the most influential blacks in America, and with the turn of each page, he shook his head in disgust.

The same group every year, he thought. Mostly chump politicians, and the only thing they influence is their own pocket, at the expense of everybody else. They're great at spending other folks' money, raising taxes every minute. Government this and government that. Who the hell do they think makes up the government?

Intermingled among the politicians and long-time civil rights leaders were photos of the black elite of private enterprise, people who represented their companies at $1,000-a-plate fund-raisers, the select few who were sought after when there was a need for a "black perspective." Smack in the middle of this grouping was a smiling LA corporate attorney, posing with his wife in front of their sprawling suburban estate. Builder recognized the man as a former college mate who was a year ahead of him. He had heard he had done well, but didn't know it was *this* well. Even in school, the guy was crooked, did a lot of underhanded things; but he was popular and got over. No telling what he was into now, thought Builder. It was people like him who get the glory—the money, the big house—they've got it all. Meanwhile, here he was, working his fingers to the bone, and yet . . .

He flung the magazine down, regretting he had picked it up. Seeing the pictures of others' success only plunged him into a deeper funk. Already today he had fought back a rush of self-pity, as he had swallowed his pride and nearly groveled before the loan sharks at Atlantic Financial. He only had half of the payment for the second mortgage, and had asked if they'd give him a little leeway as he worked to bring the mortgage current. Both Simon Weaver and his pug-faced boss had responded in a condescending manner, reminding him that he had been late or behind for the past two years, that the company had cooperated above and beyond what could be expected, and that they were clearly entitled to request the bankruptcy court to lift the stay against his house.

The bastards. He knew what they wanted: to see him bend, to hear him plead. And so, humbly, he had obliged. Through tight lips he had requested their indulgence, pointing out what they already knew—that they were receiving back payments through the bankruptcy court, that he was working out of a difficult business situation that had put him in this predicament in the first place. Finally, they had agreed to hold off from any court action, for now, but warned he'd better bring the mortgage current soon, or else they'd have no recourse.

He had never condoned violence, but today he certainly understood how it could happen—when people reach the end of their rope, when they are thwarted at every turn, when their sense of failure is so acute that they feel compelled to strike back to even the score. He had left that place with thoughts of arson and revenge running through his head.

He was at a crossroads unlike any he'd been at before, juggling back and forth the idea of how he could still make the business work, yet giving equal toss to the notion that it was a doomed enterprise. Was it him? Was it all him? Was he jinxed or something? Sure, he had made barrels of mistakes: putting his house on the line, frittering away Sasha's college money, and his and Mel's retirement fund, pumping all that plus their savings into the business in the desperate hope that things would turn around. But other people made mistakes too and seemed to rebound. Why couldn't he? Wasn't he due *some* good luck?

Just last week he had heard how his neighbor across the street had received financing for his soft drink business. The banks here in Atlanta wouldn't touch him, he had to go all the way to New York, but, still, he got the money. And then, he had heard about this white contractor who maneuvered a $300,000 signature loan—without even having to put up a dirty pair of drawers. Not a thing! Yet, Builder recalled, when he had applied for a measly ten grand, he was asked to produce all kinds of collateral and was still denied the loan. No one needs a bank when all their *i*'s are dotted and *t*'s are crossed, he thought. They need a bank to help get over the rough spots, when they're stuck in the trenches.

He went in the kitchen and came back with stale pretzels from the bare pantry, and the surviving beer from the near empty refrigerator. It was only 7:00 P.M., an unusual hour for him to be home. Normally, he'd work until 11:00 or midnight, at least, but his back had gone out earlier due to some kind of muscle pull. He had been lifting a pile of lumber, something he'd done countless times before, when excruciating pain shot up his spine, causing him to drop the lumber almost on his feet, and leaving him bent over in agony. Eventually, he made it home, recognizing that there'd be no more work today. He took some all-purpose Naprosyn from an expired prescription bottle of Mel's that he found in the medicine cabinet, and after a couple hours of rest, was feeling better. Physically. The mental torment went unabated.

You can't work a business like this without a bank backing you, he said to himself. You're a fool to keep trying. You've got to know when to throw in the towel.

He took a handful of pretzels and proceeded to self-lecture, this time in the first person.

So what do I do? Trying to get a corporate gig is insane. At forty-three? They don't even want to hire black men who are thirty. I know how that game's played.

He washed down the bland pretzels with a swallow of beer, his dream of successful entrepreneur as dark as the hole leading to the can.

Maybe I could start another business. But it's got to be something that doesn't require such a heavy outlay of cash.

Face the facts, dummy, his alter ego retorted. Any business is going to require a lot of start-up money. And you don't have it. Why not focus on something related to your experience? That way, it won't all be for naught.

Great. Any ideas?

Taking stock, he tipped his head back for an extra large swig. Out of the corner of his eye, he saw the family picture from Maxx and Nikki's wedding that was a complimentary gift from the photographer. Builder had stood it against the tall base of the lamp on top of the oblong table across the room. Gingerly, his back still aching, he rose to bring the picture closer, as though hidden among the celluloid were answers he needed to find.

They were all three smiling, Mel less so, but smiling nonetheless. He had his arm around her, and Sasha, nearly as tall as Mel, stood between them. It was astonishing how much she looked like Mel. There was something about the cheekbones and the shape of the mouth. People used to say how much Sasha favored him. But now he saw the resemblance on the maternal side, even detecting a hint of Eunice in the two of them. Sorry, Mel, he thought, knowing she wouldn't like the comparison. But it was true.

A wave of nostalgia swept over him. He missed them both, Mel and Sasha, missed them terribly, and at that moment, renewed his commitment to get his family back together. That was the problem with society today, too many families breaking up. Well, he wasn't going to let it happen to them. He was going to make sure of that.

He had called Mel several times but she still refused to speak to him. At first, he couldn't blame her, and figured it was her way of getting back at him, of making him feel bad for his behavior that night. But it had been nearly two months and his punishment had lasted long enough. There were things they had to talk about that couldn't be put off any longer. But how could he get Mel to come to the table if she wasn't even willing to listen?

He gazed at her half-smiling face in the photo. She had looked lovely that day, and despite all the activity of the wedding, had remained calm and composed. She seemed to thrive in situations like that; she was a much better organizer than he. His forte was creating ideas; hers was implementation.

Builder sighed with regret. How could he have possibly hurt her? Who'd have guessed, looking at the photo, that a few hours later the family would be in such shambles? He must have been out of his mind to have turned against Mel like that. He had relived the scene, that whole night in fact, so many times, trying to figure out where along the way he had gotten off track. Certainly, the drinking hadn't helped. He should have stayed home after the wedding, he had already had his fill. But no, he had to go out and act the fool, and then come back and . . .

Details were still fuzzy. But he remembered tearing up the kitchen looking for that bottle of Perignon. And as he started to force himself on Mel, he remembered the fear in her eyes; a palpable fear that should have stopped him, had he any sense of control. But no, he had ignored it, perhaps because he didn't want to be stopped, his pent-up rage and frustration, so long subdued, had permitted no more procrastination. Even the terrible fear in Mel's eyes had not been enough to deter him.

He had seen that look of fear twice before. Once was when he went hunting in north Georgia on a day when "either sex" tracking of deer was allowed. He had cornered a doe who, frozen in her tracks, sensed grave danger at hand. Her eyes caught his, and in that instant, locked in time, he could have let her go, given her a reprieve. But his fingers pulled the trigger.

He was not a hunter by habit. The exhilaration that he had expected from the kill didn't happen, in view of the unbalanced odds. The poor deer never had a chance. He gave the carcass to one of the guys in his group. How could he go home and tell Sasha, then three years old, that her father had shot Bambi?

The next time he saw that look of fear was in the eyes of a skinny white kid in Forsyth County.

He had taken Mel and Sasha out for a Sunday ride on one of their frequent forays into the country, an important ongoing education for Sasha, he believed, who was growing up too citified. They had stopped to look at a housing subdivision under construction, replete with tennis courts and a golf course. Shortly after they had returned to their car, they were followed by a big pickup on a deserted back road. For several minutes, the truck brazenly tailgated the Honda's bumper, just inches away from a hit. Mel and Sasha were terrified. Through the tire-spun dirt on the graveled road, they could see a washed-out Confederate flag draped across the hood and a rifle rack in the back. There were four men in the truck, two in the cab and two on the flatbed. Ignorant, uneducated rednecks, Builder deducted. He reached for the black pouch holding his father's old .32 caliber pistol.

When Mel saw him finger the gun, as he kept one hand on the steering wheel, she pleaded with him to be rational. But he told her he'd be damned if he'd let some dumb Georgia crackers terrorize his family.

The truck had pulled alongside of them, swerving perilously close. Builder couldn't see the driver clearly, but he got a good look at the jerk on the passenger side, who stuck out a tattooed arm of a naked woman to punctuate his venom.

"Git out of here, niggah. Go back where you b'long."

Southern hospitality like none other.

One punk in the flatbed dropped his pants to reveal an ashy butt. He bent over and dibbled his middle finger around his anus. Meanwhile, his partner made apelike gestures while spewing racist trash.

It was all Builder could do to hold back. He considered using the gun in his lap to shoot out the tires on the truck. He would certainly be within his rights—his family was at risk and he had to protect them. It would be due justice. But what if his aim went astray and a bullet hit someone in the truck? Next to him, Mel screamed at him to pull over to not be dragged into the ugly game of dare.

The dirt road ran out, merging into a half-paved access route dotted with people and signs of activity. With potential witnesses on the scene, the harassers closed up shop, but not before dangerously cutting in front of Builder, leaving a parting round of vitriol that could still be heard through the screech of tires.

Mel and Sasha went limp with relief; anger had become secondary. But for Builder the rage and humiliation propelled him to counterattack.

For about a mile he tried to follow the truck, ignoring Mel's request to head toward home. He *had* to respond; he couldn't let them get away with it. But when the truck turned off to a deserted road, he came to his senses. Mel was right. What good would it do at this point? Besides, it was stupid of him to place Mel and Sasha, already shaken, in further jeopardy. To these crackers, this was their turf, and he was an outsider, an intruder. A nigger. Bowing to common sense, he pocketed his unrequited rage and took his family home.

But he went back. For three straight days he went back, alone, driving up and down that dirt road, not in Mel's Honda, but in his own truck, which was more suited to the back roads and less conspicuous among the local vehicles. He couldn't afford the time away from work, spending two and three hours each day searching for a bunch of punks. But he couldn't afford not to. He had to give the message, somehow, that they had picked on the wrong guy, that they had to pay a price for their racism.

So he waited and watched and drove.

It was on the third day, during the next to last hour of his allotted time to search, that he spotted the pickup. He had just bought a soda from a tiny convenience store and was getting back into his truck, when the two-toned pickup roared to a dusty stop on the other side of the store. The skinny punk with the tattooed arm hopped out from the driver's side. He was alone.

Builder wet his lips at his good fortune. He had run through his mind many scenarios of exactly what he would do if he came across the truck and its occupants. There would be four of them and only one of him. He had devised a variety of plots over the past few days, including what he'd do if he found the pickup parked. Just disabling it would be satisfaction enough. But this—ah—this was better than he had hoped.

While the punk was inside, Builder moved quickly to implement part one of his plan, puncturing the rear tires of the pickup with a screwdriver, while keeping an eye out for passing traffic. Crouching at the back of the truck, he saw the punk emerge from the store and pause to light a cigarette. He watched him throw the match on the ground and head toward the two-toned truck.

Like a magician's rabbit, Builder appeared out of nowhere. "Hey, Billy Bob," he said, slithering alongside the truck. "We meet again." He pressed the hard nozzle of his .32 against the punk's neck. "Let's have a little chit-chat," he said amiably.

Recognition dawning, the punk let the cigarette fall from his mouth, grazing his graffiti-tattooed arm. But he seemed not to notice, more concerned was he, and rightly so, about the cold piece of metal held at the base of his head. "I—I didn't mean nothin'," he said nervously.

"Oh, I'm sure you didn't," Builder said smoothly. "Now, what I want you to do is to walk, real slow, toward them thar trees." He was enjoying being in the driver's seat, having the control, humiliating his captive. He wanted him to be so scared that he'd shake all the way down to his raggedy boots. And pee in them.

Under the cover of spruce, Builder kept his gun cocked.

"Really, mister, we was just havin' a little fun. We didn't mean no harm."

"Ah, so it's 'mister' now. Amazing how polite you can be without your backup. Where're your buddies now?"

The punk glanced from side to side, as though, by looking for them, he might make them suddenly materialize.

"Let me tell you something," Builder said tightly. "Don't you ever, ever call me or my family or any other black person—a nigger again. Understand?"

"Yes."

Builder inched the gun forward. "Yes, *sir*, you asshole."

A hard swallow. "Yesss, sir."

"Now you apologize to me."

There was a slight hesitation. Then, a quivering mouth that spoke no words.

"I said apologize," Builder demanded.

"I'm—I'm sorry."

"I can't hear you," taunted Builder, singsong.

"I'm sorry."

Builder nodded. "Good boy. Very good boy."

Perhaps it was a good thing that it had taken three days to find his prey. During all that driving and watching and waiting, much of his fury had faded, replaced by thoughts of how futile the search was, and of how much work he was leaving undone. Now that this punk was before him, and he had coerced an apology, he had won at least a partial victory, and done so without physical violence. The punk had been brought down to size, forced to look into the face of a gun. That should have been enough. But while Builder's anger had subsided, it was far from gone. He wanted to make sure that the lesson was well learned, and not soon-to-be-forgotten.

To bring the point home, he cocked the gun once more, this time pressing the nozzle against the punk's chest. "I'm one of those crazy niggers that you don't want to mess with." He deliberately bugged his eyes as he spoke. "And there's lots of us out there. Oh, yeah. Just waitin' for a reason to pluck out trash like you."

It was then that he saw the fear. That furtive, doelike look of a cornered animal with no way out.

Digging in his side pants pocket, Builder pulled out a banana, speckled and overripe from being carried around for the last three days. He pressed it against the punk's chest. "Tell your ape buddy this is from me."

From another pocket he pulled out masking tape and made the punk rip off a piece to cover his own mouth. Then, still holding the gun, Builder instructed him to put his hands behind his back, while he roped him around the trunk of a tree—which would be his prison until someone set him free.

Putting the gun in his pocket, Builder walked away with one last barb. "You got off easy, Billy Bob. All this dry wood around here—lucky for you, I don't smoke."

He had left Forsyth County feeling better than he had in a long time. But often, that look of fear had come back to haunt him. It was one thing to see it on the face of a deer in a legitimate hunt. Or on an ignorant fool who deserved to be put in his place. But now he had seen it on Mel. And he was the one who had put it there.

He returned the wedding photo to its space next to the lamp, wiping his fingerprints off the plain black frame. If Mel were here, she would have rehoused the photo by now in a wider, textured frame. She would have had the edges bordered in a dual or triple mat, creating a richer, layered effect. She believed in quality accessories, often saying how it was the fine touches, the finishing details, that enhanced a main idea. Just as she would bug him not just to mow the lawn, but to edge it; not just to make up the bed, but to smooth the sheets into a firm, even tuck. Not just to place the pillows in position, but to plump them.

If Mel were here.

If she were here, the drapes would be pulled back to let in the evening sun, giving off an orange glow to the front of the house. The vases would gleam with fresh flowers and water, rather than the mummified stalks of the once alive that now drew algae and scum underfoot. If she were here, the house would have light and spark and vim, not this mausoleum drumbeat of the dead.

He arched his back to relieve the pressure. And if Mel were here, she'd give him a massage, a long soothing rubdown that would ease his muscles and soften the pain.

At least, once upon a time she would have done that. Now, in all honesty, if she were here, there might well be a stony silence between them, harder and colder than any cement block that he had ever attempted to break.

Shoots of hunger rippled through his stomach. The pretzels and beer were a sorry substitute for wholesome food. One thing about putting in these nonstop hours, he had lost a lot of weight, he guessed about fifteen pounds. He hadn't weighed himself lately but he could move his belt a full notch over from a month before. And the pouch was gone, that telltale sign of middle age that had crept up on him due to lack of exercise. But he knew it wasn't good to lose so much so fast. He had to start eating better.

He scoured the refrigerator again, hoping the contents might have somehow improved. But there was nothing edible, just a moldy plum and a half-filled container of yogurt. Even the most imaginative of cooks would need more than that.

Greens. That's what he wanted. Fresh collard greens cooked in ham hocks. And some boiled potatoes. And a steak, medium rare. He salivated at the thought. He'd restock the pantry and fridge, and start treating himself right.

He was surprised to see so many people at Kroger during the middle of the week. There was the standard number who stopped on the way home to buy the makings for their evening meals. But Wednesday was also Senior Citizens Day, when the older set received a 5 percent discount. While the majority came in the morning on buses provided by elderly centers, the more independent types and those not fully retired made up a big portion of the evening crowd. Builder used to scoff at the droves of people looking to salvage a paltry 5 percent, and he thought it insulting that the store promoted the weekly offering under the guise of big savings. But the lessons of strife had taught him well. More than ever, he understood how every dollar counted. Down to the literal cent.

He had been in the produce section for a good ten minutes, his cart already filled with clear plastic bags of vegetables, when a young goateed man approached with a wide smile and an outstretched hand.

"Hi. Betcha don't remember me, do ya?"

The friendly face was vaguely familiar but Builder was stumped. He shook hands, not knowing with whom.

"It's the hair," the young man said, clutching his chin. "Does it every time." He almost seemed pleased that he was not recognizable. "Remember? You gave me a ride home last summer—when my car broke down on I-75."

Builder snapped his fingers. "The alternator." He chuckled at the memory. "How's it going, man?"

Johnny Gray had changed. The goatee, really a scraggly fuzz, made him look foolishly older, an unsuccessful attempt to appear more mature. He was doing fine, he said, working as the assistant manager of a large paint store across town. He and his wife Evelyn had ended up moving to Atlanta and staying with his parents. They were saving to buy their own place. And their daughter just had her second birthday.

"Looks like you're loading up," Johnny noted, pointing to Builder's full cart.

"Need to. But you're traveling light." The reference was to Johnny's empty hands.

"I just have to pick up lettuce for a salad." He slapped his forehead. "Oh! And milk. I can't forget that."

"Nope. You'd be in a heap of trouble."

"Sure would." Johnny smiled genuinely. "You know, Evelyn's been on my case for ages because I lost your card." He took a breath. "I've been wanting to talk to you to see if maybe you'd take me on at nights. As an apprentice or something."

Builder couldn't have been more surprised. "An apprentice?"

"Yes. Working for you. I'd love to learn more about contracting. I see guys coming in the store all the time, getting supplies and stuff. I talk to a lot of them, plus I've been doing some research on my own. I think it's something I'd really like to do."

No, it's not, thought Builder. You have no idea what's involved. But he listened politely as Johnny laid out his game plan.

"I figured I'll be at the paint store for another year or two, but all the while I'll be gaining experience about contracting. I mean, if I could work part-time with someone like you, that'd be great." He looked at Builder with unabashed admiration.

Builder made an involuntary jerk of the head at the compliment, so out-of-the-blue.

"Evelyn often talks about you and your wife," Johnny said sheepishly. "She wants us to be like you two in a few years."

You never know the impact you have on people, thought Builder. So, Johnny's wife often talked about them? Builder remembered her now as rather pushy and outspoken; she'd probably goaded Johnny into chasing this image of the self-made entrepreneur. She evidently saw the Burkes as the ideal couple with a solid marriage and a successful business. Man, was she mistaken. And Johnny too. They had definitely picked the wrong role models.

Builder moved his cart over to make room for a store clerk wheeling a load of melons down the aisle. "The grass is always greener on the other side," he said. "Things aren't always how they seem."

"I realize that," Johnny said.

But Builder could tell he wasn't getting the message across and decided to be more up-front. "Truth is, I'm not in a position right now to hire anybody."

As it was, he could barely pay himself and the few part-time workers he had, let alone take on someone else. If anything, what he needed was experienced help. Training Johnny would require a ton of supervision and patience—and would slow him down. Then too, Johnny didn't seem to have the knack for working with his hands. From what Builder could tell, Johnny was too absentminded, too green. The incident with the jumper cables spoke volumes; he remembered how Johnny didn't even have any. True, people can learn. But was Builder the one to teach him?

"It wouldn't have to be every day," Johnny said, sensing an outright rejection. "You know, maybe a few hours a week, only when you need me."

"It's a tough business to be in. It might look easy but it's no cakewalk."

"Oh, I know it's not something you learn overnight." Johnny tried to project that he was aware of the risks. "All I want to do is get my foot in the door. Like I said, I've been talking to people and doing a lot of research."

"And what have you learned?"

Johnny pondered slightly, wanting to do well on this pop quiz. "I've learned that you should be able to do the work yourself before you can get other people to do it." He spoke like he was reading from a script. "Because the more you know about what needs to be done, the better you can tell who can handle the job, whether their price is fair, and all that."

Builder nodded, impressed. He *had* done some homework.

"And I know you've got to do a lot of planning," Johnny continued, "and you need to have capital. I thought you might give me some tips on that."

Builder let loose a cynical laugh. He was the last person to give anybody tips on capital. As for going into contracting? Don't, would be his advice. But it wouldn't be fair to be that discouraging. Johnny already seemed a bit deflated at the news that Builder's business wasn't a roaring success. No need to burst all his bubbles.

They exchanged numbers, with Johnny vowing to give Builder's number to Evelyn this time for safekeeping, and Builder agreeing to call if things opened up.

He continued his shopping, abstractedly putting items into the cart. Funny, earlier he had leaned toward letting the business go, to closing it down for good. But the reality of not having it was too painful to endure. The conversation with young, idealistic Johnny once again provoked those nagging questions. *Was* he giving up too soon? *Could* it still be possible? Like some men addicted to women, he was addicted to owning his own business. It ran through his blood and arteries; it made up his life stuff. How could he possibly separate himself from that?

He wandered over to the beef section and selected a freshly packaged premium cut. He could already tell that he'd be up late tonight, marinating and digesting more than prime rib.

The Norcross office of Gibbons & Sons smelled of fresh paint and turpentine, and still sprouted fiber fuzz from recently installed carpet. The high gloss bouncing off the receptionist's polished desk provided a reflective sheen to the face of a new age computer which showed a detailed architectural rendering.

Builder folded Section B of the paper and sipped the last of the second cup of coffee that the receptionist had brought. He had been waiting for twenty minutes, and his patience was wearing thin. As it was, he was only here as part of a last ditch campaign to try any- and everything before throwing in the towel. He had decided that if he was going to go under, then, damn it, he'd at least get an A for effort. But if this Gibbons guy wasn't serious about seeing him . . .

When Maxx first gave him Charles Gibbons's business card a few months ago, Builder had immediately called to set up a meeting, even though his heart wasn't in it. Working on a joint venture had never been one of his goals. He had always prized his independence, and enjoyed not having to explain anything to anyone. Upon requesting to meet with Gibbons, he was told that plans to open an Atlanta office had been put on hold; nevertheless, a meeting was tentatively scheduled way in advance. Builder had forgotten all about it until he received a call last week to confirm today's appointment.

He viewed coming here as a defeat of sorts, an admission that he couldn't make it on his own—that once again, a black man was going hat in hand to Mr. Charlie (in this case, Mr. *Charles*), hoping for a bailout. That was probably a skewed way of looking at it, but it was how he felt nonetheless.

"Awfully sorry to keep you waiting." Charles Gibbons, Jr., rushed in, explaining that he had been on the phone with the Florida home office, trying to "put out a fire." He was a man of slight build and overgrown hair. His shirt sleeves were rolled halfway up his forearm and his tie sagged fashionably around his neck. He exuded a casual confidence often found in successful older executives who need no longer put up a facade, or in younger men used to having their way. Gibbons was the latter.

They moved to a small conference room, talked a moment about Maxx, assessed the Braves' chances of going to the World Series, and spoke generally about the state of the contracting industry. Then Gibbons got specific, describing the history of the company that was founded by his father, and how expansion into Atlanta and the Southeast was a logical next step.

The more Gibbons talked, the more Builder had the impression that he wasn't just another rich white boy who'd be satisfied resting on his daddy's laurels. Gibbons saw the Atlanta operations as a way of showing that he could do something on his own. In fact, he almost seemed self-conscious that he was a son of the founder, and even acknowledged that, perhaps as a result of that, people expected less of him. He wanted to prove them wrong.

Surprisingly, Builder started to feel a certain kinship with the young man across from him. He recalled his own words to Johnny: *Things aren't always what they seem.* He realized that Charles Gibbons, Jr., this privileged son of a successful entrepreneur, had his own demons to fight. Sometimes, in the most unlikely places, the appearance of well-being is merely a fragile covering for wounds invisible to the eye.

Even so, Builder reminded himself, Gibbons's struggle was of a nature different from his own, a difference that lay at the point of origin. Gibbons's father had handed him the makings for a whole business, with the backing of an established company, while Nathaniel Burke, Sr., bless his soul, had left his son a legacy of sweat equity and a box of used hand tools.

Most white folks always have a head start. A *big* head start.

"I'm interested as to why you haven't worked with any majority firms so far," Gibbons said.

"Simple," replied Builder with a smirk. "They haven't asked."

But the real answer was that he hadn't aggressively gone courting, either. Mel had urged him many times to set up appointments with the larger companies. But at the time, she didn't know that the business was in such a vulnerable position, and he didn't feel like hearing the predictable response: thanks, but no thanks.

"Seriously though," he said to Gibbons, "the major contractors work almost exclusively with people who can put in money or who can obtain bonding. I've not been able to do either." He decided to let Gibbons know that his position had deteriorated further. "Things got so bad I had to declare bankruptcy a few months ago. So I'm not exactly operating from a position of strength."

Gibbons nodded, listening.

"You should know up-front that I can't bring any money into this," Builder explained. "But I know this city, and I know my business. I can offer skills, and I can offer ideas."

"Good," Gibbons said. "But I still don't understand why you haven't worked with a majority firm before now—despite your financial situation. Many small white-owned companies are struggling too, yet they get the work."

Builder inhaled deeply. As usual, Atlanta's flowery PR had outdistanced the real state of affairs. "There's a lot of talk about working with minority businesses, but that's all it is, talk," he said. "To most major firms, their idea of a minority business person is Horace Dorsey or Lee Smallwood."

"I've heard of them."

"I'm sure you have. Their names are plastered on every joint venture in town. That's who the major firms want to deal with. Just those two. Well, that's not what the programs were set up for. The whole idea behind minority set-asides is to open the door to *small* businesses, not these guys who've become millionaires several times over. And yet, they're the ones who constantly get the work." He didn't mean to sound bitter, but it was hard to muzzle his feelings. "It's the same thing with city contracts. A few folks benefit, and that's it. The whole thing's a sham."

"Politics drives the engine, that's for sure." Gibbons reached for a bowl of hard candy and handed it to Builder. "Have one?"

"No thanks. So, is your company involved in several joint ventures in Miami?"

"Not like we should. Which is one of the changes I want to implement here." As he spoke, Gibbons meticulously unwrapped the cellophane from an orange burst. "My father and I have different philosophies about this. He thinks joint ventures weaken a company, and you end up losing some of your autonomy. I think, if done right, they can be a tremendous way to expand. And in order to be competitive, you have to be able to bid on contracts that require diverse participation. As with anything, I think the key is getting the right personnel."

"That's true. The personality mix is all-important," said Builder.

"What else do you consider important?"

"Well," Builder began thoughtfully, "that both parties enter an agreement fully understanding what each is to do, and respecting that. So many deals are on paper only. The minority contractor never shows up; in fact, he's paid to stay away. They don't want him anywhere near."

"A joint venture in name only."

"Exactly," Builder agreed. "And then, there are situations where the minority contractor gets the Mickey Mouse work, the smallest piece of the worst part of the job. They're afraid he's going to mess up so they give him cruddy stuff to do. That's not my idea of a joint venture."

"That's not my vision either. For it to work, it has to be a partnership. And there must be mutual trust."

They continued to talk for nearly an hour. Builder described some of the work he had done and the skills he could bring, and Gibbons identified potential project areas where he would need assistance. For Builder, it was the first time he had spoken to someone who seemed genuinely interested in exploring a possible joint venture and who wasn't put off by his weak financial state. He'd have to submit some financial statements and tax records, which were far from stellar, but at least Gibbons knew the overall picture.

If working with Gibbons would help keep the business alive, if it would create some consistent income, then maybe this was the best road to take, Builder thought—perhaps the only road to take. He knew about the downside of a joint venture, of a joint *anything*. It meant marching to someone else's beat. And he knew that things change real fast when people get on the job. All those good intentions of "working together" dissipate into the unyielding reality of deadlines, uncooperative weather, and short tempers. But he was running out of options, even though he was still clinging to the hope that his business might somehow, miraculously, make a comeback on its own.

Gibbons made it clear that he planned to talk with other minority contractors, but that he appreciated this initial meeting. Leaving the office, Builder felt like a tentative suitor who had mixed feelings about the first date—optimistic about the potential, but not totally sure if he wanted to call, or be called, again.

As soon as he turned the corner and saw her car, he remembered. He was thirty minutes late but she was still there, waiting in her car, her protective shield from the pounding rain. He swore at himself. How could he have forgotten? She must be fuming by now. He had too much on his mind, just too much. He had to do better.

Honking, he pulled up next to her and parked. Through the heavy rain, he could barely make out her tapping her watch. But she didn't seem too upset. He guessed that if she was, she would have left by now.

He leaped out of his truck at the same time that she left her car, and they both dashed up the long walkway to his office door, she carrying a brown paper bag close to her chest.

"I could wring your neck," Val said inside, shaking her pulled-back braids.

"A lot of water would come out if you did," he joked.

"I was about to give up on you. What happened?"

"I got held up."

She gave him a scolding look. "Honestly, I come all the way over here to feed your junky butt and—"

"I know. I'm surprised you didn't leave."

"I probably would have. Except I had a good mystery to keep me company." She set the brown bag on what used to be Fatima's desk. "And I started in on the spring rolls. The peanut sauce is *mmmwaa.*" She brought her fingers to her lips and smacked them in a little kiss of appreciation.

She had called earlier in the day, volunteering to bring dinner, since she suspected he was half eating while maintaining his usually brutal schedule. He had agreed only because the rain prevented him from working on his current project, restoring a decrepit front porch, but he had suggested she meet him at his office where he would be catching up on paperwork.

"This place has seen better days," observed Val, taking in the stacks of paper and signs of neglect.

"Yeah. I've been meaning to clean up." He was used to the clutter but seeing it now through her eyes, it did look awfully bad.

"Bet it wouldn't even recognize a dust rag," she teased. "Probably hasn't seen one since your secretary left."

He hated to admit it, but she was right. "It's a little better in here," he said, somewhat embarrassed. He switched on the light to his office where another massive mess awaited. Builder bypassed his piled-up desk and went to the sofa. He moved several books of carpet samples to one end, and swept the rest of the sofa with his cap.

"For you," he said, making a grand bow.

They set out their meal, holding paper plates in their laps and using one of the sample books as their table for beverages and condiments.

"It's probably cold by now," Val said, her grumbling not quite done.

"I like cold Chinese."

"It's not Chinese. It's Thai."

"Even better."

She pointed to the container of peanut sauce, urging him to try it. "So, what's the deal with the sale sign out front? You putting this place on the market?"

"Yep. Got to."

"Really?"

"I don't have a choice."

"You'll need to clean it up if you're hoping to sell it."

"I know."

Gingerly, she twirled noodles around her plastic fork. "I know you hate to have to sell."

"Yeah," he said wistfully. "It's been my life for so long, it's hard to let it go."

"Then don't."

"Ha! Easier said than done. Tell that to the mortgage people breathing down my neck."

She wiped her fingers with a thin napkin. "How far back are you?"

"How far back? I don't even know anymore. I'm always back. It's a perpetual state of being. It's not just this place, it's everything. I'm so sick of bills I could vomit."

"Oooh," she winced, waving her hand. "Please."

Builder chuckled. "Sorry."

"The reason I asked, I'd be glad to lend you some money. Would a couple thousand help?"

Builder hesitated, touched by the offer. "Thanks, but I couldn't take your money, Val. You're struggling like the rest of us."

"I'm not struggling quite as much as before." She put down her fork to make her announcement properly. "I finally got that settlement from Electronic World."

"Did you? Great!" He was genuinely happy for her.

"Yes, they're going to remember my name for a long time, I can assure you of that."

"I've got to hand it to you, Val. You know how to hang in there."

"Well, it's not the full amount I was asking. You know, they never give you what you really deserve."

"Sure, there's always some rope-a-dope. But you won, babe. You won. This calls for a toast."

They held up matching cans of carbonated soda.

"Anyway," said Val, affecting a highfalutin air, "as you can see, I'm certainly willing—and able—to shuffle a few dollars your way."

"Oh, 'a few dollars,' hey? Excuse me. So, now that you've hit the jackpot, a couple of grand is mere chump change, right?"

"It's all a matter of perspective."

They laughed together, enjoying Val's small victory of having caused a major corporation to blink at the righteous insistence of a determined black woman who had refused to accept an insult.

"You hold on to all your money, Val. Use it for that business you want to get off the ground. Greeting cards, right?"

"Yes."

"How's that coming, anyway?"

"Well, now that I have the start-up money, I'm ready to move on it. I can't wait forever for Mel."

Can't wait forever for Mel. That was the situation he was in too. He knew that Val would mention Mel sooner or later. But as far as he was concerned, the less said about her, the better. Out of sight, out of mind, out of discussion.

"Still haven't heard from her?" Val asked.

"Nope."

"She's got to call at some point. You all have things to work out."

"I don't know if there's anything left to work out. Or whether I even want to."

"You're just talking like that because you're still upset she left."

"No, I'm through being upset."

"Good. That's a positive sign." She picked up a small plastic container from the makeshift table. "Here, I brought some extra peanut sauce."

"Nah, I have plenty."

"I love this stuff. It's great all by itself." Val pulled out a spoon from the bag and scooped up a mouthful. But instead of an expected groan of pleasure, she let out a sharp cry and dropped the spoon.

"What is it?"

"My—lip."

A trickle of blood ran down the corner of her mouth. Val dabbed at it with her crinkled napkin.

"You really cut yourself."

"The doggone spoon." She picked it up to peer closer and noticed a sharp tab of plastic that hung over the rounded edge. "Look at this."

Builder verified the culprit. "Amazing how something that small—"

"I oughtta sue 'em," Val said resolutely.

"Sue them? Aw, come on, Val."

"I mean it. Putting out cheap stuff like this that can cut up your gums and your mouth and God knows what else. They put any old thing on the market, just to make a buck."

"Well, yeah, but—"

"What if that had happened to a little kid?" she asked. "What if a piece of plastic that's hanging over like that is bitten off by mistake and gets stuck in a child's throat?" Again, she held up the offensive cutlery. "This is dangerous. It could cause some serious damage."

He could tell where this was heading, was, in fact, already there. It was a predictable pattern: Val would suffer a slight, call the head honcho, write a letter, and then, if there was no satisfactory result, threaten legal action. In the interest of protecting the public, and of calling to task the purveyors of shoddy merchandise, she was laying the foundation for her next lawsuit. And if the folks refused to settle, then she'd try her chances in court.

"Val, this is not some major corporation. You're talking about a mom and pop store. They're from Thailand, right? They probably don't have a lot of money to begin with."

"Oh, I wouldn't sue *them*," Val said dismissively. "I'd go after the manufacturers of the spoons, of the plastic utensils. I'll bet you there're a lot of people who've had their mouths cut up because these things aren't smoothed out the way they should be."

"And it's your duty to make sure the problem gets corrected, is that it?"

"Absolutely." Val touched her lip with her finger, making sure the blood was all gone. "Now you take note of all this. I might need you later as a witness."

Builder laughed, amused by her consummate gall. "You do keep things hopping, don't you?"

Suddenly, it became hilarious—the image of Val, with her beaded braids and fiery tongue, shaking up one company after another, creating an uproar among suited-down executives through her one-woman consumer crusades.

He laughed and laughed, a transforming laughter releasing pent-up frustration and long-term angst. The laughter begot more laughter as Val joined in, caught up in its contagious spread. It spawned a feral wave of its own, and Builder was taken over by a wrenching, gut cleansing that soaked through the very core of his being.

Perhaps it was the submission, the giving in that had so emptied his body, that made it vulnerable to the unexpected jolt of pain. Builder reached for his soda, to propose another toast to Val, when he was mercilessly thrust back into the couch. His body was no longer inhabited by laughter but by searing, excruciating pain.

"What's wrong?" It had taken Val a moment to switch gears, not realizing until Builder leaned back that something was not right.

"My—my back. Maybe a p-pulled muscle." He found it hard to talk; it hurt to say the words.

"Your back?" Quickly, she placed a small square pillow behind him.

But the pain wasn't just in his back. It was unlike anything he had experienced. It clutched his side and his chest; it was like a vise that wouldn't let go.

"What if you moved to a chair? Would that help?"

He nodded feebly, the only response he could manage.

Val grabbed hold of his arm to assist him, but his weight was too much for her. As he tried to stand, the vise tightened unmercifully. He half fell to the floor, disrupting the makeshift table, uprooting the plates, and spilling the remains of the sodas onto the green and white cushions.

"Oh God, Builder!"

Frantically, Val searched for the phone, hidden beneath a stack of mail amidst the mass of clutter. She dialed 911 for an ambulance and tried to answer the questions of the emergency operator. Was there a history of heart failure? She repeated the question out loud to Builder. "I don't think so," she responded into the phone. She looked to Builder for confirmation, but he couldn't speak. When he opened his mouth, the pain gripped again, relentlessly. "Don't try to talk," she commanded.

Builder felt a warm sensation through his body. Was he having a heart attack? A stroke? It hurt even to breathe. He thought of his father, dead at fifty-three. He thought of Mel—and all that was left unsaid.

Val told him she was getting a damp cloth for his head, and disappeared from his view. From a distance, Builder heard her talking to him, trying to keep him engaged, assuring him everything would be fine.

But he could tell he was losing it. The room was becoming dim, Val's voice more faint. The last thing he remembered was her walking toward him, passing by the "Keep on Truckin'" caricature that she had drawn some time ago, now tacked to the wall. He saw his own image hanging up there, looking down on his other self, one contorted face meeting another.

CHAPTER 13

"Oh my God."

Tired from too little rest, Mel leaned toward the bathroom mirror for a fuller inspection. Her nose was red. Puffy bags sat beneath her eyes. Her face was the color of mush. Large pores, usually camouflaged, seemed to have magnified overnight. She drew back in disgust.

She couldn't stump one of those carnival age guessers today, that's for sure. She looked all of her thirty-eight years—and then some. What would Xavier say about her natural beauty now? It would take a whole lot of work to look even halfway presentable.

She sneezed heartily, a second late in grabbing a tissue to cover her mouth. Her sinuses had been giving her fits, and the over-the-counter medicine she normally took didn't help much. Last night she tried more potent pills but they had made her nervous and headachy. Then too, drinking three glasses of wine wasn't especially wise, and to make matters worse, she had topped the evening off by tripping over the fringe of a rug at Xavier's. Most of the discomfort had gone, but her ankle was still swollen, despite her getting up throughout the night to keep it elevated and to change the ice pack.

I need a whole new body, she thought miserably.

She splashed her face with cold water, hoping it would provide the boost she needed for the massive makeover job before her. Of all times to have a photo shoot. She wished she could go back to bed and sleep the day away. But Xavier had set everything up, and she had promised she'd do it.

Xavier. Things had changed between them since that night she had succumbed. There were subtle differences that were hard to define, but that she noticed nonetheless. He was not *quite* as attentive, not *quite* as complimentary. His enthusiasm for the book of photographs had waned. He was so gung-ho at first, so intent on moving ahead in photographing not just her but also the other women that would be featured. Now, he claimed to have difficulty in finding other models, although she remembered him saying earlier that he had already identified them.

And then last night, without any warning, he had shown the photographs he had taken of her to the publisher of a lingerie catalog whom he had invited over for dinner. What had angered her was not only that he had set up the encounter without consulting her, but also that the publisher seemed to know a lot about her, yet Xavier had not given her any prior information about him.

Mel didn't like the guy; he had a fast-wheeling, almost shady demeanor, and when he looked at her photographs, he seemed to see more there than met the eye. He predicted profitable repercussions should she grace the pages of a future edition of his catalog. He claimed that one of his models, whose name did sound vaguely familiar, was well on her way to film stardom, and another was doing TV commercials for a major cosmetic company.

Mel told him that she was no starry-eyed seventeen-year-old looking to hit it big, letting him know she could see through his bloated assurances of likely fame and fortune. He had responded that her youthful maturity was what was so appealing, tagging on to Xavier's contention that the "older woman" who looked younger than her years was the next big rage in his industry. With descriptive narrative, he presented some recent catalogs for her review. Several pictures were downright risqué, showing lots of cleavage and provocative poses. A photo of a model in a so-called "teaser teddy" reminded Mel of the sickening outfit she was forced to wear at Pinwheels. And in one full frontal shot, you could actually see the shadow of the model's pubic hair.

Not my style, Mel had said. But upon Xavier's urging she had finally agreed to come to the publisher's studio for audition shots this morning, provided Xavier was the photographer. The publisher promised that his selection of lingerie for Mel would be in impeccably good taste.

But now, in the light of day, doubts emerged again, and Mel wondered if she should still go through with it. It was the talk of money that had piqued her interest. Oddly, Xavier was the one who had brought it up, saying that the lingerie modeling would not only generate more interest in her when the book of photos came out, but that it was a quick and easy way to make money.

She had been surprised by his aggressive promotion. She hadn't really discussed money with him before, not intentionally, anyway. Maybe he had assumed from some of her comments about home that money was in short supply. But she couldn't recall being that specific. It was as though he was dangling this new bait out to her, intuitively knowing that the lure of money was enough of an incentive to reel her in eventually.

Maybe the disappointment was so acute because he was part American Indian, Mel reflected. Aren't Indians supposed to be somewhat spiritual, not so concerned with worldly things, closer to the earth? It must be the "other" half of him, she decided, that had showed its face last night, that had showed its face quite often during their last few times together. That other half had won out after all. The Xavier that Mel thought she knew—the Xavier that she wanted him to be always—had his tainted side too.

Mel unzipped her cosmetic case and set out the colored pencils and powders to perform her magic. She'd need a steady hand to repair all this damage. It seemed strange that, for a professional shoot, she had to apply her own makeup. It was yet another reason to question the wisdom of the arrangement. She didn't trust this publisher guy with the sleazy smile. But yes, she did need the money.

Would it ever stop—this need for money? Doing things she wasn't keen about doing? She had been in this state for so long, it was becoming hard to see herself becoming financially stable again. And even being here, in this lovely haven from all those pressures, she could not fully blot out the indisputable fact that money was a controlling factor. It took money—Anne's and Alston's—to maintain a house like this. Money—Maxx's—that had allowed her even to come here. Everything revolved around money, money, money.

"So you *are* up."

Startled, Mel turned to see Anne at the doorway.

"Sorry, I didn't mean to scare you," Anne said. "It's these soft-soled shoes."

"Maybe you should get some clunkers."

Anne laughed. "Alston has threatened me with some. He says I sneak up on him all the time." She put her weight against the jamb, observing Mel's assorted cosmetics. "Going out again?"

"Umm hmm."

"Xavier?"

"Yes. I hope he's late. It'll take me a while to get myself together."

"You didn't sleep well last night, did you?"

Mel wrinkled her brow. "It shows, huh?"

"No, it doesn't show. I thought I heard you bumping around."

"I was up a lot." She described her evening of mishaps, replete with sinusitis and a swollen ankle.

"Estelle made these fabulous boysenberry muffins. I know you're in a rush but can you spare a few minutes before you leave?"

Mel told her sure, she'd be there shortly. She was curious if there was something specific that Anne wanted to talk about. Anne could just as easily have buzzed up on the intercom, but no, she made the long walk over to this wing of the house to see personally if Mel was up and available. Maybe Anne was going to ask her to leave—not directly, but in her diplomatically charming manner. Mel couldn't blame her. She had been here for two months, and even to her it felt like she was wearing out her welcome.

A half hour later, she joined Anne at a table set up on the bricked patio outside the breakfast area. She was impressed anew at how attractive the house was for living, how well designed. It had so many nooks and crannies, albeit big ones, where one could eat or read or have a private conversation: the area adjacent to the pool, the library, the wraparound deck on the rear, and this space that opened out from the breakfast room.

A basket of muffins covered with a linen cloth awaited her, along with an assortment of preserves and fresh fruit. She had become spoiled. She was going to miss this sheltering hiatus where she was treated so royally, and which had so well insulated her from constant financial woes.

"It's a little nippy, I know," apologized Anne, seeing Mel rub her arms. "But there's a bit of sun peeping through so I think we'll be okay."

"It's gorgeous out here. Just gorgeous."

They sat for a moment, Mel with her sore ankle propped in a vacant chair, taking in the lush vegetation.

"What is it they say about Capetown—that Jesus Christ will appear there at the second coming because it's the most beautiful place in the world?" Mel breathed in the scenery around her. "It can't beat this."

Anne smiled. "I agree."

Estelle brought out glasses of juice and steaming coffee, pouring the latter into delicate cups of painted-on yellow roses.

"Well, all good things must come to an end," Mel said, raising her cup as in a toast. "I can't thank you enough for putting up with me for so long."

Her cup at her lips, Anne placed it back on the saucer, forgoing a sip. "What? You're not thinking of leaving, are you?"

Mel was surprised at Anne's surprise. "I think it's about time, wouldn't you say?"

"No, I wouldn't. You just got here."

"It's been fifty-five days exactly. I counted."

"Well, why not stay another fifty-five? Why run off all of a sudden? We haven't treated you *that* badly, have we?"

"Don't be silly. I've been living like a queen."

So, she was wrong. Anne seemed genuinely surprised to hear of her plans to leave. But if she wasn't ready to boot her out, what was it she wanted to talk about?

"When do you plan on leaving?" Anne asked.

"In a few days."

Anne picked up her cup again. "I'd hate to see you go, but I imagine Builder's glad you're coming home."

Builder. Ha! This would be news to him. In fact, she might not even call to let him know. Maybe she would just show up. No telling how he'd react; no telling how *she* would. Mel sighed heavily at the prospect.

"He *is* glad you're coming, isn't he?" persisted Anne.

"He doesn't know I'm coming," Mel admitted. "But I need to get back and tie up some loose ends. I have to get Sasha ready for school, and—" She stopped; Anne deserved to know the truth. And she herself needed to start verbalizing her decision, to hear the actual words. "The marriage is over," she said. "There's just nothing left anymore."

"Are you sure?" Anne asked forcefully. "That's such a major decision. Probably one of the most important you'll ever make."

"I've had time to think about it," Mel said.

"Only two months," Anne reminded her. "Maybe once you go back and see him and really talk to him, you'll feel differently."

"I don't think so," Mel said, not wanting to get into a more protracted explanation.

"What about Xavier?"

The question took her off guard. It was odd, after the reference to Builder, to hear Xavier's name in virtually the next breath. "What about him?"

"Well, since things didn't work out with Builder—will you and Xavier still continue to see each other?"

"I'm not leaving Builder to be with Xavier," Mel replied, feeling equally disappointed in both men.

"But isn't Xavier still working with you on that book of photos?"

"It's basically finished." Mel detected a cynicism in her own voice, the words illustrating more than face value.

"I'm sure he's going to miss you, considering you've been spending so much time together."

Mel tried to keep her voice light. "It's been fun. But like I said, all good things . . ." She deliberately took a big bite to occupy her jaw and forestall further interrogation.

"He can certainly be a charmer when he wants to, can't he?"

Her mouth full, Mel mumbled in the affirmative, but wondered where Anne was headed with her questioning.

"In one way, maybe it's a good thing you're leaving," Anne said directly, her face set in a steady gaze. "I was beginning to worry about you, that maybe you were getting too involved."

The statement startled Mel. Why should Anne have worried? Surely, she had more things on her mind than the time that Mel had spent with Xavier Lightfoot. Between her art dealings and her own personal affairs—

Suddenly, Mel knew. *Her own personal affairs.* Anne's personal affairs—*an* affair. Of course! That explained her aloofness, the undertow of chill that had recently crept into her usually open and friendly smile; it explained her many inquiries, whenever she could, about how things were going with Xavier.

"You've slept with him, haven't you?" asked Mel.

Anne looked away, her silence affirming the question.

Mel shook her head in disbelief. How could she be so dumb? So blind? Here she was staying in Anne's house, eating her food—and sleeping with her lover. She felt tainted and sordid. It wasn't right, none of it. It felt almost—incestuous. Not Anne. Not dear, Presbyterian, seemingly virginal Anne.

"So, you've been having an affair with him all the time that—"

"No, that's not true," Anne said emphatically. "It's been a long while since we were—together. It's been over now for a few years. With Alston away so much, it hasn't always been easy for me—"

"I don't want to hear it," Mel said curtly. Rationally, she had no claim to righteousness. Unfaithful herself, how could she judge Anne for doing the same thing? But it was the betrayal that angered her, even shamed her. Both Anne and Xavier knew about her; she hadn't known about them. And to her mind, that entitled her to stand on what little moral platform was left.

"Xavier can be very addictive. I tried to warn you about him."

"You did nothing of the kind," Mel snapped.

"Yes, I did," Anne said gently. "You didn't want to listen. You were captivated, and I understand that."

Mel put her fingertips to her temples, not believing what she was hearing. "I suppose the two of you had quite a few laughs on my account."

"No, it was nothing like that. He's really very fond of you."

"And you—how do you feel about me?"

"Same as always, Mel. I hope this won't hurt our friendship."

Mel left her chair and hobbled toward a beckoning clump of purple flowers. A gnat flitted around the petals, then merged inside the folds. If only she could metamorphose into some comparable life force, minuscule and invisible, where she could disappear. Out here, she felt exposed, open, and foolish.

Anne joined her in front of the purple. "I guess I was jealous of the attention he was giving you. I'm sorry. It was a mistake not to tell you. It was a while ago, and I didn't think it mattered—"

Mel rolled her eyes upward and angled her body away from Anne.

They stood there in silence, reflecting on their damaged friendship.

Anne broke the impasse. "You probably won't want to do this now, but I need to ask you a favor."

Mel stiffened. *Ask a favor? How dare she?*

Anne proceeded despite the nonresponse. "My mother's getting worse. She can't live on her own anymore. But she refuses to leave Florida and doesn't want to live here with me."

Mel heard the cracking in Anne's voice.

"It's at the point where—I have to commit her to a home. I was wondering if you could help me close out her place."

Mel turned to face her. "I don't know," she said. It was all that she could manage. What did Anne expect? That changing the subject would erase the hurt of finding out about her and Xavier? She took a deep breath. On the other hand, the situation with Xavier suddenly seemed less painful in light of the news about Anne's mother. Anne had never asked anything of her before. Not anything. And after all that she'd done for her . . .

"I'm sorry about your mother," Mel said simply.

"It's been coming for some time."

Mel nodded.

"Be grateful for the relationship you have with your mother," Anne advised, "even though it may not be the ideal. It's a terrible thing when your own mother doesn't recognize you."

"Yes. I imagine that's pretty devastating."

A few more minutes, and she would have had her arm around Anne, would have agreed to go with her for a few days, would have buried the feelings of resentment and betrayal. But at that moment the housekeeper, Estelle, called from the door of the patio, announcing that Mel had a call. From a woman, she specifically added.

"You want to take it?" asked Anne.

"I think I'd better." She glanced at her watch: 9:20. It would be 6:20 P.M. in France—dinnertime—one of the busiest times of the day at the inn. Mel had just spoken to Eunice yesterday and feared that for her to call at this hour, something must have happened to Sasha. Her heart thumping, she hurried back toward the table where Estelle held out a portable phone.

"Hello?"

"Met a BSJ lately?"

Mel swallowed in relief. "Val!"

In hearing that familiar voice and reference, Mel realized how much she had missed her. No-nonsense Val.

"I thought maybe you'd died there in Seattle. You doing okay?"

"Surviving," Mel replied quickly. "This is a surprise."

"Unfortunately, it's not a social call." Val paused a second. "It's about Builder. He's in the hospital."

"The hospital?" She was surprised that her heart skipped a beat. "What's wrong with him?"

"He's had some serious chest pains. It's not a heart attack, but something like a coronary episode. They say it's stress-related. And he's real anemic. He blacked out in front of my eyes. Scared me half to death."

"My goodness."

"He's doing better now. He might be going home today, provided he swears to take complete bed rest. Doctors say he's on the road to an early grave if he doesn't. But you know how pigheaded he is."

"When did all this happen?"

"A few nights ago. I told him to call you, but you know men and their egos. He'd never admit it, but he needs you, Mel. I think you should come home."

Builder—sick. She saw him lying in a hospital bed, pale and weak from being probed and pricked. Hadn't Maxx said some time ago that Builder didn't look well? And now, this—coronary thing. It sounded ominous.

Xavier had arrived and was listening intently to Anne on the patio. Was she telling him that their secret was out? He noticed Mel looking at them, and he waved and smiled, but Mel didn't respond.

She told Val that she'd get back in touch with her, ending the conversation. But she continued to hold the phone to her ear after Val had hung up. She needed a few minutes to pull herself together. She wasn't ready yet to face Xavier and Anne, together, with the veil of deception pulled back. Seeing them made her think of questions she should have asked

Val. Why had she been with Builder? Was it just a friendly visit? How "friendly" was friendly? And where had all this taken place? At the house? In the bedroom? *Et tu,* Val?

What was it Val had said? *He blacked out in front of my eyes.*

Mel felt an unexpected twinge of jealousy. Just tell me the truth, she thought. At least I'll know what I'm dealing with. It's the staying in the dark, the not knowing, that irked her most of all. If Anne wasn't completely honest with her, who's to say Val wasn't either? Deception by one friend now made her suspect the other. Was she too paranoid? Did she even have the right to care? A few minutes ago she had decided to call it quits with Builder. What on earth was wrong with her? She held the phone down and clicked it off.

Immediately, Anne and Xavier came toward her, advancing as a united front. It was at that instant that Mel decided what to do. There'd be no more delays, no procrastination. She'd tell Xavier that she wouldn't go on the photo shoot for the lingerie modeling. She'd tell Anne that she couldn't accompany her to Florida. She'd tell them that something had come up—an emergency that required her to leave right away.

She was going home.

The Jamaican driver pulled up to the front of the house, which revealed an unlit doorway. His passenger tipped him generously, and he rewarded her with a smile of even white teeth set against ebony skin. He whistled up the walkway with her bags, and since this was his last fare for the night, he decided he could afford to do the gentlemanly thing and wait until someone answered the door.

Even in the dark he could tell she was a fine looking woman. She reminded him of his cousin who had won a beauty contest in their village. He thought there was something foreign about her, but she spoke English with no accent. When he had asked if she had ever visited his country, and she responded no, he had sealed his lips for the rest of the trip, respecting her privacy. He wasn't one of those cabbies who yacketyyacked all the way during a ride in the hope of getting a better tip. He had learned to "read" his passengers, to let them set the pace. If they were talkative, so was he; if they wanted quiet, he obliged.

This one wanted quiet. She had only spoken once, when she first got in, and that was to tell him how to get to the house via the "back route." Following her directions, he cut off at least four minutes from the ride. So he was extra glad to see the big tip.

She rang the doorbell and knocked twice before the door was finally opened by a man in a robe, his hair uncombed.

"Oh!" he said.

"I was beginning to think you weren't here," she said to him.

There were no hugs of vigor or kisses of joy, just an awkward shuffling of places as the woman entered the house. Theirs was a tentative hello, a testing-of-the-waters greeting between people uncertain how to respond.

Strange, mused the cabby. She's such a pretty woman. If she were coming into his house, he'd be jumping up and down with excitement.

"Would you mind bringing in the bags?" she asked him.

"No problem, ma'am."

The front room was dark, save for a single corner lamp. It smelled closed in, stale, the same tight smell of his wife's windowless sewing area when she left it untended.

"Thanks again," the woman said politely.

He tipped his hat to her and left, wondering whether the man standing so stiffly at her side was her husband or boyfriend or ex-lover. Whoever he was, it sure seemed like he didn't quite know what to do.

If she were my woman, he thought, there'd be no guesswork involved.

"Were you asleep?" Mel asked.

"Uh, yeah. I must have dozed off."

"No wonder. It's almost midnight." She placed her raincoat on the arm of the couch.

"It's good to see you," he said.

"You too."

Actually, she couldn't see him very well. In the dim lighting, she could make out only the dark outline of his form rather than close-up facial details.

"How about some tea?" he volunteered.

"Fine."

She was glad to move out of the living room, and she suspected that he was too, as though, by unspoken agreement, they were both eager to vacate the unhappy scene of their last encounter.

He noticed her favoring her right side as they walked to the kitchen. "Something wrong with your leg?"

"Ankle. I tripped on a rug."

It felt strange being back, ringing the bell like a formal visitor, coming through the front door; she had dared not use her key. And now, walking into the kitchen, where the floor lay in need of a mop and the sink was loaded with dirty dishes. It was never like this when she lived here.

"Have a seat," he directed, as if she didn't know where to go.

"I'll make the tea," she offered.

"That's okay."

"No, really. I'll do it."

"But your ankle—"

"I'm not an invalid, Builder."

Giving in, he sat at the table, as Mel poured water into the teapot. She turned the knob on the stove to a medium flame, and thought of the countless hours spent in this kitchen. The meals shared, gossip exchanged, decisions made.

"So, how does it feel to be back?"

She noticed he didn't say "home"—just "back."

"Things haven't changed that much," she lied.

"If I'd known you were coming, I'd have cleaned up."

"You have a good excuse. You're not in any position to do hard labor."

He surrendered a chuckle. "Why didn't you call and let me know you'd be here?"

"I just—" She threw up her hands. "I thought it was best this way."

He brushed aside a few crumbs from the table. "Bet you heard from a certain canary, huh?"

"If you mean Val, yes. She told me you'd been in the hospital."

"You didn't have to come back for that. As you can see, I'm fit as a fiddle."

In the light of the kitchen, she could get a good look at him now. He didn't look that bad—not tired or sick, just kind of drawn and haggard.

"From what I've heard, you're far from fit as a fiddle," she said.

"Oh? And what did you hear?"

"That you blacked out, you're anemic, and under doctor's orders to stay in bed. Does that sound about right?"

"Val has a tendency to exaggerate. You know that."

"She also said that all this happened because you're under too much stress."

"Past tense. Was."

"So, it's all gone now?"

He folded, then unfolded his hands. "Just about."

Mel raised her eyebrows. "What was the remedy?"

"Several things. I've had a chance to do a lot of thinking lately. Being laid up in the hospital, I didn't have much choice."

He explained that he was hooking up with a white contractor, which should open some doors, and, most importantly, that he was hiring strictly professional crews, even if it meant hiring all-white crews. They charged more, but they generally got the job done right the first time, and in the long run would save him money. He was tired, he said, of dealing with "piecemeal brothers" whom he had to call and wake up in the morning, pick up, and take to the job site. They'd show up one day, disappear for a week, then show up again. They made him look bad and caused him to get off schedule. Often he had to finish the job himself, which put other projects even further behind, leaving his customers upset because of the slow progress. He wasn't going to work like that anymore, he said. He'd find a couple of good crews—white guys, Mexicans—whomever he could depend on to follow through.

Maybe that will help, Mel assured him. She didn't want to remind him that she had been saying that for years, that he had to hire people who were reliable. Period. And while she heard him say the words, she knew it would be difficult for him to bypass some of his workers who were extremely knowledgeable about carpentry and building, but who could not be counted on consistently.

Part of Builder's initial reason for owning a business was to help provide jobs to people who were down on their luck and passed over, not so much for lack of ability but for lack of social skills. He had talked about knowing men like that when he was growing up, riding around in his dad's pickup. Men living on the edge, not quite able to put it together. He felt sorry for them and their families, and had wanted to help them out when he could. Being black has its challenges, he had often said. If you're poor and black, you really catch hell. But trying to work with the brothers, as he put it, was detrimental to his business and had proved too costly.

"So that's one change I'm making," he said.

"That's a start."

"Yeah." He took a deep breath, as though preparing to confess. "I've also had to face up to the fact that I'm not a good manager. I've got the ideas, and I can build damn near anything. But I'm shaky on the day-to-day stuff. I know that now. I need someone to deal with the clients and suppliers and take charge of the books—handle the daily operations—so I can focus on the building part." He looked at her intently. "That's where you come in. If you're interested."

Mel wasn't sure she heard correctly. "Me?"

"You. It wouldn't have to be all day. You could still do other things. We could work out a schedule. I'll pay you, of course."

Again, he was proposing something she had mentioned when he first started out. "Let me handle the books," she had said. "I've got a nose for business." But he didn't want to relinquish any part of the business, didn't want to let her in even partially. And although he could have benefited from her strategies and ideas, he chose to run things his way, stubbornly holding tightly to the reins, out of fear that the business would become less his. Now, finally, maybe too late, he was actually seeking her help.

The teapot whistled, and Mel was glad for the diversion. It took a minute, but she found some clean mugs, remembering two that were tucked away in an upper cabinet. Builder apologized again for the condition of the kitchen, and for being out of honey and lemon.

"You still haven't given me an answer," he said, as Mel brought the mugs of steaming tea to the table.

She knew that he was experiencing a common side effect of illness—the resolve, once well, to do things differently and better. Looking at life from a sick bed, however temporarily, frequently causes people to conjure up a string of resolutions, like those made in the New Year, with the intention of breaking old habits and replacing them with healthier ones. And so it was with Builder. He had gained a new lease on life, had seen the error of his ways and was determined to shed old, dried-up skin. But how long would that resolve last? Once he had fully regained his strength, would he revert to his former self, his familiar way of doing business, just as the promise of the New Year fades? Then, too, had the business deteriorated to such a point that it was beyond repair? Was there even a possibility of an eleventh hour miracle?

Beyond the issue of saving the business, however, Mel wondered if working with Builder was even feasible in light of all that had happened. Before she could consider it, they would need to define the status of their relationship. Could they be friends, still, for Sasha's sake? Could they become business partners despite their failed marriage? Would he even want her to work with him after she told him her plans? He had freely rattled on about his plans. Well, she had plans too. Quite different from his.

She had come back for two reasons: to make sure he was all right—and to ask for a divorce. She hoped they would be able to work out an amicable arrangement. She would get a job—a decent job—using part of the money from Maxx to tide her over until something came through. That money, she knew, needed to be spent very sparingly. It was all she had to help set up a new life. Of course, she and Builder would have to decide what to do about the house. Would it be better to sell it and split the proceeds, or for one of them to continue to live in it, even though it was heavily mortgaged? Sasha, of course, would live with her, Mel had assumed, although she couldn't guarantee that would be Sasha's preference. It was the only logical choice, however, given Builder's work schedule. Right now, the main thing was to get through this period of adjustment with Builder as civilly as possible.

"Look, I don't want to pressure you into doing something you don't want to do," he said, sounding wounded that she had not responded to his offer to work with him.

"I don't feel pressure," Mel replied, taking a sip of her tea. "But first things first."

"I'm listening."

She paused. How do you tell your husband, "It's over—we need to get a divorce?" She couldn't just blurt it out. "I think we should talk about *us*," she said, as a preamble. Whatever that means.

"You first. You're the one who left, remember?"

"Yes. And you know why."

He looked down at his hands. "All right," he admitted. "Things got pretty rough. I hope you realize I didn't enjoy not having money to give you, and having to scrimp for every penny. I know I wasn't taking care of things here the way I should. It's just that the business—"

"It wasn't just the business and the money problems, Builder. You know that. Don't act like you don't know why I left."

He stared at her blankly.

If he wouldn't say it, she would. "You raped me."

"Come on, Mel," he said quietly. "Don't call it that."

"That's what it was," she insisted, her eyes widening with indignation. "Don't try to deny it."

"I'm not denying that I . . ." His voice trailed off. "Look, married people have problems. They fight."

"Fight? Is that what you'd call it? A fight?"

"Okay. So I didn't handle things right. I'm sorry about that. I truly am. That night was—crazy. I don't remember half the stuff that went on. But I tell you this: I will never, ever put my hands on you like that again. I swear."

Mel set her mouth in a disbelieving curl, like his word could not be trusted.

"What am I supposed to do?" he asked. "I've tried to apologize endless times. You wouldn't give me a chance, wouldn't even take my calls. Are you going to throw it in my face every time I turn around? What do you want from me?"

The question hung in the air, a balloon ready to pop. "I want—" Mel started. The answer was simple; yet verbalizing it required an effort she couldn't muster. They were words that needed to be said. But this wasn't the right time to say them. Not yet.

She pushed her mug toward the center of the table. "I'm tired. You're tired. Let's call it quits for the night."

He didn't object; his energy was also spent. "I guess we should both go to bed."

The way he said it surprised her. Surely he didn't expect her to sleep with him?

"I'll stay in Sasha's room," she said, warding off any assumptions by him.

He nodded, almost too readily, she thought. Was it silly of her to think that he might be a *little* disappointed?

Although tired, they lingered in the kitchen under the guise of cleaning up. Builder placed their mugs in a sink full of plates with hardened food. Since the dishwasher was already packed, he was shamed into washing by hand. Mel stacked dishes on the counter, trying to clear a space for the plastic drain board.

In joint domesticity, they talked of safer matters—Sasha mainly—which helped defuse the pent-up frustration they both felt. By the time they were midway through the mound of dishes, with Builder washing and Mel drying, they had shared a few laughs amidst an emerging rapprochement.

The phone rang intrusively at 1:05, according to the kitchen clock.

"Must be a wrong number," said Mel. She moved to answer, then held back, remembering that she had relinquished full residency rights.

"Go on, get it," urged Builder, his hands immersed in suds.

The gasping voice on the other end was unrecognizable. "It's Ma—Maa—"

"What?" Mel asked impatiently, thinking someone was playing a joke.

Again, the breathless tone, this time, more definable. Not the voice of a prankster, but of someone in paralyzed panic. "Maa—Maxx."

"Nikki? Is that you?"

"He's—hurt—" She panted between each word, as though speaking was so painful that she had to recover before moving on.

"Maxx is hurt?" Mel questioned. "How? Are you at home?"

"He's been—shot," Nikki managed.

"Oh God! Where? Where are you?"

"What is it?" Builder demanded.

"He's been shot." The words spilled out in horrifying clarity.

Mel looked helplessly at Builder, who grabbed the phone.

"Nikki? Nikki, talk to me now. Where are you?" He listened for a few seconds. "They're at Georgia Baptist," he reported to Mel, repeating the bit of news.

He listened again, winced, and pressed his forehead, more hesitant to give this update. "He was shot in the chest."

"Oh, no!" Mel's heart thumped. "How bad is it?"

He waved her off, trying to hear. "All right, Nikki. We're coming now, okay? We'll be right there."

Mel hobbled up the stairs as fast as she could, and grabbed a pair of jeans and a sweatshirt for Builder. Her brother's face flashed before her— smiling, happy-go-lucky Maxx. *How could this be? Maxx—shot? Lord, please. Let him be all right.* With shaking hands, she balled up the clothes and made her way downstairs.

Builder was hanging up the phone when Mel reentered the kitchen. His coloring had turned gray. He looked like he had aged twenty years.

"Is he going to be all right?" Mel asked nervously.

"God, I hope so. He's in surgery." Builder breathed out hard, trying to rid himself of the distressing news.

"I'll drive," she said. "You can change into these when we get there."

"Okay." He tightened the belt of his robe and headed toward the kitchen door.

"You shouldn't go down the steps," Mel cautioned. "I'll bring the car around front."

"No, don't do that." He removed his key chain from an overhead hook, and opened the door. "Let's go."

Somehow, they maneuvered the steep back steps, despite Builder's having to lean on Mel, further straining her sore ankle. The weak helping the weak. Anxiously, fearfully, they went into the night to see about Maxx.

When Nikki saw them approaching, she immediately ran to Builder, nearly collapsing in his arms. She spoke in the same breathless way as over the phone, though not as pronounced. From the scraps of information she was able to share, Mel pieced together what had happened.

On his way home from a late meeting, Maxx had stopped at a convenience store to buy a six pack of beer and a bag of roasted nuts. He was robbed while returning to his car. No one could say whether he willingly gave up his wallet or in some way resisted. But the store clerk saw the scuffle and heard a crackling noise. Maxx had fallen against his car and slid to the ground, as two nondescript males fled, their dark skins and clothing providing anonymous cover.

Maxx had been in surgery for over two hours. Prognosis: uncertain.

As they sat in the waiting room, with Builder firmly clutching Nikki's hand, Mel thought back over her last conversation with Maxx, in Seattle, and how she had demanded he leave Anne's house. He was only trying to help, he was there out of concern—yet, she had treated him like dirt. If only she could take back her stinging words. If only . . .

Builder went to change his clothes. Mel put a protective arm around Nikki. "He'll be all right," she said. "I'm sure he will."

Nikki nodded mutely, then looked at Mel as though seeing her for the first time. "When did you get back?" she asked.

"Tonight."

"Oh." She stared at the nothingness of the beige wall facing her. "I'm not handling this very well, am I?"

"You're doing just fine."

"I work in a hospital. I should know better." She looked around the sparse waiting room. "Everything seems so—normal. How could that be?" She inhaled deeply, trying to hold herself together. "I've been falling apart."

"You have a right to fall apart, honey."

Her eyes teared with desperation. "I can't lose him, Mel. I can't. I couldn't stand it."

"You're not going to lose him," Mel assured her, massaging her arm. "He's young and strong. He's a fighter. He'll pull through."

Nikki shook her head despondently. "It's too long. He's been in there much too long."

The statement jabbed at Mel's heart. If Nikki, with her medical background, was saying that, then could it really mean Maxx might not recover? She had not allowed the thought to creep in, it was too inconceivable.

"Maybe if he were at Crawford Long—" Nikki began. "At least I know the people there."

"This is one of the best hospitals in the city," Mel said. "I'm sure they're taking good care of him."

"Yes. Of course they are," Nikki said lamely, almost apologetically. "It's this waiting—it's so hard."

"I know," Mel said. "Just hold on."

But she couldn't help wondering if all that could be done for Maxx had been done as quickly as possible. In emergency situations like this, she knew that precious moments, *seconds,* can mean the difference between saving a life and losing it. Was the ambulance called right away? Did authorities respond expeditiously? Or was there some nonchalant reaction, that here lies another black man with a gunshot wound, likely shot over a drug deal gone bad? Did they assume that Maxx was a dealer, because of his expensive car? Did they make the judgment that perhaps he got what he deserved? Was his medical care in any way compromised?

A pair of uniformed officers arrived to question Nikki. Mel eyed them suspiciously, and stayed close to Nikki's side during the brief interrogation. Then, she caught herself. The police weren't the enemy. The enemy consisted of the two animals out there who had robbed Maxx. With no inkling of remorse, they were roaming free, probably using Maxx's money right now to buy drugs. They might even be the type of hustlers that Maxx himself might have defended. What a horrible irony.

She was glad when Builder returned, rid of the robe that reminded her of the sick. In his jeans and sweatshirt, he represented a new strength and optimism that she needed as much as Nikki.

But minutes later, as a nurse pointed them out to a blue-coated surgeon, Mel knew even before the doctor said the words. He wore a look that she had seen before, the look that was on the bearer of bad news about her father. There was the downward turn of the mouth, the pulled-in cheeks, the slackening of the face that forewarned fatalism.

He said what they didn't want to hear, what they had prayed would not happen.

"I'm sorry. We couldn't hold him."

We couldn't hold him.

Maxx was dead.

Nikki let out a wail of woe. Her body bent at the waist and her head dropped to her lap. Builder stooped in front of her, trying to give comfort. Mel patted Nikki's back, her own grief coming to the fore. After a moment, Nikki's sobs became muffled, which somehow made her even more pitiful.

The doctor, continuing his sad duty, explained how Maxx had lost too much blood, and that the bullet had pierced a quadrant of his heart. As he spoke, he removed his surgical cap, and twisted it with his long hands. He knew this was a difficult time, he said, but would the family consider organ donation?

Not now, thought Mel, knowing full well that now was the only time to deal with it. But the thought of Maxx being chopped up and dissected made her resent the request. Hadn't he been violated enough?

She was surprised to hear Nikki speak up in a rather strong voice. "Take what you need—it's what Maxx would have wanted."

"Are you sure?" Builder asked.

"Yes. I'm sure." Then, out of respect for Mel, she looked to her for validation. "Is that—all right with you?"

It wasn't her decision to make; it was Nikki's, as the wife—the widow now—the next of kin. But for Nikki to consider Mel's feelings and to seek her support made Mel feel closer to her at that moment than at any time before. "Yes," she whispered. "It's all right."

The doctor thanked them; then, noticing Mel's discolored ankle, he lingered a moment longer. Had she had her ankle x-rayed? he asked. Perhaps someone should look at it. It was as though he desperately wanted to find some way to vindicate himself and his hospital to this family that was so fresh with grief.

They decided that Nikki should stay with them for the night. But before they could leave the hospital, there were papers to sign, administrative matters to take care of. While Builder escorted Nikki to the office, Mel volunteered to get the car. It would give her a chance to get out of the hospital, away from the stifling air of death. Besides, she didn't want Nikki to have to walk far. Her own knees wobbled shakily, and her stomach fisted into knots as her body absorbed the news about Maxx.

Walking down the hallway, she thought of the dreaded phone call she would soon have to make to Eunice. *Lord, help me. How do I tell her that her only son—her favorite child—is dead?*

Outside, the humidity made it no easier to breathe. All around her the air hung heavy with a suffocating hold. She felt in the grips of an asthma attack, the kind she had had as a child. She tried to breathe slowly and deeply through her mouth, but that old technique brought little remedy; the compressed space only tightened further.

"Hey, Momma! Where you off to all by yourself?"

Startled, she saw three guys approaching her in the hanging-out, restless saunter of those in search of action on a Saturday night.

"Um, um, um. Looka here, looka here," one of them smacked.

Another let out a lurid whistle. "I sho would like some of *dat.*"

Mel moved closer to the brick wall on her right, her only buttress against the taunting trio.

"We can have ourselves a party right here."

"Sho 'nuff."

Cornered, Mel looked desperately for help, but saw no one. She was exposed and unprotected. *For God's sake,* she wanted to say. *Leave me alone. My brother just died.*

They completely surrounded her now, three towering figures, lording it over her in the dark. Trying to outrun them would be ludicrous, especially with her throbbing ankle.

"Get out of my way," she said, trying to sound firm.

"Aw, now. That ain't friendly, is it?"

"We just wanna talk, baby, just talk," one of them said, dragging out the words.

"Yeah," jeered another. "Talk." He formed a big ball of bubble gum, aiming it directly at Mel, as his buddies laughed.

A car turned into the parking garage and drove slowly toward them.

"Come on," one of them said. "Let's split."

They parted the way, and Mel hurriedly limped toward her car.

"Next time you better be nice, bitch," one of them shouted after her. "You don't look that good no how."

She fumbled her keys, dropping them in her panic to open the car door. From a distance, she saw the parking attendant in his hut, but that offered little solace.

Inside the car, she slumped over the steering wheel, shaking and weeping from the acute pang of emptiness, from the crushing loss of Maxx.

CHAPTER 14

"Where there is hatred, let me sow love; where there is injury, pardon."

From the overhead choir loft, the sweet voice of the soloist traveled throughout the pews of All Saints Episcopal Church. At the foot of the sanctuary stood the pall-draped casket, holding the remains of Maxximilian Bernard Lincoln—beloved son, brother, husband, uncle, friend— awaiting the final farewell.

"Where there is doubt, faith; where there is despair, hope."

Builder took Nikki's left hand, which was cold and clammy, her right hand balled up with tissues at the ready. On his other side, sat Mel, her lips quivering, her eyes moist. He patted her arm gently, then slipped his fingers into hers. He dared not glance down the pew at Eunice, who earlier, during a private viewing of the body, had nearly fallen into the casket with Maxx, imploring, "God, why didn't you take me? Not my baby, not my baby."

It had been a devastating moment for all of them, and Builder too had broken down. Up until then, he had succeeded in maintaining a calm veneer, knowing that the family looked to him for strength. He was aware that crying, like laughing, was contagious, so if he could keep his tears inside, it might help the others cope better. His philosophy about death was simple: It was a part of life that you couldn't control; you'd best accept it and move on; everyone has his or her own time. But that cut-and-dried analysis didn't work with Maxx as the subject. *Damn it, Maxx, why'd you have to go and die?* It was hard to believe he was gone. And when Eunice clung so sorrowfully to her son's dead body, Builder's own held-back tears burst through. Whoever invented funerals and wakes and ritualistic mourning didn't have the family and friends of the deceased in mind, he decided. Getting through this day would be hell for everyone.

"Where there is darkness, light; where there is sadness, joy."

Mel wanted to recross her legs, to put her left knee over her right, instead of right over left, as they were now. But to do so would be too disruptive. On one side, Builder was holding her hand in his lap; on the other, Sasha's head rested on her shoulder. So she stayed frozen in her position, listening to the soloist, thinking back over the things she should have said to Maxx.

She should have told him how much she loved him instead of harping about his faults. She should have joked with him more, laughed more, rather than played the role of the criticizing older sister. There was so much she should have done, had she only known. But it was too late now.

This all felt like a dream to her, a horrible dream, sometimes occurring in slow motion, then happening in a flurry of scenes: helping Nikki with funeral arrangements; the endless phone calls to people who knew Maxx; lining up at the house for the procession. And so much black; too much black.

"*. . . Grant that I may not, so much seek to be consoled, as to console; to be understood, as to understand.*"

"Is it almost over?" Sasha whispered.

"Almost."

Sasha raised her head and leaned to her other side to speak to Eunice, whose tear-streaked face was camouflaged by a black veil hanging over her hat. Mel had noticed how close the two of them had become. Their time together in France had cemented their kinship. They enjoyed an unspoken communication with looks and nods that could be interpreted across a room, the kind of mother-daughter connection that Mel had never had with Sasha but that Sasha had evidently found with her grandmother.

"*To be loved, as to love.*"

Mel's eye caught a flutter of beige; a funeral program had floated to the floor and Maxx's even-toothed smile stared back at her. Eunice's husband, Alfred, bent to pick up the program, then repositioned his arm around his wife. Mel was glad that Alfred had made the overseas trip to accompany Eunice and lend his support; although last night at the house, he had harshly berated himself for not coming to Maxx's wedding.

"I'm sure Maxx understood," Mel had told him. "Someone had to look after the inn."

"That's no excuse. I should have taken a holiday with Eunice. That boy was like a son to me. I should have been here."

"Don't blame yourself," Mel had said, full of her own regrets about Maxx.

"Why is it we can always show up at funerals," he had asked rhetorically, "and not the happy occasions?"

She had patted his hand, sharing his remorse. Why indeed?

"*For it is in giving, that we receive.*"

Last night, after Eunice had gone to bed, Alfred had stayed up to talk to Mel and Builder. He had expressed concern about his wife, saying it would be hard for her to recover from Maxx's death.

"Yes, I know," Mel had agreed. "Maxx was her—" She had started to say "favorite," but instead said, "heart."

"You're a big part of her heart too," he had said quietly, as if to reassure her. Mel wondered how much he knew about the friction between herself and Eunice. How much had Eunice told him about their strained relationship? How much had he figured out on his own?

"I was going to wait until the funeral was behind us before asking you this," he had said, "but—"

"What? What is it?" Mel and Builder had asked simultaneously.

"It's a lot to ask, but—would you let Sasha go back with us, for the school year?" He hurried on, without waiting for a response. "It would mean so much to Eunice. And to me."

"But she just got back here," Mel had replied, pointing out the obvious.

"She needs to be here," Builder had said firmly. "With us."

"Yes, of course you want her home," Alfred had said. "But if Sasha were around, Eunice would pull herself together more quickly. I'm convinced of that. She would help Eunice keep her mind off things, more than I or anyone else could. You should see the two of them together. Sasha is so young and full of life. Eunice lights up whenever she's around." He paused. "I think she could be Eunice's salvation."

Her salvation? What an odd choice of words, thought Mel.

"Before you say no, maybe you can pray on it," Alfred had suggested. "Please. Just pray on it."

"It is in pardoning, that we are pardoned."

Now, seeing her mother, bereaved and stripped of all semblance of glamour, Mel felt overwhelming pity. She was sorrier for her than for Nikki, the bride of two months who, in an instant turnaround, had tragically become a widow. She was sorrier for her, even, than for Maxx, whose life was senselessly cut short, yet who would not suffer the lonely torment of the living who are left to mourn the dead.

"It is in dying, that we are born, to eternal life."

Should she let Sasha go back with Eunice? Should she give up her daughter to save her mother?

As they stood to file behind the casket, being rolled down the aisle, Mel thought of the phrase that Nikki had often repeated during the past few days: "It's what Maxx would have wanted."

Perhaps this could be her gift in his name.

• • •

After Maxx was laid to rest at Westview Cemetery, people convened at the house to salvage a bit of normalcy, to eat and drink and reminisce in the midst of their mourning attire. Mel exchanged her heels for flats and went into the dining room where Val was setting out a repast. The tableful of homemade sympathy started a fresh tinkling behind her eyes; the array of cakes, casseroles, and cooked vegetables represented a neighborly spread of solace.

"So much food."

"You could open a restaurant," said Val, trying to keep the moment light. She had stayed at the house during the service, volunteering to answer the phone and receive any visitors who might drop by. Her job, as she saw it, was to provide a speck of sunshine to a sea of shipwrecked survivors. "You doing okay?"

"Yes." Mel smoothed out a small wrinkle on the edge of the table cloth. "The hardest part was when Nikki bent down and kissed the casket. And put a single rose on top of it. That just about did me in."

Val nodded, arranging the silverware in a half-moon pattern. "That's why I couldn't go. Funerals and burials and all that—we just don't mix."

"I don't think anyone *enjoys* them, Val."

Initially, she had been peeved and a little hurt when Val had told her that she wouldn't attend the ceremonies. It had seemed like a form of betrayal, that her good friend wouldn't be there for her. Even estranged Celeste, sender of the lovely fruit basket that temporarily replaced the usual centerpiece on the buffet, and Ron—whom neither Mel nor Builder had seen or spoken with in months—even they had come to the funeral. But not Val.

Over the past few days, Mel had witnessed how death begets odd reactions. Certain people whom she had expected to hear from had sent not a single word; others, whom she barely knew, had expressed an unexpected outpouring of sympathy. And Val, despite her usually tough, I-can-handle-anything facade, was a votary of the doctrine never to attend funerals, never. She believed in celebrating a person's life while they're here, to enjoy them while they're alive and kicking, and not to publicly commiserate their passing. People had different coping techniques, and this was hers.

"One of your neighbors—Ms. Lee—came by," Val said, rolling her eyes. "She wanted to make sure you knew that *this*," she pointed to a dish of macaroni and cheese, "is from her."

"That's nice," Mel noted.

"Yeah. But you should have heard her carrying on about this glass casserole dish, how it's hand-blown crystal from Princess House, and to make sure that she gets it back. She said once she made rice pudding for somebody, and she never got her plate back, and since then, she tapes her name to everything, but she still doesn't always get her stuff returned. The way she was talking, you'd think this pan was gilded in gold or something. I started to tell her, 'Look, lady, why didn't you just put it on a sheet of tin?' "

Mel chuckled, grateful to Val for poking fun and helping to distract her, at least for a while, from the emotional havoc of the day. People do bring different gifts.

"Oh, and somebody named Xavier called."

Mel's heart skipped. Xavier? How did he know?

" . . . gorgeous voice, real smooth sounding," Val said, watching her closely. "He sent his condolences."

Then, she remembered. It all seemed so long ago. Anne had called the day after Mel left, ostensibly to make sure she had arrived home safely. She had launched into an apology for any ill feelings that erupted from their last conversation. "We've been friends too long to let anything interfere with it," Anne had said, a clear reference to Xavier. But they had talked no further about it after Mel told her Maxx had been killed. She must have relayed the news to Xavier.

In the living room, Frank Kirby was telling stories about Maxx, describing him as a bon vivant, a happy-go-lucky guy with a love of fast cars and fast women, until, of course, he met Nikki. Mel stood along the fringe of the gathered group, listening. Frank could certainly weave a tale. Like Val, he knew how to place just the right emphasis on a word or phrase, how to create anticipation with a properly placed pause. At another time, these antics might seem irritating and contrived, but today, Mel appreciated Frank's special brand of humor, tempered appropriately for the occasion. She welcomed anything that precipitated a more upbeat mood. Wouldn't Maxx have wanted it that way?

On the opposite side of the room, Nikki motioned for Mel to join her and Builder, who, with his head slightly bent, was listening with measured solemnity. Reluctantly, Mel walked over, not wanting to be drawn into a conversation that looked much too intense. Please, she thought, don't let them be talking about the headstone. I can't deal with that just yet.

Nikki smiled and took her hand. "I was telling Builder that I'm going to give you a portion of the insurance money to help with Sasha's schooling."

"Oh, no," Mel objected. "We couldn't possibly take anything from you."

"You're not taking it from me. I want to do it for you. And for Sasha."

"You're going to need that money to live on."

"That's what I've been trying to tell her," Builder inserted.

"Believe me. I'll be taken care of. Maxx saw to that."

"But—" Mel said.

"Please," Nikki stopped her. "You don't know how much it will help me." She took a breath to maintain her composure. "Maxx loved Sasha so much, and I know he would have wanted this for her. She'll be going to college in a few years, and it'll be good to know the money is there for her."

"It's really sweet of you to offer this," Mel told her, "but I wish you'd think about it some more. You don't need to decide anything right now. It's way too soon."

"My mind's made up," Nikki said with finality. She squeezed their hands and walked toward the group attentively listening to Frank.

"She sounds determined," said Builder.

Mel sighed. "She's trying to do what she thinks Maxx would have wanted. That's all she talks about." She shook her head and went in search of Eunice and Sasha, whom she hadn't seen since they had all emerged from the funeral limo reserved for the family.

The door to the guest bedroom was shut tight. Mel accompanied her brisk knock with a question. "May I come in?"

A faint voice granted permission to enter. Eunice stood in the middle of undress, her black outfit pulled halfway over her head. Sasha was perched at the foot of the bed, attending.

"Do we *have* to go downstairs, Mom?" she implored.

"No. Not if you don't want to." Mel closed the door behind her. "I just came to see how you're doing."

Eunice uttered a groan of relief, free at last from the pressing confines of black. She flung the expensive fabric on the bed, next to her veiled hat. "I had to get out of these clothes."

Sasha reached for the robe lying on the back of a chair. "Here, Grandma."

As Eunice put on the robe, Mel noticed how her mother's shoulders seemed rounded and bent, burdened by the immeasurable weight of loss.

"There's plenty of food," Mel said. "You'll feel better if you eat something."

"Maybe." Eunice doubled the bed pillows for extra support, and gingerly leaned back against them. "I should go down and thank people for coming," she said limply. "Everyone has been so nice."

"Don't push yourself if you don't feel up to it. Stay here and rest."

Sasha proposed an option. "I'd be glad to fix a plate for you, Grandma."

"That's a good idea," Mel said approvingly.

"Yes. Thank you, dear," said Eunice. "I'd like that."

Mel looked at her daughter with a new perspective. She knew that Sasha was reluctant to mix with the crowd, preferring to avoid yet another round of sympathetic looks and pats on the shoulder; yet, she was willing to reimmerse herself for the sake of her grandmother. It was one more sign of Sasha's growing maturity and of her protectiveness of Eunice.

Mel went to sit at the foot of the bed, covering part of the imprint that Sasha had left.

"You've raised a lovely girl," Eunice said when they were alone. "You've done a good job."

It was one of the nicest things her mother had ever said. A pure unconditional compliment, not motivated by either guilt or the need to placate. It was genuine and sincere.

"I can tell she's grown up a lot over the summer," Mel remarked.

"Yes, she has. And she was so helpful at the inn. The guests loved her. Do you know what she liked to do best? Turn back the sheets and lay out the chocolates."

"I wonder why. I'll bet you were buying a lot more chocolate than usual."

A ghost of a smile appeared around the corners of Eunice's mouth. "You used to love chocolate too, although it never agreed with you much."

"Still doesn't," Mel acknowledged.

"And Maxx. He'd eat a pound of it at a time, if I'd let him."

Mel smiled wistfully. "I remember once when we went to Mr. Bell's store, Maxx spent all his money on four Hershey bars."

"Four?" Eunice asked, disbelieving.

"That's right. We were only allowed one, you know."

"That little rascal."

"He paid me fifty cents so I wouldn't tell you."

"And you took the bribe, did you?"

"Maxx could be very convincing."

Eunice smiled a proud mother's smile. "Yes, he could." She was silent a moment, then, "You *did* love him, didn't you?"

"Of course I did. Did you ever doubt that? He was my brother."

"I know you had trouble getting along. And you always thought I favored him."

Guiltily, Mel dropped her head. "Let's not get into that, okay? It doesn't matter."

"But it does matter. I loved you equally, Mel. You have to believe that."

She didn't. She knew that Maxx was her mother's favorite and would always be her favorite, even in death. But somehow, it really didn't matter now. Things that had loomed so important, so critical, seemed almost insignificant. The persistent debt, her failing marriage, the nagging animus that she had felt toward Eunice—none of it mattered, at least, not as before. In the face of death, that ultimate life-altering condition, previously important aspects of life are abruptly dethroned from their puffed-up positions of prominence.

"I keep thinking of the last time I was here, just a couple months ago," said Eunice. "Maxx's wedding. He was so happy. He had his whole future in front of him, his whole life—" Her voice broke off in anguished awareness of the potential that was not to be.

"Maxx lived a good life," Mel said. "Remember that. He was loved. He had a lot of friends. You can't say that about a lot of people. We have to be grateful for the time he was here. When I think of it that way, it helps, it really does."

The fleeting smile appeared again on Eunice's face. "He wanted a little girl. Did you know that?"

"No. I didn't."

"Most men want sons. But Maxx wanted a daughter. He wanted to dress her up in patent leather shoes and ruffles and lace. And when she got older—driving gloves. He wanted her to be a real hot rodder. Most women aren't into that kind of thing, you know." Eunice batted her eyes to hold back the tears. "I think that's why he doted on Sasha. She was the closest thing he had to his own daughter."

For a moment, there was silence. Then, "Take her with you," Mel said suddenly.

"What?"

"It's okay. Take her back with you."

"You mean—?" Eunice was having a hard time adjusting to the import of Mel's statement.

"You do want her to go back with you, don't you? And she wants to go?"

"Oh, yes. Of course! But I thought—she can really go? It's all right with you? And Builder?"

"I haven't talked to him yet," Mel admitted. "But I think he'll agree to it." She smiled slightly. "Maxx did teach me a few tricks of the trade, you know."

Actually, she knew she had little negotiating clout with Builder. He still resented her leaving and going off to Seattle, a move which he interpreted as unwarranted desertion. Yet, he too had changed these last few days. Maxx's death had opened up a path of communication that was previously blocked off. She and Builder had cried together, prayed together, and with Eunice and Alfred occupying the guest room, had shared the same bed. Their tentative, fledgling intimacy sprung out of mutual grief, not passionate desire. Even so, their common need for consolation enabled them to set aside momentarily the obstacles of infidelity and mistrust. Yes, she could persuade Builder to let their daughter go.

"Right now you need Sasha more than we do," Mel said solemnly. "And I think she needs you too."

"Thank you for doing this." A veil of grief seemed to have lifted from Eunice. She grasped Mel's hands. "Thank you. Thank you. You know I'll take good care of her."

Mel heard Sasha's footsteps on the stairs. "Yes, Mother. I know."

Builder upturned the bucket of suds onto the hood of the Honda and grabbed a well-used sponge to scrub away stubborn spots of tar and grease. For a minute, Mel watched in silence as he removed the dirt and grime from her car. Intent on the task, and with the portable radio providing background music to work by, he had not heard her approach from behind.

"Don't you think you're overdoing it?"

Startled, he looked up to see Mel, her hands dug deep into the two front pockets of faded jeans.

"No big deal," he said. "I've got to do something to keep from going crazy."

"But you don't want to end up back in the hospital."

He had already washed his truck this morning, and she was concerned that he was doing too much too soon. Still under doctor's orders to take it easy, he had found it increasingly difficult to remain idle.

"Is she finished packing?" he asked.

"She's getting there."

Mel had come outside to get a break from the hurricane that had swept through Sasha's room. Clothes had taken over everywhere, hanging from dresser knobs and door handles, stacked in piles on the floor and on the desk, strewn across the bed in uncategorized disarray. The storm had started last night when Mel had pulled out the trunk that would carry Sasha's belongings across the sea. What she had thought would take no more than a few hours had spilled over into a second day of sorting, sifting, and compromise. Despite Mel's organizing skills and Eunice's expert recommendations, Sasha's preferences for what was to go or stay factored heavily into the process, prompting prolonged deliberations over specific items, such as whether the blue cotton sweatshirt would be more versatile than the beige cardigan. "You can't take everything!" Mel had said, exasperated. This morning had finally brought them to the point where progress could be seen, but the task was still far from complete.

Builder hosed down the front of the car, creating new streams of water that outlined the perimeter of the wash area. "She leaves tomorrow," he said, reminding her of what they both knew so well. "Think she'll be ready?"

"Somehow, I believe she'll make it," Mel answered.

She knew this was a dream come true for Sasha, even though it was happening because of the far-reaching arms of her dead Uncle Maxx. Without Maxx's death, Sasha would never have been allowed to go to France for a whole year. And without Maxx's death, Mel herself would never have experienced that suspended moment of connectivity, which had pulled her beyond the realm of reason and convinced her that she should let Sasha go.

It had happened late last night, while Eunice was taking her bath, and Mel and Sasha were negotiating over the contents of the trunk. Even though Mel had been resigned to the decision, and had persuaded Builder to go along reluctantly—out of deference to her mother and in response to an inexplicable urge that it would somehow compensate for her not being more receptive to Maxx—still, she had held serious reservations about the wisdom of letting her daughter go so far away from home. She had told Sasha how she had not expected to do this kind of packing for at least another few years, when she would be leaving for college.

"Oh, Mom," Sasha had replied, "I'm fourteen," as though that clearly qualified her for entrance into the world of grown-up experiences.

"Fourteen!" Mel had chided. "How ancient."

It was then, at that instant, that it happened. She felt a tender pressure on her shoulders, and simultaneously, she heard a voice—gentle, distant, yet clear. Actually, she didn't hear exact words; it was more like a warm sensation that traveled through her body, transmitting a message that was immediately understood. *It's all right. It's all right to let Sasha go.*

For a frozen moment, Mel had stood in awed muteness, awaiting further communication, not knowing what to do or how to act if it came again. What did it mean? Was it an illusion? No, it couldn't be; it was too real. It *had* happened! Was it the spirit of Maxx? An echo from God? She had quivered at the thought.

She did not tell Builder, nor had she mentioned it to Eunice or Sasha. She had intuitively understood that, at least for the time being, the message was for her—and for her alone.

With Sasha's long trip spiritually sanctioned, it made it easier for Mel to watch the hours count down to the time of departure. Less than twenty-four hours to go, still so much to say and do.

"We had a long talk last night after you went to bed," Builder said now, as he wiped the windshield.

"You and Sasha?"

"Yep."

"What'd you talk about?"

"You."

"Me?" She moved in closer.

"Well, actually, you and me. She's concerned we're getting divorced."

"Oh. That again."

"So, are we?"

"What do you mean, *are* we? What'd you tell her?"

Ignoring the question, he squirted shampoo into the bucket, filling it to a foamy top.

"Builder," Mel said impatiently. "What did you tell her?"

He looked up from the bucket. "I told her that things were on shaky ground. *Real* shaky. But we were still trying to work it out. That *is* right, isn't it?"

Mel was hesitant. "Uh, sure."

"You don't sound sure."

"What do you want me to say?" she replied, hunching her shoulders. "Anything can happen. Anything at all. Just look at Maxx. If there's one thing I've learned it's that there're no guarantees."

"That's true. Which is what I told Sasha." He sloshed the soapy water onto the trunk of the car. "You do the best you can, and then—if it flies, great, if not, move on to the next deal."

"Or trade in for a new model?"

He twitched his brow, realizing she was referring to herself. "That depends."

"Depends on what?"

He concentrated on removing a recalcitrant smudge. "A really good car will fit its driver. Did you know that?" he asked, without looking at her.

"Is that so?"

"That's right. And even though the car may have a lot of mileage—if it's a good fit—it's worth hanging on to."

"I see." Mel pushed the metaphor further. "And how would you define a 'good fit'?"

He paused before answering. "Understanding, for one. That's essential." He looked up at her. "And commitment. That's an absolute given."

"I see."

"Yeah, I'm a firm believer in commitment."

"Hmmm. Remember though, it's a two-way street," Mel said. "Cars behave according to the type of driver."

"What do you mean?" he asked.

"Well, take someone who drives gently. I'm sure a car would perform well for him in the long haul. No problem. Whereas somebody who drives rough might have the best car in the world at his fingertips, but it turns into a lemon. It won't move an inch. And the driver can't figure out why. He's thinking there's something wrong with the battery or the carburetor, while all along, the problem is his own doing. Cars respond according to how they're treated. Moral of the story: Even cars don't like abuse."

He tightened his lips at her obvious reference. "Guess you have a point," he said unhappily.

"I'm glad you see it that way."

When would she let it go? *Could* she ever let it go? They were just beginning to have fun, engaging in subtle banter, a throwback to earlier times when they'd talk about each other through the personification of some unrelated object. It was nice to fall into that mode again. But she had to go and spoil it by talking about mistreatment. The flames of forgiveness which had burned brightly over the past few days were about to flicker and fade. Maxx's death had resurrected the realization of the importance of family and of getting along, something in which Mel strongly believed and felt keenly. However, there still lingered an unrequited need for payback for the wrongs done to her.

This brief exchange with Builder provided the most recent evidence.

No matter how much she may want to move to a better place with him, her feelings could not be denied, or sped through a cycle. They had to be dealt with on their own terms, in their own time. Complete healing in her marriage would require a long, long road to tread; but even before she could get on that road, she still had baby steps to take toward the rebuilding of trust with her husband.

She was thinking of how to open the lines of communication in a less vindictive way, when Sasha appeared on the overhead deck to tell Builder he had a phone call.

"Who is it, baby?" he asked, his hands dripping wet.

"I didn't get the name. Something about getting his basement remodeled."

"Wonder how he got the house number?" Builder mused out loud.

"Maybe one of your long-time clients made the referral," Mel suggested. "You know how some of those folks still don't use your office number."

"Yeah. That's probably it." He started to wipe his hands, then asked Mel, "You want to handle it?"

It was a breakthrough of sorts, one of those moments that later on might be recalled as a turning point. Builder's new strategy to have her involved in the business, actually to help run it, had until now been exclusively lip service. He had suggested a division of duties—that she'd take charge of the finances, marketing, and client follow-up, while he'd coordinate the supplies, put together the crews, and oversee the jobs on site. However, there had been no opportunity to try it out, no time to even talk about it at length, so consumed were they in the events of the past few days. The business, like everything else in their lives, had been placed on hold. But now, here it was; he wanted her to talk with a potential client. He was letting her in, upon his initiative, without her asking or reminding. He had passed the test without being put to the test.

"I'll be right there, Sasha," Mel shouted.

"*You*, Mom?" Her eyes rounded in surprise.

"Yes, me," Mel replied assuredly, heading for the steps. "Who knows?" she said, glancing back at Builder. "Today a basement, tomorrow a high-rise."

The Chevron Station on upper Roswell Road was an unlikely place to run into Larson Cook. It had been a year and a half since Mel had seen her former boss, although she had spoken with him by phone several times.

She was pumping gas, noting yet another difference between predominantly white versus black neighborhoods: how here, for instance, customers could pump before paying, whereas in most black communities you had to pay first. She was thinking of this when a powder blue '68 Mercedes rolled to a stop behind her. She'd recognize that car anywhere.

Larson maneuvered his pin-striped bulk from behind the steering wheel and emerged with a wide grin. "Mel! Of all people! How are you?"

"Living dangerously, just like you," she said airily.

He gave her an awkward bear hug, awkward because she was slightly bent over to tend to the business at hand.

"Here. Let me do that," he offered. "My lungs are already polluted." Smoothly, he took over pumping the gas. "Fill 'er up?"

"Just to fifteen."

He jiggled the hose back into the right position. "You look great, Mel. Really, great."

"Thanks. I see you and ol' Meredith are still going strong."

He nodded in the direction of his car. "The only female who's never let me down. Besides you, of course."

Mel smiled, remembering her loyalty to Larson during her years at the Chamber, despite his blustery ego and penchant for power plays.

"I was awfully sorry to hear about your brother," he said. "A damn shame."

She felt a heart twinge. "We received your lovely flowers. Thanks."

"I was out of town the day of the funeral. Otherwise, you know I would have been there."

Another twinge. Not a plummet, the plummets had finally, mercifully, stopped, but the twinges, in their own way, could be just as painful. They would surface at the slightest prodding—a belated sympathy note, a television promo for a program Maxx liked to watch, an old Harvard classmate who called to talk about him. She wanted acknowledgment, yes. It was worse when people said nothing. But the reminders stirred up emotions that lay very much on edge, raw emotions that were still too recent to have grown a scab of cover. At what point would they stop coming, these twinges, these numerous reminders that death was a recent visitor? It had been two months now. When would she no longer mark the anniversaries? How long would she continue to measure the passage of time according to when Maxx died—or when he was buried?

Ten days after. Three weeks later. Two months to the day.

"I've been meaning to call you," Larson said, hanging up the pump.

"But I wanted to wait until—well, you know—I knew you had your hands full."

She walked with him to his car as he spoke.

"It's finally ready to go, Mel. The new company I was telling you about."

"Oh, wonderful."

"Yeah. I've got a meeting in an hour with the investors. We're going to sew everything up today. I should have my shingle out within a month or two."

"That's terrific, Larson."

"I told you I'd bring you in when it's a go." He slid the fuel handle into the slot for automatic, ready to feed dear Meredith. "What do you think? Can you stand working with me again?"

Mel blinked. "Are you offering me a job, Larson?"

"You're the only person I know who can put up with me. And you're damn good too. I wouldn't have to do any on-the-job training."

"Gee. And I thought it was because you liked me."

He chuckled. "What do you say? Why don't we get together next week and talk specifics? How are you for lunch on Wednesday? Or would breakfast be better? It's your call."

Amazing how quickly things change. Not long ago, there was nothing happening, nothing even simmering. It seemed as if the long drought would never end. Now here was Larson, someone who respected her skills and business acumen, offering a new opportunity for financial stability and consistent work. And then there was Val. Since her settlement had come through, she had continued to prod Mel to get involved with her greeting card venture. "Just help with the ideas," she had said, "I'll put up the money."

In a way it was almost laughable—from being down in the dregs, from virtually nothing—to having not one, but two opportunities that could put her on the road to financial recovery and out of the clutching grip of debt. Nothing was assured, of course, and each had its share of risk. But at least they were options to ponder, they offered something to hold on to.

Larson's deal sounded especially promising. Mel knew Larson well enough to know that he wouldn't venture into anything too risky. He had set his chips in order and seemingly had the backing. It was an offer she would have eagerly snatched up just a little while ago.

But now she told Larson what she had told Val—that she was going to help Builder in his business—their business. It meant commitment and additional sacrifice but it was something she had to do. One last gargantuan effort. The business deserved that. And so did her husband.

In the last few weeks she had decided that this second time around, this last time around, she was willing to give her all—to her marriage and to the business. If either or both failed, at least she could unequivocally say that she had given it her best shot.

As an illustration of her all-out commitment, she had injected into the business most of the money Maxx had given her at his wedding. And since she now handled the bookkeeping and all the finances, she made sure that the money was well used. Part of it had been allocated toward the mortgage on Builder's Southside office, which they had decided not to sell. Another part was helping to support the new position of the part-time apprentice, Johnny Gray, who had started working last week. Mel could see the makings of an effective team. With the combination of Builder's skills, Johnny's enthusiasm, her own managerial touch, plus a likely joint venture soon with Charles Gibbons, whom she had met and found sincere, she believed they were taking the right steps to revive the business. There was reason to be optimistic. But it was all so new and fragile, and a tremendous amount of work lay ahead.

She left the gas station, continuing on her way to see a client who wanted another look at some carpet samples before making a final decision. The woman had called yesterday, sounding uncertain about her choice. Initially, Builder had taken the call, trying to convince her that the ivory color she had selected would beautifully complement her jade decor. But Mel had volunteered to take the samples over today, to allay any doubts in the client's mind. She had reminded Builder that some people needed more hand-holding, and that down the road, it might mean the difference between a referral and a dissatisfied ex-customer.

In addition to the finances, she spent much of her time handling customer relations. She discovered it was the finishing touches, the extra coddling and follow-up conversations, that equally needed attention. One change she had insisted on immediately: that someone should always be in the office to answer the phone. That's what Johnny was doing today—holding down the fort, covering the phone. People want to talk to a person, not hear some prerecorded message, Mel had told Builder. Personal touch is essential to a small business, and clients should at least be able to leave a message with a breathing body. It's an accumulation of these little things, she had said, that can make or break a business. Money is a big part of it, yes, but it isn't all about money.

She turned into a tree-lined boulevard, pecans crunching under her tires. Splashes of yellow and orange marked the beginning of early fall, and plump pumpkins decorated the front steps of several splendid houses. She would have liked to linger here, to absorb the warm colors of autumn, the comforting embrace of this dressed-up street. But she was running late. The talk with Larson had taken up the extra minutes she usually allotted for unexpecteds. She was in danger of violating her own business directive: Be on time.

The car in front of her crept along. An elderly white-haired man sat low on the driver's side. He's probably super retired, thought Mel, with nowhere to be until next week. Lightly, she tapped her horn, hoping to nudge him along. She had a client to see, a business to save, a marriage to put on track.

"Come on, pops, let's move it," she said, as much to herself as to him. "I've got a life to lead."